THE CAT THAT WALKED BY HIMSELF

& OTHER CAT STORIES

COLLINS
CLASSICS

William Collins
An imprint of HarperCollins*Publishers*
1 London Bridge Street
London SE1 9GF

WilliamCollinsBooks.com

HarperCollins*Publishers*
Macken House
39/40 Mayor Street Upper
Dublin 1
D01 C9W8
Ireland

This William Collins paperback edition published in Great Britain in 2023

1

A catalogue record for this book
is available from the British Library

ISBN 978-0-00-861993-0

The text in this edition follows that of the original publications.

Typesetting in Kalix by Palimpsest Book Production Limited,
Falkirk, Stirlingshire

Printed and Bound in the UK using 100% Renewable Electricity
at CPI Group (UK) Ltd

History of William Collins

In 1819, millworker William Collins from Glasgow, Scotland, set up a company for printing and publishing pamphlets, sermons, hymn books and prayer books. That company was Collins and was to mark the birth of HarperCollins Publishers as we know it today. The long tradition of Collins dictionary publishing can be traced back to the first dictionary William co-published in 1825, *Greek and English Lexicon*. Indeed, from 1840 onwards, he began to produce illustrated dictionaries and even obtained a licence to print and publish the Bible.

Soon after, William published the first Collins novel; however, it was the time of the Long Depression, where harvests were poor, prices were high, potato crops had failed and violence was erupting in Europe. As a result, many factories across the country were forced to close down and William chose to retire in 1846, partly due to the hardships he was facing.

Aged 30, William's son, William II, took over the business. A keen humanitarian with a warm heart and a generous spirit, William II was truly 'Victorian' in his outlook. He introduced new, up-to-date steam presses and published affordable editions of Shakespeare's works and *The Pilgrim's Progress*, making them available to the masses for the first time.

A new demand for educational books meant that success came with the publication of travel books, scientific books, encyclopedias and dictionaries. This demand to be educated led to the later publication of atlases, and Collins also held the monopoly on scripture writing at the time.

In the 1860s Collins began to expand and diversify and the idea of 'books for the millions' was developed, although the phrase wasn't coined until 1907. Affordable editions of classical literature were published, and in 1903 Collins introduced 10 titles in their Collins Handy Illustrated Pocket Novels. These proved so popular that a few years later this had increased to an output of 50 volumes, selling nearly half a million in their year of publication. In the same year, The Everyman's Library was also instituted, with the idea of publishing an affordable library of the most important classical works, biographies, religious and philosophical treatments, plays, poems, travel and adventure books. This series eclipsed all competition at the time, and the introduction of paperback books in the 1950s helped to open that market and marked a high point in the industry.

HarperCollins is and has always been a champion of the classics, and the current Collins Classics series follows in this tradition – publishing classical literature that is affordable and available to all. Beautifully packaged, highly collectible and intended to be reread and enjoyed at every opportunity.

THE CAT THAT WALKED BY HIMSELF

& OTHER CAT STORIES

CONTENTS

THE CAT THAT WALKED BY HIMSELF

RUDYARD KIPLING

Hear and attend and listen; for this befell and behappened and became and was, O my Best Beloved, when the Tame animals were wild. The Dog was wild, and the Horse was wild, and the Cow was wild, and the Sheep was wild, and the Pig was wild – as wild as wild could be – and they walked in the Wet Wild Woods by their wild lones. But the wildest of all the wild animals was the Cat. He walked by himself, and all places were alike to him.

Of course the Man was wild too. He was dreadfully wild. He didn't even begin to be tame till he met the Woman, and she told him that she did not like living in his wild ways. She picked out a nice dry Cave, instead of a heap of wet leaves, to lie down in; and she strewed clean sand on the floor; and she lit a nice fire of wood at the back of the Cave; and she hung a dried wild-horse skin, tail-down, across the opening of the Cave; and she said, "Wipe your feet, dear, when you come in, and now we'll keep house."

That night, Best Beloved, there are wild sheep roasted on the hot stones, and flavoured with wild garlic and wild pepper; and wild duck stuffed with wild rice and wild fenugreek and wild coriander; and marrow bones of wild oxen; and wild cherries, and wild grenadillas. Then the Man went to sleep in front of the fire ever so happy; but the Woman sat up, combing her hair. She took the bone of the shoulder of mutton – the big flat blade-bone – and she looked at the wonderful marks on it, and she threw more wood on the fire, and she made a Magic. She made the First Singing Magic in the world.

Out in the Wet Wild Woods all the wild animals gathered together where they could see the light of the fire a long way off, and they wondered what it meant.

Then Wild Horse stamped with his wild foot and said, "O my Friends and O my Enemies, why have the Man and the Woman made that great light in that great Cave, and what harm will it do us?"

Wild Dog lifted up his wild nose and smelled the smell of the roast mutton, and said, "I will go up and see and look, and say; for I think it is good. Cat, come with me."

"Nenni!" said the Cat. "I am the Cat who walks by himself, and all places are alike to me. I will not come."

"Then we can never be friends again," said Wild Dog, and he trotted off to the Cave. But when he had gone a little way the Cat said to himself, "All places are alike to me. Why should I not go too and see and look and come away at my own liking." So he slipped after Wild Dog softly, very softly, and hid himself where he could hear everything.

When Wild Dog reached the mouth of the Cave he lifted up the dried horse-skin with his nose and sniffed the beautiful smell of the roast mutton, and the Woman, looking at the blade-bone, heard him, and laughed, and said, "Here comes the first. Wild Thing out of the Wild Woods, what do you want?"

Wild Dog said, "O my Enemy and Wife of my Enemy, what is this that smells so good in the Wild Woods?"

Then the Woman picked up a roasted mutton-bone and

threw it to Wild Dog, and said, "Wild Thing out of the Wild Woods, taste and try." Wild Dog gnawed the bone, and it was more delicious than anything he had ever tasted, and he said, "O my Enemy and Wife of my Enemy, give me another."

The Woman said, "Wild Thing out of the Wild Woods, help my Man to hunt through the day and guard this Cave at night, and I will give you as many roast bones as you need."

"Ah!" said the Cat, listening. "This is a very wise Woman, but she is not so wise as I am."

Wild Dog crawled into the Cave and laid his head on the Woman's lap, and said, "O my Friend and Wife of my Friend, I will help your Man to hunt through the day, and at night I will guard your Cave."

"Ah!" said the Cat, listening. "That is a very foolish Dog." And he went back through the Wet Wild Woods waving his wild tail, and walking by his wild lone. But he never told anybody.

When the Man waked up he said, "What is Wild Dog doing here?" And the Woman said, "His name is not Wild Dog any more, but the First Friend, because he will be our friend for always and always and always. Take him with you when you go hunting."

Next night the Woman cut great green armfuls of fresh grass from the water-meadows, and dried it before the fire, so that it smelt like new-mown hay, and she sat at the mouth of the Cave and plaited a halter out of horse-hide, and she looked at the shoulder-of-mutton bone – at the big broad blade-bone – and she made a Magic. She made the Second Singing Magic in the world.

Out in the Wild Woods all the wild animals wondered what had happened to Wild Dog, and at last Wild Horse stamped with his foot and said, "I will go and see and say why Wild Dog has not returned. Cat, come with me."

"Nenni!" said the Cat. "I am the Cat who walks by himself, and all places are alike to me. I will not come." But all the same he followed Wild Horse softly, very softly, and hid himself where he could hear everything.

When the Woman heard Wild Horse tripping and stumbling on his long mane, she laughed and said, "Here comes the second. Wild Thing out of the Wild Woods, what do you want?"

Wild Horse said, "O my Enemy and Wife of my Enemy, where is Wild Dog?"

The Woman laughed, and picked up the blade-bone and looked at it, and said, "Wild Thing out of the Wild Woods, you did not come here for Wild Dog, but for the sake of this good grass."

And Wild Horse, tripping and stumbling on his long mane, said, "That is true; give it me to eat."

The Woman said, "Wild Thing out of the Wild Woods, bend your wild head and wear what I give you, and you shall eat the wonderful grass three times a day."

"Ah," said the Cat, listening. "This is a clever Woman, but she is not so clever as I am."

Wild Horse bent his wild head, and the Woman slipped the plaited-hide halter over it, and Wild Horse breathed on the Woman's feet and said, "O my Mistress, and Wife of my Master, I will be your servant for the sake of the wonderful grass."

"Ah," said the Cat, listening. "That is a very foolish Horse." And he went back through the Wet Wild Woods, waving his wild tail and walking by his wild lone. But he never told anybody.

When the Man and the Dog came back from hunting, the Man said, "What is Wild Horse doing here?" And the Woman said, "His name is not Wild Horse any more, but the First Servant, because he will carry us from place to place for always and always and always. Ride on his back when you go hunting."

Next day, holding her wild head high that her wild horns should not catch in the wild trees, Wild Cow came up to the

Cave, and the Cat followed, and hid himself just the same as before; and everything happened just the same as before; and the Cat said the same things as before; and when Wild Cow had promised to give her milk to the Woman every day in exchange for the wonderful grass, the Cat went back through the Wet Wild Woods waving his wild tail and walking by his wild lone, just the same as before. But he never told anybody. And when the Man and the Horse and the Dog came home from hunting and asked the same questions same as before, the Woman said, "Her name is not Wild Cow any more, but the Giver of Good Food. She will give us the warm white milk for always and always and always, and I will take care of her while you and the First Friend and the First Servant go hunting."

Next day the Cat waited to see if any other Wild Thing would go up to the Cave, but no one moved in the Wet Wild Woods, so the Cat walked there by himself; and he saw the Woman milking the Cow, and he saw the light of the fire in the Cave, and he smelt the smell of the warm white milk.

Cat said, "O my Enemy and Wife of my Enemy, where did Wild Cow go?"

The Woman laughed and said, "Wild Thing out of the Wild Woods, go back to the Woods again, for I have braided up my hair, and I have put away the magic blade-bone, and we have no more need of either friends or servants in our Cave."

Cat said, "I am not a friend, and I am not a servant. I am the Cat who walks by himself, and I wish to come into your Cave."

Woman said, "Then why did you not come with First Friend on the first night?"

Cat grew very angry and said, "Has Wild Dog told tales of me?"

Then the Woman laughed and said, "You are the Cat who walks by himself, and all places are alike to you. You are neither a friend nor a servant. You have said it yourself. Go away and walk by yourself in all places alike."

Then Cat pretended to be sorry and said, "Must I never come into the Cave? Must I never sit by the warm fire? Must I never drink the warm white milk? You are very wise and very beautiful. You should not be cruel even to a Cat."

Woman said, "I knew I was wise, but I did not know I was beautiful. So I will make a bargain with you. If ever I say one word in your praise, you may come into the Cave."

"And if you say two words in my praise?" said the Cat.

"I never shall," said the Woman, "but if I say two words in your praise, you may sit by the fire in the Cave."

"And if you say three words?" said the Cat.

"I never shall," said the Woman, "but if I say three words in your praise, you may drink the warm white milk three times a day for always and always and always."

Then the Cat arched his back and said, "Now let the Curtain at the mouth of the Cave, and the Fire at the back of the Cave, and the Milk-pots that stand beside the Fire, remember what my Enemy and the Wife of my Enemy has said." And he went away through the Wet Wild Woods waving his wild tail and walking by his wild lone.

That night when the Man and the Horse and the Dog came home from hunting, the Woman did not tell them of the bargain that she had made with the Cat, because she was afraid that they might not like it.

Cat went far and far away and hid himself in the Wet Wild Woods by his wild lone for a long time till the Woman forgot all about him. Only the Bat – the little upside-down Bat – that hung inside the Cave, knew where Cat hid; and every evening Bat would fly to Cat with news of what was happening.

One evening Bat said, "There is a Baby in the Cave. He is new and pink and fat and small, and the Woman is very fond of him."

"Ah," said the Cat, listening, "but what is the Baby fond of?"

"He is fond of things that are soft and tickle," said the Bat. "He is fond of warm things to hold in his arms when he goes to sleep. He is fond of being played with. He is fond of all those things."

"Ah," said the Cat, listening, "then my time has come."

Next night Cat walked through the Wet Wild Woods and hid very near the Cave till morning-time, and Man and Dog and Horse went hunting. The Woman was busy cooking that morning, and the Baby cried and interrupted. So she carried him outside the Cave and gave him a handful of pebbles to play with. But still the Baby cried.

Then the Cat put out his paddy paw and patted the Baby on the cheek, and it cooed; and the Cat rubbed against its fat knees and tickled it under its fat chin with his tail. And the Baby laughed; and the Woman heard him and smiled.

Then the Bat – the little upside-down Bat – that hung in the mouth of the Cave said, "O my Hostess and Wife of my Host and Mother of my Host's Son, a Wild Thing from the Wild Woods is most beautifully playing with your Baby."

"A blessing on that Wild Thing whoever he may be," said the Woman, straightening her back, "for I was a busy woman this morning and he has done me a service."

That very minute and second, Best Beloved, the dried horse-skin Curtain that was stretched tail-down at the mouth of the Cave fell down – *woosh*! – because it remembered the bargain she had made with the Cat, and when the Woman went to pick it up – lo and behold! – the Cat was sitting quite comfy inside the Cave.

"O my Enemy and Wife of my Enemy and Mother of my Enemy," said the Cat, "it is I: for you have spoken a word in my praise, and now I can sit within the Cave for always and always and always. But still I am the Cat who walks by himself, and all places are alike to me."

The Woman was very angry, and shut her lips tight and took up her spinning-wheel and began to spin.

But the Baby cried because the Cat had gone away, and the Woman could not hush it, for it struggled and kicked and grew black in the face.

"O my Enemy and Wife of my Enemy and Mother of my Enemy," said the Cat, "take a strand of the thread that you are spinning and tie it to your spindle-whorl and drag it along the floor, and I will show you a Magic that shall make your Baby laugh as loudly as he is now crying."

"I will do so," said the Woman, "because I am at my wits' end; but I will not thank you for it."

She tied the thread to the little clay spindle-whorl and drew it across the floor, and the Cat ran after it and patted it with his paws and rolled head over heels, and tossed it backward over his shoulder and chased it between his hindlegs and pretended to lose it, and pounced down upon it again, till the Baby laughed as loudly as it had been crying, and scrambled after the Cat and frolicked all over the Cave till it grew tired and settled down to sleep with the Cat in its arms.

"Now," said the Cat, "I will sing the Baby a song that shall keep him asleep for an hour". And he began to purr, loud and low, low and loud, till the Baby fell fast asleep. The Woman smiled as she looked down upon the two of them, and said, "That was wonderfully done. No question but you are very clever, O Cat."

That very minute and second, Best Beloved, the smoke of the Fire at the back of the Cave came down in clouds from the roof – *puff*! – because it remembered the bargain she had made with the Cat, and when it had cleared away – lo and behold! – the Cat was sitting quite comfy close to the fire.

"O my Enemy and Wife of my Enemy and Mother of my Enemy," said the Cat, "it is I, for you have spoken a second word in my praise, and now I can sit by the warm fire at the back of the Cave for always and always and always. But still

I am the Cat who walks by himself, and all places are alike to me."

Then the Woman was very very angry, and let down her hair and put more wood on the fire and brought out the broad blade-bone of the shoulder of mutton and began to make a Magic that should prevent her from saying a third word in praise of the Cat. It was not a Singing Magic, Best Beloved, it was a Still Magic; and by and by the Cave grew so still that a little wee-wee mouse crept out of a corner and ran across the floor.

"O my Enemy and Wife of my Enemy and Mother of my Enemy," said the Cat, "is that little mouse part of your Magic?"

"Ouh! Chee! No indeed!" said the Woman, and she dropped the blade-bone and jumped upon the footstool in front of the fire and braided up her hair very quick for fear that the mouse should run up it.

"Ah," said the Cat, watching, "then the mouse will do me no harm if I eat it?"

"No," said the Woman, braiding up her hair, "eat it quickly and I will ever be grateful to you."

Cat made one jump and caught the little mouse, and the Woman said, "A hundred thanks. Even the First Friend is not quick enough to catch little mice as you have done. You must be very wise."

That very moment and second, O Best Beloved, the Milk-pot that stood by the fire cracked in two pieces – *ffft!* – because it remembered the bargain she had made with the Cat; and when the Woman jumped down from the footstool – lo and behold! – the Cat was lapping up the warm white milk that lay in one of the broken pieces.

"O my Enemy and Wife of my Enemy and Mother of my Enemy," said the Cat, "it is I; for you have spoken three words in my praise, and now I can drink the warm white milk three times a day for always and always and always. But *still*

I am the Cat who walks by himself, and all places are alike to me."

Then the Woman laughed and set the Cat a bowl of the warm white milk and said, "O Cat, you are as clever as a man, but remember that your bargain was not made with the Man or the Dog, and I do not know what they will do when they come home."

"What is that to me?" said the Cat. "If I have my place in the Cave by the fire and my warm white milk three times a day I do not care what the Man or the Dog can do."

That evening when the Man and the Dog came into the Cave, the Woman told them all the story of the bargain while the Cat sat by the fire and smiled. Then the Man said, "Yes, but he has not made a bargain with me or with all proper Men after me." Then he took off his two leather boots and he took up his little stone axe (that makes three) and he fetched a piece of wood and a hatchet (that is five altogether), and he set them out in a row and he said, "Now we will make *our* bargain. If you do not catch mice when you are in the Cave for always and always and always, I will throw these five things at you whenever I see you, and so shall all proper Men do after me."

"Ah," said the Woman, listening, "this is a very clever Cat, but he is not so clever as my Man."

The Cat counted the five things (and they looked very knobby) and he said, "I will catch mice when I am in the Cave for always and always and always; but *still* I am the Cat who walks by himself, and all places are alike to me."

"Not when I am near," said the Man. "If you had not said that last I would have put all these things away for always and always and always; but I am now going to throw my two boots and my little stone axe (that makes three) at you whenever I meet you. And so shall all proper Men do after me!"

Then the Dog said, "Wait a minute. He has not made a bargain with *me* or with all proper Dogs after me." And he showed his teeth and said, "If you are not kind to the Baby while I am in the Cave for always and always and always, I will hunt you till I catch you, and when I catch you I will bite you. And so shall all proper Dogs do after me."

"Ah," said the Woman, listening, "this is a very clever Cat, but he is not so clever as the Dog."

Cat counted the Dog's teeth (and they looked very pointed) and he said, "I will be kind to the Baby while I am in the Cave, as long as he does not pull my tail too hard, for always and always and always. But *still* I am the Cat that walks by himself, and all places are alike to me."

"Not when I am near," said the Dog. "If you had not said that last I would have shut my mouth for always and always and always; but *now* I am going to hunt you up a tree whenever I meet you. And so shall all proper Dogs do after me."

Then the Man threw his two boots and his little stone axe (that makes three) at the Cat, and the Cat ran out of the Cave and the Dog chased him up a tree; and from that day to this, Best Beloved, three proper Men out of five will always throw things at a Cat whenever they meet him, and all proper Dogs will chase him up a tree. But the Cat keeps his side of the bargain too. He will kill mice, and he will be kind to Babies when he is in the house, just as long as they do not pull his tail too hard. But when he has done that, and between times, and when the moon gets up and night comes, he is the Cat that walks by himself, and all places are alike to him. Then he goes out to the Wet Wild Woods or up the Wet Wild Trees or on the Wet Wild Roofs, waving his wild tail and walking by his wild lone.

Pussy can sit by the fire and sing,
  Pussy can climb a tree,
Or play with a silly old cork and string
  To'muse herself, not me.

But I like Binkie my dog, because
  He knows how to behave;
So, Binkie's the same as the First Friend was,
  And I am the Man in the Cave.
Pussy will play Man Friday till
  It's time to wet her paw
And make her walk on the window-sill
  (For the footprint Crusoe saw);
Then she fluffles her tail and mews,
  And scratches and won't attend.
But Binkie will play whatever I choose,
  And he is my true First Friend.

Pussy will rub my knees with her head
  Pretending she loves me hard;
But the very minute I go to my bed
  Pussy runs out in the yard,
And there she stays till the morning-light;
  So I know it is only pretend;
But Binkie, he snores at my feet all night,
  And he is my Firstest Friend!

MASTER CAT; OR, PUSS IN BOOTS

CHARLES PERRAULT

A miller bequeathed to his three sons all he possessed of worldly goods, which consisted only of his Mill, his Ass, and his Cat. It did not take long to divide the property, and neither notary nor attorney was called in; they would soon have eaten up the poor little patrimony. The eldest son had the Mill; the second son, the Ass; and the youngest had nothing but the Cat.

The latter was very disconsolate at having such a poor share of the inheritance. "My brothers," said he, "may be able to earn an honest livelihood by entering into partnership; but, as for me, when I have eaten my Cat and made a muff of his skin, I must die of hunger." The Cat, who had heard this speech, although he had not appeared to do so, said to him with a sedate and serious air, "Do not be troubled, master; you have only to give me a bag, and get a pair of boots made for me in which I can go among the bushes, and you will see that you are not left so badly off as you believe." Though his master did not place much reliance on the Cat's words, he had seen him play such cunning tricks in catching rats and mice, when he would hang himself up by the heels, or hide in the flour pretending to be dead, that he was not altogether without hope of being helped by him out of his distress.

As soon as the Cat had what he asked for, he boldly pulled on his boots, and, hanging his bag round his neck, he took the strings of it in his fore-paws, and started off for a warren where there were a great number of rabbits. He put some bran and sow-thistles in his bag, and then, stretching himself out as if he were dead, he waited till some young rabbit, little versed in the wiles of the world, should come and poke his way into the bag, in order to eat what was inside it.

He had hardly laid himself down before he had the pleasure of seeing a young scatterbrain of a rabbit get into the bag, whereupon Master Cat pulled the strings, caught it, and killed it without mercy. Proud of his prey, he went to the palace, and asked to speak to the King. He was ushered upstairs and into the state apartment, and, after making a low bow to the King, he said, "Sire, here is a wild rabbit, which my Lord the Marquis of Carabas – for such was the title he had taken a fancy to give to his master – has ordered me to present, with his duty, to your Majesty."

"Tell your master," replied the King, "that I thank him and am pleased with his gift."

Another day he went and hid himself in the wheat, keeping the mouth of his bag open as before, and as soon as he saw that a brace of partridges had run inside, he pulled the strings, and so took them both. He went immediately and presented them to the King, as he had the rabbits. The King was equally grateful at receiving the brace of partridges, and ordered drink to be given him.

For the next two or three months, the Cat continued in this manner, taking presents of game at intervals to the King, as if from his master. One day, when he knew the King was going to drive on the banks of the river, with his daughter, the most beautiful Princess in the world, he said to his master, "If you will follow my advice, your fortune is made; you have only to go and bathe in a part of the river I will point out to you, and then leave the rest to me."

The Marquis of Carabas did as his Cat advised him, without knowing what good would come of it. While he was bathing, the King passed by, and the Cat began to call out with all his might, "Help! Help! My Lord the Marquis of Carabas is drowning!" Hearing the cry, the King looked out of the coach window, and recognising the Cat who had so often brought him game, he ordered his guards to fly to the help of my Lord the Marquis of Carabas. Whilst they were getting the poor Marquis out of the river, the Cat went up to the royal coach, and told the King that, while his master had been bathing, some robbers had come and carried off his clothes, although he had shouted, "Stop thief," as loud as he could. The rogue had hidden them himself under a large stone. The King immediately ordered the officers of his wardrobe to go and fetch one of his handsomest suits for my Lord the Marquis of Carabas. The King embraced him a thousand times, and as the fine clothes they dressed him in set off his good looks – for he was handsome and well made – the Marquis of Carabas quite took the fancy of the King's daughter, and after he had cast two or three respectful and rather tender glances towards her, she fell very much in love with him. The King insisted upon his getting into the coach, and accompanying them in their drive. The Cat, delighted to see that his plans were beginning to succeed, ran on before, and coming across some peasants who were mowing a meadow, he said to them, "You, good people, who are mowing here, if you do not tell the King that this meadow you are mowing belongs to my Lord the Marquis of Carabas, you shall all be cut in pieces as small as minced meat." The King did not fail to ask the peasants whose meadow it was they were mowing. "It belongs to my Lord the Marquis of Carabas," said they all together, for the Cat's threat had frightened them. "You have a fine property there," said the King to the Marquis of Carabas.

"As you say, sire," responded the Marquis of Carabas, "for it is a meadow which yields an abundant crop every year."

Master Cat, who still kept in advance of the party, came up to some reapers, and said to them, "You, good people, who are reaping, if you do not say that all this corn belongs to my Lord the Marquis of Carabas, you shall all be cut into pieces as small as minced meat."

The King, who passed by a minute afterwards, wished to know to whom belonged all the cornfields he saw. "To my Lord the Marquis of Carabas," repeated the reapers, and the King again congratulated the Marquis on his property.

The Cat, still continuing to run before the coach, uttered the same threat to everyone he met, and the King was astonished at the great wealth of my Lord the Marquis of Carabas. Master Cat at length arrived at a fine castle, the owner of which was an ogre, the richest ogre ever known, for all the lands through which the King had driven belonged to the Lord of this castle. The Cat took care to find out who the ogre was, and what he was able to do; then he asked to speak with him, saying that he did not like to pass so near his castle without doing himself the honour of paying his respects to him. The ogre received him as civilly as an ogre can, and made him sit down.

"I have been told," said the Cat, "that you have the power of changing yourself into all kinds of animals; that you could, for instance, transform yourself into a lion or an elephant."

"'Tis true," said the ogre, abruptly, "and to prove it to you, you shall see me become a lion." The Cat was so frightened when he saw a lion in front of him, that he quickly scrambled up into the gutter, not without difficulty and danger, on account of his boots, which were worse than useless for walking on the tiles. Shortly afterwards, seeing that the ogre had resumed his natural form, the Cat climbed down again, and admitted that he had been terribly frightened. "I have also been assured," said the Cat, "but I cannot believe it, that you have the power besides of taking the form of the smallest animal; for instance, that of a rat, or a mouse; I confess to you I hold this to be utterly impossible." "Impossible!" exclaimed the ogre, "you shall see!" and he immediately changed himself into a mouse, and began running about the floor. The cat no sooner caught sight of it, than he pounced upon it and ate it.

In the meanwhile, the King, seeing the fine castle of the ogre as he was driving past, thought he should like to go inside. The Cat, who heard the noise of the coach rolling over the draw-bridge, ran to meet it, and said to the King, "Your Majesty is welcome to the Castle of my Lord the Marquis of Carabas!"

"How, my Lord Marquis," exclaimed the King, "this castle belongs to you? Nothing could be finer than this court-yard, and all these buildings which surround it. Let us see the inside of it, if you please."

The Marquis handed out the young Princess, and following the King, who led the way upstairs, they entered a grand hall, where they found prepared a magnificent repast, which the ogre had ordered in expectation of some friends, who were to have visited him that very day, but who did not venture to enter when they heard the King was there. The King, as greatly delighted with the excellent qualities of my Lord the Marquis of Carabas as his daughter, who was more than ever in love with him, seeing what great wealth he possessed, said to him, after having drunk five or six bumpers, "It depends entirely on yourself, my Lord Marquis, whether or not you become my son-in-law." The Marquis, making several profound bows, accepted the honour the King offered him, and that same day was married to the Princess. The Cat became a great lord, and never again ran after mice, except for his amusement.

Be the advantage never so great
Of owning a superb estate,
From sire to son descended,
Young men oft find, on industry,
Combined with ingenuity,
They'd better have depended.

If the son of a miller so quickly could gain
The heart of a Princess, it seems pretty plain,
With good looks and good manners, and some
    aid from dress,
The humblest need not quite despair of success.

THE BLACK CAT

EDGAR ALLAN POE

For the most wild, yet most homely narrative which I am about to pen, I neither expect nor solicit belief. Mad indeed would I be to expect it, in a case where my very senses reject their own evidence. Yet – mad am I not – and very surely do I not dream. But tomorrow I die, and today I would unburden my soul. My immediate purpose is to place before the world plainly, succinctly, and without comment, a series of mere household events. In their consequences these events have terrified – have tortured – have destroyed me. Yet I will not attempt to expound them. To me they have presented little but horror – to many they will seem less terrible than *baroques*. Hereafter, perhaps, some intellect may be found which will reduce my phantasm to the commonplace – some intellect more calm, more logical, and far less excitable than my own, which will perceive in the circumstances I detail with awe, nothing more than an ordinary succession of very natural causes and effects.

From my infancy I was noted for the docility and humanity of my disposition. My tenderness of heart was even so conspicuous as to make me the jest of my companions. I was especially fond of animals, and was indulged by my parents with a great variety of pets. With these I spent most of my time, and never was so happy as when feeding and caressing them. This peculiarity of character grew with my growth, and in my manhood I derived from it one of my principal sources of pleasure. To those who have cherished an affection for a faithful and sagacious dog, I need hardly be at the trouble of explaining the nature or the intensity of the gratification thus derivable. There is something in the unselfish and self-sacrificing love of a brute which goes directly to the heart of him who has had frequent occasion to test the paltry friendship and gossamer fidelity of mere *Man*.

I married early, and was happy to find in my wife a disposition not uncongenial with my own. Observing my partiality for domestic pets, she lost no opportunity of procuring those of the most agreeable kind. We had birds, goldfish, a fine dog, rabbits, a small monkey, and *a cat*.

This latter was a remarkably large and beautiful animal, entirely black, and sagacious to an astonishing degree. In speaking of his intelligence, my wife, who at heart was not a little tinctured with superstition, made frequent allusion to the ancient popular notion which regarded all black cats as witches in disguise. Not that she was ever *serious* upon this point, and I mention the matter at all for no better reason than that it happens just now to be remembered.

Pluto – this was the cat's name – was my favorite pet and playmate. I alone fed him, and he attended me wherever I went about the house. It was even with difficulty that I could prevent him from following me through the streets.

Our friendship lasted in this manner for several years, during which my general temperament and character – through the instrumentality of the fiend Intemperance – had (I blush to confess it) experienced a radical alteration for the worse. I grew, day by day, more moody, more irritable, more regardless of the feelings of others. I suffered myself to use intemperate language to my wife. At length, I even offered her personal violence. My pets of course were made to feel the change in my disposition. I not only neglected, but ill-used them. For Pluto, however, I still retained sufficient regard to restrain me from maltreating him, as I made no scruple of maltreating the rabbits, the monkey, or even the dog, when by accident, or through affection, they came in my way. But my disease grew upon me – for what disease is like Alcohol? – and at length even Pluto, who was now becoming old, and consequently somewhat peevish – even Pluto began to experience the effects of my ill-temper.

One night, returning home much intoxicated, from one of my haunts about town, I fancied that the cat avoided my presence. I seized him; when, in his fright at my violence, he inflicted a slight wound upon my hand with his teeth. The fury of a demon instantly possessed me. I knew myself no longer. My original soul seemed at once to take its flight from my body, and a more than fiendish malevolence, gin-nurtured, thrilled every fiber of my frame. I took from my waistcoat-pocket a penknife, opened it, grasped the poor beast by the throat, and deliberately cut one of its eyes from the socket! I blush, I burn, I shudder, while I pen the damnable atrocity.

When reason returned with the morning – when I had slept off the fumes of the night's debauch – I experienced a sentiment half of horror, half of remorse, for the crime of which I had been guilty; but it was, at best, a feeble and equivocal feeling, and the soul remained untouched. I again plunged into excess, and soon drowned in wine all memory of the deed.

In the meantime the cat slowly recovered. The socket of the lost eye presented, it is true, a frightful appearance, but he no longer appeared to suffer any pain. He went about the house as usual, but, as might be expected, fled in extreme terror at my approach. I had so much of my old heart left as to be at first grieved by this evident dislike on the part of a creature which had once so loved me. But this feeling soon gave place to irritation. And then came, as if to my final and irrevocable overthrow, the spirit of PERVERSENESS. Of this spirit philosophy takes no account. Yet I am not more sure that my soul lives, than I am that perverseness is one of the primitive impulses of the human heart – one of the indivisible primary faculties, or sentiments, which gives direction to the character of Man. Who has not, a hundred times, found himself committing a vile or a silly action for no other reason than because he knows he should *not*? Have we not a perpetual inclination, in the teeth of our best judgment, to violate that which is *Law*, merely because we understand it to be such? This spirit of perverseness, I say, came to my final overthrow. It was this unfathomable longing of the soul *to vex itself* – to offer violence to its own nature – to do wrong for the wrong's sake only – that urged me to continue and finally to consummate the injury I had inflicted upon the unoffending brute. One morning, in cold blood, I slipped a noose about its neck and hung it to the limb of a tree; – hung it with the tears streaming from my eyes; and with the bitterest remorse at my heart; – hung it *because* I knew that it had loved me, and *because* I felt it had given me no reason of offence; – hung it *because* I knew that in so doing I was committing a sin – a deadly sin that would so jeopardise my immortal soul as to place it, if such a thing were possible, even beyond the reach of the infinite mercy of the Most Merciful and Most Terrible God.

On the night of the day on which this cruel deed was done, I was aroused from sleep by the cry of fire. The curtains of my bed were in flames. The whole house was blazing. It was with great difficulty that my wife, a servant, and myself, made our escape from the conflagration. The destruction was complete. My entire worldly wealth was swallowed up, and I resigned myself thenceforward to despair.

I am above the weakness of seeking to establish a

sequence of cause and effect, between the disaster and the atrocity. But I am detailing a chain of facts, and wish not to leave even a possible link imperfect. On the day succeeding the fire, I visited the ruins. The walls, with one exception, had fallen in. This exception was found in a compartment wall, not very thick, which stood about the middle of the house, and against which had rested the head of my bed. The plastering had here, in great measure, resisted the action of the fire, a fact which I attributed to its having been recently spread. About this wall a dense crowd were collected, and many persons seemed to be examining a particular portion of it with very minute and eager attention. The words "strange!", "singular!" and other similar expressions, excited my curiosity. I approached, and saw, as if graven in *bas-relief* upon the white surface, the figure of a gigantic *cat*. The impression was given with an accuracy truly marvelous. There was a rope about the animal's neck.

When I first beheld this apparition – for I could scarcely regard it as less – my wonder and my terror were extreme. But at length reflection came to my aid. The cat, I remembered, had been hung in a garden adjacent to the house. Upon the alarm of fire, this garden had been immediately filled by the crowd, by some one of whom the animal must have been cut from the tree and thrown, through an open window, into my chamber. This had probably been done with the view of arousing me from sleep. The falling of the other walls had compressed the victim of my cruelty into the substance of the freshly spread plaster; the lime of which, with the flames and the *ammonia* from the carcass, had then accomplished the portraiture as I saw it.

Although I thus readily accounted to my reason, if not altogether to my conscience, for the startling fact just detailed, it did not the less fail to make a deep impression upon my fancy. For months I could not rid myself of the phantasm of the cat; and during this period there came back into my spirit a half-sentiment that seemed, but was not, remorse. I went so far as to regret the loss of the animal, and to look about me, among the vile haunts which I now habitually frequented, for another pet of the same species, and of somewhat similar appearance, with which to supply its place.

One night as I sat half stupefied in a den of more than infamy, my attention was suddenly drawn to some black object reposing upon the head of one of the immense hogsheads of gin or of rum which constituted the chief furniture of the apartment. I had been looking steadily at the top of this hogshead for some minutes, and what now caused me surprise was the fact that I had not sooner perceived the object thereupon. I approached it, and touched it with my hand. It was a black cat, a very large one, fully as large as Pluto, and closely resembling him in every respect but one. Pluto had not a white hair upon any portion of his body; but this cat had a large, although indefinite, splotch of white, covering nearly the whole region of the breast.

Upon my touching him, he immediately arose, purred loudly, rubbed against my hand, and appeared delighted with my notice. This, then, was the very creature of which I was in search. I at once offered to purchase it of the landlord; but this person made no claim to it – knew nothing of it – had never seen it before.

I continued my caresses; and when I prepared to go home, the animal evinced a disposition to accompany me. I permitted it to do so, occasionally stooping and patting it as I proceeded. When it reached the house it domesticated itself at once, and became immediately a great favorite with my wife.

For my own part, I soon found a dislike to it arising within me. This was just the reverse of what I had anticipated; but – I know not how or why it was – its evident fondness for myself rather disgusted and annoyed. By slow degrees these feelings of disgust and annoyance rose into the bitterness of hatred. I avoided the creature; a certain sense of shame, and the remembrance of my former deed of cruelty, preventing me from physically abusing it. I did not for some weeks strike or otherwise violently ill-use it; but gradually – very gradually – I came to look upon it with unutterable loathing, and to flee silently from its odious presence, as from the breath of a pestilence.

What added, no doubt, to my hatred of the beast, was the discovery, on the morning after I brought it home, that, like Pluto, it also had been deprived of one of its eyes. This circumstance, however, only endeared it to my wife, who, as I have already said, possessed, in a high degree, that humanity of feeling which had once been my distinguishing trait, and the source of many of my simplest and purest pleasures.

With my aversion to this cat, however, its partiality for myself seemed to increase. It followed my footsteps with a pertinacity which it would be difficult to make the reader comprehend. Whenever I sat, it would crouch beneath my chair, or spring upon my knees, covering me with its loathsome caresses. If I arose to walk it would get between my feet, and thus nearly throw me down; or, fastening its long and sharp claws in my dress, clamber in this manner to my breast. At such times, although I longed to destroy it with a blow, I was yet withheld from so doing, partly by a memory of my former crime, but chiefly – let me confess it at once – by absolute *dread* of the beast.

This dread was not exactly a dread of physical evil – and yet I should be at a loss how otherwise to define it. I am almost ashamed to own – yes, even in this felon's cell I am almost ashamed to own – that the terror and horror with which the animal inspired me had been heightened by one of the merest chimeras it would be possible to conceive. My wife had called my attention more than once to the character of the mark of white hair of which I have spoken, and which constituted the sole visible difference between the strange beast and the one I had destroyed. The reader will remember that this mark, although large, had been originally very indefinite; but by slow degrees – degrees nearly imperceptible, and which for a long time my Reason struggled to reject as fanciful – it had at length assumed a rigorous distinctness of outline. It was now the representation of an object that I shudder to name – and for this, above all, I loathed and dreaded and would have rid myself of the monster *had I dared* – it was now, I say, the image of a hideous – of a ghastly thing – of the GALLOWS! – O mournful and terrible engine of Horror and of Crime – o Agony and of Death!

And now was I indeed wretched beyond the wretchedness of mere humanity. And *a brute beast* – whose fellow I had contemptuously destroyed – *a brute beast* to work out for *me* – for me, a man fashioned in the image of the High God – so much of insufferable woe! Alas! neither by day nor by night knew I the blessing of rest any more! During the former the creature left me no moment alone; and, in the latter, I started hourly from dreams of unutterable fear, to find the hot breath of *the thing* upon my face, and its vast weight an incarnate Nightmare that I had no power to shake off – incumbent eternally upon my *heart*!

Beneath the pressure of torments such as these, the feeble remnant of the good within me succumbed. Evil thoughts became my sole intimates – the darkest and most evil of thoughts. The moodiness of my usual temper increased to hatred of all things and of all mankind; while, from the sudden, frequent, and ungovernable outbursts of a fury to which I now blindly abandoned myself, my uncomplaining wife, alas! was the most usual and the most patient of sufferers.

One day she accompanied me, upon some household errand into the cellar of the old building which our poverty compelled us to inhabit. The cat followed me down the steep stairs, and, nearly throwing me headlong, exasperated me to madness. Uplifting an axe, and, forgetting in my wrath the childish dread which had hitherto stayed my hand, I aimed a blow at the animal, which of course would have proved instantly fatal had it descended as I wished. But this blow was arrested by the hand of my wife. Goaded, by the interference, into a rage more than demoniacal, I withdrew my arm from her grasp, and buried the axe in her brain. She fell dead upon the spot, without a groan.

This hideous murder accomplished, I set myself forthwith, and with entire deliberation, to the task of concealing the body. I knew that I could not remove it from the house, either by day or by night, without the risk of being observed by the neighbors. Many projects entered my mind. At one period I thought of cutting the corpse into minute fragments and destroying them by fire. At another, I resolved to dig a grave for it in the floor of the cellar. Again, I deliberated about casting it in the well in the yard – about packing it in a box, as if merchandise, with the usual arrangements, and so getting a porter to take it from the house. Finally I hit upon what I considered a far better expedient than either of these. I determined to wall it up in the cellar – as the monks of the Middle Ages are recorded to have walled up their victims.

For a purpose such as this the cellar was well adapted. Its walls were loosely constructed, and had lately been plastered throughout with rough plaster, which the dampness of the atmosphere had prevented from hardening. Moreover, in one of the walls was a projection, caused by a false chimney, or fireplace, that had been filled up, and made to resemble the rest of the cellar. I made no doubt that I could readily displace the bricks at this point, insert the corpse, and wall the whole up as before, so that no eye could detect anything suspicious.

And in this calculation I was not deceived. By means of a crowbar I easily dislodged the bricks; and, having carefully deposited the body against the inner wall, I propped it in that position, while with little trouble I relaid the whole structure as it originally stood. Having procured mortar, sand, and hair, with every possible precaution, I prepared a plaster which could not be distinguished from the old, and with this I very carefully went over the new brickwork. When I had finished, I felt satisfied that all was right. The wall did not present the slightest appearance of having been disturbed. The rubbish on the floor was picked up with the minutest care. I looked around triumphantly, and said to myself, "Here at last, then, my labor has not been in vain".

My next step was to look for the beast which had been the cause of so much wretchedness; for I had at length firmly resolved to put it to death. Had I been able to meet with it at the moment there could have been no doubt of its fate, but it appeared that the crafty animal had been alarmed at the violence of my previous anger, and forebore to present itself in my present mood. It is impossible to describe or to imagine the deep, the blissful sense of relief which the absence of the detested creature occasioned in my bosom. It did not make its appearance during the night; and thus for one night at least since its introduction into the house, I soundly and tranquilly slept – ay, *slept* even with the burden of murder upon my soul!

The second and third day passed, and still my tormentor came not. Once again I breathed as a free man. The monster, in terror, had fled the premises for ever! I should behold it no more! My happiness was supreme! The guilt of my dark deed disturbed me but little. Some few inquiries had been made, but these had been readily answered. Even a search had been instituted; but of course nothing was to be discovered. I looked upon my future felicity as secured.

Upon the fourth day of the assassination, a party of the police came over unexpectedly into the house, and proceeded again to make rigorous investigation of the premises. Secure, however, in the inscrutability of my place of concealment, I felt no embarrassment whatever. The officers bade me accompany them in their search. They left no nook or corner unexplored. At length, for the third or fourth time, they descended into the cellar. I quivered not in a muscle. My heart beat calmly as that of one who slumbers in innocence. I walked the cellar from end to end. I folded my arms upon my bosom, and roamed easily to and fro. The police were thoroughly satisfied, and prepared to depart. The glee of my heart was too strong to be restrained. I burned to say, if but one word, by way of triumph, and to render doubly sure their assurance of my guiltlessness.

"Gentlemen", I said at last, as the party ascended the steps, "I delight to have allayed your suspicions. I wish you all health, and a little more courtesy. By the bye, gentlemen, this – this is a very well-constructed house". (In the rabid desire to say something easily, I scarcely knew what I uttered at all.) "I may say an *excellently* well constructed house. These walls – are you going, gentlemen? – these walls are solidly put together"; and here, through the mere frenzy of bravado, I rapped heavily, with a cane which I held in my hand, upon that very portion of the brickwork behind which stood the corpse of the wife of my bosom.

But may God shield and deliver me from the fangs of the Arch-Fiend! No sooner had the reverberation of my blows sunk into silence than I was answered by a voice from within the tomb! – by a cry, at first muffled and broken, like the sobbing of a child, and then quickly swelling into one long, loud, and continuous scream, utterly anomalous and inhuman – a howl – a wailing shriek, half of horror and half of triumph, such as might have arisen only out of hell, conjointly from the throats of the damned in their agony and of the demons that exult in the damnation.

Of my own thoughts it is folly to speak. Swooning, I staggered to the opposite wall. For one instant the party upon the stairs remained motionless, through extremity of terror and of awe. In the next, a dozen stout arms were toiling at the wall. It fell bodily. The corpse, already greatly decayed and clotted with gore, stood erect before the eyes of the spectators. Upon its head, with red extended mouth and solitary eye of fire, sat the hideous beast whose craft had seduced me into murder, and whose informing voice had consigned me to the hangman. I had walled the monster up within the tomb!

CAT AND MOUSE
IN PARTNERSHIP

JACOB & WILHELM GRIMM

A certain cat had made the acquaintance of a mouse, and had said so much to her about the great love and friendship she felt for her, that at length the mouse agreed that they should live and keep house together. 'But we must make a provision for winter, or else we shall suffer from hunger,' said the cat; 'and you, little mouse, cannot venture everywhere, or you will be caught in a trap some day.' The good advice was followed, and a pot of fat was bought, but they did not know where to put it. At length, after much consideration, the cat said: 'I know no place where it will be better stored up than in the church, for no one dares take anything away from there. We will set it beneath the altar, and not touch it until we are really in need of it.' So the pot was placed in safety, but it was not long before the cat had a great yearning for it, and said to the mouse: 'I want to tell you something, little mouse; my cousin has brought a little son into the world, and has asked me to be godmother; he is white with brown spots, and I am to hold him over the font at the christening. Let me go out today, and you look after the house by yourself.' 'Yes, yes,' answered the mouse, 'by all means go, and if you get anything very good to eat, think of me. I should like a drop of sweet red christening wine myself.' All this, however, was untrue; the cat had no cousin, and had not been asked to be godmother. She went straight to the church, stole to the pot of fat, began to lick at it, and licked the top of the fat off. Then she took a walk upon the roofs of the town, looked out for opportunities, and then stretched herself in the sun, and licked her lips whenever she thought of the pot of fat, and not until it was evening did she return home. 'Well, here you are again,' said the mouse, 'no doubt you have had a merry day.' 'All went off well,' answered the cat. 'What name did they give the child?' 'Top-off!' said the cat quite coolly. 'Top-off!' cried the mouse, 'that is a very odd and uncommon name, is it a usual one in your family?' 'What does that matter,' said the cat, 'it is no worse than Crumb-stealer, as your godchildren are called.'

Before long the cat was seized by another fit of yearning. She said to the mouse: 'You must do me a favour, and once more manage the house for a day alone. I am again asked to be godmother, and, as the child has a white ring round its neck, I cannot refuse.' The good mouse consented, but the cat crept behind the town walls to the church, and devoured half the pot of fat. 'Nothing ever seems so good as what one keeps to oneself,' said she, and was quite satisfied with her day's work. When she went home the mouse inquired: 'And what was the child christened?' 'Half-done,' answered the cat. 'Half-done! What are you saying? I never heard the name in my life, I'll wager anything it is not in the calendar!'

The cat's mouth soon began to water for some more licking. 'All good things go in threes,' said she, 'I am asked to stand godmother again. The child is quite black, only it has white paws, but with that exception, it has not a single white hair on its whole body; this only happens once every few years, you will let me go, won't you?' 'Top-off! Half-done!' answered the mouse, 'they are such odd names, they make me very thoughtful.' 'You sit at home,' said the cat, 'in your dark-grey fur coat and long tail, and are filled with fancies, that's because you do not go out in the daytime.' During the cat's absence the mouse cleaned the house, and put it in order, but the greedy cat entirely emptied the pot of fat. 'When everything is eaten up one has some peace,' said she to herself, and well filled and fat she did not return home till night. The mouse at once asked what name had been given to the third child. 'It will not please you more than the others,' said the cat. 'He is called All-gone.' 'All-gone,' cried the mouse 'that is the most suspicious name of all! I have never seen it in print. All-gone; what can that mean?' and she shook her head, curled herself up, and lay down to sleep.

From this time forth no one invited the cat to be godmother, but when the winter had come and there was no longer anything to be found outside, the mouse thought of their provision, and said: 'Come, cat, we will go to our pot of fat which we have stored up for ourselves – we shall enjoy that.' 'Yes,' answered the cat, 'you will enjoy it as much as you would enjoy sticking that dainty tongue of yours out of the window.' They set out on their way, but when they arrived, the pot of fat certainly was still in its place, but it was empty. 'Alas!' said the mouse, 'now I see what has happened, now it comes to light! You a true friend! You have devoured all when you were standing godmother. First top off, then half-done, then –' 'Will you hold your tongue,' cried the cat, 'one word more, and I will eat you too.' 'All-gone' was already on the poor mouse's lips; scarcely had she spoken it before the cat sprang on her, seized her, and swallowed her down. Verily, that is the way of the world.

TOBERMORY

SAKI

It was a chill, rain-washed afternoon of a late August day, that indefinite season when partridges are still in security or cold storage, and there is nothing to hunt – unless one is bounded on the north by the Bristol Channel, in which case one may lawfully gallop after fat red stags. Lady Blemley's house-party was not bounded on the north by the Bristol Channel, hence there was a full gathering of her guests round the tea-table on this particular afternoon. And, in spite of the blankness of the season and the triteness of the occasion, there was no trace in the company of that fatigued restlessness which means a dread of the pianola and a subdued hankering for auction bridge. The undisguised openmouthed attention of the entire party was fixed on the homely negative personality of Mr Cornelius Appin. Of all her guests, he was the one who had come to Lady Blemley with the vaguest reputation. Someone had said he was "clever," and he had got his invitation in the moderate expectation, on the part of his hostess, that some portion at least of his cleverness would be contributed to the general entertainment. Until tea-time that day she had been unable to discover in what direction, if any, his cleverness lay. He was neither a wit nor a croquet champion, a hypnotic force nor a begetter of amateur theatricals. Neither did his exterior suggest the sort of man in whom women are willing to pardon a generous measure of mental deficiency. He had subsided into mere Mr Appin, and the Cornelius seemed a piece of transparent baptismal bluff. And now he was claiming to have launched on the world a discovery beside which the invention of gunpowder, of the printing press, and of steam locomotion were inconsiderable trifles. Science had made bewildering strides in many directions during recent decades, but this thing seemed to belong to the domain of miracle rather than to scientific achievement.

"And do you really ask us to believe," Sir Wilfrid was saying, "that you have discovered a means for instructing animals in the art of human speech, and that dear old Tobermory has proved your first successful pupil?"

"It is a problem at which I have worked for the last seventeen years," said Mr Appin, "but only during the last eight or nine months have I been rewarded with glimmerings of success. Of course I have experimented with thousands of animals, but latterly only with cats, those wonderful creatures which have assimilated themselves so marvellously with our civilisation while retaining all their highly developed feral instincts. Here and there among cats one comes across an outstanding superior intellect, just as one does among the ruck of human beings, and when I made the acquaintance of Tobermory a week ago I saw at once that I was in contact with a 'Beyond-cat' of extraordinary intelligence. I had gone far along the road to success in recent experiments; with Tobermory, as you call him, I have reached the goal."

Mr Appin concluded his remarkable statement in a voice which he strove to divest of a triumphant inflection. No one said "Rats," though Clovis's lips moved in a monosyllabic contortion which probably invoked those rodents of disbelief.

"And do you mean to say," asked Miss Resker, after a slight pause, "that you have taught Tobermory to say and understand easy sentences of one syllable?"

"My dear Miss Resker," said the wonder-worker patiently, "one teaches little children and savages and backward adults in that piecemeal fashion; when one has once solved the problem of making a beginning with an animal of highly developed intelligence one has no need for those halting methods. Tobermory can speak our language with perfect correctness."

This time Clovis very distinctly said, "Beyond-rats!" Sir Wilfrid was more polite, but equally sceptical.

"Hadn't we better have the cat in and judge for ourselves?" suggested Lady Blemley.

Sir Wilfrid went in search of the animal, and the company settled themselves down to the languid expectation of witnessing some more or less adroit drawing-room ventriloquism.

In a minute Sir Wilfrid was back in the room, his face white beneath its tan and his eyes dilated with excitement.

"By Gad, it's true!"

His agitation was unmistakably genuine, and his hearers started forward in a thrill of awakened interest. Collapsing into an armchair he continued breathlessly: "I found him dozing in the smoking-room, and called out to him to come for his tea. He blinked at me in his usual way, and I said, 'Come on, Toby; don't keep us waiting;' and, by Gad! he drawled out in a most horribly natural voice that he'd come when he dashed well pleased! I nearly jumped out of my skin!" Appin had preached to absolutely incredulous hearers; Sir Wilfrid's statement carried instant conviction. A Babel-like chorus of startled exclamation arose, amid which the scientist sat mutely enjoying the first fruit of his stupendous discovery.

In the midst of the clamour Tobermory entered the room

and made his way with velvet tread and studied unconcern across to the group seated round the tea-table.

A sudden hush of awkwardness and constraint fell on the company. Somehow there seemed an element of embarrassment in addressing on equal terms a domestic cat of acknowledged dental ability.

"Will you have some milk, Tobermory?" asked Lady Blemley in a rather strained voice.

"I don't mind if I do," was the response, couched in a tone of even indifference. A shiver of suppressed excitement went through the listeners, and Lady Blemley might be excused for pouring out the saucerful of milk rather unsteadily.

"I'm afraid I've spilt a good deal of it," she said apologetically.

"After all, it's not my Axminster," was Tobermory's rejoinder.

Another silence fell on the group, and then Miss Resker, in her best district-visitor manner, asked if the human language had been difficult to learn. Tobermory looked squarely at her for a moment and then fixed his gaze serenely on the middle distance. It was obvious that boring questions lay outside his scheme of life.

"What do you think of human intelligence?" asked Mavis Pellington lamely.

"Of whose intelligence in particular?" asked Tobermory coldly.

"Oh, well, mine for instance," said Mavis, with a feeble laugh.

"You put me in an embarrassing position," said Tobermory, whose tone and attitude certainly did not suggest a shred of embarrassment. "When your inclusion in this house-party was suggested Sir Wilfrid protested that you were the most brainless woman of his acquaintance, and that there was a wide distinction between hospitality and the care of the feeble-minded. Lady Blemley replied that your lack of brain-power was the precise quality which had earned you your invitation, as you were the only person she could think of who might be idiotic enough to buy their old car. You know, the one they call 'The Envy of Sisyphus,' because it goes quite nicely uphill if you push it."

Lady Blemley's protestations would have had greater effect if she had not casually suggested to Mavis only that morning that the car in question would be just the thing for her down at her Devonshire home.

Major Barfield plunged in heavily to effect a diversion.

"How about your carryings-on with the tortoiseshell puss up at the stables, eh?"

The moment he had said it everyone realised the blunder.

"One does not usually discuss these matters in public," said Tobermory frigidly. "From a slight observation of your ways since you've been in this house I should imagine you'd find it inconvenient if I were to shift the conversation on to your own little affairs."

The panic which ensued was not confined to the Major.

"Would you like to go and see if cook has got your dinner ready?" suggested Lady Blemley hurriedly, affecting to ignore the fact that it wanted at least two hours to Tobermory's dinner-time.

"Thanks," said Tobermory, "not quite so soon after my tea. I don't want to die of indigestion."

"Cats have nine lives, you know," said Sir Wilfrid heartily.

"Possibly," answered Tobermory; "but only one liver."

"Adelaide!" said Mrs Cornett, "do you mean to encourage that cat to go out and gossip about us in the servants' hall?"

The panic had indeed become general. A narrow ornamental balustrade ran in front of most of the bedroom windows at the Towers, and it was recalled with dismay that this had formed a favourite promenade for Tobermory at all hours, whence he could watch the pigeons – and heaven knew what else besides. If he intended to become reminiscent in his present outspoken strain the effect would be something more than disconcerting. Mrs Cornett, who spent much time at her toilet table, and whose complexion was reputed to be of a nomadic though punctual disposition, looked as ill at ease as the Major. Miss Scrawen, who wrote fiercely sensuous poetry and led a blameless life, merely displayed irritation; if you are methodical and virtuous in private you don't necessarily want every one to know it. Bertie van Tahn, who was so depraved at seventeen that he had long ago given up trying to be any worse, turned a dull shade of gardenia white, but he did not commit the error of dashing out of the room like Odo Finsberry, a young gentleman who was understood to be reading for the Church and who was possibly disturbed at the thought of scandals he might hear concerning other people. Clovis had the presence of mind to maintain a composed exterior; privately he was calculating how long it would take to procure a box of fancy mice through the agency of the *Exchange and Mart* as a species of hush-money. Even in a delicate situation like the present, Agnes Resker could not endure to remain too long in the background.

"Why did I ever come down here?" she asked dramatically.

Tobermory immediately accepted the opening. "Judging by what you said to Mrs Cornett on the croquet-lawn yesterday, you were out for food. You described the Blemleys as the dullest people to stay with that you knew, but said they were clever enough to employ a first-rate cook; otherwise they'd find it difficult to get anyone to come down a second time."

"There's not a word of truth in it! I appeal to Mrs Cornett—" exclaimed the discomfited Agnes.

"Mrs Cornett repeated your remark afterwards to Bertie van Tahn," continued Tobermory, "and said, 'That woman is a regular Hunger Marcher; she'd go anywhere for four square meals a day,' and Bertie van Tahn said—"

At this point the chronicle mercifully ceased. Tobermory had caught a glimpse of the big yellow Tom from the Rectory working his way through the shrubbery towards the stable wing. In a flash he had vanished through the open French window.

With the disappearance of his too brilliant pupil Cornelius Appin found himself beset by a hurricane of bitter upbraiding, anxious inquiry, and frightened entreaty. The responsibility for the situation lay with him, and he must prevent matters from becoming worse. Could Tobermory impart his dangerous gift to other cats? was the first question he had to answer. It was possible, he replied, that he might have initiated his intimate friend the stable puss into his new accomplishment, but it was unlikely that his teaching could have taken a wider range as yet.

"Then," said Mrs Cornett, "Tobermory may be a valuable cat and a great pet; but I'm sure you'll agree, Adelaide, that both he and the stable cat must be done away with without delay."

"You don't suppose I've enjoyed the last quarter of an hour, do you?" said Lady Blemley bitterly. "My husband and I are very fond of Tobermory – at least, we were before this horrible accomplishment was infused into him; but now, of course, the only thing is to have him destroyed as soon as possible."

"We can put some strychnine in the scraps he always gets at dinner-time," said Sir Wilfrid, "and I will go and drown the stable cat myself. The coachman will be very sore at losing his pet, but I'll say a very catching form of mange has broken out in both cats and we're afraid of it spreading to the kennels."

"But my great discovery!" expostulated Mr Appin; "after all my years of research and experiment—"

"You can go and experiment on the short-horns at the farm, who are under proper control," said Mrs Cornett, "or the elephants at the Zoological Gardens. They're said to be highly intelligent, and they have this recommendation, that they don't come creeping about our bedrooms and under chairs, and so forth."

An archangel ecstatically proclaiming the Millennium, and then finding that it clashed unpardonably with Henley and would have to be indefinitely postponed, could hardly have felt more crestfallen than Cornelius Appin at the reception of his wonderful achievement. Public opinion, however, was against him – in fact, had the general voice been consulted on the subject it is probable that a strong minority vote would have been in favour of including him in the strychnine diet.

Defective train arrangements and a nervous desire to see matters brought to a finish prevented an immediate dispersal of the party, but dinner that evening was not a social success. Sir Wilfrid had had rather a trying time with the stable cat and subsequently with the coachman. Agnes Resker ostentatiously limited her repast to a morsel of dry toast, which she bit as though it were a personal enemy; while Mavis Pellington maintained a vindictive silence throughout the meal. Lady Blemley kept up a flow of what she hoped was conversation, but her attention was fixed on the doorway. A plateful of carefully dosed fish scraps was in readiness on the sideboard, but sweets and savoury and dessert went their way, and no Tobermory appeared either in the dining-room or kitchen.

The sepulchral dinner was cheerful compared with the subsequent vigil in the smoking-room. Eating and drinking had at least supplied a distraction and cloak to the prevailing embarrassment. Bridge was out of the question in the general tension of nerves and tempers, and after Odo Finsberry had given a lugubrious rendering of "Melisande in the Wood" to a frigid audience, music was tacitly avoided. At eleven the servants went to bed, announcing that the small window in the pantry had been left open as usual for Tobermory's private use. The guests read steadily through the current batch of magazines, and fell back gradually, on the *Badminton Library* and bound volumes of *Punch*. Lady Blemley made periodic visits to the pantry, returning each time with an expression of listless depression which forestalled questioning.

At two o'clock Clovis broke the dominating silence.

"He won't turn up tonight. He's probably in the local newspaper office at the present moment, dictating the first instalment of his reminiscences. Lady What's-her-name's book won't be in it. It will be the event of the day."

Having made this contribution to the general cheerfulness, Clovis went to bed. At long intervals the various members of the house-party followed his example.

The servants taking round the early tea made a uniform announcement in reply to a uniform question. Tobermory had not returned.

Breakfast was, if anything, a more unpleasant function than dinner had been, but before its conclusion the situation was relieved. Tobermory's corpse was brought in from the shrubbery, where a gardener had just discovered it. From the bites on his throat and the yellow fur which coated his claws it was evident that he had fallen in unequal combat with the big Tom from the Rectory.

By midday most of the guests had quitted the Towers, and after lunch Lady Blemley had sufficiently recovered her spirits to write an extremely nasty letter to the Rectory about the loss of her valuable pet.

Tobermory had been Appin's one successful pupil, and he was destined to have no successor. A few weeks later an elephant in the Dresden Zoological Garden, which had shown no previous signs of irritability, broke loose and killed an Englishman who had apparently been teasing it. The victim's name was variously reported in the papers as Appin and Eppelin, but his front name was faithfully rendered Cornelius.

"If he was trying German irregular verbs on the poor beast," said Clovis, "he deserved all he got."

PUSS-CAT

E. F. BENSON

It was during the month of May some nine years ago that the beginning of the events that concerned Puss-cat took place. I was living at the time on the green outskirts of a country town, and my dining-room at the back of the house opened on to a small garden framed in brick walls some five feet high. Breakfasting there one morning, I saw a large black and white cat, with a sharp but serious face, observing me with studied attention. Now at the time there was an interregnum, and my house was without a mistress (in the shape of a cat), and it at once struck me that I was being interviewed by this big and pleasing stranger, to see if I would do. So, since there is nothing that a prospective mistress likes less than premature familiarity on the part of the householder whom she may be thinking of engaging, I took no direct notice of the cat, but continued to eat my breakfast carefully and tidily. After a short inspection, the cat quietly withdrew without once looking back, and I supposed that I was dismissed, or that she had decided, after all, to keep on her present household.

In that I proved to be mistaken: she had only gone away to think about it, and next morning, and for several mornings after that, I was subjected to the same embarrassing but not unfriendly scrutiny, after which she took a stroll round the garden to see if there were any flower-beds that would do to make ambushes in, and a convenient tree or two to climb should emergencies arise. On the fourth day, as far as I remember, I committed an error, and half-way through break-fast went out into the garden, to attempt to get on more familiar terms. The cat regarded me for a few moments with pained surprise, and went away; but after I had gone in again, she decided to overlook it, for she returned to her former place, and continued to observe. Next morning she made up her mind, jumped down from the wall, trotted across the grass, entered the dining-room, and, arranging herself in a great hurry round one hind-leg, which she put up in the air like a flagstaff, proceeded to make her morning toilet. That, as I knew quite well, meant that she thought I would give satisfaction, and I was therefore permitted to enter upon my duties at once. So I put down a saucer of milk for her, which she very obligingly disposed of. Then she went and sat by the door, and said "A-a-a-a," to show that she wished the door to be opened for her, so that she might inspect the rest of the house. So I called down the kitchen stairs, "There is come a cat, who I think means to stop. Don't fuss her." In this manner the real Puss-cat – though I did not know that – entered the house.

Now here I must make a short defence for my share in these things. I might, by a hasty judgment, be considered to have stolen her who soon became Puss-cat's mamma, but anyone who has any real knowledge of cats will be aware that I did nothing of the kind. Puss-cat's mamma was clearly dissatisfied with her last household and had, without the least doubt, made up her mind to leave them all and take on a fresh lot of servants; and if a cat makes up her mind about anything, no power on earth except death, or permanent confinement in a room where neither doors nor windows are ever opened, will stop her taking the contemplated step. If her last (unknown) household killed her, or permanently shut her up, of course, she could not engage fresh people, but short of that they were powerless to keep her. You may cajole or bully a dog into doing what you want, but no manner of persuasion will cause a cat to deviate one hair's breadth from the course she means to pursue. If I had driven her away she would have gone to another house, but never back to her own. For though we may own dogs and horses and other animals, it is a great mistake to think that we own cats. Cats employ us, and if we give satisfaction they may go so far as to adopt us. Besides, Puss-cat's mamma did not, as it turned out, mean to stay with me altogether: she only wanted quiet lodgings for a time.

So our new mistress went discreetly downstairs and inspected kitchen, scullery, and pantry. She spent some time in the scullery, so I was told, and felt rather doubtful. But she quite liked the new gas-stove in the kitchen, and singed her tail at it, as nobody had told her that lunch was a-cooking. Also she found a mouse-hole below the wainscoting, which appeared to decide her (for, as we soon found out, she liked work), and she trotted upstairs again and sat outside the drawing-room door till somebody opened it for her. I happened to be inside, with Jill, a young lady of the fox-terrier breed, and, of course, did not know that Puss-cat's mamma was waiting. Eventually I came out and saw her sitting there. Jill saw her, too, and eagerly ran up to her only to talk, not to fight, for Jill likes cats. But Puss-cat's mamma did not know that, so, just in case, she slapped Jill smartly first on one side the head, and then on the other. She was not angry, but only firm and strong, and wished that from the first there should be no doubt whatever about her position. Having done that, she allowed Jill to explain, which Jill did with twitchings of her stumpy tail and attitude provocative of gambols. And before many minutes were up, Puss-cat's mamma was kind enough to play with her. Then she suddenly remembered that she had not seen the rest of the house, and went upstairs, where she remained till lunch-time.

It was the manner in which she spent the first morning that gave me the key to the character of Puss-cat's mamma, and we at once settled that her name had always been Martha. She had annexed our house, it is true, but in no grabbing or belligerent spirit, but simply because she had seen from her post on the garden wall that we wanted somebody to look after us and manage the house, and she could not help knowing how wonderful she was in all things connected with a mistress's duties. Every morning when the housemaid's step was heard on the stairs during breakfast (she had a very audible step), Martha, even in the middle of fish or milk, ran to the door, said "A-a-a-a" till it was opened, and rushed after her, sitting in each bedroom in turn to see that the slops were properly emptied and the beds well and truly made. In the middle of such supervision sometimes came other calls upon her, the front-door bell would ring, and Martha had to hurry down to see that the door was nicely opened. Then perhaps she would catch sight of somebody digging in the garden, and she was forced to go out in this busiest time of the morning, to dab at the turned-up earth, in order to be sure that it was fresh. In particular, I remember the day on which the dining-room was repapered. She had to climb the step-ladder to ascertain if it was safe, and sit on the top to clean herself. Then each roll of paper had to be judged by the smell, and the paste to be touched with the end of a pink tongue. That made her sneeze (which must be the right test for paste), and she allowed it to be used. That day we lunched in the drawing-room, and it is easy to imagine how busy Martha was, for the proceeding was very irregular, and she could not tell how it would turn out. Meal-times were always busy: she had to walk in front of every dish as it was brought in, and precede it as it was taken out, and to-day these duties were complicated by the necessity of going back constantly to the real dining-room to see that the paper-hangers were not idling. To make the rush more overpowering, Jill was in the garden wanting to play (and to play with Jill was one of Martha's duties) and some young hollyhocks were being put in, certain of which, for inscrutable reasons, had to be dug up again with strong backward kicks of the hind-legs.

She had settled that there was but one cat, which was, of course, herself. Occasionally alien heads looked over the wall, and the cries of strangers sounded. Whenever that happened, whatever the stress of housework might be, Martha bounded from house into garden to expel and, if possible, kill the intruder. Once from my bedroom window I saw a terrific affair. Martha had been sitting as good as gold among hair-brushes and nail-scissors, showing me how to shave, when something feline moving in the garden caught her eye. Not waiting for the door to be opened, she made one leap of it out of the window into the apple-tree, and whirled down the trunk, even as lightning strikes and rips its way to the ground, and next moment I saw her, with paw uplifted, tearing tufts of fur from the next-door tabby. She was like one of those amazing Chinese grotesques, half-cat, half-demon, and wholly warrior. Shrill cries rent the peaceful morning air, and Martha, intoxicated with vengeance, allowed the mishandled tabby to escape. Then with awesome face and Bacchanalian eye she ate the tufts of bloodstained fur, rolling them on her tongue and swallowing them with obvious difficulty, as if performing some terrible, antique and cannibalistic rite. And all this from a lady who was so shortly to be confined. But it was no use trying to keep Martha quiet.

A second minute inspection of her house was necessary before she decided which should be the birth-chamber. She spent a long time in the woodshed that morning, and we hoped that it was going to be there; she spent a long time in the bath-room, and we hoped it wasn't. Eventually she settled

on the pantry, and when she had quite made up her mind
we made her comfortable. Next morning three dappled little
blind things were there. She ate one, for no reason, as far as
we could judge, but that she was afraid that Jill wanted to.
So, as it was her kitten, not Jill's, she ate it.

With all respect for Martha, I think that here she had
mistaken her vocation. She should never have gone in for
being a mother. The second kitten she lay down upon with
fatal results. Then, being thoroughly disgusted with maternity,
she went away and never was seen any more. She deserted
the only child she had not killed; she deserted us who had
tried so hard to give satisfaction; and in the basket there was
left, still blind, still uncertain whether it was worthwhile to
live at all, Puss-cat.

Puss-cat was her mother's own child from the first, though
with much added. She wasted no time or strength in bewailing
her orphaned condition, but took amazing quantities of milk
administered on a feather. Her eyes opened, as eyes should
do, on the seventh day, and she smiled at us all, and spat at
Jill. So Jill licked her nose with anxious care, and said quite
distinctly, "When you are a little older, I will be always ready
to do whatever you like." Jill says the same sort of thing to
everybody except the dustman.

Soon after, Puss-cat arose from her birth-bed and staggered across the pantry. Even this first expedition on her own
feet was not made without purpose, for in spite of frequent
falls she went straight up to a blind-tassel, and after looking
at it for a long time, tested it with a tiny paw to make sure
of it, thus showing, while scarcely out of the cradle, that
serious purpose which marked her throughout her dear life.
Her motto was, "Do your work," and since she remained
unmarried in spite of many very eligible offers, I think that
her unnatural mother must have impressed upon her, in those
few days before she deserted her, that the first duty of a cat

is to look after the house, and that she herself didn't think much of maternity. Puss-cat inherited also, I suppose, her fixed conviction that she ought to have been, even if she was not, the only cat in the world, and she would allow no one of her own race within eyeshot of house or garden. Some of her duties, though they were always conscientiously performed, I think rather bored her, but certainly she brought to the expulsion of cats an exquisite sense of enjoyment. On the appearance of any one of her own nation she would go hastily into ambush with twitching tail and jerking shoulder-blades, teasing and torturing herself with the postponement of that rapturous stealthy advance across the grass, if the quarry was looking the other way, or the furious hurling of herself through the air, if a frontal attack had to be delivered. And I often wondered that she did not betray her ambush by the rapture and sonorousness of her purring, as the supreme moment approached.

Jill, I am afraid, gave her a lot of worry over this duty of the expulsion of aliens, for Jill would sooner play with an alien than expel it, and her plan was to gambol up to the intruder with misplaced welcome. It is true that the effect was just the same, because a trespassing cat, seeing an alert fox-terrier rapidly approaching, seldom, if ever, stops to play, so that Jill's method was really quite effective, too. But Puss-cat had high moral purpose behind her: she wanted not only to expel, but to appal and injure, and like many moralists of our own species, she enjoyed her fulminations and onslaughts quite tremendously. She liked punishing other cats, because she was right and they were wrong, and vigorous kicks and bites would help them perhaps to understand that.

But though Puss-cat resembled her mother in the matter of the high sense of duty and moral qualities, she had what Martha lacked: that indefinable attraction which we call charm, and a great heart. She was always pleased and affectionate, and went about her duties with as near an approach to a smile as is possible for the gravest species of animal. Martha, for instance, played with Jill as a part of her duty, Puss-cat made a pleasure out of it and played with the ecstatic abandon of a child. Indeed, I have known her put dinner a quarter of an hour later, because she was in the lovely jungle of long grass at the end of the garden, and was preparing to give Jill an awful fright. This business of the jungle deserves mention, not because it was so remarkable in itself, but because it was so wonderful to Puss-cat.

The jungle in question was a space of some dozen yards, where in spring daffodils grew in clumps of sunshine and fritillaries hung their speckled bells. There were peonies also planted in the grass, and a briar-rose, and an apple-tree; nothing, as I have said, was remarkable in itself, but it was fraught with amazing possibilities to the keen imagination of Puss-cat. At the bottom of this strip of untamed jungle the lawn began, and it was one of Puss-cat's plans to hide at the edge of the jungle, flattening herself out till she looked like a shadow of something else. If luck served her, Jill, sooner or later in the pursuit of interesting smells, would pass close to the edge of the jungle without seeing her. The moment Jill had gone by, Puss-cat would stretch out a discreet paw, and just touch Jill on the hind-quarters. Jill, of course, had to turn round to see what this inexplicable thing meant, and on the moment Puss-cat would fling herself into the air and descend tiger-like on Jill's back. That was the beginning of the game, and it contained more vicissitudes than a round of golf. There were ambushes and scurryings innumerable, assaults from the apple-tree, repulsions from behind the garden roller, periods of absolute quiescence, suddenly and wildly broken by swift flanking movements through the sweet-peas, and at the end a failure of wind and limb, and Jill would lie panting on the bank, and Puss-cat, having put off dinner, proceed to clean herself for her evening duties. She had to be smart at dinner-time, whether we were dining alone, or whether there was a dinner-party, for she was never a tea-gown cat, and she dressed for her dinner, even if we were dining out. She was not responsible for that; what she was responsible for was to be tidy herself.

Puss-cat, without doubt, was a plain kitten; but again, like many children of our own inferior race, she grew up to be a very handsome cat. With great chic she did not attempt colours, but was pure black and white. Across her broad, strong back there was a black saddle, but the saddle, so to speak, had slewed round and made a black band across her left side. There was an arbitrary patch of black, too, on her left cheek, a black band on her tail, and a black tip to it. Otherwise she was pure white, except when she put out a pink tongue below her long, snowy whiskers. But her charm – the outstanding feature of Puss-cat – was independent of this fascinating colouring. Martha, for instance, had been content that dishes were carried into the dining-room, and subsequently carried out. That and no more was her notion of her duties towards dinner. But Puss-cat really began where Martha ended. Like her, she preceded the soup, but when those who were present had received their share, she always went round with loud purrings to each guest, to congratulate them and hope that they liked it. For this process, which was repeated with every dish, she had a particular walk, stepping high and treading on the tips of her toes. This congratulatory march was purely altruistic: she did not want soup herself; she was only glad that other people had got it. Then when fish came, or bird, she would make her congratulatory tour just the same, and then sit firmly down and say she would like some too. Occasionally she favoured some particular guest with marked regard, and sometimes almost forgot her duties as mistress of the house, choosing rather to sit by her *protégée* and purr loudly, so that a dish would already be half-eaten before she went her round to see that everyone was pleased with his portion. Finally, when coffee was brought, she went downstairs to the kitchen and retired for the night, usually sharing Jill's basket, where they lay together in a soft slow-breathing heap of black and white.

Puss-cat, like the ancient Greeks, was never sick or sorry; never sick, because of her robust and stalwart health; never sorry, because she never did anything to be sorry for. From living with Jill, and never seeing a cat, except for those short and painful interviews which preceded expulsion from the garden, she grew to have something of the selfless affection of a dog, and when I came home after an absence she would run out into the street to meet me, stiff-tailed, and really not attending to the debarkation of luggage, but intent only on welcoming me home. Eight busy, happy years passed thus, and then one bitter February morning, Pussy-cat disappeared.

The weeks went on, and still there came no sign of her, and when winter had passed into May I gave up all hopes of her return, and got a fresh cat, this time a young blue Persian with topaz-coloured eyes. Another month went by, and Agag (so-called from his delicate walk) had established himself in our affections, on account of his extraordinary beauty, rather than from any charm of character, when the second act of the tragedy opened.

I was sitting at breakfast one morning, with the door into the garden thrown wide, and Agag was curled up on a chair in the window (for, unlike Puss-cat and Martha, he did no housework at all, being of proud and aristocratic descent), when I saw coming slowly across the lawn a cat that I scarcely recognised. It was lean to the point of emaciation, its fur was disordered and dirty, but it was Puss-cat come home again. Then suddenly she saw me, and with a little cry of joy ran towards the open door. Then she saw Agag, and, weak and thin as she was, she woke at once to her old sense of duty, and bounded on to his chair. Never before in her time had a cat got right into the house, and such a thing, she felt determined, should not occur again. Round the room and out into the garden raged the battle before I could separate them – Puss-cat inspired by her sense of duty, Agag angry and astonished at this assault of a mere gutter-cat in his own house. At last I got hold of Puss-cat and took her up in my arms, while Agag cursed and swore in justifiable indignation. For how could he tell that this was Puss-cat?

They never fought again, but it was a miserable fortnight that followed, and all the misery was poor Puss-cat's. Agag, in spite of his beauty, had no heart, and did not mind how many cats I kept, so long as they did not molest him, or usurp his food or his cushion. But Puss-cat, though she understood that for some inscrutable reason she had to share her house with Agag, and not fight him, was a creature of strong affections, and her poor little soul was torn with agonies of jealousy. Jill, it is true, who was always treated with contemptuous unconsciousness by Agag, was certainly pleased to see her friend again, and had not forgotten her; but Puss-cat wanted so much more than Jill could give her. She took on her old duties at once, but often when she escorted the fish into the dining-room and found Agag asleep on his chair, she would be literally unable to go through with them, and would sit in a corner by herself, looking miserably and uncomprehendingly at me. Then perhaps the smell of fish would wake up Agag, and he would stretch himself and stand for a moment with superbly-arched back on his chair, before he jumped down, and with loud purrings rubbed himself against the legs of my chair to betoken his desire for food, or even would jump up on to my knees. That was the worst of all for Puss-cat, and she would often sit all dinner through in her remote corner, refusing food, and unable to take her eyes off the object of her jealousy. While Agag was present, no amount of caresses or attentions offered to her would console her, so that, when Agag had eaten, we usually turned him out of the room. Then for a little while Puss-cat had respite from her Promethean vulture; she would go her rounds again to see that everybody was pleased, and escort fresh dishes in with high-stepping walk and erect tail.

We hoped, foolishly perhaps, that in course of time the two would become friends; else, I think, I should have at once tried to find another home for Agag. But indeed, short of that, we did all we could do, lavishing attentions on dear Puss-cat, and trying to make her feel (which indeed was true) that we all loved her, and only liked and admired Agag. But while we still hoped, Puss-cat had had more than she could bear, and once again she disappeared. Jill missed her for a little while, Agag not at all. But the rest of us miss her still.

THE WHITE CAT

MADAME D'AULNOY

Once upon a time there was a king who had three sons, who were all so clever and brave that he began to be afraid that they would want to reign over the kingdom before he was dead. Now the King, though he felt that he was growing old, did not at all wish to give up the government of his kingdom while he could still manage it very well, so he thought the best way to live in peace would be to divert the minds of his sons by promises which he could always get out of when the time came for keeping them.

So he sent for them all, and, after speaking to them kindly, he added:

"You will quite agree with me, my dear children, that my great age makes it impossible for me to look after my affairs of state as carefully as I once did. I begin to fear that this may affect the welfare of my subjects, therefore I wish that one of you should succeed to my crown; but in return for such a gift as this it is only right that you should do something for me. Now, as I think of retiring into the country, it seems to me that a pretty, lively, faithful little dog would be very good company for me; so, without any regard for your ages, I promise that the one who brings me the most beautiful little dog shall succeed me at once."

The three Princes were greatly surprised by their father's sudden fancy for a little dog, but as it gave the two younger ones a chance they would not otherwise have had of being king, and as the eldest was too polite to make any objection, they accepted the commission with pleasure. They bade farewell to the King, who gave them presents of silver and precious stones, and appointed to meet them at the same hour, in the same place, after a year had passed, to see the little dogs they had brought for him.

Then they went together to a castle which was about a league from the city, accompanied by all their particular friends, to whom they gave a grand banquet, and the three brothers promised to be friends always, to share whatever good fortune befell them, and not to be parted by any envy or jealousy; and so they set out, agreeing to meet at the same castle at the appointed time, to present themselves before the King together. Each one took a different road, and the two eldest met with many adventures; but it is about the youngest that you are going to hear. He was young, and gay, and handsome, and knew everything that a prince ought to know; and as for his courage, there was simply no end to it.

Hardly a day passed without his buying several dogs – big and little, greyhounds, mastiffs, spaniels, and lapdogs. As soon as he had bought a pretty one he was sure to see a still prettier, and then he had to get rid of all the others and buy that one, as, being alone, he found it impossible to take thirty or forty thousand dogs about with him. He journeyed from day to day, not knowing where he was going, until at last, just at nightfall, he reached a great, gloomy forest. He did not know his way, and, to make matters worse, it began to thunder, and the rain poured down. He took the first path he could find, and after walking for a long time he fancied he saw a faint light, and began to hope that he was coming to some cottage where he might find shelter for the night. At length, guided by the light, he reached the door of the most splendid castle he could have imagined. This door was of gold covered with carbuncles, and it was the pure red light which shone from them that had shown him the way through the forest. The walls were of the finest porcelain in all the most delicate colours, and the Prince saw that all the stories he had ever read were pictured upon them; but as he was terribly wet, and the rain still fell in torrents, he could not stay to look about any more, but came back to the golden door. There he saw a deer's foot hanging by a chain of diamonds, and he began to wonder who could live in this magnificent castle.

"They must feel very secure against robbers," he said to himself. "What is to hinder anyone from cutting off that chain and digging out those carbuncles, and making himself rich for life?"

He pulled the deer's foot, and immediately a silver bell sounded and the door flew open, but the Prince could see nothing but numbers of hands in the air, each holding a torch. He was so much surprised that he stood quite still, until he felt himself pushed forward by other hands, so that, though he was somewhat uneasy, he could not help going on. With his hand on his sword, to be prepared for whatever might happen, he entered a hall paved with lapis-lazuli, while two lovely voices sang:

> *"The hands you see floating above*
> *Will swiftly your bidding obey;*
> *If your heart dreads not conquering Love,*
> *In this place you may fearlessly stay."*

The Prince could not believe that any danger threatened him when he was welcomed in this way, so, guided by the mysterious hands, he went towards a door of coral, which opened of its own accord, and he found himself in a vast hall of mother-of-pearl, out of which opened a number of other rooms, glittering with thousands of lights, and full of such beautiful pictures and precious things that the Prince felt quite bewildered. After passing through sixty rooms the hands that conducted him stopped, and the Prince saw a most comfortable-looking arm-chair drawn up close to the chimney-corner; at the same moment the fire lighted itself, and the pretty, soft, clever hands took off the Prince's wet, muddy clothes, and presented him with fresh ones made of the richest stuffs, all embroidered with gold and emeralds. He could not help admiring everything he saw, and the deft way in which the hands waited on him, though they sometimes appeared so suddenly that they made him jump.

When he was quite ready – and I can assure you that he looked very different from the wet and weary Prince who had stood outside in the rain, and pulled the deer's foot – the hands led him to a splendid room, upon the walls of which were painted the histories of Puss in Boots and a number of other famous cats. The table was laid for supper with two golden plates, and golden spoons and forks, and the sideboard was covered with dishes and glasses of crystal set with precious stones. The Prince was wondering who the second place could be for, when suddenly in came about a dozen cats carrying guitars and rolls of music, who took their places at one end of the room, and under the direction of a cat who beat time with a roll of paper began to mew in every imaginable key, and to draw their claws across the strings of the guitars, making the strangest kind of music that could be heard. The Prince hastily stopped up his ears, but even then the sight of these comical musicians sent him into fits of laughter.

"What funny thing shall I see next?" he said to himself, and instantly the door opened, and in came a tiny figure covered by a long black veil. It was conducted by two cats wearing black mantles and carrying swords, and a large party of cats followed, who brought in cages full of rats and mice.

The Prince was so much astonished that he thought he must be dreaming, but the little figure came up to him and threw back its veil, and he saw that it was the loveliest little white cat it is possible to imagine. She looked very young and very sad, and in a sweet little voice that went straight to his heart she said to the Prince:

"King's son, you are welcome; the Queen of the Cats is glad to see you."

"Lady Cat," replied the Prince, "I thank you for receiving me so kindly, but surely you are no ordinary pussy-cat? Indeed, the way you speak and the magnificence of your castle prove it plainly."

"King's son," said the White Cat, "I beg you to spare me these compliments, for I am not used to them. But now," she added, "let supper be served, and let the musicians be silent, as the Prince does not understand what they are saying."

So the mysterious hands began to bring in the supper, and first they put on the table two dishes, one containing stewed pigeons and the other a fricassee of fat mice. The sight of the latter made the Prince feel as if he could not enjoy his supper at all; but the White Cat, seeing this, assured him that the dishes intended for him were prepared in a separate kitchen, and he might be quite certain that they contained neither rats nor mice; and the Prince felt so sure that she would not deceive him that he had no more hesitation in beginning. Presently he noticed that on the little paw that was next him the White Cat wore a bracelet containing a portrait, and he begged to be allowed to look at it. To his great surprise he found it represented an extremely handsome young man, who was so like himself that it might have been his own portrait! The White Cat sighed as he looked at it, and seemed sadder than ever, and the Prince dared not ask any questions for fear of displeasing her; so he began to talk about other things, and found that she was interested in all the subjects he cared for himself, and seemed to know quite well what was going on in the world. After supper they went into another room, which was fitted up as a theatre, and the cats acted and danced for their amusement, and then the White Cat said good-night to him, and the hands conducted him into a room he had not seen before, hung with tapestry worked with butterflies' wings of every colour; there were mirrors that reached from the ceiling to the floor, and a little white bed with curtains of gauze tied up with ribbons. The Prince went to bed in silence, as he did not quite know how to begin a conversation with the hands that waited on him, and in the morning he was awakened by a noise and confusion outside his window, and the hands came and quickly dressed him in hunting costume. When he looked out all the cats were assembled in the courtyard, some leading greyhounds, some blowing horns, for the White Cat was going out hunting. The hands led a wooden horse up to the Prince, and seemed to expect him to mount it, at which he was very indignant; but it was no use for him to object, for he speedily found himself upon its back, and it pranced gaily off with him.

The White Cat herself was riding a monkey, which climbed even up to the eagles' nests when she had a fancy for the young eaglets. Never was there a pleasanter hunting party, and when they returned to the castle the Prince and the White Cat supped together as before, but when they had finished she offered him a crystal goblet, which must have contained a magic draught, for, as soon as he had swallowed its contents, he forgot everything, even the little dog that he was seeking for the King, and only thought how happy he was to be with the White Cat! And so the days passed, in every kind of amusement, until the year was nearly gone. The Prince had forgotten all about meeting his brothers: he did not even know what country he belonged to; but the White Cat knew when he ought to go back, and one day she said to him:

"Do you know that you have only three days left to look

for the little dog for your father, and your brothers have found lovely ones?"

Then the Prince suddenly recovered his memory, and cried:

"What can have made me forget such an important thing? My whole fortune depends upon it; and even if I could in such a short time find a dog pretty enough to gain me a kingdom, where should I find a horse who would carry me all that way in three days?" And he began to be very vexed. But the White Cat said to him: "King's son, do not trouble yourself; I am your friend, and will make everything easy for you. You can still stay here for a day, as the good wooden horse can take you to your country in twelve hours."

"I thank you, beautiful Cat," said the Prince; "but what good will it do me to get back if I have not a dog to take to my father?"

"See here," answered the White Cat, holding up an acorn; "there is a prettier one in this than in the Dogstar!"

"Oh! White Cat dear," said the Prince, "how unkind you are to laugh at me now!"

"Only listen," she said, holding the acorn to his ear.

And inside it he distinctly heard a tiny voice say: "Bow-wow!"

The Prince was delighted, for a dog that can be shut up in an acorn must be very small indeed. He wanted to take it out and look at it, but the White Cat said it would be better not to open the acorn till he was before the King, in case the tiny dog should be cold on the journey. He thanked her a thousand times, and said good-bye quite sadly when the time came for him to set out.

"The days have passed so quickly with you," he said, "I only wish I could take you with me now."

But the White Cat shook her head and sighed deeply in answer.

After all the Prince was the first to arrive at the castle

where he had agreed to meet his brothers, but they came soon after, and stared in amazement when they saw the wooden horse in the courtyard jumping like a hunter.

The Prince met them joyfully, and they began to tell him all their adventures; but he managed to hide from them what he had been doing, and even led them to think that a turnspit dog which he had with him was the one he was bringing for the King. Fond as they all were of one another, the two eldest could not help being glad to think that their dogs certainly had a better chance. The next morning they started in the same chariot. The elder brothers carried in baskets two such tiny, fragile dogs that they hardly dared to touch them. As for the turnspit, he ran after the chariot, and got so covered with mud that one could hardly see what he was like at all. When they reached the palace everyone crowded round to welcome them as they went into the King's great hall; and when the two brothers presented their little dogs nobody could decide which was the prettier. They were already arranging between themselves to share the kingdom equally, when the youngest stepped forward, drawing from his pocket the acorn the White Cat had given him. He opened it quickly, and there upon a white cushion they saw a dog so small that it could easily have been put through a ring. The Prince laid it upon the ground, and it got up at once and began to dance. The King did not know what to say, for it was impossible that anything could be prettier than this little creature. Nevertheless, as he was in no hurry to part with his crown, he told his sons that, as they had been so successful the first time, he would ask them to go once again, and seek by land and sea for a piece of muslin so fine that it could be drawn through the eye of a needle. The brothers were not very willing to set out again, but the two eldest consented because it gave them another chance, and they started as before. The youngest again mounted the wooden horse, and rode back at full speed to his beloved White Cat. Every door of the castle stood wide open, and every window and turret was illuminated, so it looked more wonderful than before. The hands hastened to meet him, and led the wooden horse off to the stable, while he hurried in to find the White Cat. She was asleep in a little basket on a white satin cushion, but she very soon started up when she heard the Prince, and was overjoyed at seeing him once more.

"How could I hope that you would come back to me King's son?" she said. And then he stroked and petted her, and told her of his successful journey, and how he had come back to ask her help, as he believed that it was impossible to find what the King demanded. The White Cat looked serious, and said she must think what was to be done, but that, luckily, there were some cats in the castle who could spin very well, and if anybody could manage it they could, and she would set them the task herself.

And then the hands appeared carrying torches, and conducted the Prince and the White Cat to a long gallery which overlooked the river, from the windows of which they saw a magnificent display of fireworks of all sorts; after which they had supper, which the Prince liked even better than the fireworks, for it was very late, and he was hungry after his long ride. And so the days passed quickly as before; it was impossible to feel dull with the White Cat, and she had quite a talent for inventing new amusements – indeed, she was cleverer than a cat has any right to be. But when the Prince asked her how it was that she was so wise, she only said:

"King's son, do not ask me; guess what you please. I may not tell you anything."

The Prince was so happy that he did not trouble himself at all about the time, but presently the White Cat told him that the year was gone, and that he need not be at all anxious about the piece of muslin, as they had made it very well.

"This time," she added, "I can give you a suitable escort"; and on looking out into the courtyard the Prince saw a superb chariot of burnished gold, enamelled in flame colour with a thousand different devices. It was drawn by twelve snow-white horses, harnessed four abreast; their trappings were flame-coloured velvet, embroidered with diamonds. A hundred chariots followed, each drawn by eight horses, and filled with officers in splendid uniforms, and a thousand guards surrounded the procession. "Go!" said the White Cat, "and when you appear before the King in such state he surely will not refuse you the crown which you deserve. Take this walnut, but do not open it until you are before him, then you will find in it the piece of stuff you asked me for."

"Lovely Blanchette," said the Prince, "how can I thank you properly for all your kindness to me? Only tell me that you wish it, and I will give up for ever all thought of being king, and will stay here with you always."

"King's son," she replied, "it shows the goodness of your heart that you should care so much for a little white cat, who is good for nothing but to catch mice; but you must not stay."

So the Prince kissed her little paw and set out. You can imagine how fast he travelled when I tell you that they reached the King's palace in just half the time it had taken the wooden horse to get there. This time the Prince was so late that he did not try to meet his brothers at their castle, so they thought he could not be coming, and were rather glad of it, and displayed their pieces of muslin to the King proudly, feeling sure of success. And indeed the stuff was very fine, and would go through the eye of a very large needle; but the King, who was only too glad to make a difficulty, sent for a particular needle, which was kept among the Crown jewels, and had such a small eye that everybody saw at once that it was impossible that the muslin should pass through it. The Princes were angry, and were beginning to complain that it was a trick, when suddenly the trumpets sounded and the youngest Prince came in. His father and brothers were quite astonished at his magnificence, and after he had greeted them he took the walnut from his pocket and opened it, fully expecting to find the piece of muslin, but instead there was only a hazel-nut. He cracked it, and there lay a cherry-stone. Everybody was looking on, and the King was chuckling to himself at the idea of finding the piece of muslin in a nutshell.

However, the Prince cracked the cherry-stone, but everyone laughed when he saw it contained only its own kernel. He opened that and found a grain of wheat, and in that was a millet seed. Then he himself began to wonder, and muttered softly:

"White Cat, White Cat, are you making fun of me?"

In an instant he felt a cat's claw give his hand quite a sharp scratch, and hoping that it was meant as an encouragement he opened the millet seed, and drew out of it a piece of muslin four hundred ells long, woven with the loveliest colours and most wonderful patterns; and when the needle was brought it went through the eye six times with the greatest ease! The King turned pale, and the other Princes stood silent and sorrowful, for nobody could deny that this was the most marvellous piece of muslin that was to be found in the world.

Presently the King turned to his sons, and said, with a deep sigh:

"Nothing could console me more in my old age than to realise your willingness to gratify my wishes. Go then once more, and whoever at the end of a year can bring back the loveliest princess shall be married to her, and shall, without further delay, receive the crown, for my successor must certainly be married." The Prince considered that he had earned the kingdom fairly twice over but still he was too well bred to argue about it, so he just went back to his gorgeous chariot, and, surrounded by his escort, returned to the White Cat faster than he had come. This time she was expecting him, the path was strewn with flowers, and a thousand braziers were burning scented woods which perfumed the air. Seated in a gallery from which she could see his arrival, the

White Cat waited for him. "Well, King's son," she said, "here you are once more, without a crown."

"Madam," said he, "thanks to your generosity I have earned one twice over; but the fact is that my father is so loth to part with it that it would be no pleasure to me to take it."

"Never mind," she answered, "it's just as well to try and deserve it. As you must take back a lovely princess with you next time I will be on the look-out for one for you. In the meantime let us enjoy ourselves; to-night I have ordered a battle between my cats and the river rats on purpose to amuse you." So this year slipped away even more pleasantly than the preceding ones. Sometimes the Prince could not help asking the White Cat how it was she could talk.

"Perhaps you are a fairy," he said. "Or has some enchanter changed you into a cat?"

But she only gave him answers that told him nothing. Days go by so quickly when one is very happy that it is certain the Prince would never have thought of its being time to go back, when one evening as they sat together the White Cat said to him that if he wanted to take a lovely princess home with him the next day he must be prepared to do what she told him.

"Take this sword," she said, "and cut off my head!"

"I!" cried the Prince, "I cut off your head! Blanchette darling, how could I do it?"

"I entreat you to do as I tell you, King's son," she replied.

The tears came into the Prince's eyes as he begged her to ask him anything but that – to set him any task she pleased as a proof of his devotion, but to spare him the grief of killing his dear Pussy. But nothing he could say altered her determination, and at last he drew his sword, and desperately, with a trembling hand, cut off the little white head. But imagine his astonishment and delight when suddenly a lovely princess stood before him, and, while he was still speechless with amazement, the door opened and a goodly company of knights and ladies entered, each carrying a cat's skin! They hastened with every sign of joy to the Princess, kissing her hand and congratulating her on being once more restored to her natural shape. She received them graciously, but after a few minutes begged that they would leave her alone with the Prince, to whom she said:

"You see, Prince, that you were right in supposing me to be no ordinary cat. My father reigned over six kingdoms. The Queen, my mother, whom he loved dearly, had a passion for travelling and exploring, and when I was only a few weeks old she obtained his permission to visit a certain mountain of which she had heard many marvellous tales, and set out, taking with her a number of her attendants. On the way they had to pass near an old castle belonging to the fairies. Nobody had ever been into it, but it was reported to be full of the most wonderful things, and my mother remembered to have heard that the fairies had in their garden such fruits as were to be seen and tasted nowhere else. She began to wish to try them for herself, and turned her steps in the direction of the garden. On arriving at the door, which blazed with gold and jewels, she ordered her servants to knock loudly, but it was useless; it seemed as if all the inhabitants of the castle must be asleep or dead. Now the more difficult it became to obtain the fruit, the more the Queen was determined that have it she would. So she ordered that they should bring ladders, and get over the wall into the garden; but though the wall did not look very high, and they tied the ladders together to make them very long, it was quite impossible to get to the top.

"The Queen was in despair, but as night was coming on she ordered that they should encamp just where they were, and went to bed herself, feeling quite ill, she was so disappointed. In the middle of the night she was suddenly awakened, and saw to her surprise a tiny, ugly old woman seated by her bedside, who said to her:

"I must say that we consider it somewhat troublesome

of your Majesty to insist upon tasting our fruit; but, to save you annoyance, my sisters and I will consent to give you as much as you can carry away, on one condition – that is, that you shall give us your little daughter to bring up as our own."

"Ah! my dear madam," cried the Queen, "is there nothing else that you will take for the fruit? I will give you my kingdoms willingly."

"No," replied the old fairy, "we will have nothing but your little daughter. She shall be as happy as the day is long, and we will give her everything that is worth having in fairyland, but you must not see her again until she is married."

"Though it is a hard condition," said the Queen, "I consent, for I shall certainly die if I do not taste the fruit, and so I should lose my little daughter either way."

"So the old fairy led her into the castle, and, though it was still the middle of the night, the Queen could see plainly that it was far more beautiful than she had been told, which you can easily believe, Prince," said the White Cat, "when I tell you that it was this castle that we are now in. "Will you gather the fruit yourself, Queen?" said the old fairy, "or shall I call it to come to you?"

"I beg you to let me see it come when it is called," cried the Queen; "that will be something quite new." The old fairy whistled twice, then she cried:

"Apricots, peaches, nectarines, cherries, plums, pears, melons, grapes, apples, oranges, lemons, gooseberries, strawberries, raspberries, come!"

"And in an instant they came tumbling in one over another, and yet they were neither dusty nor spoilt, and the Queen found them quite as good as she had fancied them. You see they grew upon fairy trees.

"The old fairy gave her golden baskets in which to take the fruit away, and it was as much as four hundred mules could carry. Then she reminded the Queen of her agreement, and led her back to the camp, and next morning she went back to her kingdom, but before she had gone very far she began to repent of her bargain, and when the King came out to meet her she looked so sad that he guessed that something had happened, and asked what was the matter. At first the Queen was afraid to tell him, but when, as soon as they reached the palace, five frightful little dwarfs were sent by the fairies to fetch me, she was obliged to confess what she had promised. The King was very angry, and had the Queen and myself shut up in a great tower and safely guarded, and drove the little dwarfs out of his kingdom; but the fairies sent a great dragon who ate up all the people he met, and whose breath burnt up everything as he passed through the country; and at last, after trying in vain to rid himself of this monster, the King, to save his subjects, was obliged to consent that I should be given up to the fairies. This time they came themselves to fetch me, in a chariot of pearl drawn by sea-horses, followed by the dragon, who was led with chains of diamonds. My cradle was placed between the old fairies, who loaded me with caresses, and away we whirled through the air to a tower which they had built on purpose for me. There I grew up surrounded with everything that was beautiful and rare, and learning everything that is ever taught to a princess, but without any companions but a parrot and a little dog, who could both talk; and receiving every day a visit from one of the old fairies, who came mounted upon the dragon. One day, however, as I sat at my window I saw a handsome young prince, who seemed to have been hunting in the forest which surrounded my prison, and who was standing and looking up at me. When he saw that I observed him he saluted me with great deference. You can imagine that I was delighted to have some one new to talk to, and in spite of the height of my window our conversation was prolonged till night fell, then my prince reluctantly bade me farewell. But after that he came again many times and at last I consented to marry him, but the question was how was I

to escape from my tower. The fairies always supplied me with
flax for my spinning, and by great diligence I made enough
cord for a ladder that would reach to the foot of the tower;
but, alas! just as my prince was helping me to descend it,
the crossest and ugliest of the old fairies flew in. Before he
had time to defend himself my unhappy lover was swallowed
up by the dragon. As for me, the fairies, furious at having
their plans defeated, for they intended me to marry the king
of the dwarfs, and I utterly refused, changed me into a white
cat. When they brought me here I found all the lords and
ladies of my father's court awaiting me under the same
enchantment, while the people of lesser rank had been made
invisible, all but their hands.

"As they laid me under the enchantment the fairies told
me all my history, for until then I had quite believed that I
was their child, and warned me that my only chance of
regaining my natural form was to win the love of a prince
who resembled in every way my unfortunate lover."

"And you have won it, lovely Princess," interrupted the
Prince.

"You are indeed wonderfully like him," resumed the
Princess – "in voice, in features, and everything; and if you
really love me all my troubles will be at an end."

"And mine too," cried the Prince, throwing himself at
her feet, "if you will consent to marry me."

"I love you already better than anyone in the world,"
she said; "but now it is time to go back to your father, and
we shall hear what he says about it."

So the Prince gave her his hand and led her out, and
they mounted the chariot together; it was even more splendid
than before, and so was the whole company. Even the horses'
shoes were of rubies with diamond nails, and I suppose that
is the first time such a thing was ever seen.

As the Princess was as kind and clever as she was beautiful, you may imagine what a delightful journey the Prince

found it, for everything the Princess said seemed to him quite charming.

When they came near the castle where the brothers were to meet, the Princess got into a chair carried by four of the guards; it was hewn out of one splendid crystal, and had silken curtains, which she drew round her that she might not be seen.

The Prince saw his brothers walking upon the terrace, each with a lovely princess, and they came to meet him, asking if he had also found a wife. He said that he had found something much rarer – a white cat! At which they laughed very much, and asked him if he was afraid of being eaten up by mice in the palace. And then they set out together for the town. Each prince and princess rode in a splendid carriage; the horses were decked with plumes of feathers, and glittered with gold. After them came the youngest prince, and last of all the crystal chair, at which everybody looked with admiration and curiosity. When the courtiers saw them coming they hastened to tell the King.

"Are the ladies beautiful?" he asked anxiously.

And when they answered that nobody had ever before seen such lovely princesses he seemed quite annoyed.

However, he received them graciously, but found it impossible to choose between them.

Then turning to his youngest son he said:

"Have you come back alone, after all?"

"Your Majesty," replied the Prince, "will find in that crystal chair a little white cat, which has such soft paws, and mews so prettily, that I am sure you will be charmed with it."

The King smiled, and went to draw back the curtains himself, but at a touch from the Princess the crystal shivered into a thousand splinters, and there she stood in all her beauty; her fair hair floated over her shoulders and was crowned with flowers, and her softly falling robe was of the purest white.

She saluted the King gracefully, while a murmur of admiration rose from all around.

"Sire," she said, "I am not come to deprive you of the throne you fill so worthily. I have already six kingdoms, permit me to bestow one upon you, and upon each of your sons. I ask nothing but your friendship, and your consent to my marriage with your youngest son; we shall still have three kingdoms left for ourselves."

The King and all the courtiers could not conceal their joy and astonishment, and the marriage of the three Princes was celebrated at once. The festivities lasted several months, and then each king and queen departed to their own kingdom and lived happily ever after.

DICK BAKER'S CAT

MARK TWAIN

One of my comrades there – another of those victims of eighteen years of unrequited toil and blighted hopes – was one of the gentlest spirits that ever bore its patient cross in a weary exile: grave and simple Dick Baker, pocket-miner of Dead-Horse Gulch. He was forty-six, grey as a rat, earnest, thoughtful, slenderly educated, slouchily dressed and clay-soiled, but his heart was finer metal than any gold his shovel ever brought to light – than any, indeed, that ever was mined or minted.

Whenever he was out of luck and a little downhearted, he would fall to mourning over the loss of a wonderful cat he used to own (for where women and children are not, men of kindly impulses take up with pets, for they must love something). And he always spoke of the strange sagacity of that cat with the air of a man who believed in his secret heart that there was something human about it – maybe even supernatural.

I heard him talking about this animal once. He said:

"Gentlemen, I used to have a cat here, by the name of Tom Quartz, which you'd 'a' took an interest in, I reckon –, most anybody would. I had him here eight year – and he was the remarkablest cat *I* ever see. He was a large grey one of the Tom specie, an' he had more hard, natchral sense than any man in this camp – 'n' a *power* of dignity – he wouldn't let the Gov'ner of Californy be familiar with him. He never ketched a rat in his life – 'peared to be above it. He never cared for nothing but mining. He knowed more about mining, that cat did, than any man *I* ever, ever see. You couldn't tell *him* noth'n' 'bout placer-diggin's – 'n' as for pocket-mining, why he was just born for it. He would dig out after me an' Jim when we went over the hills prospect'n', and he would trot along behind us for as much as five mile, if we went so fur. An' he had the best judgment about mining-ground – why you never see anything like it. When we went to work, he'd scatter a glance around, 'n' if he didn't think much of the indications, he would give a look as much as to say, "Well, I'll have to get you to excuse *me*' – 'n' without another word he'd hyste his nose into the air 'n' shove for home. But if the ground suited him, he would lay low 'n' keep dark till the first pan was washed, 'n' then he would sidle up 'n' take a look, an' if there was about six or seven grains of gold *he* was satisfied – he didn't want no better prospect 'n' that – 'n' then he would lay down on our coats and snore like a steamboat till we'd struck the pocket, an' then get up 'n' superintend. He was nearly lightnin' on superintending.

"Well, by an' by, up comes this yer quartz excitement. Everybody was into it – everybody was pick'n' 'n' blast'n' instead of shovelin' dirt on the hillside – everybody was putt'n' down a shaft instead of scrapin' the surface. Noth'n' would do Jim, but *we* must tackle the ledges, too, 'n' so we did. We commenced putt'n' down a shaft, 'n' Tom Quartz he begin to wonder what in the Dickens it was all about. *He* hadn't ever seen any mining like that before, 'n' he was all upset, as you may say – he couldn't come to a right understanding of it no way – it was too many for *him*. He was down on it too, you bet you – he was down on it powerful – 'n' always appeared to consider it the cussedest foolishness out. But that cat, you know, was *always* agin new-fangled arrangements – somehow he never could abide 'em. *You* know how it is with old habits. But by an' by Tom Quartz begin to git sort of reconciled a little, though he never *could* altogether understand that eternal sinkin' of a shaft an' never pannin' out anything. At last he got to comin' down in the shaft, hisself, to try to cipher it out. An' when he'd git the blues, 'n' feel kind o' scruffy, 'n' aggravated 'n' disgusted – knowin' as he did, that the bills was runnin' up all the time an' we warn't makin' a cent – he would curl up on a gunny-sack in the corner an' go to sleep. Well, one day when the shaft was down about eight foot, the rock got so hard that we had to put in a blast – the first blast 'n' we'd ever done since Tom Quartz was born. An' then we lit the fuse 'n' clumb out 'n' got off 'bout fifty yards – 'n' forgot 'n' left Tom Quartz sound asleep on the gunny-sack. In 'bout a minute we seen a puff of smoke bust up out of the hole, 'n' then everything let go with an awful crash, 'n' about four million ton of rocks 'n' dirt 'n' smoke 'n' splinters shot up 'bout a mile an' a half into the air, an' by George, right in the dead centre of it was old Tom Quartz a-goin' end over end, an' a-snortin' an' a-sneez'n, an' a-clawin' an' a-reach'n' for things like all possessed. But it warn't no use, you know, it warn't no use. An' that was the last we see of *him* for about two minutes 'n' a half, an' then all of a sudden it begin to rain rocks and rubbage an' directly he come down ker-whoop about ten foot off f'm where we stood. Well, I reckon he was p'raps the orneriest-lookin' beast you ever see. One ear was sot back on his neck, 'n' his tail was stove up, 'n' his eye-winkers was singed off, 'n' he was all blacked up with powder an' smoke, an' all sloppy with mud 'n' slush f'm one end to the other. Well, sir, it warn't no use to try to apologise – we couldn't say a word. He took a sort of a disgusted look at hisself, 'n' then he looked at us

– an' it was just exactly the same as if he had said – 'Gents, maybe *you* think it's smart to take advantage of a cat that ain't had no experience of quartz-minin', but *I* think *different*' – an' then he turned on his heel 'n' marched off home without ever saying another word.

"That was jest his style. An' maybe you won't believe it, but after that you never see a cat so prejudiced agin quartz-mining as what he was. An' by an' by when he *did* get to goin' down in the shaft ag'in, you'd 'a' been astonished at his sagacity. The minute we'd tetch off a blast 'n' the fuse'd begin to sizzle, he'd give a look as much as to say, "Well, I'll have to git you to excuse *me*,' an' it was supris'n' the way he'd shin out of that hole 'n' go f'r a tree. Sagacity? It ain't no name for it. 'Twas *inspiration*!"

I said, "Well, Mr. Baker, his prejudice against quartz-mining *was* remarkable, considering how he came by it. Couldn't you ever cure him of it?"

"*Cure him!* No! When Tom Quartz was sot once, he was *always* sot – and you might 'a' blowed him up as much as three million times 'n' you'd never 'a' broken him of his cussed prejudice ag'in quartz-mining."

THE CAT'S
ELOPEMENT

Once upon a time there lived a cat of marvellous beauty, with a skin as soft and shining as silk, and wise green eyes, that could see even in the dark. His name was Gon, and he belonged to a music teacher, who was so fond and proud of him that he would not have parted with him for anything in the world.

Now not far from the music master's house there dwelt a lady who possessed a most lovely little pussy cat called Koma. She was such a little dear altogether, and blinked her eyes so daintily, and ate her supper so tidily, and when she had finished she licked her pink nose so delicately with her little tongue, that her mistress was never tired of saying, "Koma, Koma, what should I do without you?"

Well, it happened one day that these two, when out for an evening stroll, met under a cherry tree, and in one moment fell madly in love with each other. Gon had long felt that it was time for him to find a wife, for all the ladies in the neighbourhood paid him so much attention that it made him quite shy; but he was not easy to please, and did not care about any of them. Now, before he had time to think, Cupid had entangled him in his net, and he was filled with love towards

Koma. She fully returned his passion, but, like a woman, she saw the difficulties in the way, and consulted sadly with Gon as to the means of overcoming them. Gon entreated his master to set matters right by buying Koma, but her mistress would not part from her. Then the music master was asked to sell Gon to the lady, but he declined to listen to any such suggestion, so everything remained as before.

At length the love of the couple grew to such a pitch that they determined to please themselves, and to seek their fortunes together. So one moonlight night they stole away, and ventured out into an unknown world. All day long they marched bravely on through the sunshine, till they had left their homes far behind them, and towards evening they found themselves in a large park. The wanderers by this time were very hot and tired, and the grass looked very soft and inviting, and the trees cast cool deep shadows, when suddenly an ogre appeared in this Paradise, in the shape of a big, big dog! He came springing towards them showing all his teeth, and Koma shrieked, and rushed up a cherry tree. Gon, however, stood his ground boldly, and prepared to give battle, for he felt that Koma's eyes were upon him, and that he must not run away. But, alas! his courage would have availed him nothing had his enemy once touched him, for he was large and powerful, and very fierce. From her perch in the tree Koma saw it all, and screamed with all her might, hoping that some one would hear, and come to help. Luckily a servant of the princess to whom the park belonged was walking by, and he drove off the dog, and picking up the trembling Gon in his arms, carried him to his mistress.

So poor little Koma was left alone, while Gon was borne away full of trouble, not in the least knowing what to do. Even the attention paid him by the princess, who was delighted with his beauty and pretty ways, did not console him, but there was no use in fighting against fate, and he could only wait and see what would turn up.

The princess, Gon's new mistress, was so good and kind that everybody loved her, and she would have led a happy life, had it not been for a serpent who had fallen in love with her, and was constantly annoying her by his presence. Her servants had orders to drive him away as often as he appeared; but as they were careless, and the serpent very sly, it sometimes happened that he was able to slip past them, and to frighten the princess by appearing before her. One day she was seated in her room, playing on her favourite musical instrument, when she felt something gliding up her sash, and saw her enemy making his way to kiss her cheek. She shrieked and threw herself backwards, and Gon, who had been curled up on a stool at her feet, understood her terror, and with one bound seized the snake by his neck. He gave him one bite and one shake, and flung him on the ground, where he lay, never to worry the princess any more. Then she took Gon in her arms, and praised and caressed him, and saw that he had the nicest bits to eat, and the softest mats to lie on; and he would have had nothing in the world to wish for if only he could have seen Koma again.

Time passed on, and one morning Gon lay before the house door, basking in the sun. He looked lazily at the world stretched out before him, and saw in the distance a big ruffian of a cat teasing and ill-treating quite a little one. He jumped up, full of rage, and chased away the big cat, and then he turned to comfort the little one, when his heart nearly burst with joy to find that it was Koma. At first Koma did not know him again, he had grown so large and stately; but when it dawned upon her who it was, her happiness knew no bounds. And they rubbed their heads and their noses again and again, while their purring might have been heard a mile off.

Paw in paw they appeared before the princess, and told her the story of their life and its sorrows. The princess wept for sympathy, and promised that they should never more be parted, but should live with her to the end of their days.

By-and-bye the princess herself got married, and brought a prince to dwell in the palace in the park. And she told him all about her two cats, and how brave Gon had been, and how he had delivered her from her enemy the serpent.

And when the prince heard, he swore they should never leave them, but should go with the princess wherever she went. So it all fell out as the princess wished; and Gon and Koma had many children, and so had the princess, and they all played together, and were friends to the end of their lives.

ABEL AND HIS GREAT ADVENTURE

L. M. MONTGOMERY

"Come out of doors, master – come out of doors. I can't talk or think right with walls around me – never could. Let's go out to the garden." These were almost the first words I ever heard Abel Armstrong say. He was a member of the board of school trustees in Stillwater, and I had not met him before this late May evening, when I had gone down to confer with him upon some small matter of business. For I was "the new schoolmaster" in Stillwater, having taken the school for the summer term.

It was a rather lonely country district – a fact of which I was glad, for life had been going somewhat awry with me and my heart was sore and rebellious over many things that have nothing to do with this narration. Stillwater offered time and opportunity for healing and counsel. Yet, looking back, I doubt if I should have found either had it not been for Abel and his beloved garden.

Abel Armstrong (he was always called "Old Abel", though he was barely sixty) lived in a quaint, gray house close by the harbour shore. I heard a good deal about him before I saw him. He was called "queer", but Stillwater folks seemed to be very fond of him. He and his sister, Tamzine, lived together; she, so my garrulous landlady informed me, had not been sound of mind at times for many years; but she was all right now, only odd and quiet. Abel had gone to college for a year when he was young, but had given it up when Tamzine "went crazy". There was no one else to look after her. Abel had settled down to it with apparent content: at least he had never complained.

"Always took things easy, Abel did," said Mrs Campbell. "Never seemed to worry over disappointments and trials as most folks do. Seems to me that as long as Abel Armstrong can stride up and down in that garden of his, reciting poetry and speeches, or talking to that yaller cat of his as if it was a human, he doesn't care much how the world wags on. He never had much git-up-and-git. His father was a hustler, but the family didn't take after him. They all favoured the mother's people – sorter shiftless and dreamy. 'Taint the way to git on in this world."

No, good and worthy Mrs Campbell. It was not the way to get on in your world; but there are other worlds where getting on is estimated by different standards, and Abel Armstrong lived in one of these – a world far beyond the ken of the thrifty Stillwater farmers and fishers. Something of this I had sensed, even before I saw him; and that night in his garden, under a sky of smoky red, blossoming into stars above the harbour, I found a friend whose personality and philosophy were to calm and harmonise and enrich my whole existence. This sketch is my grateful tribute to one of the rarest and finest souls God ever clothed with clay.

He was a tall man, somewhat ungainly of figure and homely of face. But his large, deep eyes of velvety nut-brown were very beautiful and marvellously bright and clear for a man of his age. He wore a little pointed, well-cared-for beard, innocent of gray; but his hair was grizzled, and altogether he had the appearance of a man who had passed through many sorrows which had marked his body as well as his soul. Looking at him, I doubted Mrs Campbell's conclusion that he had not "minded" giving up college. This man had given up much and felt it deeply; but he had outlived the pain and the blessing of sacrifice had come to him. His voice was very melodious and beautiful, and the brown hand he held out to me was peculiarly long and shapely and flexible.

We went out to the garden in the scented moist air of a maritime spring evening. Behind the garden was a cloudy pine wood; the house closed it in on the left, while in front and on the right a row of tall Lombardy poplars stood out in stately purple silhouette against the sunset sky.

"Always liked Lombardies," said Abel, waving a long arm at them. "They are the trees of princesses. When I was a boy they were fashionable. Anyone who had any pretensions to gentility had a row of Lombardies at the foot of his lawn or up his lane, or at any rate one on either side of his front door. They're out of fashion now. Folks complain they die at the top and get ragged-looking. So they do – so they do, if you don't risk your neck every spring climbing up a light ladder to trim them out as I do. My neck isn't worth much to anyone, which, I suppose, is why I've never broken it; and *my* Lombardies never look out-at-elbows. My mother was especially fond of them. She liked their dignity and their stand-offishness. *They* don't hobnob with every Tom, Dick and Harry. If it's pines for company, master, it's Lombardies for society."

We stepped from the front doorstone into the garden. There was another entrance – a sagging gate flanked by two branching white lilacs. From it a little dappled path led to a huge apple-tree in the centre, a great swelling cone of rosy blossom with a mossy circular seat around its trunk. But Abel's favourite seat, so he told me, was lower down the slope, under a little trellis overhung with the delicate emerald of young hop-vines. He led me to it and pointed proudly to the fine view of the harbour visible from it. The early sunset glow of rose and flame had faded out of the sky; the water was silvery and mirror-like; dim sails drifted along by the darkening shore. A bell was ringing in a small Catholic chapel across the harbour. Mellowly and dreamily sweet the chime floated through the dusk, blent with the moan of the sea. The great revolving light at the channel trembled and flashed against the opal sky, and far out, beyond the golden sand-dunes of the bar, was the crinkled gray ribbon of a passing steamer's smoke.

"There, isn't that view worth looking at?" said old Abel, with a loving, proprietary pride. "You don't have to pay anything for it, either. All that sea and sky free – 'without money and without price'. Let's sit down here in the hop-vine arbour, master. There'll be a moonrise presently. I'm never tired of finding out what a moonrise sheen can be like over that sea. There's a surprise in it every time. Now, master, you're getting your mouth in the proper shape to talk business – but don't you do it. Nobody should talk business when he's expecting a moonrise. Not that I like talking business at any time."

"Unfortunately it has to be talked of sometimes, Mr Armstrong," I said.

"Yes, it seems to be a necessary evil, master," he acknowledged. "But I know what business you've come upon, and we can settle it in five minutes after the moon's well up. I'll just agree to everything you and the other two trustees want. Lord knows why they ever put *me* on the school board. Maybe it's because I'm so ornamental. They wanted one good-looking man, I reckon."

His low chuckle, so full of mirth and so free from malice, was infectious. I laughed also, as I sat down in the hop-vine arbour.

"Now, you needn't talk if you don't want to," he said. "And I won't. We'll just sit here, sociable like, and if we think of anything worthwhile to say we'll say it. Otherwise, not. If you can sit in silence with a person for half an hour and feel comfortable, you and that person can be friends. If you can't, friends you'll never be, and you needn't waste time in trying."

Abel and I passed successfully the test of silence that evening in the hop-vine arbour. I was strangely content to sit and think – something I had not cared to do lately. A peace, long unknown to my stormy soul, seemed hovering near it. The garden was steeped in it; old Abel's personality radiated it. I looked about me and wondered whence came the charm of that tangled, unworldly spot.

"Nice and far from the market-place isn't it?" asked Abel suddenly, as if he had heard my unasked question. "No buying and selling and getting gain here. Nothing was ever sold out of *this* garden. Tamzine has her vegetable plot over yonder, but what we don't eat we give away. Geordie Marr down the harbour has a big garden like this and he sells heaps of flowers and fruit and vegetables to the hotel folks. He thinks I'm an awful fool because I won't do the same. Well, he gets money out of his garden and I get happiness out of mine. That's the difference. S'posing I could make more money – what then? I'd only be taking it from people that needed it more. There's enough for Tamzine and me. As for Geordie Marr, there isn't a more unhappy creature on God's earth – he's always stewing in a broth of trouble, poor man. O' course, he brews up most of it for himself, but I reckon that doesn't make it any easier to bear. Ever sit in a hop-vine arbour before, master?"

I was to grow used to Abel's abrupt change of subject. I answered that I never had.

"Great place for dreaming," said Abel complacently. "Being young, no doubt, you dream a-plenty."

I answered hotly and bitterly that I had done with dreams.

"No, you haven't," said Abel meditatively. "You may

think you have. What then? First thing you know you'll be dreaming again – thank the Lord for it. I ain't going to ask you what's soured you on dreaming just now. After a while you'll begin again, especially if you come to this garden as much as I hope you will. It's chockful of dreams – *any* kind of dreams. You take your choice. Now, *I* favour dreams of adventures, if you'll believe it. I'm sixty-one and I never do anything rasher than go out cod-fishing on a fine day, but I still lust after adventures. Then I dream I'm an awful fellow – blood-thirsty."

I burst out laughing. Perhaps laughter was somewhat rare in that old garden. Tamzine, who was weeding at the far end, lifted her head in a startled fashion and walked past us into the house. She did not look at us or speak to us. She was reputed to be abnormally shy. She was very stout and wore a dress of bright red-and-white striped material. Her face was round and blank, but her reddish hair was abundant and beautiful. A huge, orange-coloured cat was at her heels; as she passed us he bounded over to the arbour and sprang up on Abel's knee. He was a gorgeous brute, with vivid green eyes, and immense white double paws.

"Captain Kidd, Mr Woodley." He introduced us as seriously as if the cat had been a human being. Neither Captain Kidd nor I responded very enthusiastically.

"You don't like cats, I reckon, master," said Abel, stroking the Captain's velvet back. "I don't blame you. I was never fond of them myself until I found the Captain. I saved his life and when you've saved a creature's life you're bound to love it. It's next thing to giving it life. There are some terrible thoughtless people in the world, master. Some of those city folks who have summer homes down the harbour are so thoughtless that they're cruel. It's the worst kind of cruelty, I think – the thoughtless kind. You can't cope with it. They keep cats there in the summer and feed them and pet them and doll them up with ribbons and collars; and then in the fall they go off and leave them to starve or freeze. It makes my blood boil, master.

"One day last winter I found a poor old mother cat dead on the shore, lying against the skin and bone bodies of her three little kittens. She had died trying to shelter them. She had her poor stiff claws around them. Master, I cried. Then I swore. Then I carried those poor little kittens home and fed 'em up and found good homes for them. I know the woman who left the cat. When she comes back this summer I'm going to go down and tell her my opinion of her. It'll be rank meddling, but, lord, how I love meddling in a good cause."

"Was Captain Kidd one of the forsaken?" I asked.

"Yes. I found him one bitter cold day in winter caught in the branches of a tree by his darn-fool ribbon collar. He was almost starving. Lord, if you could have seen his eyes! He was nothing but a kitten, and he'd got his living somehow since he'd been left till he got hung up. When I loosed him he gave my hand a pitiful swipe with his little red tongue. He wasn't the prosperous free-booter you behold now. He was meek as Moses. That was nine years ago. His life has been long in the land for a cat. He's a good old pal, the Captain is."

"I should have expected you to have a dog," I said.

Abel shook his head.

"I had a dog once. I cared so much for him that when he died I couldn't bear the thought of ever getting another in his place. He was a *friend* – you understand? The Captain's only a pal. I'm fond of the Captain – all the fonder because of the spice of deviltry there is in all cats. But I *loved* my dog. There isn't any devil in a good dog. That's why they're more lovable than cats – but I'm darned if they're as interesting."

I laughed as I rose regretfully.

"Must you go, master? And we haven't talked any business after all. I reckon it's that stove matter you've come about. It's like those two fool trustees to start up a stove sputter in spring. It's a wonder they didn't leave it till dog-days and begin then."

"They merely wished me to ask you if you approved of putting in a new stove."

"Tell them to put in a new stove – any kind of a new stove – and be hanged to them," rejoined Abel. "As for you, master, you're welcome to this garden any time. If you're tired or lonely, or too ambitious or angry, come here and sit awhile, master. Do you think any man could keep mad if he sat and looked into the heart of a pansy for ten minutes? When you feel like talking, I'll talk, and when you feel like thinking, I'll let you. I'm a great hand to leave folks alone."

"I think I'll come often," I said, "perhaps too often."

"Not likely, master – not likely – not after we've watched a moonrise contentedly together. It's as good a test of compatibility as any I know. You're young and I'm old, but our souls are about the same age, I reckon, and we'll find lots to say to each other. Are you going straight home from here?"

"Yes."

"Then I'm going to bother you to stop for a moment at Mary Bascom's and give her a bouquet of my white lilacs. She loves 'em and I'm not going to wait till she's dead to send her flowers."

"She's very ill just now, isn't she?"

"She's got the Bascom consumption. That means she may die in a month, like her brother, or linger on for twenty years, like her father. But long or short, white lilac in spring is sweet, and I'm sending her a fresh bunch every day while it lasts. It's a rare night, master. I envy you your walk home in the moonlight along that shore."

"Better come part of the way with me," I suggested.

"No." Abel glanced at the house. "Tamzine never likes to be alone o' nights. So I take my moonlight walks in the garden. The moon's a great friend of mine, master. I've loved her ever since I can remember. When I was a little lad of eight I fell asleep in the garden one evening and wasn't missed. I woke up alone in the night and I was most scared to death, master. Lord, what shadows and queer noises there were! I darsn't move. I just sat there quaking, poor small mite. Then all at once I saw the moon looking down at me through the pine boughs, just like an old friend. I was comforted right off. Got up and walked to the house as brave as a lion, looking at her. Goodnight, master. Tell Mary the lilacs'll last another week yet."

From that night Abel and I were cronies. We walked and talked and kept silence and fished cod together. Stillwater people thought it very strange that I should prefer his society to that of the young fellows of my own age. Mrs Campbell was quite worried over it, and opined that there had always been something queer about me. "Birds of a feather," she quoted darkly to her husband.

I loved that old garden by the harbour shore. Even Abel himself, I think, could hardly have felt a deeper affection for it. When its gate closed behind me it shut out the world and my corroding memories and discontents. In its peace my soul emptied itself of the bitterness which had been filling and spoiling it, and grew normal and healthy again, aided thereto by Abel's wise words. He never preached, but he radiated courage and endurance and a frank acceptance of the hard things of life, as well as a cordial welcome of its pleasant things. He was the *sanest* soul I ever met. He neither minimised ill nor exaggerated good, but he held that we should never be controlled by either. Pain should not depress us unduly, nor pleasure lure us into forgetfulness and sloth. All unknowingly he made me realise that I had been a bit of a coward and a shirker. I began to understand that my personal woes were not the most important things in the universe, even to myself. In short, Abel taught me to laugh again; and when a man can laugh wholesomely things are not going too badly with him.

That old garden was always such a cheery place. Even

when the east wind sang in minor and the waves on the gray shore were sad, hints of sunshine seemed to be lurking all about it. Perhaps this was because there were so many yellow flowers in it. Tamzine liked yellow flowers. Captain Kidd, too, always paraded it in panoply of gold. He was so large and effulgent that one hardly missed the sun. Considering his presence I wondered that the garden was always so full of singing birds. But the Captain never meddled with them. Probably he understood that his master would not have tolerated it for a moment. So there was always a song or a chirp somewhere. Overhead flew the gulls and the cranes. The wind in the pines always made a glad salutation. Abel and I paced the walks, in high converse on matters beyond the ken of cat or king.

"I liked to ponder on all problems, though I can never solve them," Abel used to say. "My father held that we should never talk of things we couldn't understand. But, lord, master, if we didn't the subjects for conversation would be mighty few. I reckon the gods laugh many a time to hear us, but what matter? So long as we remember that we're only men, and don't take to fancying ourselves gods, really knowing good and evil, I reckon our discussions won't do us or anyone much harm. So we'll have another whack at the origin of evil this evening, master."

Tamzine forgot to be shy with me at last, and gave me a broad smile of welcome every time I came. But she rarely spoke to me. She spent all her spare time weeding the garden, which she loved as well as Abel did. She was addicted to bright colours and always wore wrappers of very gorgeous print. She worshipped Abel and his word was a law unto her.

"I am very thankful Tamzine is so well," said Abel one evening as we watched the sunset. The day had begun sombrely in gray cloud and mist, but it ended in a pomp of scarlet and gold. "There was a time when she wasn't, master – you've heard? But for years now she has been quite able to look after herself. And so, if I fare forth on the last great adventure some of these days Tamzine will not be left helpless."

"She is ten years older than you. It is likely she will go before you," I said.

Abel shook his head and stroked his smart beard. I always suspected that beard of being Abel's last surviving vanity. It was always so carefully groomed, while I had no evidence that he ever combed his grizzled mop of hair.

"No, Tamzine will outlive me. She's got the Armstrong heart. I have the Marwood heart – my mother was a Marwood. We don't live to be old, and we go quick and easy. I'm glad of it. I don't think I'm a coward, master, but the thought of a lingering death gives me a queer sick feeling of horror. There, I'm not going to say any more about it. I just mentioned it so that some day when you hear that old Abel Armstrong has been found dead, you won't feel sorry. You'll remember I wanted it that way. Not that I'm tired of life either. It's very pleasant, what with my garden and Captain Kidd and the harbour out there. But it's a trifle monotonous at times and death will be something of a change, master. I'm real curious about it."

"I hate the thought of death," I said gloomily.

"Oh, you're young. The young always do. Death grows friendlier as we grow older. Not that one of us really wants to die, though, master. Tennyson spoke truth when he said that. There's old Mrs Warner at the Channel Head. She's had heaps of trouble all her life, poor soul, and she's lost almost everyone she cared about. She's always saying that she'll be glad when her time comes, and she doesn't want to live any longer in this vale of tears. But when she takes a sick spell, lord, what a fuss she makes, master! Doctors from town and a trained nurse and enough medicine to kill a dog! Life may be a vale of tears, all right, master, but there are some folks who enjoy weeping, I reckon."

Summer passed through the garden with her procession of roses and lilies and hollyhocks and golden glow. The golden glow was particularly fine that year. There was a great bank of it at the lower end of the garden, like a huge billow of sunshine. Tamzine revelled in it, but Abel liked more subtly-tinted flowers. There was a certain dark wine-hued hollyhock which was a favourite with him. He would sit for hours looking steadfastly into one of its shallow satin cups. I found him so one afternoon in the hop-vine arbour.

"This colour always has a soothing effect on me," he explained. "Yellow excites me too much – makes me restless – makes me want to sail 'beyond the bourne of sunset'. I looked at that surge of golden glow down there today till I got all worked up and thought my life had been an awful failure. I found a dead butterfly and had a little funeral – buried it in the fern corner. And I thought I hadn't been any more use in the world than that poor little butterfly. Oh, I was woeful, master. Then I got me this hollyhock and sat down here to look at it alone. When a man's alone, master, he's most with God – or with the devil. The devil rampaged around me all the time I was looking at that golden glow; but God spoke to me through the hollyhock. And it seemed to me that a man who's as happy as I am and has got such a garden has made a real success of living."

"I hope I'll be able to make as much of a success," I said sincerely.

"I want you to make a different kind of success, though, master," said Abel, shaking his head. "I want you to *do* things – the things I'd have tried to do if I'd had the chance. It's in you to do them – if you set your teeth and go ahead."

"I believe I *can* set my teeth and go ahead now, thanks to you, Mr Armstrong," I said. "I was heading straight for failure when I came here last spring; but you've changed my course."

"Given you a sort of compass to steer by, haven't I?"

queried Abel with a smile. "I ain't too modest to take some credit for it. I saw I could do *you* some good. But my garden has done more than I did, if you'll believe it. It's wonderful what a garden can do for a man when he lets it have its way. Come, sit down here and bask, master. The sunshine may be gone to-morrow. Let's just sit and think."

We sat and thought for a long while. Presently Abel said abruptly:

"You don't see the folks I see in this garden, master. You don't see anybody but me and old Tamzine and Captain Kidd. I see all who used to be here long ago. It was a lively place then. There were plenty of us and we were as gay a set of youngsters as you'd find anywhere. We tossed laughter backwards and forwards here like a ball. And now old Tamzine and older Abel are all that are left."

He was silent a moment, looking at the phantoms of memory that paced invisibly to me the dappled walks and peeped merrily through the swinging boughs. Then he went on:

"Of all the folks I see here there are two that are more vivid and real than all the rest, master. One is my sister Alice. She died thirty years ago. She was very beautiful. You'd hardly believe that to look at Tamzine and me, would you? But it is true. We always called her Queen Alice – she was so stately and handsome. She had brown eyes and red-gold hair, just the colour of that nasturtium there. She was father's favourite. The night she was born they didn't think my mother would live. Father walked this garden all night. And just under that old apple-tree he knelt at sunrise and thanked God when they came to tell him that all was well.

"Alice was always a creature of joy. This old garden rang with her laughter in those years. She seldom walked – she ran or danced. She only lived twenty years, but nineteen of them were so happy I've never pitied her over much. She had everything that makes life worth living – laughter and love, and at the last sorrow. James Milburn was her lover. It's thirty-one years since his ship sailed out of that harbour and Alice waved him good-bye from this garden. He never came back. His ship was never heard of again.

"When Alice gave up hope that it would be, she died of a broken heart. They say there's no such thing; but nothing else ailed Alice. She stood at yonder gate day after day and watched the harbour; and when at last she gave up hope life went with it. I remember the day: she had watched until sunset. Then she turned away from the gate. All the unrest and despair had gone out of her eyes. There was a terrible peace in them – the peace of the dead. 'He will never come back now, Abel,' she said to me.

"In less than a week she was dead. The others mourned her, but I didn't, master. She had sounded the deeps of living and there was nothing else to linger through the years for. *My* grief had spent itself earlier, when I walked this garden in agony because I could not help her. But often, on these long warm summer afternoons, I seem to hear Alice's laughter all over this garden; though she's been dead so long."

He lapsed into a reverie which I did not disturb, and it was not until another day that I learned of the other memory that he cherished. He reverted to it suddenly as we sat again in the hop-vine arbour, looking at the glimmering radiance of the September sea.

"Master, how many of us are sitting here?"

"Two in the flesh. How many in the spirit I know not," I answered, humouring his mood.

"There is one – the other of the two I spoke of the day I told you about Alice. It's harder for me to speak of this one."

"Don't speak of it if it hurts you," I said.

"But I want to. It's a whim of mine. Do you know why I told you of Alice and why I'm going to tell you of Mercedes? It's because I want someone to remember them and think of them sometimes after I'm gone. I can't bear that their names should be utterly forgotten by all living souls.

"My older brother, Alec, was a sailor, and on his last voyage to the West Indies he married and brought home a Spanish girl. My father and mother didn't like the match. Mercedes was a foreigner and a Catholic, and differed from us in every way. But I never blamed Alec after I saw her. It wasn't that she was so very pretty. She was slight and dark and ivory-coloured. But she was very graceful, and there was a charm about her, master – a mighty and potent charm. The women couldn't understand it. They wondered at Alec's infatuation for her. I never did. I – I loved her, too, master, before I had known her a day. Nobody ever knew it. Mercedes never dreamed of it. But it's lasted me all my life. I never wanted to think of any other woman. She spoiled a man for any other kind of woman – that little pale, dark-eyed Spanish girl. To love her was like drinking some rare sparkling wine. You'd never again have any taste for a commoner draught.

"I think she was very happy the year she spent here. Our thrifty women-folk in Stillwater jeered at her because she wasn't what they called capable. They said she couldn't do anything. But she could do one thing well – she could love. She worshipped Alec. I used to hate him for it. Oh, my heart has been very full of black thoughts in its time, master. But neither Alec nor Mercedes ever knew. And I'm thankful now that they were so happy. Alec made this arbour for Mercedes – at least he made the trellis, and she planted the vines.

"She used to sit here most of the time in summer. I suppose that's why I like to sit here. Her eyes would be dreamy and far-away until Alec would flash his welcome. How that used to torture me! But now I like to remember it. And her pretty soft foreign voice and little white hands. She died after she had lived here a year. They buried her and her baby in the graveyard of that little chapel over the harbour where the bell rings every evening. She used to like sitting here and listening to it. Alec lived a long while after, but he never married again. He's gone now, and nobody remembers Mercedes but me."

Abel lapsed into a reverie – a tryst with the past which I would not disturb. I thought he did not notice my departure, but as I opened the gate he stood up and waved his hand.

Three days later I went again to the old garden by the harbour shore. There was a red light on a distant sail. In the far west a sunset city was built around a great deep harbour of twilight. Palaces were there and bannered towers of crimson and gold. The air was full of music; there was one music of the wind and another of the waves, and still another of the distant bell from the chapel near which Mercedes slept. The garden was full of ripe odours and warm colours. The Lombardies around it were tall and sombre like the priestly forms of some mystic band. Abel was sitting in the hop-vine arbour; beside him Captain Kidd slept. I thought Abel was asleep, too; his head leaned against the trellis and his eyes were shut.

But when I reached the arbour I saw that he was not asleep. There was a strange, wise little smile on his lips as if he had attained to the ultimate wisdom and were laughing in no unkindly fashion at our old blind suppositions and perplexities.

Abel had gone on his Great Adventure.

THE DRAGON TAMERS

E. NESBIT

There was once an old, old castle – it was so old that its walls
and towers and turrets and gateways and arches had crumbled
to ruins, and of all its old splendour there were only two little
rooms left; and it was here that John the blacksmith had set
up his forge. He was too poor to live in a proper house, and
no one asked any rent for the rooms in the ruin, because all
the lords of the castle were dead and gone this many a year.
So there John blew his bellows, and hammered his iron, and
did all the work which came his way. This was not much,
because most of the trade went to the mayor of the town, who
was also a blacksmith in quite a large way of business, and
had his huge forge facing the square of the town, and had
twelve apprentices, all hammering like a nest of woodpeckers,
and twelve journeymen to order the apprentices about, and a
patent forge and a self-acting hammer and electric bellows,
and all things handsome about him. So that of course the
townspeople, whenever they wanted a horse shod or a shaft
mended, went to the mayor. John the blacksmith struggled on
as best he could, with a few odd jobs from travellers and strangers who did not know what a superior forge the mayor's was.

The two rooms were warm and weather-tight, but not very large; so the blacksmith got into the way of keeping his old iron, and his odds and ends, and his fagots, and his twopenn'orths of coal, in the great dungeon down under the castle. It was a very fine dungeon indeed, with a handsome vaulted roof and big iron rings, whose staples were built into the wall, very strong and convenient for tying captives up to, and at one end was a broken flight of wide steps leading down no one knew where. Even the lords of the castle in the good old times had never known where those steps led to, but every now and then they would kick a prisoner down the steps in their lighthearted, hopeful way, and, sure enough, the prisoners never came back. The blacksmith had never dared to go beyond the seventh step, and no more have I – so I know no more than he did what was at the bottom of those stairs.

John the blacksmith had a wife and a little baby. When his wife was not doing the housework she used to nurse the baby and cry, remembering the happy days when she lived with her father, who kept seventeen cows and lived quite in the country, and when John used to come courting her in the summer evenings, as smart as smart, with a posy in his buttonhole. And now John's hair was getting gray, and there was hardly ever enough to eat.

As for the baby, it cried a good deal at odd times; but at night, when its mother had settled down to sleep, it would always begin to cry, quite as a matter of course, so that she hardly got any rest at all. This made her very tired. The baby could make up for its bad nights during the day, if it liked, but the poor mother couldn't. So whenever she had nothing to do she used to sit and cry, because she was tired out with work and worry.

One evening the blacksmith was busy with his forge. He was making a goat-shoe for the goat of a very rich lady, who wished to see how the goat liked being shod, and also whether the shoe would come to fivepence or sevenpence before she ordered the whole set. This was the only order John had had that week. And as he worked his wife sat and nursed the baby, who, for a wonder, was not crying.

Presently, over the noise of the bellows and over the clank of the iron, there came another sound. The blacksmith and his wife looked at each other.

"I heard nothing," said he.

"Neither did I," said she.

But the noise grew louder – and the two were so anxious not to hear it that he hammered away at the goat-shoe harder than he had ever hammered in his life, and she began to sing to the baby – a thing she had not had the heart to do for weeks.

But through the blowing and hammering and singing the noise came louder and louder, and the more they tried not to hear it, the more they had to. It was like the noise of some great creature purring, purring, purring – and the reason they did not want to believe they really heard it was that it came from the great dungeon down below, where the old iron was, and the firewood and the twopence worth of coal, and the broken steps that went down into the dark and ended no one knew where.

"It can't be anything in the dungeon," said the blacksmith, wiping his face. "Why, I shall have to go down there after more coals in a minute."

"There isn't anything there, of course. How could there be?" said his wife. And they tried so hard to believe that there could be nothing there that presently they very nearly did believe it.

Then the blacksmith took his shovel in one hand and his riveting hammer in the other, and hung the old stable lantern on his little finger, and went down to get the coals.

"I am not taking the hammer because I think there is something there," said he, "but it is handy for breaking the large lumps of coal."

"I quite understand," said his wife, who had brought

the coal home in her apron that very afternoon, and knew that it was all coal dust.

So he went down the winding stairs to the dungeon and stood at the bottom of the steps, holding the lantern above his head just to see that the dungeon really *was* empty, as usual. Half of it was empty as usual, except for the old iron and odds and ends, and the firewood and the coals. But the other side was not empty. It was quite full, and what it was full of was *Dragon*.

"It must have come up those nasty broken steps from goodness knows where," said the blacksmith to himself, trembling all over, as he tried to creep back up the winding stairs.

But the dragon was too quick for him – it put out a great claw and caught him by the leg, and as it moved it rattled like a great bunch of keys, or like the sheet iron they make thunder out of in pantomimes.

"No you don't," said the dragon, in a spluttering voice, like a damp squib.

"Deary, deary me," said poor John, trembling more than ever in the claw of the dragon; "here's a nice end for a respectable blacksmith!"

The dragon seemed very much struck by this remark.

"Do you mind saying that again?" said he, quite politely.

So John said again, very distinctly:

"*Here – is – a – nice – end – for – a – respectable – blacksmith.*"

"I didn't know," said the dragon. "Fancy now! You're the very man I wanted."

"So I understood you to say before," said John, his teeth chattering.

"Oh, I don't mean what you mean," said the dragon, "but I should like you to do a job for me. One of my wings has got some of the rivets out of it just above the joint. Could you put that to rights?"

"I might, sir," said John, politely, for you must always be polite to a possible customer, even if he be a dragon.

"A master craftsman – you *are* a master, of course? – can see in a minute what's wrong," the dragon went on. "Just come round here and feel my plates, will you?"

John timidly went around when the dragon took his claw away; and, sure enough, the dragon's offwing was hanging loose, and all anyhow, and several of the plates near the joint certainly wanted riveting.

The dragon seemed to be made almost entirely of iron armour – a sort of tawny, red-rust colour it was; from damp, no doubt – and under it he seemed to be covered with something furry.

All the blacksmith welled up in John's heart, and he felt more at ease.

"You could certainly do with a rivet or two, sir," said he; "in fact, you want a good many."

"Well, get to work, then," said the dragon. "You mend my wing, and then I'll go out and eat up all the town, and if you make a really smart job of it I'll eat you last. There!"

"I don't want to be eaten last, sir," said John.

"Well then, I'll eat you *first*," said the dragon.

"I don't want that, sir, either," said John.

"Go on with you, you silly man," said the dragon, "you don't know your own silly mind. Come, set to work."

"I don't like the job, sir," said John, "and that's the truth. I know how easily accidents happen. It's all fair and smooth, and 'Please rivet me, and I'll eat you last' – and then you get to work and you give a gentleman a bit of a nip or a dig under his rivets – and then it's fire and smoke, and no apologies will meet the case."

"Upon my word of honour as a dragon," said the other.

"I know you wouldn't do it on purpose, sir," said John, "but any gentleman will give a jump and a sniff if he's nipped, and one of your sniffs would be enough for me. Now, if you'd just let me fasten you up?"

"It would be so undignified," objected the dragon.

"We always fasten a horse up," said John, "and he's the 'noble animal.'"

"It's all very well," said the dragon, "but how do I know you'd untie me again when you'd riveted me? Give me something in pledge. What do you value most?"

"My hammer," said John. "A blacksmith is nothing without a hammer."

"But you'd want that for riveting me. You must think of something else, and at once, or I'll eat you first."

At this moment the baby in the room above began to scream. Its mother had been so quiet that it thought she had settled down for the night, and that it was time to begin.

"Whatever's that?" said the dragon, starting so that every plate on his body rattled.

"It's only the baby," said John.

"What's that?" asked the dragon. "Something you value?"

"Well, yes, sir, rather," said the blacksmith.

"Then bring it here," said the dragon, "and I'll take care of it till you've done riveting me, and you shall tie me up."

"All right, sir," said John, "but I ought to warn you. Babies are poison to dragons, so I don't deceive you. It's all right to touch – but don't you go putting it into your mouth. I shouldn't like to see any harm come to a nice-looking gentleman like you."

The dragon purred at this compliment and said:

"All right, I'll be careful. Now go and fetch the thing, whatever it is."

So John ran up the steps as quickly as he could, for he knew that if the dragon got impatient before it was fastened, it could heave up the roof of the dungeon with one heave of its back, and kill them all in the ruins. His wife was asleep, in spite of the baby's cries; and John picked up the baby and took it down and put it between the dragon's front paws.

"You just purr to it, sir," he said, "and it'll be as good as gold."

So the dragon purred, and his purring pleased the baby so much that it stopped crying.

Then John rummaged among the heap of old iron and found there some heavy chains and a great collar that had been made in the days when men sang over their work and put their hearts into it, so that the things they made were strong enough to bear the weight of a thousand years, let alone a dragon.

John fastened the dragon up with the collar and the chains, and when he had padlocked them all on safely he set to work to find out how many rivets would be needed.

"Six, eight, ten – twenty, forty," said he. "I haven't half enough rivets in the shop. If you'll excuse me, sir, I'll step around to another forge and get a few dozen. I won't be a minute."

And off he went, leaving the baby between the dragon's fore-paws, laughing and crowing with pleasure at the very large purr of it.

John ran as hard as he could into the town, and found the mayor and corporation.

"There's a dragon in my dungeon," he said; "I've chained him up. Now come and help to get my baby away."

And he told them all about it.

But they all happened to have engagements for that evening; so they praised John's cleverness, and said they were quite content to leave the matter in his hands.

"But what about my baby?" said John.

"Oh, well," said the mayor, "if anything should happen, you will always be able to remember that your baby perished in a good cause."

So John went home again, and told his wife some of the tale.

"You've given the baby to the dragon!" she cried. "Oh, you unnatural parent!"

"Hush," said John, and he told her some more.

"Now," he said, "I'm going down. After I've been down you can go, and if you keep your head the boy will be all right."

So down went the blacksmith, and there was the dragon purring away with all his might to keep the baby quiet.

"Hurry up, can't you?" he said. "I can't keep up this noise all night."

"I'm very sorry, sir," said the blacksmith, "but all the shops are shut. The job must wait till the morning. And don't forget you've promised to take care of that baby. You'll find it a little wearing, I'm afraid. Good night, sir."

The dragon had purred till he was quite out of breath – so now he stopped, and as soon as everything was quiet the baby thought everyone must have settled for the night, and that it was time to begin to scream. So it began.

"Oh, dear," said the dragon, "this is awful."

He patted the baby with his claw, but it screamed more than ever.

"And I am so tired too," said the dragon. "I did so hope I should have a good night."

The baby went on screaming.

"There'll be no peace for me after this," said the dragon. "It's enough to ruin one's nerves. Hush, then – did 'ums, then." And he tried to quiet the baby as if it had been a young dragon. But when he began to sing "Hush-a-bye, dragon," the baby screamed more and more and more. "I can't keep it quiet," said the dragon; and then suddenly he saw a woman sitting on the steps. "Here, I say," said he, "do you know anything about babies?"

"I do, a little," said the mother.

"Then I wish you'd take this one, and let me get some sleep," said the dragon, yawning. "You can bring it back in the morning before the blacksmith comes."

So the mother picked up the baby and took it upstairs and told her husband, and they went to bed happy, for they had caught the dragon and saved the baby.

And next day John went down and explained carefully to the dragon exactly how matters stood, and he got an iron gate with a grating to it, and set it up at the foot of the steps, and the dragon mewed furiously for days and days, but when he found it was no good he was quiet.

So now John went to the mayor, and said:

"I've got the dragon and I've saved the town."

"Noble preserver," cried the mayor, "we will get up a subscription for you, and crown you in public with a laurel wreath."

So the mayor put his name down for five pounds, and the corporation each gave three, and other people gave their guineas, and half-guineas, and half-crowns and crowns, and while the subscription was being made the mayor ordered three poems at his own expense from the town poet to celebrate the occasion. The poems were very much more admired, especially by the mayor and corporation.

The first poem dealt with the noble conduct of the mayor in arranging to have the dragon tied up. The second described the splendid assistance rendered by the corporation. And the third expressed the pride and joy of the poet in being permitted to sing such deeds, beside which the actions of St George must appear quite commonplace to all with a feeling heart or a well-balanced brain.

When the subscription was finished there was a thousand pounds, and a committee was formed to settle what should be done with it. A third of it went to pay for a banquet to the mayor and corporation; another third was spent in buying a gold collar with a dragon on it for the mayor and gold medals with dragons on them for the corporation; and what was left went in committee expenses.

So there was nothing for the blacksmith except the laurel wreath and the knowledge that it really *was* he who had saved the town. But after this things went a little better with the blacksmith. To begin with, the baby did not cry so much as it had before. Then the rich lady who owned the goat was so touched by John's noble action that she ordered a complete set of shoes at 2 shillings, 4 pence, and even made it up to 2 shillings, 6 pence, in grateful recognition of his public-spirited conduct. Then tourists used to come in breaks from quite a long way off, and pay twopence each to go down the steps and peep through the iron grating at the rusty dragon in the dungeon – and it was threepence extra for each party if the blacksmith let off coloured fire to see it by, which, as the fire was extremely short, was twopence-halfpenny clear profit every time. And the blacksmith's wife used to provide teas at ninepence a head, and altogether things grew brighter week by week.

The baby – named John, after his father, and called Johnnie for short – began presently to grow up. He was great friends with Tina, the daughter of the whitesmith, who lived nearly opposite. She was a dear little girl, with yellow pigtails and blue eyes, and she was never tired of hearing the story of how Johnnie, when he was a baby, had been minded by a real dragon.

The two children used to go together to peep through the iron grating at the dragon, and sometimes they would hear him mew piteously. And they would light a halfpenny's worth of coloured fire to look at him by. And they grew older and wiser.

Now, at last one day the mayor and corporation, hunting the hare in their gold gowns, came screaming back to the town gates with the news that a lame, humpy giant, as big as a tin church, was coming over the marshes towards the town.

"We're lost," said the mayor. "I'd give a thousand pounds to anyone who could keep that giant out of the town. *I* know what he eats – by his teeth."

No one seemed to know what to do. But Johnnie and Tina were listening, and they looked at each other, and ran off as fast as their boots would carry them.

They ran through the forge, and down the dungeon steps, and knocked at the iron door.

"Who's there?" said the dragon.

"It's only us," said the children.

And the dragon was so dull from having been alone for ten years that he said:

"Come in, dears."

"You won't hurt us, or breathe fire at us or anything?" asked Tina.

And the dragon said, "Not for worlds."

So they went in and talked to him, and told him what the weather was like outside, and what there was in the papers, and at last Johnnie said:

"There's a lame giant in the town. He wants you."

"Does he?" said the dragon, showing his teeth. "If only I were out of this!"

"If we let you loose you might manage to run away before he could catch you."

"Yes, I *might*," answered the dragon, "but then again I mightn't."

"Why – you'd never fight him?" said Tina.

"No," said the dragon; "I'm all for peace, I am. You let me out, and you'll see."

So the children loosed the dragon from the chains and the collar, and he broke down one end of the dungeon and went out – only pausing at the forge door to get the blacksmith to rivet his wing.

He met the lame giant at the gate of the town, and the giant banged on the dragon with his club as if he were banging an iron foundry, and the dragon behaved like a smelting works – all fire and smoke. It was a fearful sight, and people watched it from a distance, falling off their legs with the shock of every bang, but always getting up to look again.

At last the dragon won, and the giant sneaked away across the marshes, and the dragon, who was very tired, went home to sleep, announcing his intention of eating the town in the morning. He went back into his old dungeon because he was a stranger in the town, and he did not know of any other respectable lodging. Then Tina and Johnnie went to the mayor and corporation and said, "The giant is settled. Please give us the thousand pounds reward."

But the mayor said: "No, no, my boy. It is not you who have settled the giant, it is the dragon. I suppose you have chained him up again? When *he* comes to claim the reward he shall have it."

"He isn't chained up yet," said Johnnie. "Shall I send him to claim the reward?"

But the mayor said he need not trouble; and now he offered a thousand pounds to anyone who would get the dragon chained up again.

"I don't trust you," said Johnnie. "Look how you treated my father when he chained up the dragon."

But the people who were listening at the door interrupted, and said that if Johnnie could fasten up the dragon again they would turn out the mayor and let Johnnie be mayor in his place. For they had been dissatisfied with the mayor for some time, and thought they would like a change.

So Johnnie said, "Done," and off he went, hand in hand with Tina, and they called on all their little friends and said:

"Will you help us to save the town?"

And all the children said: "Yes, of course we will. What fun!"

"Well, then," said Tina, "you must all bring your basins of bread and milk to the forge tomorrow at breakfast time."

"And if ever I am mayor," said Johnnie, "I will give a banquet, and you shall be invited. And we'll have nothing but sweet things from beginning to end."

All the children promised, and next morning Tina and Johnnie rolled their big washing tub down the winding stair.

"What's that noise?" asked the dragon.

"It's only a big giant breathing," said Tina; "he's gone by, now."

Then, when all the town children brought their bread and milk, Tina emptied it into the wash tub, and when the tub was full Tina knocked at the iron door with the grating in it and said:

"May we come in?"

"Oh, yes," said the dragon, "it's very dull here."

So they went in, and with the help of nine other children they lifted the washing tub in and set it down by the dragon. Then all the other children went away, and Tina and Johnnie sat down and cried.

"What's this?" asked the dragon. "And what's the matter?"

"*This* is bread and milk," said Johnnie; "it's our breakfast – all of it."

"Well," said the dragon, "I don't see what you want with breakfast. I'm going to eat everyone in the town as soon as I've rested a little."

"Dear Mr Dragon," said Tina, "I wish you wouldn't eat us. How would you like to be eaten yourself?"

"Not at all," the dragon confessed, "but nobody will eat me."

"I don't know," said Johnnie, "there's a giant—"

"I know. I fought with him, and licked him—"

"Yes, but there's another come now – the one you fought was only this one's little boy. This one is half as big again."

"He's seven times as big," said Tina.

"No, nine times," said Johnnie. "He's bigger than the steeple."

"Oh, dear," said the dragon. "I never expected this."

"And the mayor has told him where you are," Tina went on, "and he is coming to eat you as soon as he has sharpened his big knife. The mayor told him you were a wild dragon – but he didn't mind. He said he only ate wild dragons – with bread sauce."

"That's tiresome," said the dragon. "And I suppose this sloppy stuff in the tub is the bread sauce?"

The children said it was. "Of course," they added, "bread sauce is only served with wild dragons. Tame ones are served with apple sauce and onion stuffing. What a pity you're not a tame one: He'd never look at you then," they said. "Good-bye, poor dragon, we shall never see you again, and now you'll know what it's like to be eaten." And they began to cry again.

"Well, but look here," said the dragon, "couldn't you pretend I was a tame dragon? Tell the giant that I'm just a poor little timid tame dragon that you kept for a pet."

"He'd never believe it," said Johnnie. "If you were our tame dragon we should keep you tied up, you know. We shouldn't like to risk losing such a dear, pretty pet."

Then the dragon begged them to fasten him up at once, and they did so: with the collar and chains that were made years ago – in the days when men sang over their work and made it strong enough to bear any strain.

And then they went away and told the people what they had done, and Johnnie was made mayor, and had a glorious feast exactly as he had said he would – with nothing in it but sweet things. It began with Turkish delight and half-penny buns, and went on with oranges, toffee, coconut ice, peppermints, jam puffs, raspberry-noyeau, ice creams, and meringues, and ended with bull's-eyes and gingerbread and acid drops.

This was all very well for Johnnie and Tina; but if you are kind children with feeling hearts you will perhaps feel sorry for the poor deceived, deluded dragon – chained up in the dull dungeon, with nothing to do but to think over the shocking untruths that Johnnie had told him.

When he thought how he had been tricked, the poor captive dragon began to weep – and the large tears fell down over his rusty plates. And presently he began to feel faint, as people sometimes do when they have been crying, especially if they have not had anything to eat for ten years or so.

And then the poor creature dried his eyes and looked about him, and there he saw the tub of bread and milk. "If giants like this damp, white stuff, perhaps *I* should like it too," and he tasted a little, and liked it so much that he ate it all up.

And the next time the tourists came, and Johnnie let off the coloured fire, the dragon said shyly:

"Excuse my troubling you, but could you bring me a little more bread and milk?"

So Johnnie arranged that people should go round with carts every day to collect the children's bread and milk for the dragon. The children were fed at the town's expense – on whatever they liked; and they ate nothing but cake and buns and sweet things, and they said the poor dragon was very welcome to their bread and milk.

Now, when Johnnie had been mayor ten years or so he married Tina, and on their wedding morning they went to see the dragon. He had grown quite tame, and his rusty plates had fallen off in places, and underneath he was soft and furry to stroke. So now they stroked him.

And he said, "I don't know how I could ever have liked eating anything but bread and milk. I *am* a tame dragon now, aren't I?" And when they said that yes, he was, the dragon said:

"I am so tame, won't you undo me?" And some people would have been afraid to trust him, but Johnnie and Tina were so happy on their wedding day that they could not believe any harm of anyone in the world. So they loosed the chains, and the dragon said: "Excuse me a moment, there are one or two little things I should like to fetch," and he moved off to those mysterious steps and went down them, out of sight into the darkness. And as he moved more and more of his rusty plates fell off.

In a few minutes they heard him clanking up the steps. He brought something in his mouth – it was a bag of gold.

"It's no good to me," he said; "perhaps you might find it useful." So they thanked him very kindly.

"More where that came from," said he, and fetched more and more and more, till they told him to stop. So now they were rich, and so were their fathers and mothers. Indeed, everyone was rich, and there were no more poor people in the town. And they all got rich without working, which is very wrong; but the dragon had never been to school, as you have, so he knew no better.

And as the dragon came out of the dungeon, following Johnnie and Tina into the bright gold and blue of their wedding day, he blinked his eyes as a cat does in the sunshine, and he shook himself, and the last of his plates dropped off, and his wings with them, and he was just like a very, very extra-sized cat. And from that day he grew furrier and furrier, and he was the beginning of all cats. Nothing of the dragon remained except the claws, which all cats have still, as you can easily ascertain.

And I hope you see now how important it is to feed your cat with bread and milk. If you were to let it have nothing to eat but mice and birds it might grow larger and fiercer, and scalier and tailier, and get wings and turn into the beginning of dragons. And then there would be all the bother over again.

THE CAT

MARY E. WILKINS FREEMAN

The snow was falling, and the Cat's fur was stiffly pointed with it, but he was imperturbable. He sat crouched, ready for the death-spring, as he had sat for hours. It was night – but that made no difference – all times were as one to the Cat when he was in wait for prey. Then, too, he was under no constraint of human will, for he was living alone that winter. Nowhere in the world was any voice calling him; on no hearth was there a waiting dish. He was quite free except for his own desires, which tyrannised over him when unsatisfied as now. The Cat was very hungry – almost famished, in fact. For days the weather had been very bitter, and all the feebler wild things which were his prey by inheritance, the born serfs to his family, had kept, for the most part, in their burrows and nests, and the Cat's long hunt had availed him nothing. But he waited with the inconceivable patience and persistency of his race; besides, he was certain. The Cat was a creature of absolute convictions, and his faith in his deductions never wavered. The rabbit had gone in there between those low-hung pine boughs. Now her little doorway had before it a shaggy curtain of snow, but in there she was. The Cat had seen her enter, so like a swift grey shadow that even his sharp and practised eyes had glanced back for the substance following, and then she was gone.

So he sat down and waited, and he waited still in the white night, listening angrily to the north wind starting in the upper heights of the mountains with distant screams, then swelling into an awful crescendo of rage, and swooping down with furious white wings of snow like a flock of fierce eagles into the valleys and ravines. The Cat was on the side of a mountain, on a wooded terrace. Above him a few feet away towered the rock ascent as steep as the wall of a cathedral. The Cat had never climbed it – trees were the ladders to his heights of life. He had often looked with wonder at the rock, and miauled bitterly and resentfully as man does in the face of a forbidding Providence. At his left was the sheer precipice. Behind him, with a short stretch of woody growth between, was the frozen perpendicular wall of a mountain stream. Before him was the way to his home. When the rabbit came out she was trapped; her little cloven feet could not scale such unbroken steeps. So the Cat waited. The place in which he was looked like a maelstrom of the wood. The tangle of trees and bushes clinging to the mountain-side with a stern clutch of roots, the prostrate trunks and branches, the vines embracing everything with strong knots and coils of growth, had a curious effect, as of things which had whirled for ages in a current of raging water, only it was not water, but wind, which had disposed everything in circling lines of yielding to its fiercest points of onset. And now over all this whirl of wood and rock and dead trunks and branches and vines descended the snow. It blew down like smoke over the rock-crest above; it stood in a gyrating column like some death-wraith of nature, on the level, then it broke over the edge of the precipice, and the Cat cowered before the fierce backward set of it. It was as if ice needles pricked his skin through his beautiful thick fur, but he never faltered and never once cried. He had nothing to gain from crying, and everything to lose; the rabbit would hear him cry and know he was waiting.

It grew darker and darker, with a strange white smother, instead of the natural blackness of night. It was a night of storm and death superadded to the night of nature. The mountains were all hidden, wrapped about, overawed, and tumultuously overborne by it, but in the midst of it waited, quite unconquered, this little, unswerving, living patience and power under a little coat of grey fur.

A fiercer blast swept over the rock, spun on one mighty foot of whirlwind athwart the level, then was over the precipice.

Then the Cat saw two eyes luminous with terror, frantic with the impulse of flight, he saw a little, quivering, dilating nose, he saw two pointing ears, and he kept still, with every one of his fine nerves and muscles strained like wires. Then the rabbit was out – there was one long line of incarnate flight and terror – and the Cat had her.

Then the Cat went home, trailing his prey through the snow.

The Cat lived in the house which his master had built, as rudely as a child's block-house, but stanchly enough. The snow was heavy on the low slant of its roof, but it would not settle under it. The two windows and the door were made fast, but the Cat knew a way in. Up a pine-tree behind the house he scuttled, though it was hard work with his heavy rabbit, and was in his little window under the eaves, then down through the trap to the room below, and on his master's bed with a spring and a great cry of triumph, rabbit and all. But his master was not there; he had been gone since early fall and it was now February. He would not return until spring, for he was an old man, and the cruel cold of the mountains clutched at his vitals like a panther, and he had gone to the village to winter. The Cat had known for a long time that his master was gone, but his reasoning was always sequential and circuitous; always for him what had been would be, and the more easily for his marvellous waiting powers so he always came home expecting to find his master.

When he saw that he was still gone, he dragged the rabbit off the rude couch which was the bed to the floor, put one little paw on the carcass to keep it steady, and began gnawing with head to one side to bring his strongest teeth to bear.

It was darker in the house than it had been in the wood, and the cold was as deadly, though not so fierce. If the Cat had not received his fur coat unquestioningly of Providence, he would have been thankful that he had it. It was a mottled grey, white on the face and breast, and thick as fur could grow.

The wind drove the snow on the windows with such force that it rattled like sleet, and the house trembled a little. Then all at once the Cat heard a noise, and stopped gnawing his rabbit and listened, his shining green eyes fixed upon a window. Then he heard a hoarse shout, a halloo of despair and entreaty; but he knew it was not his master come home, and he waited, one paw still on the rabbit. Then the halloo came again, and then the Cat answered. He said all that was essential quite plainly to his own comprehension. There was in his cry of response inquiry, information, warning, terror, and finally, the offer of comradeship; but the man outside did not hear him, because of the howling of the storm.

Then there was a great battering pound at the door, then another, and another. The Cat dragged his rabbit under the bed. The blows came thicker and faster. It was a weak arm which gave them, but it was nerved by desperation. Finally the lock yielded, and the stranger came in. Then the Cat, peering from under the bed, blinked with a sudden light, and his green eyes narrowed. The stranger struck a match and looked about. The Cat saw a face wild and blue with hunger and cold, and a man who looked poorer and older than his poor old master, who was an outcast among men for his poverty and lowly mystery of antecedents; and he heard a muttered, unintelligible voicing of distress from the harsh piteous mouth. There was in it both profanity and prayer, but the Cat knew nothing of that.

The stranger braced the door which he had forced, got some wood from the stock in the corner, and kindled a fire in the old stove as quickly as his half-frozen hands would allow. He shook so pitiably as he worked that the Cat under the bed felt the tremor of it. Then the man, who was small and feeble and marked with the scars of suffering which he had pulled down upon his own head, sat down in one of the old chairs and crouched over the fire as if it were the one love and desire of his soul, holding out his yellow hands like yellow claws, and he groaned. The Cat came out from under the bed and leaped up on his lap with the rabbit. The man gave a great shout and start of terror, and sprang, and the Cat slid clawing to the floor, and the rabbit fell inertly, and the man leaned, gasping with fright, and ghastly, against the wall. The Cat grabbed the rabbit by the slack of its neck and dragged it to the man's feet. Then he raised his shrill, insistent cry, he arched his back high, his tail was a splendid waving plume. He rubbed against the man's feet, which were bursting out of their torn shoes.

The man pushed the Cat away, gently enough, and began searching about the little cabin. He even climbed painfully the ladder to the loft, lit a match, and peered up in the darkness with straining eyes. He feared lest there might be a man, since there was a cat. His experience with men had not been pleasant, and neither had the experience of men been pleasant with him. He was an old wandering Ishmael among his kind; he had stumbled upon the house of a brother, and the brother was not at home, and he was glad.

He returned to the Cat, and stooped stiffly and stroked his back, which the animal arched like the spring of a bow.

Then he took up the rabbit and looked at it eagerly by the firelight. His jaws worked. He could almost have devoured it raw. He fumbled – the Cat close at his heels – around some rude shelves and a table, and found, with a grunt of self-gratulation, a lamp with oil in it. That he lighted; then he found a frying-pan and a knife, and skinned the rabbit, and prepared it for cooking, the Cat always at his feet.

When the odour of the cooking flesh filled the cabin, both the man and the Cat looked wolfish. The man turned the rabbit with one hand and stooped to pat the Cat with the other. The Cat thought him a fine man. He loved him with all his heart, though he had known him such a short time, and though the man had a face both pitiful and sharply set at variance with the best of things.

It was a face with the grimy grizzle of age upon it, with fever hollows in the cheeks, and the memories of wrong in the dim eyes, but the Cat accepted the man unquestioningly and loved him. When the rabbit was half cooked, neither the man nor the Cat could wait any longer. The man took it from the fire, divided it exactly in halves, gave the Cat one, and took the other himself. Then they ate.

Then the man blew out the light, called the Cat to him, got on the bed, drew up the ragged coverings, and fell asleep with the Cat in his bosom.

The man was the Cat's guest all the rest of the winter, and winter is long in the mountains. The rightful owner of the little hut did not return until May. All that time the Cat toiled hard, and he grew rather thin himself, for he shared everything except mice with his guest; and sometimes game was wary, and the fruit of patience of days was very little for two. The man was ill and weak, however, and unable to eat much, which was fortunate, since he could not hunt for himself. All day long he lay on the bed, or else sat crouched over the fire. It was a good thing that fire-wood was ready at hand for the picking up, not a stone's-throw from the door, for that he had to attend to himself.

The Cat foraged tirelessly. Sometimes he was gone for

days together, and at first the man used to be terrified, thinking he would never return; then he would hear the familiar cry at the door, and stumble to his feet and let him in. Then the two would dine together, sharing equally; then the Cat would rest and purr, and finally sleep in the man's arms.

Towards spring the game grew plentiful; more wild little quarry were tempted out of their homes, in search of love as well as food. One day the Cat had luck – a rabbit, a partridge, and a mouse. He could not carry them all at once, but finally he had them together at the house door. Then he cried, but no one answered. All the mountain streams were loosened, and the air was full of the gurgle of many waters, occasionally pierced by a bird-whistle. The trees rustled with a new sound to the spring wind; there was a flush of rose and gold-green on the breasting surface of a distant mountain seen through an opening in the wood. The tips of the bushes were swollen and glistening red, and now and then there was a flower; but the Cat had nothing to do with flowers. He stood beside his booty at the house door, and cried and cried with his insistent triumph and complaint and pleading, but no one came to let him in. Then the Cat left his little treasures at the door, and went around to the back of the house to the pine-tree, and was up the trunk with a wild scramble, and in through his little window, and down through the trap to the room, and the man was gone.

The Cat cried again – that cry of the animal for human companionship which is one of the sad notes of the world; he looked in all the corners; he sprang to the chair at the window and looked out; but no one came. The man was gone and he never came again.

The Cat ate his mouse out on the turf beside the house; the rabbit and the partridge he carried painfully into the house, but the man did not come to share them. Finally, in the course of a day or two, he ate them up himself; then he slept a long time on the bed, and when he waked the man was not there.

Then the Cat went forth to his hunting-grounds again, and came home at night with a plump bird, reasoning with his tireless persistency in expectancy that the man would be there; and there was a light in the window, and when he cried his old master opened the door and let him in.

His master had strong comradeship with the Cat, but not affection. He never patted him like that gentler outcast, but he had a pride in him and an anxiety for his welfare, though he had left him alone all winter without scruple. He feared lest some misfortune might have come to the Cat, though he was so large of his kind, and a mighty hunter. Therefore, when he saw him at the door in all the glory of his glossy winter coat, his white breast and face shining like snow in the sun, his own face lit up with welcome, and the Cat embraced his feet with his sinuous body vibrant with rejoicing purrs.

The Cat had his bird to himself, for his master had his own supper already cooking on the stove. After supper the Cat's master took his pipe, and sought a small store of tobacco which he had left in his hut over winter. He had thought often of it; that and the Cat seemed something to come home to in the spring. But the tobacco was gone; not a dust left. The man swore a little in a grim monotone, which made the profanity lose its customary effect. He had been, and was, a hard drinker; he had knocked about the world until the marks of its sharp corners were on his very soul, which was thereby calloused, until his very sensibility to loss was dulled. He was a very old man.

He searched for the tobacco with a sort of dull combativeness of persistency; then he stared with stupid wonder around the room. Suddenly many features struck him as being changed. Another stove-lid was broken; an old piece of carpet was tacked up over a window to keep out the cold; his firewood was gone. He looked and there was no oil left in his can. He looked at the coverings on his bed; he took them up, and again he made that strange remonstrant noise in his throat. Then he looked again for his tobacco.

Finally he gave it up. He sat down beside the fire, for May in the mountains is cold; he held his empty pipe in his mouth, his rough forehead knitted, and he and the Cat looked at each other across that impassable barrier of silence which has been set between man and beast from the creation of the world.

THE PHILANTHROPIST AND THE HAPPY CAT

SAKI

Jocantha Bessbury was in the mood to be serenely and graciously happy. Her world was a pleasant place, and it was wearing one of its pleasantest aspects. Gregory had managed to get home for a hurried lunch and a smoke afterwards in the little snuggery; the lunch had been a good one, and there was just time to do justice to the coffee and cigarettes. Both were excellent in their way, and Gregory was, in his way, an excellent husband. Jocantha rather suspected herself of making him a very charming wife, and more than suspected herself of having a first-rate dressmaker.

"I don't suppose a more thoroughly contented personality is to be found in all Chelsea," observed Jocantha in allusion to herself; "except perhaps Attab," she continued, glancing towards the large tabby-marked cat that lay in considerable ease in a corner of the divan. "He lies there, purring and dreaming, shifting his limbs now and then in an ecstasy of cushioned comfort. He seems the incarnation of everything soft and silky and velvety, without a sharp edge in his composition, a dreamer whose philosophy is sleep and let sleep; and then, as evening draws on, he goes out into the garden with a red glint in his eyes and slays a drowsy sparrow."

"As every pair of sparrows hatches out ten or more young ones in the year, while their food supply remains stationary, it is just as well that the Attabs of the community should have that idea of how to pass an amusing afternoon," said Gregory. Having delivered himself of this sage comment he lit another cigarette, bade Jocantha a playfully affectionate good-bye, and departed into the outer world.

"Remember, dinner's a wee bit earlier to-night, as we're going to the Haymarket," she called after him.

Left to herself, Jocantha continued the process of looking at her life with placid, introspective eyes. If she had not everything she wanted in this world, at least she was very well pleased with what she had got. She was very well pleased, for instance, with the snuggery, which contrived somehow to be cosy and dainty and expensive all at once. The porcelain was rare and beautiful, the Chinese enamels took on wonderful tints in the firelight, the rugs and hangings led the eye through sumptuous harmonies of colouring. It was a room in which one might have suitably entertained an ambassador or an archbishop, but it was also a room in which one could cut out pictures for a scrap-book without feeling that one was scandalising the deities of the place with one's litter. And as with the snuggery, so with the rest of the house, and as with the house, so with the other departments of Jocantha's life; she really had good reason for being one of the most contented women in Chelsea.

From being in a mood of simmering satisfaction with her lot she passed to the phase of being generously commiserating for those thousands around her whose lives and circumstances were dull, cheap, pleasureless, and empty. Work girls, shop assistants and so forth, the class that have neither the happy-go-lucky freedom of the poor nor the leisured freedom of the rich, came specially within the range of her sympathy. It was sad to think that there were young people who, after a long day's work, had to sit alone in chill, dreary bedrooms because they could not afford the price of a cup of coffee and a sandwich in a restaurant, still less a shilling for a theatre gallery.

Jocantha's mind was still dwelling on this theme when she started forth on an afternoon campaign of desultory shopping; it would be rather a comforting thing, she told herself, if she could do something, on the spur of the moment, to bring a gleam of pleasure and interest into the life of even one or two wistful-hearted, empty-pocketed workers; it would add a good deal to her sense of enjoyment at the theatre that night. She would get two upper circle tickets for a popular play, make her way into some cheap tea-shop, and present the tickets to the first couple of interesting work girls with whom she could casually drop into conversation. She could explain matters by saying that she was unable to use the tickets herself and did not want them to be wasted, and, on the other hand, did not want the trouble of sending them back. On further reflection she decided that it might be better to get only one ticket and give it to some lonely-looking girl sitting eating her frugal meal by herself; the girl might scrape acquaintance with her next-seat neighbour at the theatre and lay the foundations of a lasting friendship.

With the Fairy Godmother impulse strong upon her, Jocantha marched into a ticket agency and selected with immense care an upper circle seat for the "Yellow Peacock," a play that was attracting a considerable amount of discussion and criticism. Then she went forth in search of a tea-shop and philanthropic adventure, at about the same time that Attab sauntered into the garden with a mind attuned to sparrow stalking. In a corner of an A.B.C. shop she found an unoccupied table, whereat she promptly installed herself, impelled by the fact that at the next table was sitting a young girl, rather plain of feature, with tired, listless eyes, and a general air of uncomplaining forlornness. Her dress was of poor material, but aimed at being in the fashion, her hair was pretty, and her complexion bad; she was finishing a modest meal of tea and scone, and she was not very different in her way from thousands of other girls who were finishing, or beginning, or continuing their teas in London tea-shops at that exact moment. The odds were enormously in favour of the supposition that she had never seen the "Yellow Peacock"; obviously she supplied excellent material for Jocantha's first experiment in haphazard benefaction.

Jocantha ordered some tea and a muffin, and then turned a friendly scrutiny on her neighbour with a view to catching her eye. At that precise moment the girl's face lit up with sudden pleasure, her eyes sparkled, a flush came into her cheeks, and she looked almost pretty. A young man, whom she greeted with an affectionate "Hello, Bertie," came up to her table and took his seat in a chair facing her. Jocantha looked hard at the new-comer; he was in appearance a few years younger than herself, very much better looking than Gregory, rather better looking, in fact, than any of the young men of her set. She guessed him to be a well-mannered young clerk in some wholesale warehouse, existing and amusing himself as best he might on a tiny salary, and commanding a holiday of about two weeks in the year. He was aware, of course, of his good looks, but with the shy self-consciousness of the Anglo-Saxon, not the blatant complacency of the Latin or Semite. He was obviously on terms of friendly intimacy with the girl he was talking to, probably they were drifting towards a formal engagement. Jocantha pictured the boy's home, in a rather narrow circle, with a tiresome mother who always wanted to know how and where he spent his evenings. He would exchange that humdrum thraldom in due course for a home of his own, dominated by a chronic scarcity of pounds, shillings, and pence, and a dearth of most of the things that made life attractive or comfortable. Jocantha felt extremely sorry for him. She wondered if he had seen the

"Yellow Peacock"; the odds were enormously in favour of the supposition that he had not. The girl had finished her tea and would shortly be going back to her work; when the boy was alone it would be quite easy for Jocantha to say: "My husband has made other arrangements for me this evening; would you care to make use of this ticket, which would otherwise be wasted?" Then she could come there again one afternoon for tea, and, if she saw him, ask him how he liked the play. If he was a nice boy and improved on acquaintance he could be given more theatre tickets, and perhaps asked to come one Sunday to tea at Chelsea. Jocantha made up her mind that he would improve on acquaintance, and that Gregory would like him, and that the Fairy Godmother business would prove far more entertaining than she had originally anticipated. The boy was distinctly presentable; he knew how to brush his hair, which was possibly an imitative faculty; he knew what colour of tie suited him, which might be intuition; he was exactly the type that Jocantha admired, which of course was accident. Altogether she was rather pleased when the girl looked at the clock and bade a friendly but hurried farewell to her companion. Bertie nodded "good-bye," gulped down a mouthful of tea, and then produced from his overcoat pocket a paper-covered book, bearing the title "Sepoy and Sahib, a tale of the great Mutiny."

The laws of tea-shop etiquette forbid that you should offer theatre tickets to a stranger without having first caught the stranger's eye. It is even better if you can ask to have a sugar basin passed to you, having previously concealed the fact that you have a large and well-filled sugar basin on your own table; this is not difficult to manage, as the printed menu is generally nearly as large as the table, and can be made to stand on end. Jocantha set to work hopefully; she had a long and rather high-pitched discussion with the waitress concerning alleged defects in an altogether blameless muffin, she made loud and plaintive inquiries about the tube service to some impossibly remote suburb, she talked with brilliant insincerity to the tea-shop kitten, and as a last resort she upset a milk-jug and swore at it daintily. Altogether she attracted a good deal of attention, but never for a moment did she attract the attention of the boy with the beautifully-brushed hair, who was some thousands of miles away in the baking plains of Hindostan, amid deserted bungalows, seething bazaars, and riotous barrack squares, listening to the throbbing of tom-toms and the distant rattle of musketry.

Jocantha went back to her house in Chelsea, which struck her for the first time as looking dull and over-furnished. She had a resentful conviction that Gregory would be uninteresting at dinner, and that the play would be stupid after dinner. On the whole her frame of mind showed a marked divergence from the purring complacency of Attab, who was again curled up in his corner of the divan with a great peace radiating from every curve of his body.

But then he had killed his sparrow.

THE CAT WHO COULD EAT SO MUCH

Once upon a time there was a man who had a cat, and she ate so very much that he did not want to keep her any longer. So he decided to tie a stone around her neck, and throw her into the river; but before he did so she was to have something to eat just once more. The woman offered her a dish of mush and a little potful of fat. These she swallowed, and then jumped out of the window. There stood the man on the threshing-floor.

"Good-day, man in the house," said the cat.

"Good-day, cat," said the man. "Have you had anything to eat yet to-day?"

"O, only a little, but my fast has hardly been broken," said the cat. "I have had no more than a dish of mush and a little potful of fat, and I am thinking over whether I ought not to eat you as well," said she, and she seized the man and ate him up. Then she went into the stable. There sat the woman, milking.

"Good-day, woman in the stable," said the cat.

"Good-day, cat, is that you?" said the woman. "Have you eaten your food?" she asked.

"O, only a little to-day. My fast has hardly been broken," said the cat. "I have had no more than a dish of mush and a little potful of fat and the man in the house, and I'm thinking over whether I ought not to eat you as well," said she, and she seized the woman and ate her up.

"Good-day, cow at the manger," said the cat to the bell-cow.

"Good-day, cat," said the bell-cow. "Have you had anything to eat yet to-day?"

"O, only a little. My fast has hardly been broken," said the cat. "I have had no more than a dish of mush and a little potful of fat and the man in the house and the woman in the stable, and I'm thinking over whether I ought not to eat you as well," said the cat, and seized the bell-cow and ate her up. Then she went up to the orchard, and there stood a man who was sweeping up leaves.

"Good-day, leaf-sweeper in the orchard," said the cat.

"Good-day, cat," said the man. "Have you had anything to eat yet to-day?"

"O, only a little. My fast has hardly been broken," said the cat. "I have had no more than a dish of mush and a little potful of fat and the man in the house and the woman in the stable and the bell-cow at the manger, and I'm thinking over whether I ought not to eat you up as well," said she, and seized the leaf-sweeper and ate him up.

Then she came to a stone-pile. There stood the weasel, looking about him.

"Good-day, weasel on the stone-pile," said the cat.

"Good-day, cat," said the weasel. "Have you had anything to eat yet to-day?"

"O, only a little. My fast has hardly been broken," said the cat. "I have had no more than a dish of mush and a little potful of fat and the man in the house and the woman in the stable and the bell-cow at the manger and the leaf-sweeper in the orchard, and I'm thinking over whether I ought not to eat you as well," said the cat, and seized the weasel and ate him up.

After she had gone a while, she came to a hazel-bush. There sat the squirrel, gathering nuts.

"Good-day, squirrel in the bush," said the cat.

"Good-day, cat! Have you already had anything to eat yet to-day?" said the squirrel.

"O, only a little. My fast has hardly been broken," said the cat. "I have had no more than a dish of mush and a little potful of fat and the man in the house and the woman in the stable and the bell-cow at the manger and the leaf-sweeper in the orchard and the weasel on the stone-pile, and I'm thinking over whether I ought not to eat you up as well," said she, and seized the squirrel and ate him up.

After she had gone a little while longer, she met Reynard the fox, who was peeping out of the edge of the forest.

"Good-day, fox, you sly-boots," said the cat.

"Good-day, cat! Have you had anything to eat yet to-day?" said the fox.

"O, only a little. My fast has hardly been broken," said the cat. "I have had no more than a dish of mush and a little potful of fat and the man in the house and the woman in the stable and the bell-cow at the manger and the leaf-sweeper in the orchard and the weasel on the stone-pile and the squirrel in the hazel-bush, and I'm thinking over whether I ought not to eat you as well," said she, and seized the fox and ate him up too.

When she had gone a little further, she met a hare.

"Good-day, you hopping hare," said the cat.

"Good-day, cat! Have you had anything to eat yet to-day?" said the hare.

"O, only a little. My fast has hardly been broken," said the cat. "I have had no more than a dish of mush and a little potful of fat and the man in the house and the woman in the stable and the bell-cow at the manger and the leaf-sweeper in the orchard and the weasel on the stone-pile and the squirrel in the hazel-bush and the fox, the sly-boots, and I'm thinking over whether I ought not to eat you up as well," said she, and seized the hare and ate him up.

When she had gone a little further, she met a wolf.

"Good-day, you wild wolf," said the cat.

"Good-day, cat! Have you had anything to eat yet to-day?" said the wolf.

"O, only a little. My fast has hardly been broken," said the cat. "I have had no more than a dish of mush and a little potful of fat and the man in the house and the woman in the stable and the bell-cow at the manger and the leaf-sweeper in the orchard and the weasel on the stone-pile and the squirrel in the hazel-bush and the fox, the sly-boots, and the hopping hare, and I'm thinking over whether I ought not to eat you up as well," said she, and seized the wolf and ate him up, too.

Then she went into the wood, and when she had gone far and farther than far, over hill and dale, she met a young bear.

"Good-day, little bear brown-coat," said the cat.

"Good-day, cat! Have you had anything to eat yet to-day?" said the bear.

"O, only a little. My fast has hardly been broken," said the cat. "I have had no more than a dish of mush and a little pot of fat and the man in the house and the woman in the stable and the bell-cow at the manger and the leaf-sweeper in the orchard and the weasel on the stone-pile and the squirrel in the hazel-bush and the fox, the sly-boots, and the hopping hare and the wild wolf, and I'm thinking over whether I ought not to eat you up as well," said she, and seized the little bear and ate him up.

When the cat had gone a bit further, she met the mother bear, who was clawing at the tree-stems so that the bark flew, so angry was she to have lost her little one.

"Good-day, you biting mother bear," said the cat.

"Good-day, cat! Have you had anything to eat yet to-day?" said the mother bear.

"O, only a little. My fast has hardly been broken," said the cat. "I have had no more than a dish of mush and a little potful of fat and the man in the house and the woman in the stable and the bell-cow at the manger and the leaf-sweeper in the orchard and the weasel on the stone-pile and the squirrel in the hazel-bush and the fox, the sly-boots, and the hopping hare and the wild wolf and the little bear brown-coat, and I'm thinking over whether I ought not to eat you as well," said she, and seized the mother bear and ate her, too.

When the cat had gone on a little further, she met the bear himself.

"Good-day, Bruin Good-fellow," said she.

"Good-day, cat! Have you had anything to eat yet to-day?" asked the bear.

"O, only a little. My fast has hardly been broken," said the cat. "I have had no more than a dish of mush and a little potful of fat and the man in the house and the woman in the stable and the bell-cow at the manger and the leaf-sweeper in the orchard and the weasel in the stone-pile and the squirrel in the hazel-bush and the fox, the sly-boots, and the hopping hare and the wild wolf and the little bear brown-coat and the biting mother bear, and now I'm thinking over whether I ought not to eat you as well," said she, and she seized the bear and ate him up, too.

Then the cat went far and farther than far, until she came into the parish. And there she met a bridal party on the road.

"Good-day, bridal party on the road," said the cat.

"Good-day, cat! Have you had anything to eat yet to-day?"

"O, only a little. My fast is hardly broken," said the cat. "I have had no more than a dish of mush and a little potful of fat and the man in the house and the woman in the stable and the bell-cow at the manger and the leaf-sweeper in the orchard and the weasel on the stone-pile and the squirrel in the hazel-bush and the fox, the sly-boots, and the hopping hare and the wild wolf and the little bear brown-coat and the biting mother bear and bruin good-fellow and now I'm thinking whether I ought not to eat you up as well," said she, and she pounced on the whole bridal party, and ate it up, with the cook, the musicians, the horses and all.

When she had gone a bit farther, she came to the church. And there she met a funeral procession.

"Good-day, funeral procession at the church," said the cat.

"Good-day, cat! Have you had anything to eat yet to-day?" said the funeral procession.

"O, only a little. My fast has hardly been broken," said the cat. "I have had no more than a dish of mush and a little potful of fat and the man in the house and the woman in the stable and the bell-cow at the manger and the leaf-sweeper in the orchard and the weasel on the stone-pile and the squirrel in the hazel-bush and the fox, the sly-boots, and the hopping hare and the wild wolf and little bear brown-coat and the biting mother bear and bruin good-fellow and the bridal party on the road, and now I'm thinking over whether I ought not to eat you up as well," said she, and pounced on the funeral procession, and ate up corpse and procession.

When the cat had swallowed it all, she went straight on up to the sky, and when she had gone far and farther than far, she met the moon in a cloud.

"Good-day, moon in a cloud," said the cat.

"Good-day, cat! Have you had anything to eat yet to-day?" said the moon.

"O, only a little. My fast has hardly been broken," said the cat. "I have had no more than a dish of mush and a little potful of fat and the man in the house and the woman in the stable and the bell-cow at the manger and the leaf-sweeper in the orchard and the weasel on the stone-pile and the squirrel in the hazel-bush and the fox, the sly-boots, and the wild wolf and little bear brown-coat and the biting mother bear and bruin good-fellow and the bridal party on the road and the funeral procession at the church, and now I'm thinking over whether I ought not to eat you up as well," said she, and pounced on the moon and ate him up, half and full.

Then the cat went far and farther than far, and met the sun.

"Good morning, cat! Have you had anything to eat yet to-day?" said the sun.

"O, only a little," said the cat. "I have had no more than a dish of mush and a little potful of fat and the man in the house and the woman in the stable and the bell-cow at the manger and the leaf-sweeper in the orchard and the weasel on the stone-pile and the squirrel in the hazel-bush and the fox, the sly-boots, and the hopping hare and the wild wolf and little bear brown-coat and the biting mother bear and bruin good-fellow and the bridal party on the road and the funeral procession at the church and the moon in a cloud, and now I'm thinking over whether I ought not to eat you up as well," said she, and pounced on the sun in the sky and ate him up.

Then the cat went far and farther than far, until she came to a bridge, and there she met a large billy-goat.

"Good morning, billy-goat on the broad bridge," said the cat.

"Good morning, cat! Have you had anything to eat yet to-day?" said the goat.

"O, only a little. My fast has hardly been broken," said the cat. "I had no more than a dish of mush and a little potful of fat and the man in the house and the woman in the stable and the bell-cow at the manger and the leaf-sweeper in the orchard and the weasel on the stone-pile and the squirrel in the hazel-bush and the fox, the sly-boots, and the hopping hare and the wild wolf and little bear brown-coat and the biting mother bear and bruin good-fellow and the bridal party on the road and the funeral procession at the church and the moon in a cloud and the sun in the sky, and now I'm thinking over whether I ought not to eat you up as well," said she.

"We'll fight about that first of all," said the goat, and butted the cat with his horns so that she rolled off the bridge, and fell into the water, and there she burst.

Then they all crawled out, and each went to his own place, all whom the cat had eaten up, and were every one of them as lively as before, the man in the house and the woman in the stable and the bell-cow at the manger and the leaf-sweeper in the orchard and the weasel on the stone-pile and the squirrel in the hazel-bush and the fox, the sly-boots, and the hopping hare and the wild wolf and little bear brown-coat and the biting mother bear and bruin good-fellow and the bridal party on the road and the funeral procession at the church and the moon in a cloud and the sun in the sky.

THE STALLS OF BARCHESTER CATHEDRAL

M. R. JAMES

This matter began, as far as I am concerned, with the reading of a notice in the obituary section of the *Gentleman's Magazine* for an early year in the nineteenth century:

"On February 26th, at his residence in the Cathedral Close of Barchester, the Venerable John Benwell Haynes, D.D., aged 57, Archdeacon of Sowerbridge and Rector of Pickhill and Candley. He was of – College, Cambridge, and where, by talent and assiduity, he commanded the esteem of his seniors; when, at the usual time, he took his first degree, his name stood high in the list of *wranglers*. These academical honours procured for him within a short time a Fellowship of his College. In the year 1783 he received Holy Orders, and was shortly afterwards presented to the perpetual Curacy of Ranxton-sub-Ashe by his friend and patron the late truly venerable Bishop of Lichfield ... His speedy preferments, first to a Prebend, and subsequently to the dignity of Precentor in the Cathedral of Barchester, form an eloquent testimony to the respect in which he was held and to his eminent qualifications. He succeeded to the Archdeaconry upon the sudden decease of Archdeacon Pulteney in 1810. His sermons, ever conformable to the principles of the religion and Church which he adorned, displayed in no ordinary degree, without the least trace of enthusiasm, the refinement of the scholar united with the graces of the Christian. Free from sectarian violence, and informed by the spirit of the truest charity, they will long dwell in the memories of his hearers. (Here a further omission.) The productions of his pen include an able defence of Episcopacy, which, though often perused by the author of this tribute to his memory, afford but one additional instance of the want of liberality and enterprise which is a too common characteristic of the publishers of our generation. His published works are, indeed, confined to a spirited and elegant version of the *Argonautica* of Valerius Flaccus, a volume of *Discourses upon the Several Events in the Life of Joshua*, delivered in his Cathedral, and a number of the charges which he pronounced at various visitations to the clergy of his Archdeaconry. These are distinguished by etc., etc. The urbanity and hospitality of the subject of these lines will not readily be forgotten by those who enjoyed his acquaintance. His interest in the venerable and awful pile under whose hoary vault he was so punctual an attendant, and particularly in the musical portion of its rites, might be termed filial, and formed a strong and delightful contrast to the polite indifference displayed by too many of our Cathedral dignitaries at the present time."

The final paragraph, after informing us that Dr Haynes died a bachelor, says:

"It might have been augured that an existence so placid and benevolent would have been terminated in a ripe old age by a dissolution equally gradual and calm. But how unsearchable are the workings of Providence! The peaceful and retired seclusion amid which the honoured evening of Dr Haynes' life was mellowing to its close was destined to be disturbed, nay, shattered, by a tragedy as appalling as it was unexpected. The morning of the 26th of February –"

But perhaps I shall do better to keep back the remainder of the narrative until I have told the circumstances which led up to it. These, as far as they are now accessible, I have derived from another source.

I had read the obituary notice which I have been quoting, quite by chance, along with a great many others of the same period. It had excited some little speculation in my mind, but, beyond thinking that, if I ever had an opportunity of examining the local records of the period indicated, I would try to remember Dr Haynes, I made no effort to pursue his case.

Quite lately I was cataloguing the manuscripts in the library of the college to which he belonged. I had reached the end of the numbered volumes on the shelves, and I proceeded to ask the librarian whether there were any more books which he thought I ought to include in my description. "I don't think there are," he said, "but we had better come and look at the manuscript class and make sure. Have you time to do that now?" I had time. We went to the library, checked off the manuscripts, and, at the end of our survey arrived at a shelf of which I had seen nothing. Its contents consisted for the most part of sermons, bundles of fragmentary papers, college exercises, *Cyrus*, an epic poem in several cantos, the product of a country clergyman's leisure, mathematical tracts by a deceased professor, and other similar material of a kind with which I am only too familiar. I took brief notes of these. Lastly, there was a tin box, which was pulled out and dusted. Its label, much faded, was thus inscribed: "Papers of the Ven. Archdeacon Haynes. Bequeathed in 1834 by his sister, Miss Letitia Haynes."

I knew at once that the name was one which I had somewhere encountered, and could very soon locate it. "That must be the Archdeacon Haynes who came to a very odd end at Barchester. I've read his obituary in the *Gentleman's Magazine*. May I take the box home? Do you know if there is anything interesting in it?"

The librarian was very willing that I should take the box and examine it at leisure. "I never looked inside it myself," he said, "but I've always been meaning to. I am pretty sure that is the box which our old Master once said ought never to have been accepted by the college. He said that to Martin years ago; and he said also that as long as he had control over the library it should never be opened. Martin told me about it, and said that he wanted terribly to know what was in it; but the Master was librarian, and always kept the box in the lodge, so there was no getting at it in his time, and when he died it was taken away by mistake by his heirs, and only returned a few years ago. I can't think why I haven't opened it; but, as I have to go away from Cambridge this afternoon, you had better have first go at it. I think I can trust you not to publish anything undesirable in our catalogue."

I took the box home and examined its contents, and thereafter consulted the librarian as to what should be done about publication, and, since I have his leave to make a story out of it, provided I disguise the identity of the people concerned, I will try what can be done.

The materials are, of course, mainly journals and letters. How much I shall quote and how much epitomise must be determined by considerations of space. The proper under-standing of the situation has necessitated a little – not very arduous – research, which has been greatly facilitated by the excellent illustrations and text of the Barchester volume in Bell's *Cathedral Series*.

When you enter the choir of Barchester Cathedral now, you pass through a screen of metal and coloured marbles, designed by Sir Gilbert Scott, and find yourself in what I must call a very bare and odiously furnished place. The stalls are modern, without canopies. The places of the dignitaries and the names of the prebends have fortunately been allowed to survive, and are inscribed on small brass plates affixed to the stalls. The organ is in the triforium, and what is seen of the case is Gothic. The reredos and its surroundings are like every other.

Careful engravings of a hundred years ago show a very different state of things. The organ is on a massive classical screen. The stalls are also classical and very massive. There is a baldacchino of wood over the altar, with urns upon its corners. Further east is a solid altar screen, classical in design, of wood, with a pediment, in which is a triangle surrounded by rays, enclosing certain Hebrew letters in gold. Cherubs contemplate these. There is a pulpit with a great sounding-board at the eastern end of the stalls on the north side, and there is a black and white marble pavement. Two ladies and a gentleman are admiring the general effect. From other sources I gather that the archdeacon's stall then, as now, was next to the bishop's throne at the south-eastern end of the stalls. His house almost faces the western part of the church, and is a fine red-brick building of William III's time.

Here Dr Haynes, already a mature man, took up his abode with his sister in the year 1810. The dignity had long been the object of his wishes, but his predecessor refused to depart until he had attained the age of ninety-two. About a week after he had held a modest festival in celebration of that ninety-second birthday, there came a morning, late in the year, when Dr Haynes, hurrying cheerfully into his break-fast-room, rubbing his hands and humming a tune, was greeted, and checked in his genial flow of spirits, by the sight of his sister, seated, indeed, in her usual place behind the tea-urn, but bowed forward and sobbing unrestrainedly into her handkerchief. "What – what is the matter? What bad news?" he began. "Oh, Johnny, you've not heard? The poor dear archdeacon!" "The archdeacon, yes? What is it – ill, is he?" "No, no; they found him on the staircase this morning;

it is so shocking." "Is it possible! Dear, dear, poor Pulteney! Had there been any seizure?" "They don't think so, and that is almost the worst thing about it. It seems to have been all the fault of that stupid maid of theirs, Jane." Dr Haynes paused. "I don't quite understand, Letitia. How was the maid at fault?" "Why, as far as I can make out, there was a stair-rod missing, and she never mentioned it, and the poor archdeacon set his foot quite on the edge of the step – you know how slippery that oak is – and it seems he must have fallen almost the whole flight and broken his neck. It *is* so sad for poor Miss Pulteney. Of course, they will get rid of the girl at once. I never liked her." Miss Haynes's grief resumed its sway, but eventually relaxed so far as to permit of her taking some breakfast. Not so her brother, who, after standing in silence before the window for some minutes, left the room, and did not appear again that morning.

I need only add that the careless maid-servant was dismissed forthwith, but that the missing stair-rod was very shortly afterwards found *under* the stair-carpet – an additional proof, if any were needed, of extreme stupidity and careless-ness on her part.

For a good many years Dr Haynes had been marked out by his ability, which seems to have been really considerable, as the likely successor of Archdeacon Pulteney, and no disap-pointment was in store for him. He was duly installed, and entered with zeal upon the discharge of those functions which are appropriate to one in his position. A considerable space in his journals is occupied with exclamations upon the confu-sion in which Archdeacon Pulteney had left the business of his office and the documents appertaining to it. Dues upon Wringham and Barnswood have been uncollected for some-thing like twelve years, and are largely irrecoverable; no visitation has been held for seven years; four chancels are almost past mending. The persons deputised by the arch-deacon have been nearly as incapable as himself. It was almost a matter for thankfulness that this state of things had not been permitted to continue, and a letter from a friend confirms this view. "[Greek: ὁ κατέχων]," it says (in rather cruel allusion to the Second Epistle to the Thessalonians), "is removed as last. My poor friend! Upon what a scene of confusion will you be entering! I give you my word that, on the last occasion of my crossing his threshold, there was no single paper that he could lay hands upon, no syllable of mine that he could hear, and no fact in connection with my business that he could remember. But now, thanks to a negligent maid and a loose stair-carpet, there is some prospect that necessary business will be transacted without a complete loss alike of voice and temper." This letter was tucked into a pocket in the cover of one of the diaries.

There can be no doubt of the new archdeacon's zeal and enthusiasm. "Give me but time to reduce to some semblance of order the innumerable errors and complications with which I am confronted, and I shall gladly and sincerely join with the aged Israelite in the canticle which too many, I fear, pronounce but with their lips." This reflection I find, not in a diary, but a letter; the doctor's friends seem to have returned his correspondence to his surviving sister. He does not confine himself, however, to reflections. His investigation of the rights and duties of his office are very searching and businesslike, and there is a calculation in one place that a period of three years will just suffice to set the business of the Archdeaconry upon a proper footing. The estimate appears to have been an exact one. For just three years he is occupied in reforms; but I look in vain at the end of that time for the promised *Nunc dimittis*. He has now found a new sphere of activity. Hitherto his duties have precluded him from more than an occasional attendance at the Cathedral services. Now he begins to take an interest in the fabric and the music. Upon his struggles with the organist, an old gentleman who had been in office since 1786, I have no time to dwell; they were not attended with any marked success. More to the purpose is his sudden growth of enthusiasm for the Cathedral itself and its furniture. There is a draft of a letter to Sylvanus Urban (which I do not think was ever sent) describing the stalls in the choir. As I have said, these were of fairly late date – of about the year 1700, in fact.

"The archdeacon's stall, situated at the south-east end, west of the episcopal throne (now so worthily occupied by the truly excellent prelate who adorns the See of Barchester), is distinguished by some curious ornamentation. In addition to the arms of Dean West, by whose efforts the whole of the internal furniture of the choir was completed, the prayer-desk is terminated at the eastern extremity by three small but remarkable statuettes in the grotesque manner. One is an exquisitely modelled figure of a cat, whose crouching posture suggests with admirable spirit the suppleness, vigilance, and craft of the redoubted adversary of the genus *Mus*. Opposite to this is a figure seated upon a throne and invested with the attributes of royalty; but it is no earthly monarch whom the carver has sought to portray. His feet are studiously concealed by the long robe in which he is draped: but neither the crown nor the cap which he wears suffice to hide the prick-ears and curving horns which betray his Tartarean origin; and the hand which rests upon his knee is armed with talons of horrifying length and sharpness. Between these two figures stands a shape muffled in a long mantle. This might at first sight be mistaken for a monk or 'friar of orders grey,' for the head is cowled and a knotted cord depends from somewhere about the waist. A slight inspection, however, will lead to a very different conclusion. The knotted cord is quickly seen to be a halter, held by a hand all but concealed within the draperies; while the sunken features and, horrid to relate, the rent flesh upon the cheek-bones, proclaim the King of Terrors. These figures are evidently the production of no unskilled chisel; and should it chance that any of your correspondents are able to throw light upon their origin and significance, my obligations to your valuable miscellany will be largely increased."

There is more description in the paper, and, seeing that the woodwork in question has now disappeared, it has a considerable interest. A paragraph at the end is worth quoting:

"Some late researches among the Chapter accounts have shown me that the carving of the stalls was not, as was very usually reported, the work of Dutch artists, but was executed by a native of this city or district named Austin. The timber was procured from an oak copse in the vicinity, the property of the Dean and Chapter, known as Holywood. Upon a recent visit to the parish within whose boundaries it is situated, I learned from the aged and truly respectable incumbent that traditions still lingered amongst the inhabitants of the great size and age of the oaks employed to furnish the materials of the stately structure which has been, however imperfectly, described in the above lines. Of one in particular, which stood near the centre of the grove, it is remembered that it was known as the Hanging Oak. The propriety of that title is confirmed by the fact that a quantity of human bones was found in the soil about its roots, and that at certain times of the year it was the custom for those who wished to secure a successful issue to their affairs, whether of love or the ordinary business of life, to suspend from its boughs small images or puppets rudely fashioned of straw, twigs, or the like rustic materials."

So much for the archdeacon's archaeological investigations. To return to his career as it is to be gathered from his diaries. Those of his first three years of hard and careful work show him throughout in high spirits, and, doubtless, during this time, that reputation for hospitality and urbanity which is mentioned in his obituary notice was well deserved. After that, as time goes on, I see a shadow coming over him – destined to develop into utter blackness – which I cannot but think must have been reflected in his outward demeanour. He commits a good deal of his fears and troubles to his diary; there was no other outlet for them. He was unmarried, and his sister was not always with him. But I am much mistaken if he has told all that he might have told. A series of extracts shall be given:

"*August 30, 1816.* The days begin to draw in more perceptibly than ever. Now that the Archdeaconry papers are reduced to order, I must find some further employment for the evening hours of autumn and winter. It is a great blow that Letitia's health will not allow her to stay through these months. Why not go on with my *Defence of Episcopacy*? It may be useful.

"*September 15.* Letitia has left me for Brighton.

"*Octpber 11.* Candles lit in the choir for the first time at evening prayers. It came as a shock: I find that I absolutely shrink from the dark season.

"*November 17.* Much struck by the character of the carving on my desk: I do not know that I had ever carefully noticed it before. My attention was called to it by an accident. During the *Magnificat* I was, I regret to say, almost overcome with sleep. My hand was resting on the back of the carved figure of a cat which is the nearest to me of the three figures on the end of my stall. I was not aware of this, for I was not looking in that direction, until I was startled by what seemed a softness, a feeling as of rather rough and coarse fur, and a sudden movement, as if the creature were twisting round its head to bite me. I regained complete consciousness in an instant, and I have some idea that I must have uttered a suppressed exclamation, for I noticed that Mr Treasurer turned his head quickly in my direction. The impression of the unpleasant feeling was so strong that I found myself rubbing my hand upon my surplice. This accident led me to examine the figures after prayers more carefully than I had done before, and I realised for the first time with what skill they are executed.

"*December 6.* I do indeed miss Letitia's company. The

evenings, after I have worked as long as I can at my *Defence*, are very trying. The house is too large for a lonely man, and visitors of any kind are too rare. I get an uncomfortable impression when going to my room that there *is* company of some kind. The fact is (I may as well formulate it to myself) that I hear voices. This, I am well aware, is a common symptom of incipient decay of the brain – and I believe that I should be less disquieted than I am if I had any suspicion that this was the cause. I have none – none whatever, nor is there anything in my family history to give colour to such an idea. Work, diligent work, and a punctual attention to the duties which fall to me is my best remedy, and I have little doubt that it will prove efficacious.

"*January 1.* My trouble is, I must confess it, increasing upon me. Last night, upon my return after midnight from the Deanery, I lit my candle to go upstairs. I was nearly at the top when something whispered to me, 'Let me wish you a happy New Year.' I could not be mistaken: it spoke distinctly and with a peculiar emphasis. Had I dropped my candle, as I all but did, I tremble to think what the consequences must have been. As it was, I managed to get up the last flight, and was quickly in my room with the door locked, and experienced no other disturbance.

"*January 15.* I had occasion to come downstairs last night to my workroom for my watch, which I had inadvertently left on my table when I went up to bed. I think I was at the top of the last flight when I had a sudden impression of a sharp whisper in my ear '*Take care.*' I clutched the balusters and naturally looked round at once. Of course, there was nothing. After a moment I went on – it was no good turning back – but I had as nearly as possible fallen: a cat – a large one by the feel of it – slipped between my feet, but again, of course, I saw nothing. It *may* have been the kitchen cat, but I do not think it was.

"*February 27.* A curious thing last night, which I should

like to forget. Perhaps if I put it down here I may see it in its true proportion. I worked in the library from about nine to ten. The hall and staircase seemed to be unusually full of what I can only call movement without sound: by this I mean that there seemed to be continuous going and coming, and that whenever I ceased writing to listen, or looked out into the hall, the stillness was absolutely unbroken. Nor, in going to my room at an earlier hour than usual – about half-past ten – was I conscious of anything that I could call a noise. It so happened that I had told John to come to my room for the letter to the bishop which I wished to have delivered early in the morning at the Palace. He was to sit up, therefore, and come for it when he heard me retire. This I had for the moment forgotten, though I had remembered to carry the letter with me to my room. But when, as I was winding up my watch, I heard a light tap at the door, and a low voice saying, 'May I come in?' (which I most undoubtedly did hear), I recollected the fact, and took up the letter from my dressing-table, saying, 'Certainly: come in.' No one, however, answered my summons, and it was now that, as I strongly suspect, I committed an error: for I opened the door and held the letter out. There was certainly no one at that moment in the passage, but, in the instant of my standing there, the door at the end opened and John appeared carrying a candle. I asked him whether he had come to the door earlier; but am satisfied that he had not. I do not like the situation; but although my senses were very much on the alert, and though it was some time before I could sleep, I must allow that I perceived nothing further of an untoward character."

With the return of spring, when his sister came to live with him for some months, Dr Haynes's entries became more cheerful, and, indeed, no symptom of depression is discernible unto the early part of September, when he was again left alone. And now, indeed, there is evidence that he was incommoded again, and that more pressingly. To this matter I will return in a moment, but I digress to put in a document which, rightly or wrongly, I believe to have a bearing on the thread of the story.

The account-books of Dr Haynes, preserved along with his other papers, show, from a date but little later than that of his institution as archdeacon, a quarterly payment of £25 to J. L. Nothing could have been made of this, had it stood by itself. But I connect with it a very dirty and ill-written letter, which, like another that I have quoted, was in a pocket in the cover of a diary. Of date or postmark there is no vestige, and the decipherment was not easy. It appears to run:

> "Dr Sr
> "I have bin expctin to her off you theis last
> wicks, and not Haveing done so must supose you
> have not got mine witch was saying how me and
> my man had met in with bad times this season
> all seems to go cross with us on the farm and
> which way to look for the rent we have no
> knowledge of it this been the sad case with us if
> you would have the great [liberality *probably, but
> the exact spelling defies reproduction*] to send
> fourty pounds otherwise steps will have to be
> took which I should not wish. Has you was the
> Means of my losing my place with Dr Pulteney I
> think it is only just what I am asking and you
> know best what I could say if I was Put to it but
> I do not wish anything of that unpleasant Nature
> being one that always wish to have everything
> Pleasant about me.
> "Your obedt Servt,
> "JANE LEE."

About the time at which I suppose this letter to have been written there is, in fact, a payment of £40 to J.L.

We return to the diary:

"*October 22.* At evening prayers, during the Psalms, I had that same experience which I recollect from last year. I was resting my hand on one of the carved figures, as before (I usually avoid that of the cat now), and – I was going to have said – a change came over it, but that seems attributing too much importance to what must, after all, be due to some physical affection in myself: at any rate, the wood seemed to become chilly and soft as if made of wet linen. I can assign the moment at which I became sensible of this. The choir was singing the words (*Set thou an ungodly man to be ruler over him and*) *let Satan stand at his right hand*.

"The whispering in my house was more persistent tonight. I seemed not to be rid of it in my room. I have not noticed this before. A nervous man, which I am not, and hope I am not becoming, would have been much annoyed, if not alarmed, by it. The cat was on the stairs tonight. I think it sits there always. There *is* no kitchen cat.

"*November 15.* Here again I must note a matter I do not understand. I am much troubled in sleep. No definite image presented itself, but I was pursued by the very vivid impression that wet lips were whispering into my ear with great rapidity and emphasis for some time together. After this, I suppose, I fell asleep, but was awakened with a start by a feeling as if a hand were laid on my shoulder. To my intense alarm I found myself standing at the top of the lowest flight of the first staircase. The moon was shining brightly enough through the large window to let me see that there was a large cat on the second or third step. I can make no comment. I crept up to bed again, I do not know how. Yes, mine is a heavy burden. [Then follows a line or two which has been scratched out. I fancy I read something like 'acted for the best.']"

Not long after this it is evident to me that the archdeacon's firmness began to give way under the pressure of these phenomena. I omit as unnecessarily painful and distressing the ejaculations and prayers which, in the months of December and January, appear for the first time and become increasingly frequent. Throughout this time, however, he is obstinate in clinging to his post. Why he did not plead ill-health and take refuge at Bath or Brighton I cannot tell; my impression is that it would have done him no good; that he was a man who, if he had confessed himself beaten by the annoyances, would have succumbed at once, and that he was conscious of this. He did seek to palliate them by inviting visitors to his house. The result he has noted in this fashion:

"*January 7.* I have prevailed on my cousin Allen to give me a few days, and he is to occupy the chamber next to mine.

"*January 8.* A still night. Allen slept well, but complained of the wind. My own experiences were as before: still whispering and whispering: what is it that he wants to say?

"*January 9.* Allen thinks this a very noisy house. He thinks, too, that my cat is an unusually large and fine specimen, but very wild.

"*January 10.* Allen and I in the library until eleven. He left me twice to see what the maids were doing in the hall: returning the second time he told me he had seen one of them passing through the door at the end of the passage, and said if his wife were here she would soon get them into better order. I asked him what coloured dress the maid wore; he said grey or white. I supposed it would be so.

"*January 11.* Allen left me today. I must be firm."

These words, *I must be firm*, occur again and again on subsequent days; sometimes they are the only entry. In these cases they are in an unusually large hand, and dug into the paper in a way which must have broken the pen that wrote them.

Apparently the archdeacon's friends did not remark any change in his behaviour, and this gives me a high idea of his courage and determination. The diary tells us nothing more than I have indicated of the last days of his life. The end of it all must be told in the polished language of the obituary notice:

"The morning of the 26th of February was cold and tempestuous. At an early hour the servants had occasion to go into the front hall of the residence occupied by the lamented subject of these lines. What was their horror upon observing the form of their beloved and respected master lying upon the landing of the principal staircase in an attitude which inspired the gravest fears. Assistance was procured, and an universal consternation was experienced upon the discovery that he had been the object of a brutal and a murderous attack. The vertebral column was fractured in more than one place. This might have been the result of a fall: it appeared that the stair-carpet was loosened at one point. But, in addition to this, there were injuries inflicted upon the eyes, nose and mouth, as if by the agency of some savage animal, which, dreadful to relate, rendered those features unrecognisable. The vital spark was, it is needless to add, completely extinct, and had been so, upon the testimony of respectable medical authorities, for several hours. The author or authors of this mysterious outrage are alike buried in mystery, and the most active conjecture has hitherto failed to suggest a solution of the melancholy problem afforded by this appalling occurrence."

The writer goes on to reflect upon the probability that the writings of Mr Shelley, Lord Byron, and M Voltaire may have been instrumental in bringing about the disaster, and concludes by hoping, somewhat vaguely, that this event may "operate as an example to the rising generation"; but this portion of his remarks need not be quoted in full.

I had already formed the conclusion that Dr Haynes was responsible for the death of Dr Pulteney. But the incident connected with the carved figure of death upon the archdeacon's stall was a very perplexing feature. The conjecture that it had been cut out of the wood of the Hanging Oak was not difficult, but seemed impossible to substantiate. However, I paid a visit to Barchester, partly with the view of finding out whether there were any relics of the woodwork to be heard of. I was introduced by one of the canons to the curator of the local museum, who was, my friend said, more likely to be able to give me information on the point than anyone else. I told this gentleman of the description of certain carved figures and arms formerly on the stalls, and asked whether any had survived. He was able to show me the arms of Dean West and some other fragments. These, he said, had been got from an old resident, who had also once owned a figure – perhaps one of those which I was inquiring for. There was a very odd thing about that figure, he said. "The old man who had it told me that he picked it up in a wood-yard, whence he had obtained the still extant pieces, and had taken it home for his children. On the way home he was fiddling about with it and it came in two in his hands, and a bit of paper dropped out. This he picked up and, just noticing that there was writing on it, put it into his pocket, and subsequently into a vase on his mantelpiece. I was at his house not very long ago, and happened to pick up the vase and turn it over to see whether there were any marks on it, and the paper fell into my hand. The old man, on my handing it to him, told me the story I have told you, and said I might keep the paper. It was crumpled and rather torn, so I have mounted it on a card, which I have here. If you can tell me what it means I shall be very glad, and also, I may say, a good deal surprised."

He gave me the card. The paper was quite legibly inscribed in an old hand, and this is what was on it:

When I grew in the Wood
I was water'd wth Blood
Now in the Church I stand
Who that touches me with his Hand
If a Bloody hand he bear
I councell him to be ware

Lest he be fetcht away
Whether by night or day,
But chiefly when the wind blows high
In a night of February.
This I drempt, 26 Febr. A° 1699.

JOHN AUSTIN.

"I suppose it is a charm or a spell: wouldn't you call it something of that kind?" said the curator.

"Yes," I said, "I suppose one might. What became of the figure in which it was concealed?"

"Oh, I forgot," said he. "The old man told me it was so ugly and frightened his children so much that he burnt it."

WHITTINGTON
AND HIS CAT

In the reign of the famous King Edward III there was a little boy called Dick Whittington, whose father and mother died when he was very young. As poor Dick was not old enough to work, he was very badly off; he got but little for his dinner, and sometimes nothing at all for his breakfast; for the people who lived in the village were very poor indeed, and could not spare him much more than the parings of potatoes, and now and then a hard crust of bread.

Now Dick had heard many, many very strange things about the great city called London; for the country people at that time thought that folks in London were all fine gentlemen and ladies; and that there was singing and music there all day long; and that the streets were all paved with gold.

One day a large waggon and eight horses, all with bells at their heads, drove through the village while Dick was standing by the sign-post. He thought that this waggon must be going to the fine town of London; so he took courage, and asked the waggoner to let him walk with him by the side of the waggon. As soon as the waggoner heard that poor Dick had no father or mother, and saw by his ragged clothes that he could not be worse off than he was, he told him he might go if he would, so off they set together.

So Dick got safe to London, and was in such a hurry to see the fine streets paved all over with gold, that he did not even stay to thank the kind waggoner; but ran off as fast as his legs would carry him, through many of the streets, thinking every moment to come to those that were paved with gold; for Dick had seen a guinea three times in his own little village, and remembered what a deal of money it brought in change; so he thought he had nothing to do but to take up some little bits of the pavement, and should then have as much money as he could wish for.

Poor Dick ran till he was tired, and had quite forgot his friend the waggoner; but at last, finding it grow dark, and that every way he turned he saw nothing but dirt instead of gold, he, sat down in a dark corner and cried himself to sleep.

Little Dick was all night in the streets; and next morning, being very hungry, he got up and walked about, and asked everybody he met to give him a halfpenny to keep him from starving; but nobody stayed to answer him, and only two or three gave him a halfpenny; so that the poor boy was soon quite weak and faint for the want of victuals.

In this distress he asked charity of several people, and one of them said crossly: "Go to work for an idle rogue." "That I will," says Dick, "I will to go work for you, if you will let me." But the man only cursed at him and went on.

At last a good-natured looking gentleman saw how hungry he looked. "Why don't you go to work, my lad?" said he to Dick. "That I would, but I do not know how to get any," answered Dick. "If you are willing, come along with me," said the gentleman, and took him to a hay-field, where Dick worked briskly, and lived merrily till the hay was made.

After this he found himself as badly off as before; and being almost starved again, he laid himself down at the door of Mr Fitzwarren, a rich merchant. Here he was soon seen by the cook-maid, who was an ill-tempered creature, and happened just then to be very busy dressing dinner for her master and mistress; so she called out to poor Dick: "What business have you there, you lazy rogue? there is nothing else but beggars; if you do not take yourself away, we will see how you will like a sousing of some dish-water; I have some here hot enough to make you jump."

Just at that time Mr Fitzwarren himself came home to dinner; and when he saw a dirty ragged boy lying at the door, he said to him: "Why do you lie there, my boy? You seem old enough to work; I am afraid you are inclined to be lazy."

"No, indeed, sir," said Dick to him, "that is not the case, for I would work with all my heart, but I do not know anybody, and I believe I am very sick for the want of food."

"Poor fellow, get up; let me see what ails you."

Dick now tried to rise, but was obliged to lie down again, being too weak to stand, for he had not eaten any food for three days, and was no longer able to run about and beg a halfpenny of people in the street. So the kind merchant ordered him to be taken into the house, and have a good dinner given him, and be kept to do what work he was able to do for the cook.

Little Dick would have lived very happy in this good family if it had not been for the ill-natured cook. She used to say: "You are under me, so look sharp; clean the spit and the dripping-pan, make the fires, wind up the jack, and do all the scullery work nimbly, or –" and she would shake the ladle at him. Besides, she was so fond of basting, that when she had no meat to baste, she would baste poor Dick's head and shoulders with a broom, or anything else that happened to fall in her way. At last her ill-usage of him was told to Alice, Mr Fitzwarren's daughter, who told the cook she should be turned away if she did not treat him kinder.

The behaviour of the cook was now a little better; but besides this Dick had another hardship to get over. His bed stood in a garret, where there were so many holes in the floor and the walls that every night he was tormented with rats and mice. A gentleman having given Dick a penny for cleaning his shoes, he thought he would buy a cat with it. The next day he saw a girl with a cat, and asked her, "Will you let me have that cat for a penny?" The girl said: "Yes, that I will, master, though she is an excellent mouser."

Dick hid his cat in the garret, and always took care to carry a part of his dinner to her; and in a short time he had no more trouble with the rats and mice, but slept quite sound every night.

Soon after this, his master had a ship ready to sail; and as it was the custom that all his servants should have some chance for good fortune as well as himself, he called them all into the parlour and asked them what they would send out.

They all had something that they were willing to venture except poor Dick, who had neither money nor goods, and therefore could send nothing. For this reason he did not come into the parlour with the rest; but Miss Alice guessed what was the matter, and ordered him to be called in. She then said: "I will lay down some money for him, from my own purse;" but her father told her: "This will not do, for it must be something of his own."

When poor Dick heard this, he said: "I have nothing but a cat which I bought for a penny some time since of a little girl."

"Fetch your cat then, my lad," said Mr Fitzwarren, "and let her go."

Dick went upstairs and brought down poor puss, with tears in his eyes, and gave her to the captain; "For," he said, "I shall now be kept awake all night by the rats and mice." All the company laughed at Dick's odd venture; and Miss Alice, who felt pity for him, gave him some money to buy another cat.

This, and many other marks of kindness shown him by Miss Alice, made the ill-tempered cook jealous of poor Dick, and she began to use him more cruelly than ever, and always made game of him for sending his cat to sea.

She asked him: "Do you think your cat will sell for as much money as would buy a stick to beat you?"

At last poor Dick could not bear this usage any longer, and he thought he would run away from his place; so he packed up his few things, and started very early in the morning, on All-hallows Day, the first of November. He walked as far as Holloway; and there sat down on a stone, which to this day is called "Whittington's Stone," and began to think to himself which road he should take.

While he was thinking what he should do, the Bells of Bow Church, which at that time were only six, began to ring, and their sound seemed to say to him: "Turn again, Whittington, Thrice Lord Mayor of London."

"Lord Mayor of London!" said he to himself. "Why, to be sure, I would put up with almost anything now, to be Lord Mayor of London, and ride in a fine coach, when I grow to be a man! Well, I will go back, and think nothing of the cuffing and scolding of the old cook, if I am to be Lord Mayor of London at last."

Dick went back, and was lucky enough to get into the house, and set about his work, before the old cook came downstairs.

We must now follow Miss Puss to the coast of Africa. The ship with the cat on board, was a long time at sea; and was at last driven by the winds on a part of the coast of Barbary, where the only people were the Moors, unknown to the English. The people came in great numbers to see the sailors, because they were of different colour to themselves, and treated them civilly; and, when they became better acquainted, were very eager to buy the fine things that the ship was loaded with.

When the captain saw this, he sent patterns of the best things he had to the king of the country; who was so much pleased with them, that he sent for the captain to the palace. Here they were placed, as it is the custom of the country, on rich carpets flowered with gold and silver. The king and queen were seated at the upper end of the room; and a number of dishes were brought in for dinner. They had not sat long, when a vast number of rats and mice rushed in, and devoured all the meat in an instant. The captain wondered at this, and asked if these vermin were not unpleasant.

"Oh yes," said they, "very offensive, and the king would give half his treasure to be freed of them, for they not only destroy his dinner, as you see, but they assault him in his chamber, and even in bed, and so that he is obliged to be watched while he is sleeping, for fear of them."

The captain jumped for joy; he remembered poor Whittington and his cat, and told the king he had a creature on board the ship that would despatch all these vermin immediately. The king jumped so high at the joy which the news gave him, that his turban dropped off his head. "Bring this creature to me," says he; "vermin are dreadful in a court, and if she will perform what you say, I will load your ship with gold and jewels in exchange for her."

The captain, who knew his business, took this opportunity to set forth the merits of Miss Puss. He told his majesty; "It is not very convenient to part with her, as, when she is gone, the rats and mice may destroy the goods in the ship – but to oblige your majesty, I will fetch her."

"Run, run!" said the queen; "I am impatient to see the dear creature."

Away went the captain to the ship, while another dinner was got ready. He put Puss under his arm, and arrived at the place just in time to see the table full of rats. When the cat saw them, she did not wait for bidding, but jumped out of the captain's arms, and in a few minutes laid almost all the rats and mice dead at her feet. The rest of them in their fright scampered away to their holes.

The king was quite charmed to get rid so easily of such plagues, and the queen desired that the creature who had done them so great a kindness might be brought to her, that she might look at her. Upon which the captain called: "Pussy, pussy, pussy!" and she came to him. He then presented her to the queen, who started back, and was afraid to touch a creature who had made such a havoc among the rats and mice. However, when the captain stroked the cat and called: "Pussy, pussy," the queen also touched her and cried: "Putty, putty," for she had not learned English. He then put her down on the queen's lap, where she purred and played with her majesty's hand, and then purred herself to sleep.

The king, having seen the exploits of Mrs. Puss, and being informed that her kittens would stock the whole country, and keep it free from rats, bargained with the captain for the whole ship's cargo, and then gave him ten times as much for the cat as all the rest amounted to.

The captain then took leave of the royal party, and set sail with a fair wind for England, and after a happy voyage arrived safe in London.

One morning, early, Mr Fitzwarren had just come to his counting-house and seated himself at the desk, to count over the cash, and settle the business for the day, when somebody came tap, tap, at the door. "Who's there?" said Mr Fitzwarren. "A friend," answered the other; "I come to bring you good news of your ship *Unicorn*." The merchant, bustling up in such a hurry that he forgot his gout, opened the door, and who should he see waiting but the captain and factor, with a cabinet of jewels, and a bill of lading; when he looked at this the merchant lifted up his eyes and thanked Heaven for sending him such a prosperous voyage.

They then told the story of the cat, and showed the rich present that the king and queen had sent for her to poor Dick. As soon as the merchant heard this, he called out to his servants:

"Go send him in, and tell him of his fame;
Pray call him Mr Whittington by name."

Mr Fitzwarren now showed himself to be a good man; for when some of his servants said so great a treasure was too much for him, he answered: "God forbid I should deprive him of the value of a single penny, it is his own, and he shall have it to a farthing."

He then sent for Dick, who at that time was scouring pots for the cook, and was quite dirty. He would have excused himself from coming into the counting-house, saying, "The room is swept, and my shoes are dirty and full of hob-nails." But the merchant ordered him to come in.

Mr Fitzwarren ordered a chair to be set for him, and so he began to think they were making game of him, at the same time said to them: "Do not play tricks with a poor simple boy, but let me go down again, if you please, to my work."

"Indeed, Mr Whittington," said the merchant, "we are all quite in earnest with you, and I most heartily rejoice in the news that these gentlemen have brought you; for the captain has sold your cat to the King of Barbary, and brought you in return for her more riches than I possess in the whole world; and I wish you may long enjoy them!"

Mr Fitzwarren then told the men to open the great treasure they had brought with them; and said: "Mr Whittington has nothing to do but to put it in some place of safety."

Poor Dick hardly knew how to behave himself for joy. He begged his master to take what part of it he pleased, since he owed it all to his kindness. "No, no," answered Mr Fitzwarren, "this is all your own; and I have no doubt but you will use it well."

Dick next asked his mistress, and then Miss Alice, to accept a part of his good fortune; but they would not, and at the same time told him they felt great joy at his good success. But this poor fellow was too kind-hearted to keep it all to himself; so he made a present to the captain, the mate, and the rest of Mr Fitzwarren's servants; and even to the ill-natured old cook.

After this Mr Fitzwarren advised him to send for a proper tailor and get himself dressed like a gentleman; and told him he was welcome to live in his house till he could provide himself with a better.

When Whittington's face was washed, his hair curled, his hat cocked, and he was dressed in a nice suit of clothes he was as handsome and genteel as any young man who visited at Mr Fitzwarren's; so that Miss Alice, who had once been so kind to him, and thought of him with pity, now looked upon him as fit to be her sweetheart; and the more so, no doubt, because Whittington was now always thinking what he could do to oblige her, and making her the prettiest presents that could be.

Mr Fitzwarren soon saw their love for each other, and proposed to join them in marriage; and to this they both readily agreed. A day for the wedding was soon fixed; and they were attended to church by the Lord Mayor, the court of aldermen, the sheriffs, and a great number of the richest merchants in London, whom they afterwards treated with a very rich feast.

History tells us that Mr Whittington and his lady lived in great splendour, and were very happy. They had several children. He was Sheriff of London, thrice Lord Mayor, and received the honour of knighthood by Henry V.

He entertained this king and his queen at dinner after his conquest of France so grandly, that the king said "Never had prince such a subject;" when Sir Richard heard this, he said: "Never had subject such a prince."

The figure of Sir Richard Whittington with his cat in his arms, carved in stone, was to be seen till the year 1780 over the archway of the old prison of Newgate, which he built for criminals.

THERE AROSE
A KING

E. F. BENSON

Agag, though of undoubtedly royal blood, was never a real
king. He was no more than one of the Hyksos, a shepherd-king,
bound by the limitations of his race, and no partaker in its
magnificence. Naturally, he did not work as the late house-
keeper had done (and no one expected that of him), but he
had neither the splendour nor the vivacity, possessed, let us
say, by Henry VIII or George IV, to make up for his indolence
in affairs of state. Henry VIII, anyhow, busied himself in
marriages, whereas Agag was merely terrified at the idea of
wooing, not to say winning, any of the princesses that were
brought to his notice; and they, on their part, only made the
rudest faces at him. Again George IV, though unkingly in
many respects, used to plunge about in the wild pursuit of
pleasure, and was supposed to have a kind heart. Agag, on
the contrary, never plunged: a cushion and some fish and
plenty of repose were the sum of his desires, and as for a kind
heart, he never had a heart at all. An unkind heart would
have given him some semblance of personality, but there was
not the faintest room to suppose that any emotion, other than
the desire for food and sleep and warmth, came within

measurable distance of him. He died in his sleep, probably of apoplexy, after a large meal, and beautiful in death as in life, was buried and forgotten. I have never known a cat so completely devoid of character, and I sometimes wonder whether he was a real cat at all, and not some sort of inflated dormouse in cat's clothing.

There followed a republican regime in this matter of cats. We went back, after Agag, to working cats, who would sit at mouse-holes for hours together, pounce and devour, and clean themselves and sleep, but among them all there was no "character" which ever so faintly resembled even Martha, far less Puss-cat.

I suppose the royalty of Agag, stupid and dull though he was, had infected me with a certain snobbishness as regards cats, and secretly – given that there were to be no more of those splendid plebeians, like Puss-cat – I longed for somebody who combined royal descent (for the sake of beauty and pride) with character, good or bad. Nero or Heliogabalus or Queen Elizabeth, or even the Emperor William II of Germany would have done, but I didn't want George I on the one side or a mere mild president of a small republic on the other.

Just after Agag's death I had moved up to London, and for a time there was this succession of unnoticeable heads of the state. They were born – those presidents of my republic – from respectable hard-working families, and never gave themselves out (though they knew quite well that they were the heads of the state) to be anything else but what they were: good, hard-working cats, with, of course, not only a casting, but a determining vote on all questions that concerned them or anybody else.

We were democratic in those days, and I am afraid "freedom broadened slowly down" from president to president. We were loyal, law-abiding citizens under their rule, but when our president was sitting at the top of the area steps, taking the air after his morning's work, it used to be no shock to me to see him tickled on the top of his head by people like tradesmen coming for orders, or a policeman or a nursery-maid. The president, in these circumstances, would arch a back, make poker of a tail, and purr. Being at leisure and unoccupied with cares of State, he did not pretend to be anything but *bourgeois*. The *bourgeoisie* had access to him; he would play with them, without any sense of inequality, through the area railings. There was a nursery-maid, I remember, whom our last president was very much attached to. He used to make the most terrific onslaughts at her shoe-laces.

But now all that regime is past. We are royalist again to the core, and Cyrus, of undoubtedly royal descent, is on the throne. The revolution was accomplished in the most pacific manner conceivable. A friend, on my birthday, two years ago, brought a small wicker basket, and the moment it was opened the country, which for a month or two had been in a state of darkest anarchy, without president or any ruler, was a civilised state again, with an acknowledged king. There was no war; nothing sanguinary occurred. Only by virtue of the glory of our king we became a great Power again. Cyrus had arranged that his pedigree should come with him; this was much bigger than Cyrus, and, being written on parchment (with a large gold crown painted at the head of it), was far more robust than he whose ancestors it enumerated. For his majesty, as he peered over the side of the royal cradle, did not seem robust at all. He put two little weak paws on the edge of his basket and tried to look like a lion, but he had no spirit to get farther. Then he wrinkled up his august face, and gave a sneeze so prodigious that he tumbled out of the basket alto-gether, and by accident (or at the most by catarrh) set foot in the dominions where he still reigns. Of course, I was not quite so stupid as not to recognise a royal landing, though made in so unconventional a manner; it was only as if George IV, in one of his numerous landings on some pier (so fitly commemorated by the insertion of a large brass boot print), had fallen flat on his face instead, and was commemorated by a full-length brass, with top-hat a little separate.

Babies of the human species, it is true, are all like each other, and I would defy any professor of Eugenics or of allied and abstruse schools of investigation to say, off-hand, whether a particular baby, divorced from his surroundings, is the Prince of Wales or Master Jones. But, quite apart from his pedigree, there was never any question at all about Cyrus. There was no single hair on his lean little body that was not of the true and royal blue, and his ears already were tufted inside with downy growth, and his poor little eyes, sadly screened by the moisture of his catarrh, showed their yellow topaz irises, that were never seen on Master Jones. So he tumbled upside down into his new kingdom, and, recovering himself, sat up and blinked, and said, "Ah-h-h." I took him up very reverently in both hands, and put him on my knee. He made an awful face, like a Chinese grotesque instead of a Persian king, but anyhow it was an Oriental face. Then he put a large paw in front of his diminutive nose and went fast asleep. It had been a most fatiguing sneeze.

Royal Persian babies, as you perhaps know, must never, after they have said good-bye to their royal mammas, be given milk. When they are thirsty they must have water; when they are hungry they have little finely chopped-up dishes of flesh and fish and fowl. As Cyrus slept, little chopped-up things were hastily prepared for him, and when he woke, his food and drink were waiting his royal pleasure. They seemed to please him a good deal, but at a crucial moment, when his mouth was quite full, he sneezed again. There was an explosion of awful violence, but the royal baby licked up the fragments... We knew at once that we had a tidy king to rule over us.

Cyrus was two months old when he became king, and the next four months were spent in growing and eating and sneezing. His general manner of life was to eat largely and instantly fall asleep, and it was then, I think, that he grew. Eventually a sneeze plucked him from his slumber, and this first alarum was a storm-cone, so to speak, that betokened the coming tornado. Once, after I began to count, he sneezed seventeen times... Then, when that was over, he sat quiet and recuperated; then he jumped straight up in the air, purred loudly, and ate again. The meal was succeeded by more slumber, and the cycle of his day was complete.

His first refreshment he took about seven in the morning – as soon as anybody was dressed – and an hour later, heavily slumbering, he was brought up to my room when I called, buttoned up in my servant's coat, and placed on my bed. He at once guessed that there must be a pleasant warm cave underneath the bedclothes, and, with stampings and purrings, penetrated into this abyss, curled himself against my side, and resumed his interrupted slumbers. After a while I would feel an internal stirring begin in my bed, and usually managed to deposit the king on the floor before his first sneeze. His second breakfast, of course, had come upstairs with my hot water, and after the sneezing was over he leaped into the air, espied and stalked some new and unfamiliar object, and did his duty with his victuals. He then looked round for a convenient resting-place, choosing one, if possible, that resembled an ambush, the definition of which may be held to be a place with a small opening and spaciousness within.

That gave us the second clue (tidiness being the first) towards the king's character. He had a tactical mind, and should make a good general. As soon as I observed this, I used to make an ambush for him among the sheets of the morning paper, providing it with a small spy-hole. If I scratched the paper in the vicinity of the spy-hole, a little silver-blue paw made wild dabs at the seat of the disturbance. Having thus frustrated any possible enemy, he went to sleep.

But the ambush he liked best was a half-opened drawer,

such as he found one morning for himself. There among flannel shirts and vests he made himself exceedingly comfortable, pending attacks. But before he went to sleep he made a point of putting out a small and awe-inspiring head to terrify any marauding bands who might be near. This precaution was usually successful, and he slept for the greater part of the morning.

For six months he stuffed and sneezed and slept, and then, one morning, like Lord Byron and the discovery of his fame, Cyrus woke and discovered the responsibilities of kingship. His sneezing fits suddenly ceased, and the Cyropaidaia (or education of Cyrus) began. He conducted his own education, of course, entirely by himself; he knew, by heredity, what a king had to learn, and proceeded to learn it. Hitherto the pantry and my bedroom were the only territories of his dominion that he had any acquaintance with, and a royal progress was necessary. The dining-room did not long detain him, and presented few points of interest, but in a small room adjoining he found on the table a telephone with a long green cord attached to the receiver. This had to be investigated, since his parents had not told him about telephones, but he soon grasped the principle of it, and attempted to get the ear-piece off its hook, no doubt with a view to issuing orders of some kind. It would not yield to gentle methods, and, after crouching behind a book and wriggling his body a great deal, he determined to rush the silly thing. A wild leap in the air, and Cyrus and the green cord and the receiver were all mingled up together in hopeless confusion... He did not telephone again for weeks.

The drawing-room was less dangerous. There was a bear-skin on the floor, and Cyrus sat down in front of the head, prepared to receive homage. This, I suppose, was duly tendered, because he tapped it on the nose (as the King entering the City of London touches the sword presented by the Lord Mayor), and passed on to the piano. He did not care about the keyboard, but liked the pedals, and also caught sight of a reflection of himself in the black shining front of it.

This was rather a shock, and entailed a few swift fandango-like steps with fore-paws waving wildly in the air. Horror! The silent image opposite did exactly the same thing ... it was nearly as bad as the telephone. But the piano stood at an angle to the wall, offering a suitable ambush, and he scampered behind it. And there he found the great ambush of all, for the back cloth of the piano was torn, and he could get completely inside it. Tactically, it was a perfect ambush, for it commanded the only route into the room from the door; but his delight in it was such that whenever he was ambushed there, he could not resist putting his head out and glaring, if anybody came near, thus giving the secret completely away. Or was it only indulgence towards our weak intellects, that were so incapable of imagining that there was a king inside the piano?

The exploration of the kitchen followed; the only point of interest was a fox-terrier at whom the king spat; but in the scullery there was a very extraordinary affair – namely, a brass tap, conveniently placed over a sink, half-covered with a board. On the nozzle of this tap an occasional drop of water appeared, which at intervals fell off. Cyrus could not see what happened to it, but when next the drop gathered he put his paw to it and licked it off. After doing this for nearly an hour he came to the conclusion that it was the same water as he drank after his meals. The supply seemed constant, though exiguous ... it might have to be seen to. After that he just looked in at the linen cupboard, and the door blew to while he was inside. He was not discovered till six hours later, and was inclined to be stiff about it.

Next day the royal progress continued, and Cyrus discovered the garden (forty feet by twenty, but large enough for Mr Lloyd George to have his eye on it, and demand a valuation of the mineral rights therein). But it was not large enough for Cyrus (I don't know what he expected), for after looking at it closely for a morning, he decided that he could run up the brick walls that bounded it. This was an infringement of his prerogative, for the king is bound to give notice to his ministers, when he proposes to quit the country, and Cyrus had said nothing about it. Consequently I ran out and pulled him quietly but firmly back by the tail, which was the only part of him that I could reach. He signified his disapproval in what is called "the usual manner," and tried to bite me. Upon which I revolted and drove the king indoors, and bought some rabbit wire. This I fastened down along the top of the wall, so that it projected horizontally inwards. Then I let the king out again and sat down on the steps to see what would happen.

Cyrus pretended that the walls were of no interest to him, and stalked a few dead leaves. But even a king is bounded, not only by rabbit wire, but by the limitations of cat-nature, which compelled him to attempt again what he has been thwarted over. So, after massacring a few leaves (already dead), he sprang up the wall, and naturally hit his nose against the rabbit wire, and was cast back from the frontier into his own dominions. Once again he tried and failed, appealed to an obdurate prime minister, and then sat down and devoted the whole power of his tactical mind to solving this baffling affair. And three days afterwards I saw him again run up the wall, and instead of hitting his nose against the rabbit wire, he clung to it with his claws. It bent with his weight, and he got one claw on the upper side of it, then the other, wriggled round it, and stood triumphant with switching tail on the frontier.

So in turn I had to sit and think; but, short of building up the whole garden wall to an unscalable height, or erecting a *cheval de frise* on the top of it, I had a barren brain. After all, foreign travel is an ineradicable instinct in cat-nature, and I infinitely preferred that the king should travel among small back-gardens than out of the area gate into the street. Perhaps, if he had full licence (especially since I could not prevent him) to explore the hinter-lands, he might leave the more dangerous coast alone... And then I thought of a plan, which perhaps might recall my *Reise-Kaiser*, when on his travels. This I instantly proceeded to test.

Now I had been told by my Cabinet that the one noise which would pluck the king out of his deepest slumber, and would bring him bouncing and ecstatic to the place where this sound came from, was the use of the knife-sharpener. This, it appeared, was the earliest piece of household ritual performed in the morning, when Cyrus was hungriest, and the sound of the knife-sharpener implied to him imminent food. I borrowed the knife-sharpener and ran out into the garden. Cyrus was already four garden walls away, and paid not the slightest attention to my calling him. So I vigorously began stropping the knife. The effect was instantaneous; he turned and fled along the walls that separated him from that beloved and welcome noise. He jumped down into his own dominion with erect and bushy tail ... and I gave him three little oily fragments of sardine-skin. And up till now, at any rate, that metallic chirruping of the sharpened knife has never failed. Often I have seen him a mere speck on some horizon roof, but there appears to be no incident or interest in the whole range of foreign travel that can compete with this herald of food.

On the other hand, too, if Cyrus is not quite well (this very seldom happens), though he does not care for food, he does not, either, feel up to foreign travel, and, therefore, the knife-sharpener may repose in its drawer. Indeed, there are advantages in having a greedy king that I had never suspected...

As the months went on and Cyrus grew larger and longer-haired, he gradually, as befitted a king who had come to rule over men, renounced all connexion with other animals, especially cats. He used to lie *perdu* in a large flower-pot which he had overturned (ejecting the hydrangea with scuffles of backward-kicking hind legs), and watch for the appearance of his discarded race. If so much as an ear or a tail appeared on the frontier walls, he hurled himself, his face a mask of fury, at the intruder. The same ambush, I am sorry to say, served him as a butt for the destruction of sparrows. He did not kill them, but brought them indoors to the kitchen, and presented them, as a token of his prowess as a hunter, to the cook. Dogs, similarly, were not allowed, when he sat at the area gate. Once I saw, returning home from a few doors off, a brisk Irish terrier gambol down my area steps (Cyrus's area steps, I mean), and quickened my pace, fearing for Cyrus, if he happened to be sitting there. He was sitting there, but I need not have been afraid, for before I had reached the house a prolonged and dismal yell rent the air, and an astonished Irish terrier shot up, as from a gun, through the area gate again with a wild and hunted expression. When I got there I found Cyrus seated on the top step calm and firm, delicately licking the end of his silvery paw.

Once only, as far as I remember, was Cyrus ever routed by anything with four legs, but that was not a question of lack of physical courage, but a collapse of nerves in the presence of a sort of hobgoblin, something altogether uncanny and elfin. For a visitor had brought inside her muff an atrocious little griffon, and Cyrus had leaped on to this lady's knee and rather liked the muff. Then, from inside it, within an inch or two of Cyrus's face, there looked out a half-fledged little head, of a new and nerve-shattering type. Cyrus stared for one moment at this dreadful apparition, and then bolted inside the piano-ambush. The griffon thought this was the first manœuvre in a game of play, so jumped down and sniffed round the entrance to the ambush. Panic-stricken scufflings and movements came from within... Then a diabolical thought struck me: Cyrus had never yet been in his ambush when the piano was played, and the griffon being stowed back again in the muff, for fear of accidents, I went very softly to the keys and played one loud chord. As the Irish terrier came out of the area gate, so came Cyrus out of his violated sanctuary...

Cyrus was now just a year old; his kitten-coat had been altogether discarded; he already weighed eleven pounds, and he was clad from nose to tail-tip in his complete royal robes. His head was small, and looked even smaller framed in the magnificent ruff that curled outwards from below his chin. In colour he was like a smoky shadow, with two great topaz lights gleaming in the van; the tips of his paws were silvery, as if wood-ash smouldered whitely through the smoke. That year we enjoyed a summer of extraordinary heat, and Cyrus made the unique discovery about the refrigerator, a large tin box, like a safe, that stood in the scullery. The germ of the discovery, I am afraid, was a fluke, for he had snatched a steak of salmon from the tray which the fishmonger had most imprudently left on the area steps, and, with an instinct for secrecy which this unusual treasure-trove awoke in him, he bore it to the nearest dark place, which happened to be the refrigerator. Here he ate as much as it was wise to gobble at one sitting, and then, I must suppose, instead of going to sleep, he pondered. For days he had suffered from the excessive heat; his flower-pot ambush in the garden was unendurable, so also was his retreat under my bedclothes. But here was a far more agreeable temperature... This is all the reconstruction of motive that I can give, and it is but guesswork. But day after day, while the heat lasted, Cyrus sat opposite the refrigerator and bolted into it whenever he found opportunity. The heat also increased his somnolence, and one morning, when he came up to breakfast with me, he fell asleep on the sofa before I had time to cut off the little offering of kidney which I had meant to be my homage. When I put it quite close to his nose he opened his mouth to receive it, but was again drowned in gulfs of sleep before he could masticate it. So it stuck out of the corner of his mouth like a cigarette. But eventually, I knew, he "would wake and remember and understand."

And now Cyrus is two years old, and has reigned a year and ten months. I think he has completed his own education, and certainly he has cleared his frontiers of cats, and, I am afraid, his dominion of sparrows. One misguided bird this year built in a small bush in his garden. A series of distressing unfledged objects were presented to the cook... He has appropriated the chair I was accustomed to use in my sitting-room, and he has torn open the new back-cloth that I had caused to be put on my piano. I dare say he was right about that, for there is no use in having an ambush if you cannot get into it. In other ways, too, I do not think he is strictly constitutional. But whenever I return to his kingdom after some absence, as soon as the door is open Cyrus runs down the steps to meet me (even as Puss-cat used to do) and makes a poker of his tail, and says "Ah-h-h-h." That makes up for a good deal of what appears to be tyranny. And only this morning he gave me a large spider, precious and wonderful, and still faintly stirring...

THE LION
AND THE CAT

Far away on the other side of the world there lived, long ago, a lion and his younger brother, the wild cat, who were so fond of each other that they shared the same hut. The lion was much the bigger and stronger of the two – indeed, he was much bigger and stronger than any of the beasts that dwelt in the forest; and, besides, he could jump father and run faster than all the rest. If strength and swiftness could gain him a dinner he was sure never to be without one, but when it came to cunning, both the grizzly bear and the serpent could get the better of him, and he was forced to call in the help of the wild cat.

Now the young wild cat had a lovely golden ball, so beautiful that you could hardly look at it except through a piece of smoked glass, and he kept it hidden in the thick fur muff that went round his neck. A very large old animal, since dead, had given it to him when he was hardly more than a baby, and had told him never to part with it, for as long as he kept it no harm could ever come near him.

In general the wild cat did not need to use his ball, for the lion was fond of hunting, and could kill all the food that they needed; but now and then his life would have been in danger had it not been for the golden ball.

One day the two brothers started to hunt at daybreak, but as the cat could not run nearly as fast as the lion, he had quite a long start. At least he *thought* it was a long one, but in a very few bounds and springs the lion reached his side.

"There is a bear sitting on that tree," he whispered softly. "He is only waiting for us to pass, to drop down on my back."

"Ah, you are so big that he does not see I am behind you," answered the wild cat. And, touching the ball, he just said: "Bear, die!" And the bear tumbled dead out of the tree, and rolled over just in front of them.

For some time they trotted on without any adventures, till just as they were about to cross a strip of long grass on the edge of the forest, the lion's quick ears detected a faint rustling noise.

"That is a snake," he cried, stopping short, for he was much more afraid of snakes than of bears.

"Oh, it is all right," answered the cat. "Snake, die!" And the snake died, and the two brothers skinned it. They then folded the skin up into a very small parcel, and the cat tucked it into his mane, for snakes' skins can do all sorts of wonderful things, if you are lucky enough to have one of them.

All this time they had had no dinner, for the snake's flesh was not nice, and the lion did not like eating bear – perhaps because he never felt sure that the bear was *really* dead, and would not jump up alive when his enemy went near him. Most people are afraid of *some* thing, and bears and serpents were the only creatures that caused the lion's heart to tremble. So the two brothers set off again and soon reached the side of a hill where some fine deer were grazing.

"Kill one of those deer for your own dinner," said the boy-brother, "but catch me another alive. I want him."

The lion at once sprang towards them with a loud roar,

but the deer bounded away, and they were all three soon lost to sight. The cat waited for a long while, but finding that the lion did not return, went back to the house where they lived.

It was quite dark when the lion came home, where his brother was sitting curled up in one corner.

"Did you catch the deer for me?" asked the boy-brother, springing up.

"Well, no," replied the man-brother. "The fact is, that I did not get up to them till we had run half way across the world and left the wind far behind us. Think what a trouble it would have been to drag it here! So – I just ate them both."

The cat said nothing, but he did not feel that he loved his big brother. He had thought a great deal about that deer, and had meant to get on his back to ride him as a horse, and go to see all the wonderful places the lion talked to him about when he was in a good temper. The more he thought of it the more sulky he grew, and in the morning, when the lion said that it was time for them to start to hunt, the cat told him that he might kill the bear and snake by himself, as *he* had a headache, and would rather stay at home. The little fellow knew quite well that the lion would not dare to go out without him and his ball for fear of meeting a bear or a snake.

The quarrel went on, and for many days neither of the brothers spoke to each other, and what made them still more cross was, that they could get very little to eat, and we know that people are often cross when they are hungry. At last it occurred to the lion that if he could only steal the magic ball he could kill bears and snakes for himself, and then the cat might be as sulky as he liked for anything that it would matter. But how was the stealing to be done? The cat had the ball hung round his neck day and night, and he was such a light sleeper that it was useless to think of taking it while he slept. No! The only thing was to get him to lend it of his own accord, and after some days the lion (who was not at all clever) hit upon a plan that he thought would do.

"Dear me, how dull it is here!" said the lion one afternoon, when the rain was pouring down in such torrents that, however sharp your eyes or your nose might be, you could not spy a single bird or beast among the bushes. "Dear me, how dull, how dreadfully dull I am. Couldn't we have a game of catch with that golden ball of yours?"

"I don't care about playing catch, it does not amuse me," answered the cat, who was as cross as ever; for no cat, even to this day, ever forgets an injury done to him.

"Well, then, lend me the ball for a little, and I will play by myself," replied the lion, stretching out a paw as he spoke.

"You can't play in the rain, and if you did, you would only lose it in the bushes," said the cat.

"Oh, no, I won't; I will play in here. Don't be so ill-natured." And with a very bad grace the cat untied the string and threw the golden ball into the lion's lap, and composed himself to sleep again.

For a long while the lion tossed it up and down gaily, feeling that, however sound asleep the boy-brother might *look*, he was sure to have one eye open; but gradually he began to edge closer to the opening, and at last gave such a toss that the ball went up high into the air, and he could not see what became of it.

"Oh, how stupid of me!" he cried, as the cat sprang up angrily, "let us go at once and search for it. It can't really have fallen very far." But though they searched that day and the next, and the next after that, they never found it, because it never came down.

After the loss of his ball the cat refused to live with the lion any longer, but wandered away to the north, always hoping he might meet with his ball again. But months passed, and years passed, and though he travelled over hundreds of miles, he never saw any traces of it.

At length, when he was getting quite old, he came to a place unlike any that he had ever seen before, where a big river rolled right to the foot of some high mountains. The ground all about the river bank was damp and marshy, and as no cat likes to wet its feet, this one climbed a tree that rose high above the water, and thought sadly of his lost ball, which would have helped him out of this horrible place. Suddenly he saw a beautiful ball, for all the world like his own, dangling from a branch of the tree he was on. He longed to get at it; but was the branch strong enough to bear his weight? It was no use, after all he had done, getting drowned in the water. However, it could do no harm, if he was to go a little way; he could always manage to get back somehow.

So he stretched himself at full length upon the branch, and wriggled his body cautiously along. To his delight it seemed thick and stout. Another movement, and, by stretching out his paw, he would be able to draw the string towards him, when the branch gave a loud crack, and the cat made haste to wriggle himself back the way he had come.

But when cats make up their minds to do anything they generally *do* it; and this cat began to look about to see if there was really no way of getting at his ball. Yes! there was, and it was much surer than the other, though rather more difficult. Above the bough where the ball was hung was another bough much thicker, which he knew could not break with his weight; and by holding on tight to this with all his four paws, he could just manage to touch the ball with his tail. He would thus be able to whisk the ball to and fro till, by-and-by, the string would become quite loose, and it would fall to the ground. It might take some time, but the lion's little brother was patient, like most cats.

Well, it all happened just as the cat intended it should, and when the ball dropped on the ground the cat ran down the tree like lightning, and, picking it up, tucked it away in the snake's skin round his neck. Then he began jumping along the shore of the Big Water from one place to another, trying to find a boat, or even a log of wood, that would take him across. But there was nothing; only, on the other side, he saw two girls cooking, and though he shouted to them at the top of his voice, they were too far off to hear what he said. And, what was worse, the ball suddenly fell out of its snake's skin bag right into the river.

Now, it is not at all an uncommon thing for balls to tumble into rivers, but in that case they generally either fall to the bottom and stay there, or else bob about on the top of the water close to where they first touched it. But this ball, instead of doing either of these things, went straight across to the other side, and there one of the girls saw it when she stooped to dip some water into her pail.

"Oh! what a lovely ball!" cried she, and tried to catch it in her pail; but the ball always kept bobbing just out of her reach.

"Come and help me!" she called to her sister, and after a long while they had the ball safe inside the pail. They were delighted with their new toy, and one or the other held it in her hand till bedtime came, and then it was a long time before they could make up their minds where it would be safest for the night. At last they locked it in a cupboard in one corner of their room, and as there was no hole anywhere the ball could not possibly get out. After that they went to sleep.

In the morning the first thing they both did was to run to the cupboard and unlock it, but when the door opened they started back, for, instead of the ball, there stood a handsome young man.

"Ladies," he said, "how can I thank you for what you have done for me? Long, long ago, I was enchanted by a wicked fairy, and condemned to keep the shape of a ball till I should meet with two maidens, who would take me to their own home. But where was I to meet them? For hundreds of years I have lived in the depths of the forest, where nothing but wild beasts ever came, and it was only when the lion threw me into the sky that I was able to fall to earth near this river. Where there is a river, sooner or later people will come; so, hanging myself on a tree, I watched and waited. For a moment I lost heart when I fell once more into the hands of my old master the wild cat, but my hopes rose again as I saw he was making for the river bank opposite where you were standing. That was my chance, and I took it. And now, ladies, I have only to say that, if ever I can do anything to help you, go to the top of that high mountain and knock three times at the iron door at the north side, and I will come to you."

So, with a low bow, he vanished from before them, leaving the maidens weeping at having lost in one moment both the ball and the prince.

HOW THE LEOPARD
GOT HIS SPOTS

RUDYARD KIPLING

In the days when everybody started fair, Best Beloved, the
Leopard lived in a place called the High Veldt. 'Member it
wasn't the Low Veldt, or the Bush Veldt, or the Sour Veldt,
but the 'sclusively bare, hot, shiny High Veldt, where there
was sand and sandy-coloured rock and 'sclusively tufts of
sandy-yellowish grass. The Giraffe and the Zebra and the
Eland and the Koodoo and the Hartebeest lived there; and
they were 'sclusively sandy-yellow-brownish all over; but the
Leopard, he was the 'sclusivest sandiest-yellowest-brownest
of them all – a greyish-yellowish catty-shaped kind of beast,
and he matched the 'sclusively yellowish-greyish-brownish
colour of the High Veldt to one hair. This was very bad for
the Giraffe and the Zebra and the rest of them; for he would
lie down by a 'sclusively yellowish-greyish-brownish stone or
clump of grass, and when the Giraffe or the Zebra or the
Eland or the Koodoo or the Bush-Buck or the Bonte-Buck
came by he would surprise them out of their jumpsome lives.
He would indeed! And, also, there was an Ethiopian with
bows and arrows (a 'sclusively greyish-brownish-yellowish
man he was then), who lived on the High Veldt with the

Leopard; and the two used to hunt together – the Ethiopian with his bows and arrows, and the Leopard 'sclusively with his teeth and claws – till the Giraffe and the Eland and the Koodoo and the Quagga and all the rest of them didn't know which way to jump, Best Beloved. They didn't indeed!

After a long time – things lived for ever so long in those days – they learned to avoid anything that looked like a Leopard or an Ethiopian; and bit by bit – the Giraffe began it, because his legs were the longest – they went away from the High Veldt. They scuttled for days and days and days till they came to a great forest, 'sclusively full of trees and bushes and stripy, speckly, patchy-blatchy shadows, and there they hid: and after another long time, what with standing half in the shade and half out of it, and what with the slippery-slidy shadows of the trees falling on them, the Giraffe grew blotchy, and the Zebra grew stripy, and the Eland the the Koodoo grew darker, with little wavy grey lines on their backs like bark on a tree trunk; and so, though you could hear them and smell them, you could very seldom see them, and then only when you knew precisely where to look. They had a beautiful time in the 'sclusively speckly-spickly shadows of the forest, while the Leopard and the Ethiopian ran about over the 'sclusively greyish-yellowish-reddish High Veldt outside, wondering where all their breakfasts and their dinners and their teas had gone. At last they were so hungry that they ate rats and beetles and rock-rabbits, the Leopard and the Ethiopian, and then they had the Big Tummy-ache, both together; and then they met Baviaan – the dog-headed, barking Baboon, who is Quite the Wisest Animal in All South Africa.

This is Wise Baviaan, the dog-headed Baboon, who is Quite the Wisest Animal in All South Africa. I have drawn him from a statue that I made up out of my own head, and I have written his name on his belt and on his shoulder and on the thing he is sitting on. I have written it in what is not called Coptic and Hieroglyphic and Cuneiformic and Bengalic and Burmic and Hebric, all because he is so wise. He is not beautiful, but he is very wise; and I should like to paint him with paint-box colours, but I am not allowed. The umbrella-ish thing about his head is his Conventional Mane.

Said Leopard to Baviaan (and it was a very hot day), 'Where has all the game gone?'

And Baviaan winked. *He* knew.

Said the Ethiopian to Baviaan, 'Can you tell me the present habitat of the aboriginal Fauna?' (That meant just the same thing, but the Ethiopian always used long words. He was a grown-up.)

And Baviaan winked. *He* knew.

Then said Baviaan, 'The game has gone into other spots; and my advice to you, Leopard, is to go into other spots as soon as you can.'

And the Ethiopian said, 'That's is all very fine, but I wish to know whither the aboriginal Fauna has migrated.'

Then said Baviaan, 'The aboriginal Fauna has joined the aboriginal Flora because it was high time for a change; and my advice to you, Ethiopian, is to change as soon as you can.'

That puzzled the Leopard and the Ethiopian, but they set off to look for the aboriginal Flora, and presently, after ever so many days, they saw a great, high, tall forest full of tree trunks all 'sclusively speckled and sprottled and spotted, dotted and splashed and slashed and hatched and cross-hatched with shadows. (Say that quickly aloud, and you will see how *very* shadowy the forest must have been.)

'What is this,' said the Leopard, 'that is so 'sclusively dark, and yet so full of little pieces of light?'

'I don't know,' said the Ethiopian, 'but it ought to be the aboriginal Flora. I can smell Giraffe, and I can hear Giraffe, but I can't see Giraffe.'

'That's curious,' said the Leopard. 'I suppose it is because we have just come out of the sunshine. I can smell Zebra, and I can hear Zebra, but I can't see Zebra.'

'Wait a bit,' said the Ethiopian. 'It's a long time since we've hunted 'em. Perhaps we've forgotten what they were like.'

'Fiddle!' said the Leopard. 'I remember them perfectly on the High Veldt, especially their marrow-bones. Giraffe is about seventeen feet high, of a 'sclusively fulvous golden-yellow from head to heel; and Zebra is about four and a half feet high, of a 'sclusively grey-fawn colour from head to heel.'

'Umm,' said the Ethiopian, looking into the speckly-spickly shadows of the aboriginal Flora-forest. 'Then they ought to show up in this dark place like ripe bananas in a smoke-house.'

But they didn't. The Leopard and the Ethiopian hunted all day; and though they could smell them and hear them, they never saw one of them.

'For goodness' sake,' said the Leopard at tea-time, 'let us wait till it gets dark. This daylight hunting is a perfect scandal.'

So they waited till dark, and then the Leopard heard

something breathing sniffily in the starlight that fell all stripy through the branches, and he jumped at the noise, and it smelt like Zebra, and it felt like Zebra, and when he knocked it down it kicked like Zebra, but he couldn't see it. So he said, 'Be quiet, O you person without any form. I am going to sit on your head till morning, because there is something about you that I don't understand.'

Presently he heard a grunt and a crash and a scramble, and the Ethiopian called out, 'I've caught a thing that I can't see. It smells like Giraffe, and it kicks like Giraffe, but it hasn't any form.'

'Don't you trust it,' said the Leopard. 'Sit on its head till the morning – same as me. They haven't any form – any of 'em.'

So they sat down on them hard till bright morning-time, and then Leopard said, 'What have you at your end of the table, Brother?'

The Ethiopian scratched his head and said, 'It ought to be 'sclusively a rich fulvous orange-tawny from head to heel, and it ought to be Giraffe; but it is covered all over with chestnut blotches. What have you at *your* end of the table, Brother?'

And the Leopard scratched his head and said, 'It ought to be 'sclusively a delicate greyish-fawn, and it ought to be Zebra; but it is covered all over with black and purple stripes. What in the world have you been doing to yourself, Zebra? Don't you know that if you were on the High Veldt I could see you ten miles off? You haven't any form.'

'Yes,' said the Zebra, 'but this isn't the High Veldt. Can't you see?'

'I can now,' said the Leopard. 'But I couldn't all yesterday. How is it done?'

'Let us up,' said the Zebra, 'and we will show you.'

They let the Zebra and the Giraffe get up; and Zebra moved away to some little thorn-bushes where the sunlight fell all stripy, and Giraffe moved off to some tallish trees where the shadows fell all blotchy.

'Now watch,' said the Zebra and the Giraffe. 'This is the way it's done. One – two – three! And where's your breakfast?'

Leopard stared, and Ethiopian stared, but all they could see were stripy shadows and blotched shadows in the forest, but never a sign of Zebra and Giraffe. They had just walked off and hidden themselves in the shadowy forest.

'Hi! Hi!' said the Ethiopian. 'That's a trick worth learning. Take a lesson by it, Leopard. You show up in this dark place like a bar of soap in a coal-scuttle.'

'Ho! Ho!' said the Leopard. 'Would it surprise you very much to know that you show up in this dark place like a mustard-plaster on a sack of coals?'

'Well, calling names won't catch dinner,' said the Ethiopian. 'The long and the little of it is that we don't match our backgrounds. I'm going to take Baviaan's advice. He told me I ought to change; and as I've nothing to change except my skin I'm going to change that.'

'What to?' said the Leopard, tremendously excited.

'To a nice working blackish-brownish colour, with a little purple in it, and touches of slaty-blue. It will be the very thing for hiding in hollows and behind trees.'

So he changed his skin then and there, and the Leopard was more excited than ever; he had never seen a man change his skin before.

'But what about me?' he said, when the Ethiopian had worked his last little finger into his fine new black skin.

'You take Baviaan's advice too. He told you to go into spots.'

'So I did,' said the Leopard. 'I went into other spots as fast as I could. I went into this spot with you, and a lot of good it has done me.'

'Oh,' said the Ethiopian, 'Baviaan didn't mean spots in South Africa. He meant spots on your skin.'

'What's the use of that?' said the Leopard.

'Think of Giraffe,' said the Ethiopian. 'Or if you prefer stripes, think of Zebra. They find their spots and stripes give them per-fect satisfaction.'

'Umm,' said the Leopard. 'I wouldn't look like Zebra – not for ever so.'

'Well, make up your mind,' said the Ethiopian, 'because I'd hate to go hunting without you, but I must if you insist on looking like a sun-flower against a tarred fence.'

'I'll take spots, then,' said the Leopard; 'but don't make 'em too vulgar-big. I wouldn't look like Giraffe – not for ever so.'

'I'll make 'em with the tips of my fingers,' said the Ethiopian. 'There's plenty of black left on my skin still. Stand over!'

Then the Ethiopian put his five fingers close together (there was plenty of black left on his new skin still) and pressed them all over the Leopard, and wherever the five fingers touched they left five little black marks, all close together. You can see them on any Leopard's skin you like, Best Beloved. Sometimes the fingers slipped and the marks got a little blurred; but if you look closely at any Leopard now you will see that there are always five spots – off five fat black finger-tips.

'Now you *are* a beauty!' said the Ethiopian. 'You can lie out on the bare ground and look like a heap of pebbles. You can lie out on the naked rocks and look like a piece of pudding-stone. You can lie out on a leafy branch and look like sunshine sifting through the leaves; and you can lie right across the centre of a path and look like nothing in particular. Think of that and purr!'

'But if I'm all this,' said the Leopard, 'why didn't you go spotty too?'

'Oh, plain black's best for me,' said the Ethiopian. 'Now come along and we'll see if we can't get even with Mr One-Two-Three-Where's-your-Breakfast!'

So they went away and lived happily ever afterward, Best Beloved. That is all.

Oh, now and then you will hear grown-ups say, 'Can the Ethiopian change his skin or the Leopard his spots?' I don't think even grown-ups would keep on saying such a silly thing if the Leopard and the Ethiopian hadn't done it once – do you? But they will never do it again, Best Beloved. They are quite contented as they are.

> I am the Most Wise Baviaan, saying in most wise
> > tones,
> 'Let us melt into the landscape – just us two by
> > our lones.'
> People have come – in a carriage – calling. But
> > Mummy is there . . .
> Yes, I can go if you take me – Nurse says *she*
> > don't care.
> Let's go up to the pig-sties and sit on the
> > farmyard rails!
> Let's say things to the bunnies, and watch 'em
> > skitter their tails!
> Let's – oh, *anything*, daddy, so long as it's you
> > and me,
> And going truly exploring, and not being in till
> > tea!
> Here's your boots (I've brought 'em), and here's
> > your cap and stick,
> And here's your pipe and tobacco. Oh, come
> > along out of it – quick!

This is the picture of the Leopard and Ethiopian after they had taken Wise Baviaan's advice and the Leopard had gone into other spots and the Ethiopian had changed his skin. They are out hunting in the spickly-speckly forest, and they are looking for Mr One-Two-Three-Where's-your-Breakfast. If you look a little you will see Mr One-Two-Three not far away. The Ethiopian has hidden behind a splotchy-blotchy tree because it matches his skin, and the Leopard is lying beside a spickly-speckly bank of stones because it matches his spots. Mr One-Two-Three-Where's-your-Breakfast is standing up eating leaves from a tall tree. This is really a puzzle-picture like 'Find-the-Cat.'

THE CATS OF ULTHAR

H. P. LOVECRAFT

It is said that in Ulthar, which lies beyond the river Skai, no man may kill a cat; and this I can verily believe as I gaze upon him who sitteth purring before the fire. For the cat is cryptic, and close to strange things which men cannot see. He is the soul of antique Ægyptus, and bearer of tales from forgotten cities in Meroe and Ophir. He is the kin of the jungle's lords and heir to the secrets of hoary and sinister Africa. The Sphinx is his cousin, and he speaks her language; but he is more ancient than the Sphinx, and remembers that which she hath forgotten.

In Ulthar, before ever the burgesses forbade the killing of cats, there dwelt an old cotter and his wife who delighted to trap and slay the cats of their neighbours. Why they did this I know not; save that many hate the voice of the cat in the night, and take it ill that cats should run stealthily about yards and gardens at twilight. But whatever the reason, this old man and woman took pleasure in trapping and slaying every cat which came near to their hovel; and from some of the sounds heard after dark, many villagers fancied that the manner of slaying was exceedingly peculiar.

But the villagers did not discuss such things with the old man and his wife; because of the habitual expression on the withered faces of the two, and because their cottage was so small and so darkly hidden under spreading oaks at the back of a neglected yard. In truth, much as the owners of cats hated these odd folk, they feared them more; and instead of berating them as brutal assassins, merely took care that no cherished pet or mouser should stray towards the remote hovel under the dark trees. When through some unavoidable oversight a cat was missed, and sounds heard after dark, the loser would lament impotently; or console himself by thanking Fate that it was not one of his children who had thus vanished. For the people of Ulthar were simple, and knew not whence it is that all cats first came.

One day a caravan of strange wanderers from the South entered the narrow cobbled streets of Ulthar. Dark wanderers they were, and unlike the other roving folk who passed through the village twice every year. In the market-place they told fortunes for silver, and bought gay beads from the merchants. What was the land of these wanderers none could tell; but it was seen that they were given to strange prayers and that they had painted on the sides of their wagons strange figures with human bodies and the heads of cats, hawks, rams and lions. And the leader of the caravan wore a headdress with two horns and a curious disc between the horns.

There was in this singular caravan a little boy with no father or mother, but only a tiny black kitten to cherish. The plague had not been kind to him, yet had left him this small furry thing to mitigate his sorrow; and when one is very young, one can find great relief in the lively antics of a black kitten. So the boy whom the dark people called Menes smiled more often than he wept as he sat playing with his graceful kitten on the steps of an oddly painted wagon.

On the third morning of the wanderers' stay in Ulthar,

Menes could not find his kitten; and as he sobbed aloud in the market place certain villagers told him of the old man and his wife, and of sounds heard in the night. And when he heard these things his sobbing gave place to meditation, and finally to prayer. He stretched out his arms towards the sun and prayed in a tongue no villager could understand; though indeed the villagers did not try very hard to understand, since their attention was mostly taken up by the sky and the odd shapes the clouds were assuming. It was very peculiar, but as the little boy uttered his petition there seemed to form overhead the shadowy, nebulous figures of exotic things; of hybrid creatures crowned with horn-flanked discs. Nature is full of such illusions to impress the imaginative.

That night the wanderers left Ulthar, and were never seen again. And the householders were troubled when they noticed that in all the village there was not a cat to be found. From each hearth the familiar cat had vanished; cats large and small, black, grey, striped, yellow and white. Old Kranon, the burgomaster, swore that the dark folk had taken the cats away in revenge for the killing of Menes' kitten; and cursed the caravan and the little boy. But Nith, the lean notary, declared that the old cotter and his wife were more likely persons to suspect; for their hatred of cats was notorious and increasingly bold.

Still, no one durst complain to the sinister couple; even when little Atal, the innkeeper's son, vowed that he had at twilight seen all the cats of Ulthar in that accursed yard under the trees, pacing very slowly and solemnly in a circle around the cottage, two abreast, as if in performance of some unheard-of rite of beasts. The villagers did not know how much to believe from so small a boy; and though they feared that the evil pair had charmed the cats to their death, they preferred not to chide the old cotter till they met him outside his dark and repellent yard.

So Ulthar went to sleep in vain anger; and when the people awakened at dawn – behold! every cat was back at his accustomed hearth! Large and small, black, grey, striped, yellow and white, none was missing. Very sleek and fat did the cats appear, and sonorous with purring content. The citizens talked with one another of the affair, and marvelled not a little. Old Kranon again insisted that it was the dark folk who had taken them, since cats did not return alive from the cottage of the ancient man and his wife. But all agreed on one thing; that the refusal of all the cats to eat their portions of meat or drink their saucers of milk was exceedingly curious. And for two whole days the sleek, lazy cats of Ulthar would touch no food, but only doze by the fire or in the sun.

It was fully a week before the villagers noticed that no lights were appearing at dusk in the windows of the cottage under the trees. Then the lean Nith remarked that no one had seen the old man or his wife since the night the cats were away. In another week the burgomaster decided to overcome his fears and call at the strangely silent dwelling as a matter of duty, though in doing so he was careful to take with him Shang the blacksmith and Thul the cutter of stone as witnesses. And when they had broken down the frail door they found only this: two cleanly picked human skeletons on the earthen floor, and a number of singular beetles crawling in the shadowy corners.

There was subsequently much talk among the burgesses of Ulthar. Zath, the coroner, disputed at length with Nith, the lean notary; and Kranon and Shang and Thul were overwhelmed with questions. Even little Atal, the innkeeper's son, was closely questioned and given a sweetmeat as reward. They talked of the old cotter and his wife, of the caravan of dark wanderers, of small Menes and his black kitten, of the prayer of Menes and of the sky during that prayer, of the doings of the cats on the night the caravan left, and of what was later found in the cottage under the dark trees in the repellent yard.

And in the end the burgesses passed that remarkable law which is told of by traders in Hatheg and discussed by travellers in Nir; namely, that in Ulthar no man may kill a cat.

KISA THE CAT

Once upon a time there lived a queen who had a beautiful cat, the colour of smoke, with china-blue eyes, which she was very fond of. The cat was constantly with her, and ran after her wherever she went, and even sat up proudly by her side when she drove out in her fine glass coach.

"Oh, pussy," said the queen one day, "you are happier than I am! For you have a dear little kitten just like yourself, and I have nobody to play with but you."

"Don't cry," answered the cat, laying her paw on her mistress's arm. "Crying never does any good. I will see what can be done."

The cat was as good as her word. As soon as she returned from her drive she trotted off to the forest to consult a fairy who dwelt there, and very soon after the queen had a little girl, who seemed made out of snow and sunbeams. The queen was delighted, and soon the baby began to take notice of the kitten as she jumped about the room, and would not go to sleep at all unless the kitten lay curled up beside her.

Two or three months went by, and though the baby was still a baby, the kitten was fast becoming a cat, and one evening when, as usual, the nurse came to look for her, to put her in the baby's cot, she was nowhere to be found. What a hunt there was for that kitten, to be sure! The servants, each anxious to find her, as the queen was certain to reward the lucky man, searched in the most impossible places. Boxes were opened that would hardly have held the kitten's paw; books were taken from bookshelves, lest the kitten should have got behind them, drawers were pulled out, for perhaps the kitten might have got shut in. But it was all no use. The kitten had plainly run away, and nobody could tell if it would ever choose to come back.

Years passed away, and one day, when the princess was playing ball in the garden, she happened to throw her ball farther than usual, and it fell into a clump of rose-bushes. The princess of course ran after it at once, and she was stooping down to feel if it was hidden in the long grass, when she heard a voice calling her: "Ingibjörg! Ingibjörg!" it said, "have you forgotten me? I am Kisa, your sister!"

"But I never *had* a sister," answered Ingibjörg, very much puzzled; for she knew nothing of what had taken place so long ago.

"Don't you remember how I always slept in your cot beside you, and how you cried till I came? But girls have no memories at all! Why, I could find my way straight up to that cot this moment, if I was once inside the palace."

"Why did you go away then?" asked the princess. But before Kisa could answer, Ingibjörg's attendants arrived breathless on the scene, and were so horrified at the sight of a strange cat, that Kisa plunged into the bushes and went back to the forest.

The princess was very much vexed with her ladies-in-waiting for frightening away her old playfellow, and told the queen who came to her room every evening to bid her good-night.

"Yes, it is quite true what Kisa said," answered the queen;

"I should have liked to see her again. Perhaps, some day, she will return, and then you must bring her to me."

Next morning it was very hot, and the princess declared that she must go and play in the forest, where it was always cool, under the big shady trees. As usual, her attendants let her do anything she pleased, and, sitting down on a mossy bank where a little stream tinkled by, soon fell sound asleep. The princess saw with delight that they would pay no heed to her, and wandered on and on, expecting every moment to see some fairies dancing round a ring, or some little brown elves peeping at her from behind a tree. But, alas! she met none of these; instead, a horrible giant came out of his cave and ordered her to follow him. The princess felt much afraid, as he was so big and ugly, and began to be sorry that she had not stayed within reach of help; but as there was no use in disobeying the giant, she walked meekly behind.

They went a long way, and Ingibjörg grew very tired, and at length began to cry.

"I don't like girls who make horrid noises," said the giant, turning round. "But if you *want* to cry, I will give you something to cry for." And drawing an axe from his belt, he cut off both her feet, which he picked up and put in his pocket. Then he went away.

Poor Ingibjörg lay on the grass in terrible pain, and wondering if she should stay there till she died, as no one would know where to look for her. How long it was since she had set out in the morning she could not tell – it seemed years to her, of course; but the sun was still high in the heavens when she heard the sound of wheels, and then, with a great effort, for her throat was parched with fright and pain, she gave a shout.

"I am coming!" was the answer; and in another moment a cart made its way through the trees, driven by Kisa, who used her tail as a whip to urge the horse to go faster. Directly Kisa saw Ingibjörg lying there, she jumped quickly down, and lifting the girl carefully in her two front paws, laid her upon some soft hay, and drove back to her own little hut.

In the corner of the room was a pile of cushions, and these Kisa arranged as a bed. Ingibjörg, who by this time was nearly fainting from all she had gone through, drank greedily some milk, and then sank back on the cushions while Kisa fetched some dried herbs from a cupboard, soaked them in warm water and tied them on the bleeding legs. The pain vanished at once, and Ingibjörg looked up and smiled at Kisa.

"You will go to sleep now," said the cat, "and you will not mind if I leave you for a little while. I will lock the door, and no one can hurt you." But before she had finished the princess was asleep. Then Kisa got into the cart, which was standing at the door, and catching up the reins, drove straight to the giant's cave.

Leaving her cart behind some trees, Kisa crept gently up to the open door, and, crouching down, listened to what the giant was telling his wife, who was at supper with him.

"The first day that I can spare I shall just go back and kill her," he said; "it would never do for people in the forest to know that a mere girl can defy me!" And he and his wife were so busy calling Ingibjörg all sorts of names for her bad behaviour, that they never noticed Kisa stealing into a dark corner, and upsetting a whole bag of salt into the great pot before the fire.

"Dear me, how thirsty I am!" cried the giant by-and-by.

"So am I," answered his wife. "I do wish I had not taken that last spoonful of broth; I am sure something was wrong with it."

"If I don't get some water I shall die," went on the giant. And rushing out of the cave, followed by his wife, he ran down the path which led to the river.

Then Kisa entered the hut, and lost no time in searching every hole till she came upon some grass, under which

Ingibjörg's feet were hidden, and putting them in her cart, drove back again to her own hut.

Ingibjörg was thankful to see her, for she had lain, too frightened to sleep, trembling at every noise.

"Oh, is it you?" she cried joyfully, as Kisa turned the key. And the cat came in, holding up the two neat little feet in their silver slippers.

"In two minutes they shall be as tight as ever they were!" said Kisa. And taking some strings of the magic grass which the giant had carelessly heaped on them, she bound the feet on to the legs above.

"Of course you won't be able to walk for some time; you must not expect *that*," she continued. "But if you are very good, perhaps, in about a week, I may carry you home again."

And so she did; and when the cat drove the cart up to the palace gate, lashing the horse furiously with her tail, and the king and queen saw their lost daughter sitting beside her, they declared that no reward could be too great for the person who had brought her out of the giant's hands.

"We will talk about that by-and-by," said the cat, as she made her best bow, and turned her horse's head.

The princess was very unhappy when Kisa left her without even bidding her farewell. She would neither eat nor drink, nor take any notice of all the beautiful dresses her parents bought for her.

"She will die, unless we can make her laugh," one whispered to the other. "Is there anything in the world that we have left untried?"

"Nothing, except marriage," answered the king. And he invited all the handsomest young men he could think of to the palace, and bade the princess choose a husband from among them.

It took her some time to decide which she admired the most, but at last she fixed upon a young prince, whose eyes were like the pools in the forest, and his hair of bright gold.

The king and the queen were greatly pleased, as the young man was the son of a neighbouring king, and they gave orders that a splendid feast should be got ready.

When the marriage was over, Kisa suddenly stood before them, and Ingibjörg rushed forward and clasped her in her arms.

"I have come to claim my reward," said the cat. "Let me sleep for this night at the foot of your bed."

"Is that *all?*" asked Ingibjörg, much disappointed.

"It is enough," answered the cat. And when the morning dawned, it was no cat that lay upon the bed, but a beautiful princess.

"My mother and I were both enchanted by a spiteful fairy," said she, "and we could not free ourselves till we had done some kindly deed that had never been wrought before. My mother died without ever finding a chance of doing anything new, but I took advantage of the evil act of the giant to make you as whole as ever."

Then they were all more delighted than before, and the princess lived in the court until she, too, married, and went away to govern one of her own.

MADAME JOLICŒUR'S CAT

THOMAS A. JANVIER

Being somewhat of an age, and a widow of dignity – the late
Monsieur Jolicœur has held the responsible position under
Government of Ingénieur des Ponts et Chaussées – yet being
also of a provocatively fresh plumpness, and a Marseillaise, it
was of necessity that Madame Veuve Jolicœur, on being left
lonely in the world save for the companionship of her adored
Shah de Perse, should entertain expectations of the future
that were antipodal and antagonistic: on the one hand, of an
austere life suitable to a widow of a reasonable maturity and
of an assured position; on the other hand, of a life, not austere,
suitable to a widow still of a provocatively fresh plumpness
and by birth a Marseillaise.

Had Madame Jolicœur possessed a severe temperament
and a resolute mind – possessions inherently improbable, in
view of her birthplace – she would have made her choice
between these equally possible futures with a promptness and
with a finality that would have left nothing at loose ends. So
endowed, she would have emphasised her not excessive age
by a slightly excessive gravity of dress and of deportment; and
would have adorned it, and her dignified widowhood, by

becoming dévote: and thereafter, clinging with a modest ostentation only to her piety, would have radiated, as time made its marches, an always increasingly exemplary grace. But as Madame Jolicœur did not possess a temperament that even bordered on severity, and as her mind was a sort that made itself up in at least twenty different directions in a single moment – as she was, in short, an entirely typical and therefore an entirely delightful Provençale – the situation was so much too much for her that, by the process of formulating a great variety of irreconcilable conclusions, she left everything at loose ends by not making any choice at all.

In effect, she simply stood attendant upon what the future had in store for her: and meanwhile avowedly clung only, in default of piety, to her adored Shah de Perse – to whom was given, as she declared in disconsolate negligence of her still provocatively fresh plumpness, all of the bestowable affection that remained in the devastated recesses of her withered heart.

To preclude any possibility of compromising misunderstanding, it is but just to Madame Jolicœur to explain at once that the personage thus in receipt of the contingent remainder of her blighted affections – far from being, as his name would suggest, an Oriental potentate temporarily domiciled in Marseille to whom she had taken something more than a passing fancy – was a Persian superb black cat; and a cat of such rare excellencies of character and of acquirements as fully to deserve all of the affection that any heart of the right sort – withered, or otherwise – was disposed to bestow upon him.

Cats of his perfect beauty, of his perfect grace, possibly might be found, Madame Jolicœur grudgingly admitted, in the Persian royal catteries; but nowhere else in the Orient, and nowhere at all in the Occident, she declared with an energetic conviction, possibly could there be found a cat who even approached him in intellectual development, in wealth of interesting accomplishments, and, above all, in natural sweetness of disposition – a sweetness so marked that even under extreme provocation he never had been known to thrust out an angry paw. This is not to say that the Shah de Perse was a characterless cat, a lymphatic nonentity. On occasion – usually in connection with food that was distasteful to him – he could have his resentments; but they were manifested always with a dignified restraint. His nearest approach to ill-mannered abruptness was to bat with a contemptuous paw the offending morsel from his plate; which brusque act he followed by fixing upon the bestower of unworthy food a coldly, but always politely, contemptuous stare. Ordinarily, however, his displeasure – in the matter of unsuitable food, or in other matters – was exhibited by no more overt action than his retirement to a corner – he had his choices in corners, governed by the intensity of his feelings – and there seating himself with his back turned scornfully to an offending world. Even in his kindliest corner, on such occasions, the expression of his scornful back was as a whole volume of wingéd words!

But the rare little cat tantrums of the Shah de Perse – if to his so gentle excesses may be applied so strong a term – were but as sun-spots on the effulgence of his otherwise constant amiability. His regnant desires, by which his worthy little life was governed, were to love and to please. He was the most cuddlesome cat, Madame Jolicœur unhesitatingly asserted, that ever had lived; and he had a purr – softly thunderous and winningly affectionate – that was in keeping with his cuddlesome ways. When, of his own volition, he would jump into her abundant lap and go to burrowing with his little soft round head beneath her soft round elbows, the while gurglingly purring forth his love for her, Madame Jolicœur, quite justifiably, at times was moved to tears. Equally was his sweet nature exhibited in his always eager willingness to show off his little train of

cat accomplishments. He would give his paw with a courteous grace to any lady or gentleman – he drew the caste
line rigidly – who asked for it. For his mistress, he would
spring to a considerable height and clutch with his two soft
paws – never by any mistake scratching – her outstretched
wrist, and so would remain suspended while he delicately
nibbled from between his fingers her edible offering. For
her, he would make an almost painfully real pretence of
being a dead cat: extending himself upon the rug with an
exaggeratedly death-like rigidity – and so remaining until
her command to be alive again brought him briskly to rub
himself, rising on his hind legs and purring mellowly, against
her comfortable knees.

All of these interesting tricks, with various others that
may be passed over, he would perform with a lively zest
whenever set at them by a mere word of prompting; but his
most notable trick was a game in which he engaged with his
mistress not at word of command, but – such was his intelligence – simply upon her setting the signal for it. The signal
was a close-fitting white cap – to be quite frank, a night-cap
– that she tied upon her head when it was desired that the
game should be played.

It was of the game that Madame Jolicœur should assume
her cap with an air of detachment and aloofness: as though
no such entity as the Shah de Perse existed, and with an
insisted-upon disregard of the fact that he was watching her
alertly with his great golden eyes. Equally was it of the game
that the Shah de Perse should affect – save for his alert
watching – a like disregard of the doings of Madame Jolicœur:
usually by an ostentatious pretence of washing his upraised
hind leg, or by a like pretence of scrubbing his ears. These
conventions duly having been observed, Madame Jolicœur
would seat herself in her especial easy-chair, above the rela-
tively high back of which her night-capped head a little rose.
Being so seated, always with the air of aloofness and

detachment, she would take a book from the table and make a show of becoming absorbed in its contents. Matters being thus advanced, the Shah de Perse would make a show of becoming absorbed in searchings for an imaginary mouse – but so would conduct his fictitious quest for that supposititious animal as eventually to achieve for himself a strategic position close behind Madame Jolicœur's chair. Then, dramatically, the pleasing end of the game would come: as the Shah de Perse – leaping with the distinguishing grace and lightness of his Persian race – would flash upward and "surprise" Madame Jolicœur by crowning her white-capped head with his small black person, all a-shake with triumphant purrs! It was a charming little comedy – and so well understood by the Shah de Perse that he never ventured to essay it under other, and more intimate, conditions of night-cap use; even as he never failed to engage in it with spirit when his white lure properly was set for him above the back of Madame Jolicœur's chair. It was as though to the Shah de Perse the white night-cap of Madame Jolicœur, displayed in accordance with the rules of the game, were an oriflamme: akin to, but in minor points differing from, the helmet of Navarre.

Being such a cat, it will be perceived that Madame Jolicœur had reason in her avowed intention to bestow upon him all of the bestowable affection remnant in her withered heart's devastated recesses; and, equally, that she would not be wholly desolate, having such a cat to comfort her, while standing impartially attendant upon the decrees of fate.

To assert that any woman not conspicuously old and quite conspicuously of a fresh plumpness could be left in any city isolate, save for a cat's company, while the fates were spinning new threads for her, would be to put a severe strain upon credulity. To make that assertion specifically of Madame Jolicœur, and specifically – of all cities in the world! – of

Marseille, would be to strain credulity fairly to the breaking point. On the other hand, to assert that Madame Jolicœur, in defence of her isolation, was disposed to plant machine-guns in the doorway of her dwelling – a house of modest elegance on the Pavé d'Amour, at the crossing of the Rue Bausset – would be to go too far. Nor indeed – aside from the fact that the presence of such engines of destruction would not have been tolerated by the other residents of the quietly respectable Pavé d'Amour – was Madame Jolicœur herself, as has been intimated, temperamentally inclined to go to such lengths as machine-guns in maintenance of her somewhat waveringly desired privacy in a merely cat-enlivened solitude.

Between these widely separated extremes of conjectural possibility lay the mediate truth of the matter: which truth – thus resembling precious gold in its valueless rock matrix – lay embedded in, and was to be extracted from, the irresponsible utterances of the double row of loosely hung tongues, always at hot wagging, ranged along the two sides of the Rue Bausset.

Madame Jouval, a milliner of repute – delivering herself with the generosity due to a good customer from whom an order for a trousseau was a not unremote possibility, yet with the acumen perfected by her professional experiences – summed her views of the situation, in talk with Madame Vic, proprietor of the Vic bakery, in these words: "It is of the convenances, and equally is it of her own melancholy necessities, that this poor Madame retires for a season to sorrow in a suitable seclusion in the company of her sympathetic cat. Only in such retreat can she give vent fitly to her desolating grief. But after storm comes sunshine: and I am happily assured by her less despairing appearance, and by the new mourning that I have been making for her, that even now, from the bottomless depth of her affliction, she looks beyond the storm."

"I well believe it!" snapped Madame Vic. "That the appearance of Madame Jolicœur at any time has been despairing is a matter that has escaped my notice. As to the mourning that she now wears, it is a defiance of all propriety. Why, with no more than that of colour in her frock" – Madame Vic upheld her thumb and finger infinitesimally separated – "and with a mere pin-point of a flower in her bonnet, she would be fit for the opera!"

Madame Vic spoke with a caustic bitterness that had its roots. Her own venture in second marriage had been catastrophic – so catastrophic that her neglected bakery had gone very much to the bad. Still more closely to the point, Madame Jolicœur – incident to finding entomologic specimens misplaced in her breakfast-rolls – had taken the leading part in an interchange of incivilities with the bakery's proprietor, and had withdrawn from it her custom.

"And even were her mournings not a flouting of her short year of widowhood," continued Madame Vic, with an acrimony that abbreviated the term of widowhood most unfairly – "the scores of eligible suitors who openly come streaming to her door, and are welcomed there, are as trumpets proclaiming her audacious intentions and her indecorous desires. Even Monsieur Brisson is in that outrageous procession! Is it not enough that she should entice a repulsively bald-headed notary and an old rake of a major to make their brazen advances, without suffering this anatomy of a pharmacien to come treading on their heels? – he with his hands imbrued in the life-blood of the unhappy old woman whom his mismade prescription sent in agony to the tomb! Pah! I have no patience with her! She and her grief and her seclusion and her sympathetic cat, indeed! It all is a tragedy of indiscretion – that shapes itself as a revolting farce!"

It will be observed that Madame Vic, in framing her bill of particulars, practically reduced her alleged scores of

Madame Jolicœur's suitors to precisely two – since the bad third was handicapped so heavily by that notorious matter of the mismade prescription as to be a negligible quantity, quite out of the race. Indeed, it was only the preposterous temerity of Monsieur Brisson – despairingly clutching at any chance to retrieve his broken fortunes – that put him in the running at all. With the others, in such slighting terms referred to by Madame Vic – Monsieur Peloux, a notary of standing, and the Major Gontard, of the Twenty-ninth of the Line – the case was different. It had its sides.

"That this worthy lady reasonably may desire again to wed," declared Monsieur Fromagin, actual proprietor of the Épicerie Russe – an establishment liberally patronised by Madame Jolicœur – "is as true as that when she goes to make her choosings between these estimable gentlemen she cannot make a choice that is wrong."

Madame Gauthier, a clear-starcher of position, to whom Monsieur Fromagin thus addressed himself, was less broadly positive. "That is a matter of opinion," she answered; and added: "To go no further than the very beginning, Monsieur should perceive that her choice has exactly fifty chances in the hundred of going wrong: lying, as it does, between a meagre, sallow-faced creature of a death-white baldness, and a fine big pattern of a man, strong and ruddy, with a close-clipped but abundant thatch on his head, and a moustache that admittedly is superb!"

"Ah, there speaks the woman!" said Monsieur Fromagin, with a patronising smile distinctly irritating. "Madame will recognise – if she will but bring herself to look a little beyond the mere outside – that what I have advanced is not a matter of opinion but of fact. Observe: Here is Monsieur Peloux – to whose trifling leanness and aristocratic baldness the thoughtful give no attention – easily a notary in the very first rank. As we all know, his services are sought in cases of the most exigent importance—"

"For example," interpolated Madame Gauthier, "the case of the insurance solicitor, in whose countless defraudings my own brother was a sufferer: a creature of a vileness, whose deserts were unnumbered ages of dungeons – and who, thanks to the chicaneries of Monsieur Peloux, at this moment walks free as air!"

"It is of the professional duty of advocates," replied Monsieur Fromagin, sententiously, "to defend their clients; on the successful discharge of that duty – irrespective of minor details – depends their fame. Madame neglects the fact that Monsieur Peloux, by his masterly conduct of the case that she specifies, won for himself from his legal colleagues an immense applause."

"The more shame to his legal colleagues!" commented Madame Gauthier curtly.

"But leaving that affair quite aside," continued Monsieur Fromagin airily, but with insistence, "here is this notable advocate who reposes his important homages at Madame Jolicœur's feet: he a man of an age that is suitable, without being excessive; who has in the community an assured position; whose more than moderate wealth is known. I insist, therefore, that should she accept his homages she would do well."

"And I insist," declared Madame Gauthier stoutly, "that should she turn her back upon the Major Gontard she would do most ill!"

"Madame a little disregards my premises," Monsieur Fromagin spoke in a tone of forbearance, "and therefore a little argues – it is the privilege of her sex – against the air. Distinctly, I do not exclude from Madame Jolicœur's choice that gallant Major: whose rank – now approaching him to the command of a regiment, and fairly equalling the position at the bar achieved by Monsieur Peloux – has been won, grade by grade, by deeds of valour in his African campaignings which have made him conspicuous even in the army that stands first in such matters of all the armies of the world. Moreover – although, admittedly, in that way Monsieur Peloux makes a better showing – he is of an easy affluence. On the Camargue he has his excellent estate in vines, from which comes a revenue more than sufficing to satisfy more than modest wants. At Les Martigues he has his charming coquette villa, smothered in the flowers of his own planting, to which at present he makes his agreeable escapes from his military duties; and in which, when his retreat is taken, he will pass softly his sunset years. With these substantial points in his favour, the standing of the Major Gontard in this matter practically is of a parity with the standing of Monsieur Peloux. Equally, both are worthy of Madame Jolicœur's consideration: both being able to continue her in the life of elegant comfort to which she is accustomed; and both being on a social plane – it is of her level accurately – to which the widow of an ingénieur des ponts et chaussées neither steps up nor steps down. Having now made clear, I trust, my reasonings, I repeat the proposition with which Madame took issue: When Madame Jolicœur goes to make her choosings between these estimable gentlemen she cannot make a choice that is wrong."

"And I repeat, Monsieur," said Madame Gauthier, lifting her basket from the counter, "that in making her choosings Madame Jolicœur either goes to raise herself to the heights of a matured happiness, or to plunge herself into bald-headed abysses of despair. Yes, Monsieur, that far apart are her choosings!" And Madame Gauthier added, in communion with herself as she passed to the street with her basket: "As for me, it would be that adorable Major by a thousand times!"

As was of reason, since hers was the first place in the matter, Madame Jolicœur herself carried on debatings – in the portion of her heart that had escaped complete devastation – identical in essence with the debatings of her case which went up and down the Rue Bausset.

Not having become dévote – in the year and more of opportunity open to her for a turn in that direction – one horn of her original dilemma had been eliminated, so to say, by atrophy. Being neglected, it had withered: with the practical result that out of her very indecisions had come a decisive choice. But to her new dilemma, of which the horns were the Major and the Notary – in the privacy of her secret thoughts she made no bones of admitting that this dilemma confronted her – the atrophying process was not applicable; at least, not until it could be applied with a sharp finality. Too long dallied with, it very well might lead to the atrophy of both of them in dudgeon; and thence onward, conceivably, to her being left to cling only to the Shah de Perse for all the remainder of her days.

Therefore, to the avoidance of that too radical conclusion, Madame Jolicœur engaged in her debatings briskly: offering to herself, in effect, the balanced arguments advanced by Monsieur Fromagin in favour equally of Monsieur Peloux and of the Major Gontard; taking as her own, with moderating exceptions and emendations, the views of Madame Gauthier as to the meagreness and pallid baldness of the one and the sturdiness and gallant bearing of the other; considering, from the standpoint of her own personal knowledge in the premises, the Notary's disposition toward a secretive reticence that bordered upon severity, in contrast with the cordially frank and debonair temperament of the Major; and, at the back of all, keeping well in mind the fundamental truths that opportunity ever is evanescent and that time ever is on the wing.

As the result of her debatings, and not less as the result of experience gained in her earlier campaigning, Madame Jolicœur took up a strategic position nicely calculated to inflame the desire for, by assuming the uselessness of, an assault. In set terms, confirming particularly her earlier and more general avowal, she declared equally to the Major and to the Notary that absolutely the whole of her bestowable affection – of the remnant in her withered heart available for distribution – was bestowed upon the Shah de Perse: and so, with an alluring nonchalance, left them to draw the logical conclusion that their strivings to win that desirable quantity were idle – since a definite disposition of it already had been made.

The reply of the Major Gontard to this declaration was in keeping with his known amiability, but also was in keeping with his military habit of command. "Assuredly," he said, "Madame shall continue to bestow, within reason, her affections upon Monsieur le Shah; and with them that brave animal – he is a cat of ten thousand – shall have my affections as well. Already, knowing my feeling for him, we are friends – as Madame shall see to her own convincing." Addressing himself in tones of kindly persuasion to the Shah de Perse, he added: "Viens, Monsieur!" – whereupon the Shah de Perse instantly jumped himself to the Major's knee and broke forth, in response to a savant rubbing of his soft little jowls, into his gurgling purr. "Voilà, Madame!" continued the Major. "It is to be perceived that we have our good understandings, the Shah de Perse and I. That we all shall live happily together tells itself without words. But observe" – of a sudden the voice of the Major thrilled with a deep earnestness, and his style of address changed to a familiarity that only the intensity of his feeling condoned – "I am resolved that to me, above all, shall be given thy dear affections. Thou shalt give me the perfect flower of them – of that fact rest thou assured. In thy heart I am to be the very first – even as in my heart thou thyself art the very first of all the world. In Africa I have had my successes in my conquests and holdings of fortresses. Believe me, I shall have an equal success in conquering and in holding the sweetest fortress in France!"

Certainly, the Major Gontard had a bold way with him.

But that it had its attractions, not to say its compellings, Madame Jolicœur could not honestly deny.

On the part of the Notary – whose disposition, fostered by his profession, was toward subtlety rather than toward boldness – Madame Jolicœur's declaration of cat rights was received with no such belligerent blare of trumpets and beat of drums. He met it with a light show of banter – beneath which, to come to the surface later, lay hidden dark thoughts.

"Madame makes an excellent pleasantry," he said with a smile of the blandest. "Without doubt, not a very flattering pleasantry – but I know that her denial of me in favour of her cat is but a jesting at which we both may laugh. And we may laugh together the better because, in the roots of her jesting, we have our sympathies. I also have an intensity of affection for cats" – to be just to Monsieur Peloux, who loathed cats, it must be said that he gulped as he made this flagrantly untruthful statement – "and with this admirable cat, so dear to Madame, it goes to make itself that we speedily become enduring friends."

Curiously enough – a mere coincidence, of course – as the Notary uttered these words so sharply at points with veracity, in the very moment of them, the Shah de Perse stiffly retired into his sulkiest corner and turned what had every appearance of being a scornful back upon the world.

Judiciously ignoring this inopportunely equivocal incident, Monsieur Peloux reverted to the matter in chief and concluded his deliverance in these words: "I well understand, I repeat, that Madame for the moment makes a comedy of herself and of her cat for my amusing. But I persuade myself that her droll fancyings will not be lasting, and that she will be serious with me in the end. Until then – and then most of all – I am at her feet humbly: an unworthy, but a very earnest, suppliant for her good-will. Should she have the cruelty to refuse my supplication, it will remain with me to die in an unmerited despair!"

Certainly, this was an appeal – of a sort. But even without perceiving the mitigating subtlety of its comminative final clause – so skilfully worded as to leave Monsieur Peloux free to bring off his threatened unmeritedly despairing death quite at his own convenience – Madame Jolicœur did not find it satisfying. In contrast with the Major Gontard's ringingly audacious declarations of his habits in dealing with fortresses, she felt that it lacked force. And, also – this, of course, was a sheer weakness – she permitted herself to be influenced appreciably by the indicated preferences of the Shah de Perse: who had jumped to the knee of the Major with an affectionate alacrity; and who undeniably had turned on the Notary – either by chance or by intention – a back of scorn.

As the general outcome of these several developments, Madame Jolicœur's debatings came to have in them – if I so may state the trend of her mental activities – fewer bald heads and more moustaches; and her never severely set purpose to abide in a loneliness relieved only by the Shah de Perse was abandoned root and branch.

While Madame Jolicœur continued her debatings – which, in their modified form, manifestly were approaching her to conclusions – water was running under bridges elsewhere.

In effect, her hesitancies produced a period of suspense that gave opportunity for, and by the exasperating delay of it stimulated, the resolution of the Notary's dark thoughts into darker deeds. With reason, he did not accept at its face value Madame Jolicœur's declaration touching the permanent bestowal of her remnant affections; but he did believe that there was enough in it to make the Shah de Perse a delaying obstacle to his own acquisition of them. When obstacles got in this gentleman's way it was his habit to kick them out of it – a habit that had not been unduly stunted by half a lifetime of successful practice at the criminal bar.

Because of his professional relations with them, Monsieur

Peloux had an extensive acquaintance among criminals of varying shades of intensity – at times, in his dubious doings, they could be useful to him – hidden away in the shadowy nooks and corners of the city; and he also had his emissaries through whom they could be reached. All the conditions thus standing attendant upon his convenience, it was a facile matter for him to make an appointment with one of these disreputables at a cabaret of bad record in the Quartier de la Tourette: a region – bordering upon the north side of the Vieux Port – that is at once the oldest and the foulest quarter of Marseille.

In going to keep this appointment – as was his habit on such occasions, in avoidance of possible spying upon his movements – he went deviously: taking a cab to the Bassin de Carènage, as though some maritime matter engaged him, and thence making the transit of the Vieux Port in a bateau mouche. It was while crossing in the ferryboat that a sudden shuddering beset him: as he perceived with horror – but without repentance – the pit into which he descended. In his previous, always professional, meetings with criminals his position had been that of unassailable dominance. In his pending meeting – since he himself would be not only a criminal but an inciter to crime – he would be, in the essence of the matter, the under dog. Beneath his seemly black hat his bald head went whiter than even its normal deathly whiteness, and perspiration started from its every pore. Almost with a groan, he removed his hat and dried with his handkerchief what were in a way his tears of shame.

Over the interview between Monsieur Peloux and his hireling – cheerfully moistened, on the side of the hireling, with absinthe of a vileness in keeping with its place of purchase – decency demands the partial drawing of a veil. In brief, Monsieur Peloux – his guilty eyes averted, the shame-tears streaming afresh from his bald head – presented his criminal demand and stated the sum that he would pay for its gratification. This sum – being in keeping with his own estimate of what it paid for – was so much in excess of the hireling's views concerning the value of a mere cat-killing that he fairly jumped at it.

"Be not disturbed, Monsieur!" he replied, with the fervour of one really grateful, and with the expansive extravagance of a Marseillais keyed up with exceptionally bad absinthe. "Be not disturbed in the smallest! In this very coming moment this camel of a cat shall die a thousand deaths; and in but another moment immeasurable quantities of salt and ashes shall obliterate his justly despicable grave! To an instant accomplishment of Monsieur's wishes I pledge whole-heartedly the word of an honest man."

Actually – barring the number of deaths to be inflicted on the Shah de Perse, and the needlessly defiling concealment of his burial-place – this radical treatment of the matter was precisely what Monsieur Peloux desired; and what, in terms of innuendo and euphuism, he had asked for. But the brutal frankness of the hireling, and his evident delight in sinning for good wages, came as an arousing shock to the enfeebled remnant of the Notary's better nature – with a resulting vacillation of purpose to which he would have risen superior had he been longer habituated to the ways of crime.

"No! No!" he said weakly. "I did not mean that – by no means all of that. At least – that is to say – you will understand me, my good man, that enough will be done if you remove the cat from Marseille. Yes, that is what I mean – take it somewhere. Take it to Cassis, to Arles, to Avignon – where you will – and leave it there. The railway ticket is my charge – and, also, you have an extra napoléon for your refreshment by the way. Yes, that suffices. In a bag, you know – and soon!"

Returning across the Vieux Port in the bateau mouche, Monsieur Peloux no longer shuddered in dread of crime to be committed – his shuddering was for accomplished crime.

On his bald head, unheeded, the gushing tears of shame accumulated in pools.

When leaves of absence permitted him to make retirements to his coquette little estate at Les Martigues, the Major Gontard was as another Cincinnatus: with the minor differences that the lickerish cookings of the brave Marthe – his old femme de ménage: a veritable protagonist among cooks, even in Provence – checked him on the side of severe simplicity; that he would have welcomed with effusion lictors, or others, come to announce his advance to a regiment; and that he made no use whatever of a plow.

In the matter of the plow, he had his excuses. His two or three acres of land lay on a hillside banked in tiny terraces – quite unsuited to the use of that implement – and the whole of his agricultural energies were given to the cultivation of flowers. Among his flowers, intelligently assisted by old Michel, he worked with a zeal bred of his affection for them; and after his workings, when the cool of evening was come, smoked his pipe refreshingly while seated on the vine-bowered estrade before his trim villa on the crest of the slope: the while sniffing with a just interest at the fumes of old Marthe's cookings, and placidly delighting in the ever-new beauties of the sunsets above the distant mountains and their near-by reflected beauties in the waters of the Étang de Berre.

Save in his professional relations with recalcitrant inhabitants of Northern Africa, he was of a gentle nature, this amiable warrior: ever kindly, when kindliness was deserved, in all his dealings with mankind. Equally, his benevolence was extended to the lower orders of animals – that it was understood, and reciprocated, the willing jumping of the Shah de Perse to his friendly knee made manifest – and was exhibited in practical ways. Naturally, he was a liberal contributor to the funds of the Société protectrice des animaux; and, what was more to the purpose, it was his well-rooted habit to do such protecting as was necessary, on his own account, when he chanced upon any suffering creature in trouble or in pain.

Possessing these commendable characteristics, it follows that the doings of the Major Gontard in the railway station at Pas de Lanciers – on the day sequent to the day on which Monsieur Peloux was the promoter of a criminal conspiracy – could not have been other than they were. Equally does it follow that his doings produced the doings of the man with the bag.

Pas de Lanciers is the little station at which one changes trains in going from Marseille to Les Martigues. Descending from a first-class carriage, the Major Gontard awaited the Martigues train – his leave was for two days, and his thoughts were engaged pleasantly with the breakfast that old Marthe would have ready for him and with plans for his flowers. From a third-class carriage descended the man with the bag, who also awaited the Martigues train. Presently – the two happening to come together in their saunterings up and down the platform – the Major's interest was aroused by observing that within the bag went on a persistent wriggling; and his interest was quickened into characteristic action when he heard from its interior, faintly but quite distinctly, a very pitiful half-strangled little mew!

"In another moment," said the Major, addressing the man sharply, "that cat will be suffocated. Open the bag instantly and give it air!"

"Pardon, Monsieur," replied the man, starting guiltily. "This excellent cat is not suffocating. In the bag it breathes freely with all its lungs. It is a pet cat, having the habitude to travel in this manner; and, because it is of a friendly disposition, it is accustomed thus to make its cheerful little remarks." By way of comment upon this explanation, there came from the bag another half-strangled mew that was not at all suggestive of cheerfulness. It was a faint miserable mew – that told of cat despair!

At that juncture a down train came in on the other side of the platform, a train on its way to Marseille.

"Thou art a brute!" said the Major, tersely. "I shall not suffer thy cruelties to continue!" As he spoke, he snatched away the bag from its uneasy possessor and applied himself to untying its confining cord. Oppressed by the fear that goes with evil-doing, the man hesitated for a moment before attempting to retrieve what constructively was his property.

In that fateful moment the bag opened and a woebegone little black cat-head appeared; and then the whole of a delighted little black cat-body emerged – and cuddled with joy-purrs of recognition in its deliverer's arms! Within the sequent instant the recognition was mutual. "Thunder of guns!" cried the Major. "It is the Shah de Perse!"

Being thus caught red-handed, the hireling of Monsieur Peloux cowered. "Brigand!" continued the Major. "Thou hast ravished away this charming cat by the foulest of robberies. Thou art worse than the scum of Arab camp-followings. And if I had thee to myself, over there in the desert," he added grimly, "thou shouldst go the same way!"

All overawed by the Major's African attitude, the hireling took to whining. "Monsieur will believe me when I tell him that I am but an unhappy tool – I, an honest man whom a rich tempter, taking advantage of my unmerited poverty, has betrayed into crime. Monsieur himself shall judge me when I have told him all!" And then – with creditably imaginative variations on the theme of a hypothetical dying wife in combination with six supposititious starving children – the man came close enough to telling all to make clear that his backer in cat-stealing was Monsieur Peloux!

With a gasp of astonishment, the Major again took the word. "What matters it, animal, by whom thy crime was prompted? Thou art the perpetrator of it – and to thee comes punishment! Shackles and prisons are in store for thee! I shall—"

But what the Major Gontard had in mind to do toward assisting the march of retributive justice is immaterial – since he did not do it. Even as he spoke – in these terms of doom that qualifying conditions rendered doomless – the man suddenly dodged past him, bolted across the platform, jumped to the foot-board of a carriage of the just-starting train, cleverly bundled himself through an open window, and so was gone: leaving the Major standing lonely, with impotent rage filling his heart, and with the Shah de Perse all a purring cuddle in his arms!

Acting on a just impulse, the Major Gontard sped to the telegraph office. Two hours must pass before he could follow the miscreant; but the departed train ran express to Marseille, and telegraphic heading-off was possible. To his flowers, and to the romance of a breakfast that old Marthe by then was in the very act of preparing for him, his thoughts went in bitter relinquishment: but his purpose was stern! Plumping the Shah de Perse down anyway on the telegraph table, and seizing a pen fiercely, he began his writings. And then, of a sudden, an inspiration came to him that made him stop in his writings – and that changed his flames of anger into flames of joy.

His first act under the influence of this new and better emotion was to tear his half-finished dispatch into fragments. His second act was to assuage the needs, physical and psychical, of the Shah de Perse – near to collapse for lack of food and drink, and his little cat feelings hurt by his brusque deposition on the telegraph table – by carrying him tenderly to the buffet; and there – to the impolitely over-obvious amusement of the buffetière – purchasing cream without stint for the allaying of his famishings. To his feasting the Shah de Perse went with the avid energy begotten of his bag-compelled long fast. Dipping his little red tongue deep into the saucer, he lapped with a vigour that all cream-splattered his little black nose. Yet his admirable little cat manners were not forgotten: even in the very thick of his eager lappings – pathetically eager, in view of the cause of them – he purred forth gratefully, with a gurgling chokiness, his earnest little cat thanks.

As the Major Gontard watched this pleasing spectacle his heart was all aglow within him and his face was of a radiance comparable only with that of an Easter-morning sun. To himself he was saying: "It is a dream that has come to me! With the disgraced enemy in retreat, and with the Shah de Perse for my banner, it is that I hold victoriously the whole universe in the hollow of my hand!"

While stopping appreciably short of claiming for himself a clutch upon the universe, Monsieur Peloux also had his satisfactions on the evening of the day that had witnessed the enlèvement of the Shah de Perse. By his own eyes he knew certainly that that iniquitous kidnapping of a virtuous cat had been effected. In the morning the hireling had brought to him in his private office the unfortunate Shah de Perse – all unhappily bagged, and even then giving vent to his pathetic complainings – and had exhibited him, as a pièce justificatif, when making his demand for railway fare and the promised extra napolèon. In the mid-afternoon the hireling had returned, with the satisfying announcement that all was accomplished: that he had carried the cat to Pas de Lanciers, of an adequate remoteness, and there had left him with a person in need of a cat who received him willingly. Being literally true, this statement had in it so convincing a ring of sincerity that Monsieur Peloux paid down in full the blood-money and dismissed his bravo with commendation. Thereafter, being alone, he rubbed his hands – gladly thinking of what was in the way to happen in sequence to the permanent removal of this cat stumbling-block from his path. Although professionally accustomed to consider the possibilities of permutation, the known fact that petards at times are retroactive did not present itself to his mind.

And yet – being only an essayist in crime, still unhardened – certain compunctions beset him as he approached himself, on the to-be eventful evening of that eventful day, to the door of Madame Jolicœur's modestly elegant dwelling on the Pavé d'Amour. In the back of his head were justly self-condemnatory thoughts, to the general effect that he was a blackguard and deserved to be kicked. In the dominant front of his head, however, were thoughts of a more agreeable sort: of how he would find Madame Jolicœur all torn and rent by the bitter sorrow of her bereavement; of how he would pour into her harried heart a flood of sympathy by which that injured organ would be soothed and mollified; of how she would be lured along gently to requite his tender condolence with a softening gratitude – that presently would merge easily into the yet softer phrase of love! It was a well-made programme, and it had its kernel of reason in his recognised ability to win bad causes – as that of the insurance solicitor – by emotional pleadings which in the same breath lured to lenience and made the intrinsic demerits of the cause obscure.

"Madame dines," was the announcement that met Monsieur Peloux when, in response to his ring, Madame Jolicœur's door was opened for him by a trim maid-servant. "But Madame already has continued so long her dining," added the maid-servant, with a glint in her eyes that escaped his preoccupied attention, "that in but another instant must come the end. If M'sieu' will have the amiability to await her in the salon, it will be for but a point of time!"

Between this maid-servant and Monsieur Peloux no love was lost. Instinctively he was aware of, and resented, her views – practically identical with those expressed by Madame Gauthier to Monsieur Fromagin – touching his deserts as compared with the deserts of the Major Gontard.

Moreover, she had personal incentives to take her revenges. From Monsieur Peloux, her only vail had been a miserable two-franc Christmas box. From the Major, as from a perpetually verdant Christmas-tree, boxes of bonbons and five-franc pieces at all times descended upon her in showers.

Without perceiving the curious smile that accompanied this young person's curiously cordial invitation to enter, he accepted the invitation and was shown into the salon: where he seated himself – a left-handedness of which he would have been incapable had he been less perturbed – in Madame Jolicœur's own special chair. An anatomical vagary of the Notary's meagre person was the undue shortness of his body and the undue length of his legs. Because of this eccentricity of proportion, his bald head rose above the back of the chair to a height approximately identical with that of its normal occupant.

His waiting time – extending from its promised point to what seemed to him to be a whole geographical meridian – went slowly. To relieve it, he took a book from the table, and in a desultory manner turned the leaves. While thus perfunctorily engaged, he heard the clicking of an opening door, and then the sound of voices: of Madame Jolicœur's voice, and of a man's voice – which latter, coming nearer, he recognised beyond all doubting as the voice of the Major Gontard. Of other voices there was not a sound: whence the compromising fact was obvious that the two had gone through that long dinner together, and alone! Knowing, as he did, Madame Jolicœur's habitual disposition toward the convenances – willingly to be boiled in oil rather than in the smallest particular to abrade them – he perceived that only two explanations of the situation were possible: either she had lapsed of a sudden into madness; or – the thought was petrifying – the Major Gontard had won out in his French campaigning on his known conquering African lines. The cheerfully sane tone of the lady's voice forbade him to clutch at the poor solace to be found in the first alternative – and so forced him to accept the second. Yielding for a moment to his emotions, the death-whiteness of his bald head taking on a still deathlier pallor, Monsieur Peloux buried his face in his hands and groaned.

In that moment of his obscured perception a little black personage trotted into the salon on soundless paws. Quite possibly, in his then overwrought condition, had Monsieur Peloux seen this personage enter he would have shrieked – in the confident belief that before him was a cat ghost! Pointedly, it was not a ghost. It was the happy little Shah de Perse himself – all a-frisk with the joy of his blessed home-coming and very much alive! Knowing, as I do, many of the mysterious ways of little cat souls, I even venture to believe that his overbubbling gladness largely was due to his sympathetic perception of the gladness that his home-coming had brought to two human hearts.

Certainly, all through that long dinner the owners of those hearts had done their best, by their pettings and their pamperings of him, to make him a participant in their deep happiness; and he, gratefully respondent, had made his affectionate thankings by going through all of his repertory of tricks – with one exception – again and again. Naturally, his great trick, while unexhibited, repeatedly had been referred to. Blushing delightfully, Madame Jolicœur had told about the night-cap that was a necessary part of it; and had promised – blushing still more delightfully – that at some time, in the very remote future, the Major should see it performed. For my own part, because of my knowledge of little cat souls, I am persuaded that the Shah de Perse, while missing the details of this love-laughing talk, did get into his head the general trend of it; and therefore did trot on in advance into the salon with his little cat mind full of the notion that Madame Jolicœur immediately would follow him – to seat herself, duly night-capped, book in hand, in signal for their game of surprises to begin.

Unconscious of the presence of the Shah de Perse, tortured by the gay tones of the approaching voices, clutching his book vengefully as though it were a throat, his bald head beaded with the sweat of agony and the pallor of it intensified by his poignant emotion, Monsieur Peloux sat rigid in Madame Jolicœur's chair!

"It is declared," said Monsieur Brisson, addressing himself to Madame Jouval, for whom he was in the act of preparing what was spoken of between them as "the tonic," a courteous euphuism, "that that villain Notary, aided by a bandit hired to his assistance, was engaged in administering poison to the cat; and that the brave animal, freeing itself from the bandit's holdings, tore to destruction the whole of his bald head – and then triumphantly escaped to its home!"

"A sight to see is that head of his!" replied Madame Jouval. "So swathed is it in bandages, that the turban of the Grand Turk is less!" Madame Jouval spoke in tones of satisfaction that were of reason – already she had held conferences with Madame Jolicœur in regard to the trousseau.

"And all," continued Monsieur Brisson, with rancour, "because of his jealousies of the cat's place in Madame Jolicœur's affections – the affections which he so hopelessly hoped, forgetful of his own repulsiveness, to win for himself!"

"Ah, she has done well, that dear lady," said Madame Jouval warmly. "As between the Notary – repulsive, as Monsieur justly terms him – and the charming Major, her instincts rightly have directed her. To her worthy cat, who aided in her choosing, she has reason to be grateful. Now her cruelly wounded heart will find solace. That she should wed again, and happily, was Heaven's will."

"It was the will of the baggage herself!" declared Monsieur Brisson with bitterness. "Hardly had she put on her travesty of a mourning than she began her oglings of whole armies of men!"

Aside from having confected with her own hands the mourning to which Monsieur Brisson referred so disparagingly, Madame Jouval was not one to hear calmly the ascription of the term baggage – the word has not lost in its native French, as it has lost in its naturalised English, its original epithetical intensity – to a patroness from whom she was in the very article of receiving an order for an exceptionally rich trousseau. Naturally, she bristled. "Monsieur must admit at least," she said sharply, "that her oglings did not come in his direction;" and with an irritatingly smooth sweetness added: "As to the dealings of Monsieur Peloux with the cat, Monsieur doubtless speaks with an assured knowledge. Remembering, as we all do, the affair of the unhappy old woman, it is easy to perceive that to Monsieur, above all others, any one in need of poisonings would come!"

The thrust was so keen that for the moment Monsieur Brisson met it only with a savage glare. Then the bottle that he handed to Madame Jouval inspired him with an answer. "Madame is in error," he said with politeness. "For poisons it is possible to go variously elsewhere – as, for example, to Madame's tongue." Had he stopped with that retort courteous, but also searching, he would have done well. He did ill by adding to it the retort brutal: "But that old women of necessity come to me for their hair-dyes is another matter. That much I grant to Madame with all good will."

Admirably restraining herself, Madame Jouval replied in tones of sympathy: "Monsieur receives my commiserations in his misfortunes." Losing a large part of her restraint, she continued, her eyes glittering: "Yet Monsieur's temperament clearly is over-sanguine. It is not less than a miracle of absurdity that he imagined: that he, weighted down with his infamous murderings of scores of innocent old women, had even a chance the most meagre of realising his ridiculous aspirations of Madame Jolicœur's hand!" Snatching up her bottle and making for the door, without any restraint whatever she added: "Monsieur and his aspirations are a tragedy of stupidity – and equally are abounding in all the materials for a farce at the Palais de Cristal!"

Monsieur Brisson was cut off from opportunity to reply to this outburst by Madame Jouval's abrupt departure. His loss of opportunity had its advantages. An adequate reply to her discharge of such a volley of home truths would have been difficult to frame.

In the Vic bakery, between Madame Vic and Monsieur Fromagin, a discussion was in hand akin to that carried on between Monsieur Brisson and Madame Jouval – but marked with a somewhat nearer approach to accuracy in detail. Being sequent to the settlement of Monsieur Fromagin's monthly bill – always a matter of nettling dispute – it naturally tended to develop its own asperities.

"They say," observed Monsieur Fromagin, "that the cat – it was among his many tricks – had the habitude to jump on Madame Jolicœur's head when, for that purpose, she covered it with a night-cap. The use of the cat's claws on such a covering, and, also, her hair being very abundant –"

"*Very* abundant!" interjected Madame Vic; and added: "She, she is of a richness to buy wigs by the scores!"

"It was his custom, I say," continued Monsieur Fromagin with insistence, "to steady himself after his leap by using lightly his claws. His illusion in regard to the bald head of the Notary, it would seem, led to the catastrophe. Using his claws at first lightly, according to his habit, he went on to use them with a truly savage energy – when he found himself as on ice on that slippery eminence and verging to a fall."

"They say that his scalp was peeled away in strips and strings!" said Madame Vic. "And all the while that woman and that reprobate of a Major standing by in shrieks and roars of laughter – never raising a hand to save him from the beast's ferocities! The poor man has my sympathies. He, at least, in all his doings – I do not for a moment believe the story that he caused the cat to be stolen – observed rigidly the convenances: so recklessly shattered by Madame Jolicœur in her most compromising dinner with the Major alone!"

"But Madame forgets that their dinner was in celebration of their betrothal – following Madame Jolicœur's glad yielding, in just gratitude, when the Major heroically had rescued her deserving cat from the midst of its enemies and triumphantly had restored it to her arms."

"It is the man's part," responded Madame Vic, "to make the best of such matters. In the eyes of all right-minded women her conduct has been of a shamelessness from first to last: tossing and balancing the two of them for months upon months; luring them, and countless others with them, to her feet; declaring always that for her disgusting cat's sake she will have none of them; and ending by pretending brazenly that for her cat's sake she bestows herself – second-hand remnant that she is – on the handsomest man for his age, concerning his character it is well to be silent; that she could find for herself in all Marseille! On such actions, on such a woman, Monsieur, the saints in heaven look down with an agonised scorn!"

"Only those of the saints, Madame," said Monsieur Fromagin, warmly taking up the cudgels for his best customer, "as in the matter of second marriages, prior to their arrival in heaven, have had regrettable experiences. Equally, I venture to assert, a like qualification applies to a like attitude on earth. That Madame has her prejudices, incident to her misfortunes, is known."

"That Monsieur has his brutalities, incident to his regrettable bad breeding, also is known. His present offensiveness, however, passes all limits. I request him to remove himself from my sight." Madame Vic spoke with dignity.

Speaking with less dignity, but with conviction – as Monsieur Fromagin left the bakery – she added: "Monsieur, effectively, is a camel! I bestow upon him my disdain!"

THE WHITE CAT

E. NESBIT

The White Cat lived at the back of a shelf at the darkest end of the inside attic which was nearly dark all over. It had lived there for years, because one of its white china ears was chipped, so that it was no longer a possible ornament for the spare bedroom.

Tavy found it at the climax of a wicked and glorious afternoon. He had been left alone. The servants were the only other people in the house. He had promised to be good. He had meant to be good. And he had not been. He had done everything you can think of. He had walked into the duck pond, and not a stitch of his clothes but had had to be changed. He had climbed on a hay rick and fallen off it, and had not broken his neck, which, as cook told him, he richly deserved to do. He had found a mouse in the trap and put it in the kitchen tea-pot, so that when cook went to make tea it jumped out at her, and affected her to screams followed by tears. Tavy was sorry for this, of course, and said so like a man. He had only, he explained, meant to give her a little start. In the confusion that followed the mouse, he had eaten all the blackcurrant jam that was put out for kitchen tea, and for this too, he apologised handsomely as soon as it was pointed out to him. He had broken a pane of the greenhouse with a stone and... But why pursue the painful theme? The last thing he had done was to explore the attic, where he was never allowed to go, and to knock down the White Cat from its shelf.

The sound of its fall brought the servants. The cat was not broken – only its other ear was chipped. Tavy was put to bed. But he got out as soon as the servants had gone downstairs, crept up to the attic, secured the Cat, and washed it in the bath. So that when mother came back from London, Tavy, dancing impatiently at the head of the stairs, in a very wet night-gown, flung himself upon her and cried, "I've been awfully naughty, and I'm frightfully sorry, and please may I have the White Cat for my very own?"

He was much sorrier than he had expected to be when he saw that mother was too tired even to want to know, as she generally did, exactly how naughty he had been. She only kissed him, and said:

"I am sorry you've been naughty, my darling. Go back to bed now. Good-night."

Tavy was ashamed to say anything more about the China Cat, so he went back to bed. But he took the Cat with him, and talked to it and kissed it, and went to sleep with its smooth shiny shoulder against his cheek.

In the days that followed, he was extravagantly good. Being good seemed as easy as being bad usually was. This may have been because mother seemed so tired and ill; and gentlemen in black coats and high hats came to see mother, and after they had gone she used to cry. (These things going on in a house sometimes make people good; sometimes they act just the other way.) Or it may have been because he had the China Cat to talk to. Anyhow, whichever way it was, at the end of the week mother said:

"Tavy, you've been a dear good boy, and a great comfort to me. You must have tried very hard to be good."

It was difficult to say, "No, I haven't, at least not since the first day," but Tavy got it said, and was hugged for his pains.

"You wanted," said mother, "the China Cat. Well, you may have it."

"For my very own?"

"For your very own. But you must be very careful not to break it. And you mustn't give it away. It goes with the house. Your Aunt Jane made me promise to keep it in the family. It's very, very old. Don't take it out of doors for fear of accidents."

"I love the White Cat, mother," said Tavy. "I love it better'n all my toys."

Then mother told Tavy several things, and that night when he went to bed Tavy repeated them all faithfully to the China Cat, who was about six inches high and looked very intelligent.

"So you see," he ended, "the wicked lawyer's taken nearly all mother's money, and we've got to leave our own lovely big White House, and go and live in a horrid little house with another house glued on to its side. And mother does hate it so."

"I don't wonder," said the China Cat very distinctly.

"*What!*" said Tavy, half-way into his night-shirt.

"I said, I don't wonder, Octavius," said the China Cat, and rose from her sitting position, stretched her china legs and waved her white china tail.

"You can speak?" said Tavy.

"Can't you see I can? – hear I mean?" said the Cat. "I belong to you now, so I can speak to you. I couldn't before. It wouldn't have been manners."

Tavy, his night-shirt round his neck, sat down on the edge of the bed with his mouth open.

"Come, don't look so silly," said the Cat, taking a walk along the high wooden mantelpiece, "any one would think you didn't *like* me to talk to you."

"I *love* you to," said Tavy recovering himself a little.

"Well then," said the Cat.

"May I touch you?" Tavy asked timidly.

"Of course! I belong to you. Look out!" The China Cat gathered herself together and jumped. Tavy caught her.

It was quite a shock to find when one stroked her that the China Cat, though alive, was still china, hard, cold, and smooth to the touch, and yet perfectly brisk and absolutely bendable as any flesh and blood cat.

"Dear, dear white pussy," said Tavy, "I do love you."

"And I love you," purred the Cat, "otherwise I should never have lowered myself to begin a conversation."

"I wish you were a real cat," said Tavy.

"I am," said the Cat. "Now how shall we amuse ourselves? I suppose you don't care for sport – mousing, I mean?"

"I never tried," said Tavy, "and I think I rather wouldn't."

"Very well then, Octavius," said the Cat. "I'll take you to the White Cat's Castle. Get into bed. Bed makes a good travelling carriage, especially when you haven't any other. Shut your eyes."

Tavy did as he was told. Shut his eyes, but could not keep them shut. He opened them a tiny, tiny chink, and sprang up. He was not in bed. He was on a couch of soft beast-skin, and the couch stood in a splendid hall, whose walls were of gold and ivory. By him stood the White Cat, no longer china, but real live cat – and fur – as cats should be.

"Here we are," she said. "The journey didn't take long, did it? Now we'll have that splendid supper, out of the fairy tale, with the invisible hands waiting on us."

She clapped her paws – paws now as soft as white velvet – and a table-cloth floated into the room; then knives and forks and spoons and glasses, the table was laid, the dishes drifted in, and they began to eat. There happened to be every single thing Tavy liked best to eat. After supper there was music and singing, and Tavy, having kissed a white, soft, furry forehead, went to bed in a gold four-poster with a counterpane of butterflies' wings. He awoke at home. On the mantelpiece sat the White Cat, looking as though butter would not melt in her mouth. And all her furriness had gone with her voice. She was silent – and china.

Tavy spoke to her. But she would not answer. Nor did she speak all day. Only at night when he was getting into bed she suddenly mewed, stretched, and said:

"Make haste, there's a play acted tonight at my castle."

Tavy made haste, and was rewarded by another glorious evening in the castle of the White Cat.

And so the weeks went on. Days full of an ordinary little boy's joys and sorrows, goodnesses and badnesses. Nights spent by a little Prince in the Magic Castle of the White Cat.

Then came the day when Tavy's mother spoke to him, and he, very scared and serious, told the China Cat what she had said.

"I knew this would happen," said the Cat. "It always does. So you're to leave your house next week. Well, there's only one way out of the difficulty. Draw your sword, Tavy, and cut off my head and tail."

"And then will you turn into a Princess, and shall I have to marry you?" Tavy asked with horror.

"No, dear – no," said the Cat reassuringly. "I shan't turn into anything. But you and mother will turn into happy people. I shall just not *be* any – for you."

"Then I won't do it," said Tavy.

"But you must. Come, draw your sword, like a brave fairy Prince, and cut off my head."

The sword hung above his bed, with the helmet and breast-plate Uncle James had given him last Christmas.

"I'm not a fairy Prince," said the child. "I'm Tavy – and I love you."

"You love your mother better," said the Cat. "Come cut

my head off. The story always ends like that. You love mother best. It's for her sake."

"Yes." Tavy was trying to think it out. "Yes, I love mother best. But I love *you*. And I won't cut off your head – no, not even for mother.'

"Then," said the Cat, "I must do what I can!"

She stood up, waving her white china tail, and before Tavy could stop her she had leapt, not, as before, into his arms, but on to the wide hearthstone.

It was all over – the China Cat lay broken inside the high brass fender. The sound of the smash brought mother running.

"What is it?" she cried. "Oh, Tavy – the China Cat!"

"She would do it," sobbed Tavy. "She wanted me to cut off her head'n I wouldn't."

"Don't talk nonsense, dear," said mother sadly. "That only makes it worse. Pick up the pieces."

"There's only two pieces," said Tavy. "Couldn't you stick her together again?"

"Why," said mother, holding the pieces close to the candle. "She's been broken before. And mended."

"*I* knew that," said Tavy, still sobbing. "Oh, my dear White Cat, oh, oh, oh!" The last "oh" was a howl of anguish.

"Come, crying won't mend her," said mother. "Look, there's another piece of her, close to the shovel."

Tavy stooped.

"That's not a piece of cat," he said, and picked it up.

It was a pale parchment label, tied to a key. Mother held it to the candle and read: "*Key of the lock behind the knot in the mantelpiece panel in the white parlour.*"

"Tavy! I wonder! But … where did it come from?"

"Out of my White Cat, I s'pose," said Tavy, his tears stopping. "Are you going to see what's in the mantelpiece panel, mother? Are you? Oh, do let me come and see too!"

"You don't deserve," mother began, and ended, "Well, put your dressing-gown on then."

They went down the gallery past the pictures and the stuffed birds and tables with china on them and downstairs on to the white parlour. But they could not see any knot in the mantelpiece panel, because it was all painted white. But mother's fingers felt softly all over it, and found a round raised spot. It was a knot, sure enough. Then she scraped round it with her scissors, till she loosened the knot, and poked it out with the scissors point.

"I don't suppose there's any keyhole there really," she said. But there was. And what is more, the key fitted. The panel swung open, and inside was a little cupboard with two shelves. What was on the shelves? There were old laces and old embroideries, old jewellery and old silver; there was money, and there were dusty old papers that Tavy thought most uninteresting. But mother did not think them uninteresting. She laughed, and cried, or nearly cried, and said:

"Oh, Tavy, this was why the China Cat was to be taken such care of!" Then she told him how, a hundred and fifty years before, the Head of the House had gone out to fight for the Pretender, and had told his daughter to take the greatest care of the China Cat. "I will send you word of the reason by a sure hand," he said, for they parted on the open square, where any spy might have overheard anything. And he had been killed by an ambush not ten miles from home – and his daughter had never known. But she had kept the Cat.

"And now it has saved us," said mother. "We can stay in the dear old house, and there are two other houses that will belong to us too, I think. And, oh, Tavy, would you like some pound-cake and ginger-wine, dear?"

Tavy did like. And had it.

The China Cat was mended, but it was put in the glass-fronted corner cupboard in the drawing-room, because it had saved the house.

Now I dare say you'll think this is all nonsense, and a made-up story. Not at all. If it were, how would you account for Tavy's finding, the very next night, fast asleep on his pillow, his own white Cat – the furry friend that the China Cat used to turn into every evening – the dear hostess who had amused him so well in the White Cat's fairy Palace?

It was she, beyond a doubt, and that was why Tavy didn't mind a bit about the China Cat being taken from him and kept under glass. You may think that it was just any old stray white cat that had come in by accident. Tavy knows better. It has the very same tender tone in its purr that the magic White Cat had. It will not talk to Tavy, it is true; but Tavy can and does talk to it. But the thing that makes it perfectly certain that it is the White Cat is that the tips of its two ears are missing – just as the China Cat's ears were. If you say that it might have lost its ear-tips in battle you are the kind of person who always *makes* difficulties, and you may be quite sure that the kind of splendid magics that happened to Tavy will never happen to *you*.

CLASSIC LITERATURE: WORDS AND PHRASES
adapted from the Collins English Dictionary

Accoucheur NOUN a male midwife or doctor ❑ *I think my sister must have had some general idea that I was a young offender whom an Accoucheur Policemen had taken up (on my birthday) and delivered over to her* (*Great Expectations* by Charles Dickens)

addled ADJ confused and unable to think properly ❑ *But she counted and counted till she got that addled* (*The Adventures of Huckleberry Finn* by Mark Twain)

admiration NOUN amazement or wonder ❑ *lifting up his hands cnd eyes by way of admiration* (*Gulliver's Travels* by Jonathan Swift)

afeard ADJ afeard means afraid ❑ *shake it–and don't be afeard* (*The Adventures of Huckleberry Finn* by Mark Twain)

affected VERB affected means to assume the appearance of ❑ *Hadst thou affected sweet divinity* (*Doctor Faustus 5.2* by Christopher Marlowe)

aground ADV when a boat runs aground, it touches the ground in a shallow part of the water and gets stuck ❑ *what kep' you?–boat get aground?* (*The Adventures of Huckleberry Finn* by Mark Twain)

ague NOUN a fever in which the patient has alternate hot and cold shivering fits ❑ *his exposure to the wet and cold had brought on fever and ague* (*Oliver Twist* by Charles Dickens)

alchemy ADJ false or worthless ❑ *all wealth alchemy* (*The Sun Rising* by John Donne)

all alike PHRASE the same all the time ❑ *Love, all alike* (*The Sun Rising* by John Donne)

alow and aloft PHRASE alow means in the lower part or bottom, and aloft means on the top, so alow and aloft means on the top and in the bottom or throughout ❑ *Someone's turned the chest out alow and aloft* (*Treasure Island* by Robert Louis Stevenson)

ambuscade NOUN ambuscade is not a proper word. Tom means an ambush, which is when a group of people attack their enemies, after hiding and waiting for them ❑ *and so we would lie in ambuscade, as he called it* (*The Adventures of Huckleberry Finn* by Mark Twain)

amiable ADJ likeable or pleasant ❑ *Such amiable qualities must speak for themselves* (*Pride and Prejudice* by Jane Austen)

amulet NOUN an amulet is a charm thought to drive away evil spirits. ❑ *uttered phrases at once occult and familiar, like the amulet worn on the heart* (*Silas Marner* by George Eliot)

amusement NOUN here amusement means a strange and disturbing puzzle ❑ *this was an amusement the other way* (*Robinson Crusoe* by Daniel Defoe)

ancient NOUN an ancient was the flag displayed on a ship to show which country it belongs to. It is also called the ensign ❑ *her ancient and pendants out* (*Robinson Crusoe* by Daniel Defoe)

antic ADJ here antic means horrible or grotesque ❑ *armed and dressed after a very antic manner* (*Gulliver's Travels* by Jonathan Swift)

antics NOUN antics is an old word meaning clowns, or people who do silly things to make other people laugh ❑ *And point like antics at his triple crown* (*Doctor Faustus 3.2* by Christopher Marlowe)

appanage NOUN an appanage is a living allowance ❑ *As if loveliness were not the special prerogative of woman–her legitimate appanage and heritage!* (*Jane Eyre* by Charlotte Brontë)

appended VERB appended means attached or added to ❑ *and these words appended* (*Treasure Island* by Robert Louis Stevenson)

approver NOUN an approver is someone who gives evidence against someone he used to work with ❑ *Mr Noah Claypole: receiving a free pardon from the Crown in consequence of being admitted approver against Fagin* (*Oliver Twist* by Charles Dickens)

areas NOUN the areas is the space, below street level, in front of the basement of a house ❑ *The Dodger had a vicious propensity, too, of pulling the caps from the heads of small boys and tossing them down areas* (*Oliver Twist* by Charles Dickens)

argument NOUN theme or important idea or subject which runs through a piece of writing ❑ *Thrice needful to the argument which now* (*The Prelude* by William Wordsworth)

artificially ADV artfully or cleverly ❑ *and he with a sharp flint sharpened very artificially* (*Gulliver's Travels* by Jonathan Swift)

artist NOUN here artist means a skilled workman ❑ *This man was a most ingenious artist* (*Gulliver's Travels* by Jonathan Swift)

assizes NOUN assizes were regular court sessions which a visiting judge was in charge of ❑ *you shall hang at the next assizes* (*Treasure Island* by Robert Louis Stevenson)

attraction NOUN gravitation, or Newton's theory of gravitation ❑ *he predicted the same fate to attraction* (*Gulliver's Travels* by Jonathan Swift)

aver VERB to aver is to claim something strongly ❑ *for Jem Rodney, the mole catcher, averred that one evening as he was returning homeward* (*Silas Marner* by George Eliot)

baby NOUN here baby means doll, which is a child's toy that looks like a small person ❑ *and skilful dressing her baby* (*Gulliver's Travels* by Jonathan Swift)

bagatelle NOUN bagatelle is a game rather like billiards and pool ❑ *Breakfast had been ordered at a pleasant little tavern, a mile or so away upon the rising ground beyond the green; and there was a bagatelle board in the room, in case we should desire to unbend our minds after the solemnity.* (*Great Expectations* by Charles Dickens)

bah EXCLAM Bah is an exclamation of frustration or anger ❑ *'Bah,' said Scrooge.* (*A Christmas Carol* by Charles Dickens)

bairn NOUN a northern word for child ❑ *Who has taught you those fine words, my bairn?* (*Wuthering Heights* by Emily Brontë)

bait VERB to bait means to stop on a journey to take refreshment ❑ *So, when they stopped to bait the horse, and ate and drank and enjoyed themselves, I could touch nothing that they touched, but kept my fast unbroken.* (*David Copperfield* by Charles Dickens)

balustrade NOUN a balustrade is a row of vertical columns that form railings ❑ *but I mean to say you might have got a hearse up that staircase, and taken it broadwise, with the splinter-bar towards the wall, and the door towards the balustrades: and done it easy* (*A Christmas Carol* by Charles Dickens)

bandbox NOUN a large lightweight box for carrying bonnets or hats ❑ *I am glad I bought my bonnet, if it is only for the fun of having another bandbox* (*Pride and Prejudice* by Jane Austen)

barren NOUN a barren here is a stretch or expanse of barren land ❑ *a line of upright stones, continued the* *length of the barren* (*Wuthering Heights* by Emily Brontë)

basin NOUN a basin was a cup without a handle ❑ *who is drinking his tea out of a basin* (*Wuthering Heights* by Emily Brontë)

battalia NOUN the order of battle ❑ *till I saw part of his army in battalia* (*Gulliver's Travels* by Jonathan Swift)

battery NOUN a Battery is a fort or a place where guns are positioned ❑ *You bring the lot to me, at that old Battery over yonder* (*Great Expectations* by Charles Dickens)

battledore and shuttlecock NOUN The game battledore and shuttlecock was an early version of the game now known as badminton. The aim of the early game was simply to keep the shuttlecock from hitting the ground. ❑ *Battledore and shuttlecock's a wery good game when you an't the shuttlecock and two lawyers the battledores, in which case it gets too excitin' to be pleasant* (*Pickwick Papers* by Charles Dickens)

beadle NOUN a beadle was a local official who had power over the poor ❑ *But these impertinences were speedily checked by the evidence of the surgeon, and the testimony of the beadle* (*Oliver Twist* by Charles Dickens)

bearings NOUN the bearings of a place are the measurements or directions that are used to find or locate it ❑ *the bearings of the island* (*Treasure Island* by Robert Louis Stevenson)

beaufet NOUN a beaufet was a sideboard ❑ *and sweet-cake from the beaufet* (*Emma* by Jane Austen)

beck NOUN a beck is a small stream ❑ *a beck which follows the bend of the glen* (*Wuthering Heights* by Emily Brontë)

bedight VERB decorated ❑ *and bedight with Christmas holly stuck into the top.* (*A Christmas Carol* by Charles Dickens)

Bedlam NOUN Bedlam was a lunatic asylum in London which had statues carved by Caius Gabriel Cibber at its entrance ❑ *Bedlam, and those carved maniacs at the gates* (*The Prelude* by William Wordsworth)

beeves NOUN oxen or castrated bulls which are animals used for pulling vehicles or carrying things ❑ *to deliver in every morning six beeves* (*Gulliver's Travels* by Jonathan Swift)

begot VERB created or caused ❑ *Begot in thee* (*On His Mistress* by John Donne)

behoof NOUN behoof means benefit ❑ *'Yes, young man,' said he, releasing the handle of the article in question, retiring a step or two from my table, and speaking for the behoof of the landlord and waiter at the door* (*Great Expectations* by Charles Dickens)

berth NOUN a berth is a bed on a boat ❑ *this is the berth for me* (*Treasure Island* by Robert Louis Stevenson)

bevers NOUN a bever was a snack, or small portion of food, eaten between main meals ❑ *that buys me thirty meals a day and ten bevers* (*Doctor Faustus 2.1* by Christopher Marlowe)

bilge water NOUN the bilge is the widest part of a ship's bottom, and the bilge water is the dirty water that collects there ❑ *no gush of bilge-water had turned it to fetid puddle* (*Jane Eyre* by Charlotte Brontë)

bills NOUN bills is an old term meaning prescription. A prescription is the piece of paper on which your doctor writes an order for medicine and which you give to a chemist to get the medicine ❑ *Are not thy bills hung up as monuments* (*Doctor Faustus 1.1* by Christopher Marlowe)

black cap NOUN a judge wore a black cap when he was about to sentence a prisoner to death ❑ *The judge assumed the black cap, and the prisoner still stood with the same air and gesture.* (*Oliver Twist* by Charles Dickens)

boot-jack NOUN a wooden device to help take boots off ❑ *The speaker appeared to throw a boot-jack, or some such article, at the person he addressed* (*Oliver Twist* by Charles Dickens)

booty NOUN booty means treasure or prizes ❑ *would be inclined to give up their booty in payment of the dead man's debts* (*Treasure Island* by Robert Louis Stevenson)

Bow Street runner PHRASE Bow Street runners were the first British police force, set up by the author Henry Fielding in the eighteenth century ❑ *as would have convinced a judge or a Bow Street runner* (*Treasure Island* by Robert Louis Stevenson)

brawn NOUN brawn is a dish of meat which is set in jelly ❑ *Heaped up upon the floor, to form a kind of throne, were turkeys, geese, game, poultry, brawn, great joints of meat, suckling-pigs* (*A Christmas Carol* by Charles Dickens)

bray VERB when a donkey brays, it makes a loud, harsh sound ❑ *and she doesn't bray like a jackass* (*The Adventures of Huckleberry Finn* by Mark Twain)

break VERB in order to train a horse you first have to break it ❑ *'If a high-mettled creature like this,' said he, 'can't be broken by fair means, she will never be good for anything'* (*Black Beauty* by Anna Sewell)

bullyragging VERB bullyragging is an old word which means bullying. To bullyrag someone is to threaten or force someone to do something they don't want to do ❑ *and a lot of loafers bullyragging him for sport* (*The Adventures of Huckleberry Finn* by Mark Twain)

but PREP except for (this) ❑ *but this, all pleasures fancies be* (*The Good-Morrow* by John Donne)

by hand PHRASE by hand was a common expression of the time meaning that baby had been fed either using a spoon or a bottle rather than by breast-feeding ❑ *My sister, Mrs. Joe Gargery, was more than twenty years older than I, and had established a great reputation with herself . . . because she had bought me up 'by hand'* (*Great Expectations* by Charles Dickens)

bye-spots NOUN bye-spots are lonely places ❑ *and bye-spots of tales rich with indigenous produce* (*The Prelude* by William Wordsworth)

calico NOUN calico is plain white fabric made from cotton ❑ *There was two old dirty calico dresses* (*The Adventures of Huckleberry Finn* by Mark Twain)

camp-fever NOUN camp-fever was another word for the disease typhus ❑ *during a severe camp-fever* (*Emma* by Jane Austen)

cant NOUN cant is insincere or empty talk ❑ *'Man,' said the Ghost, 'if man you be in heart, not adamant, forbear that wicked cant until you have discovered What the surplus is, and Where it is.'* (*A Christmas Carol* by Charles Dickens)

canty ADJ canty means lively, full of life ❑ *My mother lived til eighty, a canty dame to the last* (*Wuthering Heights* by Emily Brontë)

canvas VERB to canvas is to discuss ❑ *We think so very differently on this point Mr Knightley, that there can be no use in canvassing it* (*Emma* by Jane Austen)

capital ADJ capital means excellent or extremely good ❑ *for it's capital, so shady, light, and big* (*Little Women* by Louisa May Alcott)

capstan NOUN a capstan is a device used on a ship to lift sails and anchors ❑ *capstans going, ships going out to sea, and unintelligible sea creatures roaring curses over the* *bulwarks at respondent lightermen* (*Great Expectations* by Charles Dickens)

case-bottle NOUN a square bottle designed to fit with others into a case ❑ *The spirit being set before him in a huge case-bottle, which had originally come out of some ship's locker* (*The Old Curiosity Shop* by Charles Dickens)

casement NOUN casement is a word meaning window. The teacher in *Nicholas Nickleby* misspells window showing what a bad teacher he is ❑ *W-i-n, win, d-e-r, der, winder, a casement.* (*Nicholas Nickleby* by Charles Dickens)

cataleptic ADJ a cataleptic fit is one in which the victim goes into a trancelike state and remains still for a long time ❑ *It was at this point in their history that Silas's cataleptic fit occurred during the prayer-meeting* (*Silas Marner* by George Eliot)

cauldron NOUN a cauldron is a large cooking pot made of metal ❑ *stirring a large cauldron which seemed to be full of soup* (*Alice's Adventures in Wonderland* by Lewis Carroll)

cephalic ADJ cephalic means to do with the head ❑ *with ink composed of a cephalic tincture* (*Gulliver's Travels* by Jonathan Swift)

chaise and four NOUN a closed four-wheel carriage pulled by four horses ❑ *he came down on Monday in a chaise and four to see the place* (*Pride and Prejudice* by Jane Austen)

chamberlain NOUN the main servant in a household ❑ *In those times a bed was always to be got there at any hour of the night, and the chamberlain, letting me in at his ready wicket, lighted the candle next in order on his shelf* (*Great Expectations* by Charles Dickens)

characters NOUN distinguishing marks ❑ *Impressed upon all forms the characters* (*The Prelude* by William Wordsworth)

chary ADJ cautious ❑ *I should have been chary of discussing my guardian too freely even with her* (*Great Expectations* by Charles Dickens)

cherishes VERB here cherishes means cheers or brightens ❑ *some philosophic song of Truth that cherishes our daily life* (*The Prelude* by William Wordsworth)

chickens' meat PHRASE chickens' meat is an old term which means chickens' feed or food ❑ *I had shook a bag of chickens' meat out in that place* (*Robinson Crusoe* by Daniel Defoe)

chimeras NOUN a chimera is an unrealistic idea or a wish which is unlikely to be fulfilled ❑ *with many other wild impossible chimeras* (*Gulliver's Travels* by Jonathan Swift)

chines NOUN chine is a cut of meat that includes part or all of the backbone of the animal ❑ *and they found hams and chines uncut* (*Silas Marner* by George Eliot)

chits NOUN chits is a slang word which means girls ❑ *I hate affected, niminy-piminy chits!* (*Little Women* by Louisa May Alcott)

chopped VERB chopped means come suddenly or accidentally ❑ *if I had chopped upon them* (*Robinson Crusoe* by Daniel Defoe)

chute NOUN a narrow channel ❑ *One morning about day-break, I found a canoe and crossed over a chute to the main shore* (*The Adventures of Huckleberry Finn* by Mark Twain)

circumspection NOUN careful observation of events and circumstances; caution ❑ *I honour your circumspection* (*Pride and Prejudice* by Jane Austen)

clambered VERB clambered means to climb somewhere with difficulty, usually using your hands and your feet ❑ *he clambered up and down stairs* (*Treasure Island* by Robert Louis Stevenson)

clime NOUN climate ❑ *no season knows nor clime* (*The Sun Rising* by John Donne)

clinched VERB clenched ❑ *the tops whereof I could but just reach with my fist clinched* (*Gulliver's Travels* by Jonathan Swift)

close chair NOUN a close chair is a sedan chair, which is an covered chair which has room for one person. The sedan chair is carried on two poles by two men, one in front and one behind ❑ *persuaded even the Empress herself to let me hold her in her close chair* (*Gulliver's Travels* by Jonathan Swift)

clown NOUN clown here means peasant or person who lives off the land ❑ *In ancient days by emperor and clown* (*Ode to a Nightingale* by John Keats)

coalheaver NOUN a coalheaver loaded coal onto ships using a spade ❑ *Good, strong, wholesome medicine, as was given with great success to two Irish labourers and a coalheaver* (*Oliver Twist* by Charles Dickens)

coal-whippers NOUN men who worked at docks using machines to load coal onto ships ❑ *here, were colliers by the score and score, with the coal-whippers plunging off stages on deck* (*Great Expectations* by Charles Dickens)

cobweb NOUN a cobweb is the net which a spider makes for catching insects ❑ *the walls and ceilings were all hung round with cobwebs* (*Gulliver's Travels* by Jonathan Swift)

coddling VERB coddling means to treat someone too kindly or protect them too much ❑ *and I've been coddling the fellow as if I'd been his grand-mother* (*Little Women* by Louisa May Alcott)

coil NOUN coil means noise or fuss or disturbance ❑ *What a coil is there?* (*Doctor Faustus 4.7* by Christopher Marlowe)

collared VERB to collar something is a slang term which means to capture.

In this sentence, it means he stole it [the money] ❑ *he collared it* (*The Adventures of Huckleberry Finn* by Mark Twain)

colling VERB colling is an old word which means to embrace and kiss ❑ *and no clasping and colling at all* (*Tess of the D'Urbervilles* by Thomas Hardy)

colloquies NOUN colloquy is a formal conversation or dialogue ❑ *Such colloquies have occupied many a pair of pale-faced weavers* (*Silas Marner* by George Eliot)

comfit NOUN sugar-covered pieces of fruit or nut eaten as sweets ❑ *and pulled out a box of comfits* (*Alice's Adventures in Wonderland* by Lewis Carroll)

coming out VERB when a girl came out in society it meant she was of marriageable age. In order to 'come out' girls were expecting to attend balls and other parties during a season ❑ *The younger girls formed hopes of coming out a year or two sooner than they might otherwise have done* (*Pride and Prejudice* by Jane Austen)

commit VERB commit means arrest or stop ❑ *Commit the rascals* (*Doctor Faustus 4.7* by Christopher Marlowe)

commodious ADJ commodious means convenient ❑ *the most commodious and effectual ways* (*Gulliver's Travels* by Jonathan Swift)

commons NOUN commons is an old term meaning food shared with others ❑ *his pauper assistants ranged themselves behind him; the gruel was served out; and a long grace was said over the short commons.* (*Oliver Twist* by Charles Dickens)

complacency NOUN here complacency means a desire to please others. To-day complacency means feeling pleased with oneself without good reason. ❑ *Twas thy power that raised the first complacency in me* (*The Prelude* by William Wordsworth)

complaisance NOUN complaisance was eagerness to please ❑ *we cannot wonder at his complaisance* (*Pride and Prejudice* by Jane Austen)

complaisant ADJ complaisant means polite ❑ *extremely cheerful and complaisant to their guest* (*Gulliver's Travels* by Jonathan Swift)

conning VERB conning means learning by heart ❑ *Or conning more* (*The Prelude* by William Wordsworth)

consequent NOUN consequence ❑ *as avarice is the necessary consequent of old age* (*Gulliver's Travels* by Jonathan Swift)

consorts NOUN concerts ❑ *The King, who delighted in music, had frequent consorts at Court* (*Gulliver's Travels* by Jonathan Swift)

conversible ADJ conversible meant easy to talk to, companionable ❑ *He can be a conversible companion* (*Pride and Prejudice* by Jane Austen)

copper NOUN a copper is a large pot that can be heated directly over a fire ❑ *He gazed in stupefied astonishment on the small rebel for some seconds, and then clung for support to the copper* (*Oliver Twist* by Charles Dickens)

copper-stick NOUN a copper-stick is the long piece of wood used to stir washing in the copper (or boiler) which was usually the biggest cooking pot in the house ❑ *It was Christmas Eve, and I had to stir the pudding for next day, with a copper-stick, from seven to eight by the Dutch clock* (*Great Expectations* by Charles Dickens)

counting-house NOUN a counting-house is a place where accountants work ❑ *Once upon a time–of all the good days in the year, on Christmas Eve–old Scrooge sat busy in his counting-house* (*A Christmas Carol* by Charles Dickens)

courtier NOUN a courtier is someone who attends the king or queen–a member of the court ❑ *next the ten courtiers;* (*Alice's Adventures in Wonderland* by Lewis Carroll)

covies NOUN covies were flocks of partridges ❑ *and will save all of the best covies for you* (*Pride and Prejudice* by Jane Austen)

cowed VERB cowed means frightened or intimidated ❑ *it cowed me more than the pain* (*Treasure Island* by Robert Louis Stevenson)

cozened VERB cozened means tricked or deceived ❑ *Do you remember, sir, how you cozened me* (*Doctor Faustus 4.7* by Christopher Marlowe)

cravats NOUN a cravat is a folded cloth that a man wears wrapped around his neck as a decorative item of clothing ❑ *we'd 'a' slept in our cravats to-night* (*The Adventures of Huckleberry Finn* by Mark Twain)

crock and dirt PHRASE crock and dirt is an old expression meaning soot and dirt ❑ *and the mare catching cold at the door, and the boy grimed with crock and dirt* (*Great Expectations* by Charles Dickens)

crockery NOUN here crockery means pottery ❑ *By one of the parrots was a cat made of crockery* (*The Adventures of Huckleberry Finn* by Mark Twain)

crooked sixpence PHRASE it was considered unlucky to have a bent sixpence ❑ *You've got the beauty, you see, and I've got the luck, so you must keep me by you for your crooked sixpence* (*Silas Marner* by George Eliot)

croquet NOUN croquet is a traditional English summer game in which players try to hit wooden balls through hoops ❑ *and once she remembered trying to box her own ears for having cheated herself in a game of croquet* (*Alice's Adventures in Wonderland* by Lewis Carroll)

cross PREP across ❑ *The two great streets, which run cross and divide it into four quarters* (*Gulliver's Travels* by Jonathan Swift)

culpable ADJ if you are culpable for something it means you are to blame ❑ *deep are the sorrows that spring from false ideas for which no man is culpable.* (*Silas Marner* by George Eliot)

cultured ADJ cultivated ❑ *Nor less when spring had warmed the cultured Vale* (*The Prelude* by William Wordsworth)

cupidity NOUN cupidity is greed ❑ *These people hated me with the hatred of cupidity and disappointment.* (*Great Expectations* by Charles Dickens)

curricle NOUN an open two-wheeled carriage with one seat for the driver and space for a single passenger ❑ *and they saw a lady and a gentleman in a curricle* (*Pride and Prejudice* by Jane Austen)

cynosure NOUN a cynosure is something that strongly attracts attention or admiration ❑ *Then I thought of Eliza and Georgiana; I beheld one the cynosure of a ballroom, the other the inmate of a convent cell* (*Jane Eyre* by Charlotte Brontë)

dalliance NOUN someone's dalliance with something is a brief involvement with it ❑ *nor sporting in the dalliance of love* (*Doctor Faustus Chorus* by Christopher Marlowe)

darkling ADV darkling is an archaic way of saying in the dark ❑ *Darkling I listen* (*Ode to a Nightingale* by John Keats)

delf-case NOUN a sideboard for holding dishes and crockery ❑ *at the pewter dishes and delf-case* (*Wuthering Heights* by Emily Brontë)

determined ■ VERB here determined means ended ❑ *and be out of vogue when that was determined* (*Gulliver's Travels* by Jonathan Swift) ■ VERB determined can mean to have been learned or found especially by investigation or experience ❑ *All the sensitive feelings it wounded so cruelly, all the shame and misery it kept alive within my breast, became more poignant as I thought of this; and I determined that the life was unendurable* (*David Copperfield* by Charles Dickens)

Deuce NOUN a slang term for the Devil ❑ *Ah, I dare say I did. Deuce take me, he added suddenly, I know I did. I find I am not quite unscrewed yet.* (*Great Expectations* by Charles Dickens)

diabolical ADJ diabolical means devilish or evil ❑ *and with a thousand diabolical expressions* (*Treasure Island* by Robert Louis Stevenson)

direction NOUN here direction means address ❑ *Elizabeth was not surprised at it, as Jane had written the direction remarkably ill* (*Pride and Prejudice* by Jane Austen)

discover VERB to make known or announce ❑ *the Emperor would discover the secret while I was out of his power* (*Gulliver's Travels* by Jonathan Swift)

dissemble VERB hide or conceal ❑ *Dissemble nothing* (*On His Mistress* by John Donne)

dissolve VERB dissolve here means to release from life, to die ❑ *Fade far away, dissolve, and quite forget* (*Ode to a Nightingale* by John Keats)

distrain VERB to distrain is to seize the property of someone who is in debt in compensation for the money owed ❑ *for he's threatening to distrain for it* (*Silas Marner* by George Eliot)

Divan NOUN a Divan was originally a Turkish council of state–the name was transferred to the couches they sat on and is used to mean this in English ❑ *Mr Brass applauded this picture very much, and the bed being soft and comfortable, Mr Quilp determined to use it, both as a sleeping place by night and as a kind of Divan by day.* (*The Old Curiosity Shop* by Charles Dickens)

divorcement NOUN separation ❑ *By all pains which want and divorcement* *hath* (*On His Mistress* by John Donne)

dog in the manger, PHRASE this phrase describes someone who prevents you from enjoying something that they themselves have no need for ❑ *You are a dog in the manger, Cathy, and desire no one to be loved but yourself* (*Wuthering Heights* by Emily Brontë)

dolorifuge NOUN dolorifuge is a word which Thomas Hardy invented. It means pain-killer or comfort ❑ *as a species of dolorifuge* (*Tess of the D'Urbervilles* by Thomas Hardy)

dome NOUN building ❑ *that river and that mouldering dome* (*The Prelude* by William Wordsworth)

domestic NOUN here domestic means a person's management of the house ❑ *to give some account of my domestic* (*Gulliver's Travels* by Jonathan Swift)

dunce NOUN a dunce is another word for idiot ❑ *Do you take me for a dunce? Go on?* (*Alice's Adventures in Wonderland* by Lewis Carroll)

Ecod EXCLAM a slang exclamation meaning 'oh God!' ❑ *'Ecod,' replied Wemmick, shaking his head, 'that's not my trade.'* (*Great Expectations* by Charles Dickens)

egg-hot NOUN an egg-hot (see also 'flip' and 'negus') was a hot drink made from beer and eggs, sweetened with nutmeg ❑ *She fainted when she saw me return, and made a little jug of egg-hot afterwards to console us while we talked it over.* (*David Copperfield* by Charles Dickens)

encores NOUN an encore is a short extra performance at the end of a longer one, which the entertainer gives because the audience has enthusiastically asked for it ❑ *we want a little something to answer encores with, anyway* (*The Adventures of Huckleberry Finn* by Mark Twain)

equipage NOUN an elegant and impressive carriage ❑ *and besides, the equipage did not answer to any of*

their neighbours (*Pride and Prejudice* by Jane Austen)

exordium NOUN an exordium is the opening part of a speech ❑ *'Now, Handel,' as if it were the grave beginning of a portentous business exordium, he had suddenly given up that tone* (*Great Expectations* by Charles Dickens)

expect VERB here expect means to wait for ❑ *to expect his farther commands* (*Gulliver's Travels* by Jonathan Swift)

familiars NOUN familiars means spirits or devils who come to someone when they are called ❑ *I'll turn all the lice about thee into familiars* (*Doctor Faustus 1.4* by Christopher Marlowe)

fantods NOUN a fantod is a person who fidgets or can't stop moving nervously ❑ *It most give me the fantods* (*The Adventures of Huckleberry Finn* by Mark Twain)

farthing NOUN a farthing is an old unit of British currency which was worth a quarter of a penny ❑ *Not a farthing less. A great many back-payments are included in it, I assure you.* (*A Christmas Carol* by Charles Dickens)

farthingale NOUN a hoop worn under a skirt to extend it ❑ *A bell with an old voice–which I dare say in its time had often said to the house, Here is the green farthingale* (*Great Expectations* by Charles Dickens)

favours NOUN here favours is an old word which means ribbons ❑ *A group of humble mourners entered the gate: wearing white favours* (*Oliver Twist* by Charles Dickens)

feigned VERB pretend or pretending ❑ *not my feigned page* (*On His Mistress* by John Donne)

fence ■ NOUN a fence is someone who receives and sells stolen goods ❑ *What are you up to? Ill-treating the boys, you covetous, avaricious, in-sa-ti-a-ble old fence?* (*Oliver Twist* by

Charles Dickens) ■ NOUN defence or protection ❑ *but honesty hath no fence against superior cunning* (Gulliver's Travels by Jonathan Swift)

fess ADJ fess is an old word which means pleased or proud ❑ *You'll be fess enough, my poppet* (Tess of the D'Urbervilles by Thomas Hardy)

fettered ADJ fettered means bound in chains or chained ❑ *'You are fettered,' said Scrooge, trembling. 'Tell me why?'* (A Christmas Carol by Charles Dickens)

fidges VERB fidges means fidgets, which is to keep moving your hands slightly because you are nervous or excited ❑ *Look, Jim, how my fingers fidges* (Treasure Island by Robert Louis Stevenson)

finger-post NOUN a finger-post is a sign-post showing the direction to different places ❑ *'The gallows,' continued Fagin, 'the gallows, my dear, is an ugly finger-post, which points out a very short and sharp turning that has stopped many a bold fellow's career on the broad highway.'* (Oliver Twist by Charles Dickens)

fire-irons NOUN fire-irons are tools kept by the side of a fire to either cook with or look after the fire ❑ *the fire-irons came first* (Alice's Adventures in Wonderland by Lewis Carroll)

fire-plug NOUN a fire-plug is another word for a fire hydrant ❑ *The pony looked with great attention into a fire-plug, which was near him, and appeared to be quite absorbed in contemplating it* (The Old Curiosity Shop by Charles Dickens)

flank NOUN flank is the side of an animal ❑ *And all her silken flanks with garlands dressed* (Ode on a Grecian Urn by John Keats)

flip NOUN a flip is a drink made from warmed ale, sugar, spice and beaten egg ❑ *The events of the day, in combination with the twins, if not with the flip, had made Mrs Micawber hysterical, and she shed tears as she replied* (David Copperfield by Charles Dickens)

flit VERB flit means to move quickly ❑ *and if he had meant to flit to Thrushcross Grange* (Wuthering Heights by Emily Brontë)

floorcloth NOUN a floorcloth was a hard-wearing piece of canvas used instead of carpet ❑ *This avenging phantom was ordered to be on duty at eight on Tuesday morning in the hall (it was two feet square, as charged for floorcloth)* (Great Expectations by Charles Dickens)

fly-driver NOUN a fly-driver is a carriage drawn by a single horse ❑ *The fly-drivers, among whom I inquired next, were equally jocose and equally disrespectful* (David Copperfield by Charles Dickens)

fob NOUN a small pocket in which a watch is kept ❑ *'Certain,' replied the man, drawing a gold watch from his fob* (Oliver Twist by Charles Dickens)

folly NOUN folly means foolishness or stupidity ❑ *the folly of beginning a work* (Robinson Crusoe by Daniel Defoe)

fond ADJ fond means foolish ❑ *Fond worldling* (Doctor Faustus 5.2 by Christopher Marlowe)

fondness NOUN silly or foolish affection ❑ *They have no fondness for their colts or foals* (Gulliver's Travels by Jonathan Swift)

for his fancy PHRASE for his fancy means for his liking or as he wanted ❑ *and as I did not obey quick enough for his fancy* (Treasure Island by Robert Louis Stevenson)

forlorn ADJ lost or very upset ❑ *you are from that day forlorn* (Gulliver's Travels by Jonathan Swift)

foster-sister NOUN a foster-sister was someone brought up by the same nurse or in the same household ❑ *I had been his foster-sister* (Wuthering Heights by Emily Brontë)

fox-fire NOUN fox-fire is a weak glow that is given off by decaying, rotten wood ❑ *what we must have was a lot of them rotten chunks that's called fox-fire* (*The Adventures of Huckleberry Finn* by Mark Twain)

frozen sea PHRASE the Arctic Ocean ❑ *into the frozen sea* (*Gulliver's Travels* by Jonathan Swift)

gainsay VERB to gainsay something is to say it isn't true or to deny it ❑ *'So she had,' cried Scrooge. 'You're right. I'll not gainsay it, Spirit. God forbid!'* (*A Christmas Carol* by Charles Dickens)

gaiters NOUN gaiters were leggings made of a cloth or piece of leather which covered the leg from the knee to the ankle ❑ *Mr Knightley was hard at work upon the lower buttons of his thick leather gaiters* (*Emma* by Jane Austen)

galluses NOUN galluses is an old spelling of gallows, and here means suspenders. Suspenders are straps worn over someone's shoulders and fastened to their trousers to prevent the trousers falling down ❑ *and home-knit galluses* (*The Adventures of Huckleberry Finn* by Mark Twain)

galoot NOUN a sailor but also a clumsy person ❑ *and maybe a galoot on it chopping* (*The Adventures of Huckleberry Finn* by Mark Twain)

gayest ADJ gayest means the most lively and bright or merry ❑ *Beth played her gayest march* (*Little Women* by Louisa May Alcott)

gem NOUN here gem means jewellery ❑ *the mountain shook off turf and flower, had only heath for raiment and crag for gem* (*Jane Eyre* by Charlotte Brontë)

giddy ADJ giddy means dizzy ❑ *and I wish you wouldn't keep appearing and vanishing so suddenly; you make one quite giddy.* (*Alice's Adventures in Wonderland* by Lewis Carroll)

gig NOUN a light two-wheeled carriage ❑ *when a gig drove up to the garden gate: out of which there jumped a fat gentleman* (*Oliver Twist* by Charles Dickens)

gladsome ADJ gladsome is an old word meaning glad or happy ❑ *Nobody ever stopped him in the street to say, with gladsome looks* (*A Christmas Carol* by Charles Dickens)

glen NOUN a glen is a small valley; the word is used commonly in Scotland ❑ *a beck which follows the bend of the glen* (*Wuthering Heights* by Emily Brontë)

gravelled VERB gravelled is an old term which means to baffle or defeat someone ❑ *Gravelled the pastors of the German Church* (*Doctor Faustus 1.1* by Christopher Marlowe)

grinder NOUN a grinder was a private tutor ❑ *but that when he had had the happiness of marrying Mrs Pocket very early in his life, he had impaired his prospects and taken up the calling of a Grinder* (*Great Expectations* by Charles Dickens)

gruel NOUN gruel is a thin, watery cornmeal or oatmeal soup ❑ *and the little saucepan of gruel (Scrooge had a cold in his head) upon the hob.* (*A Christmas Carol* by Charles Dickens)

guinea, half a NOUN half a guinea was ten shillings and sixpence ❑ *but lay out half a guinea at Ford's* (*Emma* by Jane Austen)

gull VERB gull is an old term which means to fool or deceive someone ❑ *Hush, I'll gull him supernaturally* (*Doctor Faustus 3.4* by Christopher Marlowe)

gunnel NOUN the gunnel, or gunwale, is the upper edge of a boat's side ❑ *But he put his foot on the gunnel and rocked her* (*The Adventures of Huckleberry Finn* by Mark Twain)

gunwale NOUN the side of a ship ❑ *He dipped his hand in the water over the boat's gunwale* (*Great Expectations* by Charles Dickens)

Gytrash NOUN a Gytrash is an omen of misfortune to the superstitious, usually taking the form of a hound ❑ *I remembered certain of Bessie's tales, wherein figured a North-of-England spirit, called a 'Gytrash'* (*Jane Eyre* by Charlotte Brontë)

hackney-cabriolet NOUN a two-wheeled carriage with four seats for hire and pulled by a horse ❑ *A hackney-cabriolet was in waiting; with the same vehemence which she had exhibited in addressing Oliver, the girl pulled him in with her, and drew the curtains close.* (*Oliver Twist* by Charles Dickens)

hackney-coach NOUN a four-wheeled horse-drawn vehicle for hire ❑ *The twilight was beginning to close in, when Mr Brownlow alighted from a hackney-coach at his own door, and knocked softly.* (*Oliver Twist* by Charles Dickens)

haggler NOUN a haggler is someone who travels from place to place selling small goods and items ❑ *when I be plain Jack Durbeyfield, the haggler* (*Tess of the D'Urbervilles* by Thomas Hardy)

halter NOUN a halter is a rope or strap used to lead an animal or to tie it up ❑ *I had of course long been used to a halter and a headstall* (*Black Beauty* by Anna Sewell)

hamlet NOUN a hamlet is a small village or a group of houses in the countryside ❑ *down from the hamlet* (*Treasure Island* by Robert Louis Stevenson)

hand-barrow NOUN a hand-barrow is a device for carrying heavy objects. It is like a wheelbarrow except that it has handles, rather than wheels, for moving the barrow ❑ *his sea chest following behind him in a hand-barrow* (*Treasure Island* by Robert Louis Stevenson)

handspike NOUN a handspike was a stick which was used as a lever ❑ *a bit of stick like a handspike* (*Treasure Island* by Robert Louis Stevenson)

haply ADV haply means by chance or perhaps ❑ *And haply the Queen-Moon is on her throne* (*Ode to a Nightingale* by John Keats)

harem NOUN the harem was the part of the house where the women lived ❑ *mostly they hang round the harem* (*The Adventures of Huckleberry Finn* by Mark Twain)

hautboys NOUN hautboys are oboes ❑ *sausages and puddings resembling flutes and hautboys* (*Gulliver's Travels* by Jonathan Swift)

hawker NOUN a hawker is someone who sells goods to people as he travels rather than from a fixed place like a shop ❑ *to buy some stockings from a hawker* (*Treasure Island* by Robert Louis Stevenson)

hawser NOUN a hawser is a rope used to tie up or tow a ship or boat ❑ *Again among the tiers of shipping, in and out, avoiding rusty chain-cables, frayed hempen hawsers* (*Great Expectations* by Charles Dickens)

headstall NOUN the headstall is the part of the bridle or halter that goes around a horse's head ❑ *I had of course long been used to a halter and a headstall* (*Black Beauty* by Anna Sewell)

hearken VERB hearken means to listen ❑ *though we sometimes stopped to lay hold of each other and hearken* (*Treasure Island* by Robert Louis Stevenson)

heartless ADJ here heartless means without heart or dejected ❑ *I am not heartless* (*The Prelude* by William Wordsworth)

hebdomadal ADJ hebdomadal means weekly ❑ *It was the hebdomadal treat to which we all looked forward from Sabbath to Sabbath* (*Jane Eyre* by Charlotte Brontë)

highwaymen NOUN highwaymen were people who stopped travellers and robbed them ❑ *We are high-waymen* (*The Adventures of Huckleberry Finn* by Mark Twain)

hinds NOUN hinds means farm hands, or people who work on a farm ❏ *He called his hinds about him* (*Gulliver's Travels* by Jonathan Swift)

histrionic ADJ if you refer to someone's behaviour as histrionic, you are being critical of it because it is dramatic and exaggerated ❏ *But the histrionic muse is the darling* (*The Adventures of Huckleberry Finn* by Mark Twain)

hogs NOUN hogs is another word for pigs ❏ *Tom called the hogs 'ingots'* (*The Adventures of Huckleberry Finn* by Mark Twain)

horrors NOUN the horrors are a fit, called delirium tremens, which is caused by drinking too much alcohol ❏ *I'll have the horrors* (*Treasure Island* by Robert Louis Stevenson)

huffy ADJ huffy means to be obviously annoyed or offended about something ❏ *They will feel that more than angry speeches or huffy actions* (*Little Women* by Louisa May Alcott)

hulks NOUN hulks were prison-ships ❏ *The miserable companion of thieves and ruffians, the fallen outcast of low haunts, the associate of the scourings of the jails and hulks* (*Oliver Twist* by Charles Dickens)

humbug NOUN humbug means nonsense or rubbish ❏ *'Bah,' said Scrooge. 'Humbug!'* (*A Christmas Carol* by Charles Dickens)

humours NOUN it was believed that there were four fluids in the body called humours which decided the temperament of a person depending on how much of each fluid was present ❏ *other peccant humours* (*Gulliver's Travels* by Jonathan Swift)

husbandry NOUN husbandry is farming animals ❏ *bad husbandry were plentifully anointing their wheels* (*Silas Marner* by George Eliot)

huswife NOUN a huswife was a small sewing kit ❏ *but I had put my huswife on it* (*Emma* by Jane Austen)

ideal ADJ ideal in this context means imaginary ❏ *I discovered the yell was not ideal* (*Wuthering Heights* by Emily Brontë)

If our two PHRASE if both our ❏ *If our two loves be one* (*The Good-Morrow* by John Donne)

ignis-fatuus NOUN ignis-fatuus is the light given out by burning marsh gases, which lead careless travellers into danger ❏ *it is madness in all women to let a secret love kindle within them, which, if unreturned and unknown, must devour the life that feeds it; and, if discovered and responded to, must lead ignis-fatuus-like, into miry wilds whence there is no extrication.* (*Jane Eyre* by Charlotte Brontë)

imaginations NOUN here imaginations means schemes or plans ❏ *soon drove out those imaginations* (*Gulliver's Travels* by Jonathan Swift)

impressible ADJ impressible means open or impressionable ❏ *for Marner had one of those impressible, self-doubting natures* (*Silas Marner* by George Eliot)

in good intelligence PHRASE friendly with each other ❏ *that these two persons were in good intelligence with each other* (*Gulliver's Travels* by Jonathan Swift)

inanity NOUN inanity is silliness or dull stupidity ❏ *Do we not wile away moments of inanity* (*Silas Marner* by George Eliot)

incivility NOUN incivility means rudeness or impoliteness ❏ *if it's only for a piece of incivility like to-night's* (*Treasure Island* by Robert Louis Stevenson)

indigenae NOUN indigenae means natives or people from that area ❏ *an exotic that the surly indigenae will not recognise for kin* (*Wuthering Heights* by Emily Brontë)

indocible ADJ unteachable ❏ *so they were the most restive and indocible* (*Gulliver's Travels* by Jonathan Swift)

ingenuity NOUN inventiveness ❑ *entreated me to give him something as an encouragement to ingenuity* (*Gulliver's Travels* by Jonathan Swift)

ingots NOUN an ingot is a lump of a valuable metal like gold, usually shaped like a brick ❑ *Tom called the hogs 'ingots'* (*The Adventures of Huckleberry Finn* by Mark Twain)

inkstand NOUN an inkstand is a pot which was put on a desk to contain either ink or pencils and pens ❑ *throwing an inkstand at the Lizard as she spoke* (*Alice's Adventures in Wonderland* by Lewis Carroll)

inordinate ADJ without order. To-day inordinate means 'excessive'. ❑ *Though yet untutored and inordinate* (*The Prelude* by William Wordsworth)

intellectuals NOUN here intellectuals means the minds (of the workmen) ❑ *those instructions they give being too refined for the intellectuals of their workmen* (*Gulliver's Travels* by Jonathan Swift)

interview NOUN meeting ❑ *By our first strange and fatal interview* (*On His Mistress* by John Donne)

jacks NOUN jacks are rods for turning a spit over a fire ❑ *It was a small bit of pork suspended from the kettle hanger by a string passed through a large door key, in a way known to primitive housekeepers unpossessed of jacks* (*Silas Marner* by George Eliot)

jews-harp NOUN a jews-harp is a small, metal, musical instrument that is played by the mouth ❑ *A jews-harp's plenty good enough for a rat* (*The Adventures of Huckleberry Finn* by Mark Twain)

jorum NOUN a large bowl ❑ *while Miss Skiffins brewed such a jorum of tea, that the pig in the back premises became strongly excited* (*Great Expectations* by Charles Dickens)

jostled VERB jostled means bumped or pushed by someone or some people

❑ *being jostled himself into the kennel* (*Gulliver's Travels* by Jonathan Swift)

keepsake NOUN a keepsake is a gift which reminds someone of an event or of the person who gave it to them. ❑ *books and ornaments they had in their boudoirs at home: keepsakes that different relations had presented to them* (*Jane Eyre* by Charlotte Brontë)

kenned VERB kenned means knew ❑ *though little kenned the lamplighter that he had any company but Christmas!* (*A Christmas Carol* by Charles Dickens)

kennel NOUN kennel means gutter, which is the edge of a road next to the pavement, where rain water collects and flows away ❑ *being jostled himself into the kennel* (*Gulliver's Travels* by Jonathan Swift)

knock-knee ADJ knock-knee means slanted, at an angle. ❑ *LOT 1 was marked in whitewashed knock-knee letters on the brewhouse* (*Great Expectations* by Charles Dickens)

ladylike ADJ to be ladylike is to behave in a polite, dignified and graceful way ❑ *No, winking isn't ladylike* (*Little Women* by Louisa May Alcott)

lapse NOUN flow ❑ *Stealing with silent lapse to join the brook* (*The Prelude* by William Wordsworth)

larry NOUN larry is an old word which means commotion or noisy celebration ❑ *That was all a part of the larry!* (*Tess of the D'Urbervilles* by Thomas Hardy)

laths NOUN laths are strips of wood ❑ *The panels shrunk, the windows cracked; fragments of plaster fell out of the ceiling, and the naked laths were shown instead* (*A Christmas Carol* by Charles Dickens)

leer NOUN a leer is an unpleasant smile ❑ *with a kind of leer* (*Treasure Island* by Robert Louis Stevenson)

lenitives NOUN these are different kinds of drugs or medicines: lenitives and palliatives were pain relievers; aperitives were laxatives; abstersives caused vomiting; corrosives destroyed human tissue; restringents caused constipation; cephalalgics stopped headaches; icterics were used as medicine for jaundice; apophlegmatics were cough medicine, and acoustics were cures for the loss of hearing ❑ *lenitives, aperitives, abstersives, corrosives, restringents, palliatives, laxatives, cephalalgics, icterics, apophlegmatics, acoustics (Gulliver's Travels* by Jonathan Swift)

lest CONJ in case. If you do something lest something (usually) unpleasant happens you do it to try to prevent it happening ❑ *She went in without knocking, and hurried upstairs, in great fear lest she should meet the real Mary Ann (Alice's Adventures in Wonderland* by Lewis Carroll)

levee NOUN a levee is an old term for a meeting held in the morning, shortly after the person holding the meeting has got out of bed ❑ *I used to attend the King's levee once or twice a week (Gulliver's Travels* by Jonathan Swift)

life-preserver NOUN a club which had lead inside it to make it heavier and therefore more dangerous ❑ *and with no more suspicious articles displayed to view than two or three heavy bludgeons which stood in a corner, and a 'life-preserver' that hung over the chimney-piece. (Oliver Twist* by Charles Dickens)

lighterman NOUN a lighterman is another word for sailor ❑ *in and out, hammers going in ship-builders' yards, saws going at timber, clashing engines going at things unknown, pumps going in leaky ships, capstans going, ships going out to sea, and unintelligible sea creatures roaring curses over the bulwarks at respondent lightermen (Great Expectations* by Charles Dickens)

livery NOUN servants often wore a uniform known as a livery ❑ *suddenly a footman in livery came running out of the wood (Alice's Adventures in Wonderland* by Lewis Carroll)

livid ADJ livid means pale or ash coloured. Livid also means very angry ❑ *a dirty, livid white (Treasure Island* by Robert Louis Stevenson)

lottery-tickets NOUN a popular card game ❑ *and Mrs Philips protested that they would have a nice comfortable noisy game of lottery tickets (Pride and Prejudice* by Jane Austen)

lower and upper world PHRASE the earth and the heavens are the lower and upper worlds ❑ *the changes in the lower and upper world (Gulliver's Travels* by Jonathan Swift)

lustres NOUN lustres are chandeliers. A chandelier is a large, decorative frame which holds light bulbs or candles and hangs from the ceiling ❑ *the lustres, lights, the carving and the guilding (The Prelude* by William Wordsworth)

lynched VERB killed without a criminal trial by a crowd of people ❑ *He'll never know how nigh he come to getting lynched (The Adventures of Huckleberry Finn* by Mark Twain)

malingering VERB if someone is malingering they are pretending to be ill to avoid working ❑ *And you stand there malingering (Treasure Island* by Robert Louis Stevenson)

managing PHRASE treating with consideration ❑ *to think the honour of my own kind not worth managing (Gulliver's Travels* by Jonathan Swift)

manhood PHRASE manhood means human nature ❑ *concerning the nature of manhood (Gulliver's Travels* by Jonathan Swift)

man-trap NOUN a man-trap is a set of steel jaws that snap shut when trodden on and trap a person's leg

❑ *'Don't go to him,' I called out of the window, 'he's an assassin! A man-trap!'* (*Oliver Twist* by Charles Dickens)

maps NOUN charts of the night sky ❑ *Let maps to others, worlds on worlds have shown* (*The Good-Morrow* by John Donne)

mark VERB look at or notice ❑ *Mark but this flea, and mark in this* (*The Flea* by John Donne)

maroons NOUN A maroon is someone who has been left in a place which it is difficult for them to escape from, like a small island ❑ *if schooners, islands, and maroons* (*Treasure Island* by Robert Louis Stevenson)

mast NOUN here mast means the fruit of forest trees ❑ *a quantity of acorns, dates, chestnuts, and other mast* (*Gulliver's Travels* by Jonathan Swift)

mate VERB defeat ❑ *Where Mars did mate the warlike Carthigens* (*Doctor Faustus Chorus* by Christopher Marlowe)

mealy ADJ Mealy when used to describe a face meant pallid, pale or colourless ❑ *I only know two sorts of boys. Mealy boys, and beef-faced boys* (*Oliver Twist* by Charles Dickens)

middling ADV fairly or moderately ❑ *I she worked me middling hard for about an hour* (*The Adventures of Huckleberry Finn* by Mark Twain)

mill NOUN a mill, or treadmill, was a device for hard labour or punishment in prison ❑ *Was you never on the mill?* (*Oliver Twist* by Charles Dickens)

milliner's shop NOUN a milliner's sold fabrics, clothing, lace and accessories; as time went on they specialized more and more in hats ❑ *to pay their duty to their aunt and to a milliner's shop just over the way* (*Pride and Prejudice* by Jane Austen)

minching un' munching PHRASE how people in the north of England used to describe the way people from the south speak ❑ *Minching un' munching!* (*Wuthering Heights* by Emily Brontë)

mine NOUN gold ❑ *Whether both th'Indias of spice and mine* (*The Sun Rising* by John Donne)

mire NOUN mud ❑ *Tis my fate to be always ground into the mire under the iron heel of oppression* (*The Adventures of Huckleberry Finn* by Mark Twain)

miscellany NOUN a miscellany is a collection of many different kinds of things ❑ *under that, the miscellany began* (*Treasure Island* by Robert Louis Stevenson)

mistarshers NOUN mistarshers means moustache, which is the hair that grows on a man's upper lip ❑ *when he put his hand up to his mistarshers* (*Tess of the D'Urbervilles* by Thomas Hardy)

morrow NOUN here good-morrow means tomorrow and a new and better life ❑ *And now good-morrow to our waking souls* (*The Good-Morrow* by John Donne)

mortification NOUN mortification is an old word for gangrene which is when part of the body decays or 'dies' because of disease ❑ *Yes, it was a mortification–that was it* (*The Adventures of Huckleberry Finn* by Mark Twain)

mought VERB mought is an old spelling of might ❑ *what you mought call me? You mought call me captain* (*Treasure Island* by Robert Louis Stevenson)

move VERB move me not means do not make me angry ❑ *Move me not, Faustus* (*Doctor Faustus 2.1* by Christopher Marlowe)

muffin-cap NOUN a muffin-cap is a flat cap made from wool ❑ *the old one, remained stationary in the muffin-cap and leathers* (*Oliver Twist* by Charles Dickens)

mulatter NOUN a mulatter was another word for mulatto, which is a person with parents who are from different races ❏ *a mulatter, most as white as a white man* (*The Adventures of Huckleberry Finn* by Mark Twain)

mummery NOUN mummery is an old word that meant meaningless (or pretentious) ceremony ❏ *When they were all gone, and when Trabb and his men–but not his boy: I looked for him–had crammed their mummery into bags, and were gone too, the house felt wholesomer.* (*Great Expectations* by Charles Dickens)

nap NOUN the nap is the woolly surface on a new item of clothing. Here the surface has been worn away so it looks bare ❏ *like an old hat with the nap rubbed off* (*The Adventures of Huckleberry Finn* by Mark Twain)

natural ◼ NOUN a natural is a person born with learning difficulties ❏ *though he had been left to his particular care by their deceased father, who thought him almost a natural.* (*David Copperfield* by Charles Dickens) ◼ ADJ natural meant illegitimate ❏ *Harriet Smith was the natural daughter of somebody* (*Emma* by Jane Austen)

navigator NOUN a navigator was originally someone employed to dig canals. It is the origin of the word 'navvy' meaning a labourer ❏ *She ascertained from me in a few words what it was all about, comforted Dora, and gradually convinced her that I was not a labourer–from my manner of stating the case I believe Dora concluded that I was a navigator, and went balancing myself up and down a plank all day with a wheelbarrow–and so brought us together in peace.* (*David Copperfield* by Charles Dickens)

necromancy NOUN necromancy means a kind of magic where the magician speaks to spirits or ghosts to find out what will happen in the future ❏ *He surfeits upon cursed necromancy* (*Doctor Faustus chorus* by Christopher Marlowe)

negus NOUN a negus is a hot drink made from sweetened wine and water ❏ *He sat placidly perusing the newspaper, with his little head on one side, and a glass of warm sherry negus at his elbow.* (*David Copperfield* by Charles Dickens)

nice ADJ discriminating. Able to make good judgements or choices ❏ *consequently a claim to be nice* (*Emma* by Jane Austen)

nigh ADV nigh means near ❏ *He'll never know how nigh he come to getting lynched* (*The Adventures of Huckleberry Finn* by Mark Twain)

nimbleness NOUN nimbleness means being able to move very quickly or skilfully ❏ *and with incredible accuracy and nimbleness* (*Treasure Island* by Robert Louis Stevenson)

noggin NOUN a noggin is a small mug or a wooden cup ❏ *you'll bring me one noggin of rum* (*Treasure Island* by Robert Louis Stevenson)

none ADJ neither ❏ *none can die* (*The Good-Morrow* by John Donne)

notices NOUN observations ❏ *Arch are his notices* (*The Prelude* by William Wordsworth)

occiput NOUN occiput means the back of the head ❏ *saw off the occiput of each couple* (*Gulliver's Travels* by Jonathan Swift)

officiously ADV kindly ❏ *the governess who attended Glumdalclitch very officiously lifted me up* (*Gulliver's Travels* by Jonathan Swift)

old salt PHRASE old salt is a slang term for an experienced sailor ❏ *a 'true sea-dog', and a 'real old salt'* (*Treasure Island* by Robert Louis Stevenson)

or ere PHRASE before ❏ *or ere the Hall was built* (*The Prelude* by William Wordsworth)

ostler NOUN one who looks after horses at an inn ❏ *The bill paid, and the waiter remembered, and the ostler not forgotten, and the chambermaid taken into consideration* (*Great Expectations* by Charles Dickens)

ostry NOUN an ostry is an old word for a pub or hotel ❑ *lest I send you into the ostry with a vengeance* (*Doctor Faustus 2.2* by Christopher Marlowe)

outrunning the constable PHRASE outrunning the constable meant spending more than you earn ❑ *but I shall by this means be able to check your bills and to pull you up if I find you outrunning the constable.* (*Great Expectations* by Charles Dickens)

over ADV across ❑ *It is in length six yards, and in the thickest part at least three yards over* (*Gulliver's Travels* by Jonathan Swift)

over the broomstick PHRASE this is a phrase meaning 'getting married without a formal ceremony' ❑ *They both led tramping lives, and this woman in Gerrard-street here, had been married very young, over the broomstick (as we say), to a tramping man, and was a perfect fury in point of jealousy.* (*Great Expectations* by Charles Dickens)

own VERB own means to admit or to acknowledge ❑ *It's my old girl that advises. She has the head. But I never own to it before her. Discipline must be maintained* (*Bleak House* by Charles Dickens)

page NOUN here page means a boy employed to run errands ❑ *not my feigned page* (*On His Mistress* by John Donne)

paid pretty dear PHRASE paid pretty dear means paid a high price or suffered quite a lot ❑ *I paid pretty dear for my monthly fourpenny piece* (*Treasure Island* by Robert Louis Stevenson)

pannikins NOUN pannikins were small tin cups ❑ *of lifting light glasses and cups to his lips, as if they were clumsy pannikins* (*Great Expectations* by Charles Dickens)

pards NOUN pards are leopards ❑ *Not charioted by Bacchus and his pards* (*Ode to a Nightingale* by John Keats)

parlour boarder NOUN a pupil who lived with the family ❑ *and somebody had lately raised her from the condition of scholar to parlour boarder* (*Emma* by Jane Austen)

particular, a London PHRASE London in Victorian times and up to the 1950s was famous for having very dense fog–which was a combination of real fog and the smog of pollution from factories ❑ *This is a London particular . . . A fog, miss* (*Bleak House* by Charles Dickens)

patten NOUN pattens were wooden soles which were fixed to shoes by straps to protect the shoes in wet weather ❑ *carrying a basket like the Great Seal of England in plaited straw, a pair of pattens, a spare shawl, and an umbrella, though it was a fine bright day* (*Great Expectations* by Charles Dickens)

paviour NOUN a paviour was a labourer who worked on the street pavement ❑ *the paviour his pickaxe* (*Oliver Twist* by Charles Dickens)

peccant ADJ peccant means unhealthy ❑ *other peccant humours* (*Gulliver's Travels* by Jonathan Swift)

penetralium NOUN penetralium is a word used to describe the inner rooms of the house ❑ *and I had no desire to aggravate his impatience previous to inspecting the penetralium* (*Wuthering Heights* by Emily Brontë)

pensive ADV pensive means deep in thought or thinking seriously about something ❑ *and she was leaning pensive on a tomb-stone on her right elbow* (*The Adventures of Huckleberry Finn* by Mark Twain)

penury NOUN penury is the state of being extremely poor ❑ *Distress, if not penury, loomed in the distance* (*Tess of the D'Urbervilles* by Thomas Hardy)

perspective NOUN telescope ❑ *a pocket perspective* (*Gulliver's Travels* by Jonathan Swift)

phaeton NOUN a phaeton was an open carriage for four people ❑ *often* condescends to drive by my humble abode in her little phaeton and ponies (*Pride and Prejudice* by Jane Austen)

phantasm NOUN a phantasm is an illusion, something that is not real. It is sometimes used to mean ghost ❑ *Experience had bred no fancies in him that could raise the phantasm of appetite* (*Silas Marner* by George Eliot)

physic NOUN here physic means medicine ❑ *there I studied physic two years and seven months* (*Gulliver's Travels* by Jonathan Swift)

pinioned VERB to pinion is to hold both arms so that a person cannot move them ❑ *But the relentless Ghost pinioned him in both his arms, and forced him to observe what happened next.* (*A Christmas Carol* by Charles Dickens)

piquet NOUN piquet was a popular card game in the C18th ❑ *Mr Hurst and Mr Bingley were at piquet* (*Pride and Prejudice* by Jane Austen)

plaister NOUN a plaister is a piece of cloth on which an apothecary (or pharmacist) would spread ointment. The cloth is then applied to wounds or bruises to treat them ❑ *Then, she gave the knife a final smart wipe on the edge of the plaister, and then sawed a very thick round off the loaf: which she finally, before separating from the loaf, hewed into two halves, of which Joe got one, and I the other.* (*Great Expectations* by Charles Dickens)

plantations NOUN here plantations means colonies, which are countries controlled by a more powerful country ❑ *besides our plantations in America* (*Gulliver's Travels* by Jonathan Swift)

plastic ADJ here plastic is an old term meaning shaping or a power that was forming ❑ *A plastic power abode with me* (*The Prelude* by William Wordsworth)

players NOUN actors ❑ *of players which upon the world's stage be* (*On His Mistress* by John Donne)

plump ADV all at once, suddenly ❑ *But it took a bit of time to get it well round, the change come so uncommon plump, didn't it?* (*Great Expectations* by Charles Dickens)

plundered VERB to plunder is to rob or steal from ❑ *These crosses stand for the names of ships or towns that they sank or plundered* (*Treasure Island* by Robert Louis Stevenson)

pommel ■ VERB to pommel someone is to hit them repeatedly with your fists ❑ *hug him round the neck, pommel his back, and kick his legs in irrepressible affection!* (*A Christmas Carol* by Charles Dickens) ■ NOUN a pommel is the part of a saddle that rises up at the front ❑ *He had his gun across his pommel* (*The Adventures of Huckleberry Finn* by Mark Twain)

poor's rates NOUN poor's rates were property taxes which were used to support the poor ❑ *'Oh!' replied the undertaker; 'why, you know, Mr. Bumble, I pay a good deal towards the poor's rates.'* (*Oliver Twist* by Charles Dickens)

popular ADJ popular means ruled by the people, or Republican, rather than ruled by a monarch ❑ *With those of Greece compared and popular Rome* (*The Prelude* by William Wordsworth)

porringer NOUN a porringer is a small bowl ❑ *Of this festive composition each boy had one porringer, and no more* (*Oliver Twist* by Charles Dickens)

postboy NOUN a postboy was the driver of a horse-drawn carriage ❑ *He spoke to a postboy who was dozing under the gateway* (*Oliver Twist* by Charles Dickens)

post-chaise NOUN a fast carriage for two or four passengers ❑ *Looking round, he saw that it was a post-chaise, driven at great speed* (*Oliver Twist* by Charles Dickens)

postern NOUN a small gate usually at the back of a building ❑ *The little servant happening to be entering the* *fortress with two hot rolls, I passed through the postern and crossed the drawbridge, in her company* (*Great Expectations* by Charles Dickens)

pottle NOUN a pottle was a small basket ❑ *He had a paper-bag under each arm and a pottle of strawberries in one hand . . .* (*Great Expectations* by Charles Dickens)

pounce NOUN pounce is a fine powder used to prevent ink spreading on untreated paper ❑ *in that grim atmosphere of pounce and parchment, red-tape, dusty wafers, ink-jars, brief and draft paper, law reports, writs, declarations, and bills of costs* (*David Copperfield* by Charles Dickens)

pox NOUN pox means sexually transmitted diseases like syphilis ❑ *how the pox in all its consequences and denominations* (*Gulliver's Travels* by Jonathan Swift)

prelibation NOUN prelibation means a foretaste of or an example of something to come ❑ *A prelibation to the mower's scythe* (*The Prelude* by William Wordsworth)

prentice NOUN an apprentice ❑ *and Joe, sitting on an old gun, had told me that when I was 'prentice to him regularly bound, we would have such Larks there!* (*Great Expectations* by Charles Dickens)

presently ADV immediately ❑ *I presently knew what they meant* (*Gulliver's Travels* by Jonathan Swift)

pumpion NOUN pumpkin ❑ *for it was almost as large as a small pumpion* (*Gulliver's Travels* by Jonathan Swift)

punctual ADJ kept in one place ❑ *was not a punctual presence, but a spirit* (*The Prelude* by William Wordsworth)

quadrille ■ NOUN a quadrille is a dance invented in France which is usually performed by four couples ❑ *However, Mr Swiveller had Miss Sophy's hand for the first quadrille (country-dances being low, were utterly proscribed)* (*The Old Curiosity Shop* by Charles Dickens) ■ NOUN quadrille was a card game for four people ❑ *to make up her pool of quadrille in the evening* (*Pride and Prejudice* by Jane Austen)

quality NOUN gentry or upper-class people ❑ *if you are with the quality* (*The Adventures of Huckleberry Finn* by Mark Twain)

quick parts PHRASE quick-witted ❑ *Mr Bennet was so odd a mixture of quick parts* (*Pride and Prejudice* by Jane Austen)

quid NOUN a quid is something chewed or kept in the mouth, like a piece of tobacco ❑ *rolling his quid* (*Treasure Island* by Robert Louis Stevenson)

quit VERB quit means to avenge or to make even ❑ *But Faustus's death shall quit my infamy* (*Doctor Faustus 4.3* by Christopher Marlowe)

rags NOUN divisions ❑ *Nor hours, days, months, which are the rags of time* (*The Sun Rising* by John Donne)

raiment NOUN raiment means clothing ❑ *the mountain shook off turf and flower, had only heath for raiment and crag for gem* (*Jane Eyre* by Charlotte Brontë)

rain cats and dogs PHRASE an expression meaning rain heavily. The origin of the expression is unclear ❑ *But it'll perhaps rain cats and dogs to-morrow* (*Silas Marner* by George Eliot)

raised Cain PHRASE raised Cain means caused a lot of trouble. Cain is a character in the Bible who killed his brother Abel ❑ *and every time he got drunk he raised Cain around town* (*The Adventures of Huckleberry Finn* by Mark Twain)

rambling ADJ rambling means confused and not very clear ❑ *my head began to be filled very early with rambling thoughts* (*Robinson Crusoe* by Daniel Defoe)

raree-show NOUN a raree-show is an old term for a peep-show or a fairground entertainment ❑ *A raree-show is here, with children gathered round* (*The Prelude* by William Wordsworth)

recusants NOUN people who resisted authority ❑ *hardy recusants* (*The Prelude* by William Wordsworth)

redounding VERB eddying. An eddy is a movement in water or air which goes round and round instead of flowing in one direction ❑ *mists and steam-like fogs redounding everywhere* (*The Prelude* by William Wordsworth)

redundant ADJ here redundant means overflowing but Wordsworth also uses it to mean excessively large or too big ❑ *A tempest, a redundant energy* (*The Prelude* by William Wordsworth)

reflex NOUN reflex is a shortened version of reflexion, which is an alternative spelling of reflection ❑ *To cut across the reflex of a star* (*The Prelude* by William Wordsworth)

Reformatory NOUN a prison for young offenders/criminals ❑ *Even when I was taken to have a new suit of clothes, the tailor had orders to make them like a kind of Reformatory, and on no account to let me have the free use of my limbs.* (*Great Expectations* by Charles Dickens)

remorse NOUN pity or compassion ❑ *by that remorse* (*On His Mistress* by John Donne)

render VERB in this context render means give. ❑ *and Sarah could render no reason that would be sanctioned by the feeling of the community.* (*Silas Marner* by George Eliot)

repeater NOUN a repeater was a watch that chimed the last hour when a button was pressed–as a result it was useful in the dark ❑ *And his watch is a gold repeater, and worth a hundred pound if it's worth a penny.* (*Great Expectations* by Charles Dickens)

repugnance NOUN repugnance means a strong dislike of something or someone ❑ *overcoming a strong repugnance* (*Treasure Island* by Robert Louis Stevenson)

reverence NOUN reverence means bow. When you bow to someone, you briefly bend your body towards them as a formal way of showing them respect ❑ *made my reverence* (*Gulliver's Travels* by Jonathan Swift)

reverie NOUN a reverie is a daydream ❑ *I can guess the subject of your reverie* (*Pride and Prejudice* by Jane Austen)

revival NOUN a religious meeting held in public ❑ *well I'd ben a-running' a little temperance revival thar' bout a week* (*The Adventures of Huckleberry Finn* by Mark Twain)

revolt VERB revolt means turn back or stop your present course of action and go back to what you were doing before ❑ *Revolt, or I'll in piecemeal tear thy flesh* (*Doctor Faustus* 5.1 by Christopher Marlowe)

rheumatics/rheumatism NOUN rheumatics [rheumatism] is an illness that makes your joints or muscles stiff and painful ❑ *a new cure for the rheumatics* (*Treasure Island* by Robert Louis Stevenson)

riddance NOUN riddance is usually used in the form good riddance which you say when you are pleased that something has gone or been left behind ❑ *I'd better go into the house, and die and be a riddance* (*David Copperfield* by Charles Dickens)

rimy ADJ rimy is an adjective which means covered in ice or frost ❑ *It was a rimy morning, and very damp* (*Great Expectations* by Charles Dickens)

riper ADJ riper means more mature or older ❑ *At riper years to Wittenberg he went* (*Doctor Faustus chorus* by Christopher Marlowe)

rubber NOUN a set of games in whist or backgammon ❏ *her father was sure of his rubber* (*Emma* by Jane Austen)

ruffian NOUN a ruffian is a person who behaves violently ❏ *and when the ruffian had told him* (*Treasure Island* by Robert Louis Stevenson)

sadness NOUN sadness is an old term meaning seriousness ❏ *But I prithee tell me, in good sadness* (*Doctor Faustus 2.2* by Christopher Marlowe)

sailed before the mast PHRASE this phrase meant someone who did not look like a sailor ❏ *he had none of the appearance of a man that sailed before the mast* (*Treasure Island* by Robert Louis Stevenson)

scabbard NOUN a scabbard is the covering for a sword or dagger ❏ *Girded round its middle was an antique scabbard; but no sword was in it, and the ancient sheath was eaten up with rust* (*A Christmas Carol* by Charles Dickens)

schooners NOUN A schooner is a fast, medium-sized sailing ship ❏ *if schooners, islands, and maroons* (*Treasure Island* by Robert Louis Stevenson)

science NOUN learning or knowledge ❏ *Even Science, too, at hand* (*The Prelude* by William Wordsworth)

scrouge VERB to scrouge means to squeeze or to crowd ❏ *to scrouge in and get a sight* (*The Adventures of Huckleberry Finn* by Mark Twain)

scrutore NOUN a scrutore, or escritoire, was a writing table ❏ *set me gently on my feet upon the scrutore* (*Gulliver's Travels* by Jonathan Swift)

scutcheon/escutcheon NOUN an escutcheon is a shield with a coat of arms, or the symbols of a family name, engraved on it ❏ *On the scutcheon we'll have a bend* (*The Adventures of Huckleberry Finn* by Mark Twain)

sea-dog PHRASE sea-dog is a slang term for an experienced sailor or pirate ❏ *a 'true sea-dog', and a 'real old salt,'* (*Treasure Island* by Robert Louis Stevenson)

see the lions PHRASE to see the lions was to go and see the sights of London. Originally the phrase referred to the menagerie in the Tower of London and later in Regent's Park ❏ *We will go and see the lions for an hour or two–it's something to have a fresh fellow like you to show them to,* Copperfield (*David Copperfield* by Charles Dickens)

self-conceit NOUN self-conceit is an old term which means having too high an opinion of oneself, or deceiving yourself ❏ *Till swollen with cunning, of a self-conceit* (*Doctor Faustus chorus* by Christopher Marlowe)

seneschal NOUN a steward ❏ *where a grey-headed seneschal sings a funny chorus with a funnier body of vassals* (*Oliver Twist* by Charles Dickens)

sensible ADJ if you were sensible of something you are aware or conscious of something ❏ *If my children are silly I must hope to be always sensible of it* (*Pride and Prejudice* by Jane Austen)

sessions NOUN court cases were heard at specific times of the year called sessions ❏ *He lay in prison very ill, during the whole interval between his committal for trial, and the coming round of the Sessions.* (*Great Expectations* by Charles Dickens)

shabby ADJ shabby places look old and in bad condition ❏ *a little bit of a shabby village named Pikesville* (*The Adventures of Huckleberry Finn* by Mark Twain)

shay-cart NOUN a shay-cart was a small cart drawn by one horse ❏ *'I were at the Bargemen t'other night, Pip;' whenever he subsided into affection, he called me Pip, and whenever he relapsed into politeness he called me Sir; 'when there come up in his* *shay-cart Pumblechook.' (Great Expectations* by Charles Dickens)

shilling NOUN a shilling is an old unit of currency. There were twenty shillings in every British pound ❑ *'Ten shillings too much,' said the gentleman in the white waistcoat.* (*Oliver Twist* by Charles Dickens)

shines NOUN tricks or games ❑ *well, it would make a cow laugh to see the shines that old idiot cut* (*The Adventures of Huckleberry Finn* by Mark Twain)

shirking VERB shirking means not doing what you are meant to be doing, or evading your duties ❑ *some of you shirking lubbers* (*Treasure Island* by Robert Louis Stevenson)

shiver my timbers PHRASE shiver my timbers is an expression which was used by sailors and pirates to express surprise ❑ *why, shiver my timbers, if I hadn't forgotten my score!* (*Treasure Island* by Robert Louis Stevenson)

shoe-roses NOUN shoe-roses were roses made from ribbons which were stuck on to shoes as decoration ❑ *the very shoe-roses for Netherfield were got by proxy* (*Pride and Prejudice* by Jane Austen)

singular ADJ singular means very great and remarkable or strange ❑ *'Singular dream,' he says* (*The Adventures of Huckleberry Finn* by Mark Twain)

sire NOUN sire is an old word which means lord or master or elder ❑ *She also defied her sire* (*Little Women* by Louisa May Alcott)

sixpence NOUN a sixpence was half of a shilling ❑ *if she had only a shilling in the world, she would be very likely to give away sixpence of it* (*Emma* by Jane Austen)

slavey NOUN the word slavey was used when there was only one servant in a house or boarding-house–so she had to perform all the duties of a larger staff ❑ *Two distinct knocks, sir, will produce the slavey at any*

time (*The Old Curiosity Shop* by Charles Dickens)

slender ADJ weak ❑ *In slender accents of sweet verse* (*The Prelude* by William Wordsworth)

slop-shops NOUN slop-shops were shops where cheap ready-made clothes were sold. They mainly sold clothes to sailors ❑ *Accordingly, I took the jacket off, that I might learn to do without it; and carrying it under my arm, began a tour of inspection of the various slop-shops.* (*David Copperfield* by Charles Dickens)

sluggard NOUN a lazy person ❑ *'Stand up and repeat "Tis the voice of the sluggard",' said the Gryphon.* (*Alice's Adventures in Wonderland* by Lewis Carroll)

smallpox NOUN smallpox is a serious infectious disease ❑ *by telling the men we had smallpox aboard* (*The Adventures of Huckleberry Finn* by Mark Twain)

smalls NOUN smalls are short trousers ❑ *It is difficult for a large-headed, small-eyed youth, of lumbering make and heavy countenance, to look dignified under any circumstances; but it is more especially so, when superadded to these personal attractions are a red nose and yellow smalls* (*Oliver Twist* by Charles Dickens)

sneeze-box NOUN a box for snuff was called a sneeze-box because sniffing snuff makes the user sneeze ❑ *To think of Jack Dawkins–lummy Jack–the Dodger–the Artful Dodger–going abroad for a common twopenny-halfpenny sneeze-box!* (*Oliver Twist* by Charles Dickens)

snorted VERB slept ❑ *Or snorted we in the Seven Sleepers' den?* (*The Good-Morrow* by John Donne)

snuff NOUN snuff is tobacco in powder form which is taken by sniffing ❑ *as he thrust his thumb and fore-finger into the proffered snuff-box of the undertaker: which was an ingenious little model of a patent* *coffin.* (*Oliver Twist* by Charles Dickens)

soliloquized VERB to soliloquize is when an actor in a play speaks to himself or herself rather than to another actor ❏ *'A new servitude! There is something in that,' I soliloquized (mentally, be it understood; I did not talk aloud)* (*Jane Eyre* by Charlotte Brontë)

sough NOUN a sough is a drain or a ditch ❏ *as you may have noticed the sough that runs from the marshes* (*Wuthering Heights* by Emily Brontë)

spirits NOUN a spirit is the nonphysical part of a person which is believed to remain alive after their death ❏ *that I might raise up spirits when I please* (*Doctor Faustus 1.5* by Christopher Marlowe)

spleen ■ NOUN here spleen means a type of sadness or depression which was thought to only affect the wealthy ❏ *yet here I could plainly discover the true seeds of spleen* (*Gulliver's Travels* by Jonathan Swift) ■ NOUN irritability and low spirits ❏ *Adieu to disappointment and spleen* (*Pride and Prejudice* by Jane Austen)

spondulicks NOUN spondulicks is a slang word which means money ❏ *not for all his spondulicks and as much more on top of it* (*The Adventures of Huckleberry Finn* by Mark Twain)

stalled of VERB to be stalled of something is to be bored with it ❏ *I'm stalled of doing naught* (*Wuthering Heights* by Emily Brontë)

stanchion NOUN a stanchion is a pole or bar that stands upright and is used as a building support ❏ *and slid down a stanchion* (*The Adventures of Huckleberry Finn* by Mark Twain)

stang NOUN stang is another word for pole was an old measurement ❏ *These fields were intermingled with woods of half a stang* (*Gulliver's Travels* by Jonathan Swift)

starlings NOUN a starling is a wall built around the pillars that support a bridge to protect the pillars ❏ *There were states of the tide when, having been down the river, I could not get back through the eddy-chafed arches and starlings of old London Bridge* (*Great Expectations* by Charles Dickens)

startings NOUN twitching or night-time movements of the body ❏ *with midnight's startings* (*On His Mistress* by John Donne)

stomacher NOUN a panel at the front of a dress ❏ *but send her aunt the pattern of a stomacher* (*Emma* by Jane Austen)

stoop VERB swoop ❏ *Once a kite hovering over the garden made a stoop at me* (*Gulliver's Travels* by Jonathan Swift)

succedaneum NOUN a succedaneum is a substitute ❏ *But as a succedaneum* (*The Prelude* by William Wordsworth)

suet NOUN a hard animal fat used in cooking ❏ *and your jaws are too weak For anything tougher than suet* (*Alice's Adventures in Wonderland* by Lewis Carroll)

sultry ADJ sultry weather is hot and damp. Here sultry means unpleasant or risky ❏ *for it was getting pretty sultry for us* (*The Adventures of Huckleberry Finn* by Mark Twain)

summerset NOUN summerset is an old spelling of somersault. If someone does a somersault, they turn over completely in the air ❏ *I have seen him do the summerset* (*Gulliver's Travels* by Jonathan Swift)

supper NOUN supper was a light meal taken late in the evening. The main meal was dinner which was eaten at four or five in the afternoon ❏ *and the supper table was all set out* (*Emma* by Jane Austen)

surfeits VERB to surfeit in something is to have far too much of it, or to overindulge in it to an unhealthy degree ❏ *He surfeits upon cursed* necromancy (*Doctor Faustus chorus* by Christopher Marlowe)

surtout NOUN a surtout is a long close-fitting overcoat ❑ *He wore a long black surtout reaching nearly to his ankles* (*The Old Curiosity Shop* by Charles Dickens)

swath NOUN swath is the width of corn cut by a scythe ❑ *while thy hook Spares the next swath* (*Ode to Autumn* by John Keats)

sylvan ADJ sylvan means belonging to the woods ❑ *Sylvan historian* (*Ode on a Grecian Urn* by John Keats)

taction NOUN taction means touch. This means that the people had to be touched on the mouth or the ears to get their attention ❑ *without being roused by some external taction upon the organs of speech and hearing* (*Gulliver's Travels* by Jonathan Swift)

Tag and Rag and Bobtail PHRASE the riff-raff, or lower classes. Used in an insulting way ❑ *'No,' said he; 'not till it got about that there was no protection on the premises, and it come to be considered dangerous, with convicts and Tag and Rag and Bobtail going up and down.'* (*Great Expectations* by Charles Dickens)

tallow NOUN tallow is hard animal fat that is used to make candles and soap ❑ *and a lot of tallow candles* (*The Adventures of Huckleberry Finn* by Mark Twain)

tan VERB to tan means to beat or whip ❑ *and if I catch you about that school I'll tan you good* (*The Adventures of Huckleberry Finn* by Mark Twain)

tanyard NOUN the tanyard is part of a tannery, which is a place where leather is made from animal skins ❑ *hid in the old tanyard* (*The Adventures of Huckleberry Finn* by Mark Twain)

tarry ADJ tarry means the colour of tar or black ❑ *his tarry pig-tail* (*Treasure Island* by Robert Louis Stevenson)

thereof PHRASE from there ❑ *By all desires which thereof did ensue* (*On His Mistress* by John Donne)

thick with, be PHRASE if you are 'thick with someone' you are very close, sharing secrets–it is often used to describe people who are planning something secret ❑ *Hasn't he been thick with Mr Heathcliff lately?* (*Wuthering Heights* by Emily Brontë)

thimble NOUN a thimble is a small cover used to protect the finger while sewing ❑ *The paper had been sealed in several places by a thimble* (*Treasure Island* by Robert Louis Stevenson)

thirtover ADJ thirtover is an old word which means obstinate or that someone is very determined to do want they want and can not be persuaded to do something in another way ❑ *I have been living on in a thirtover, lackadaisical way* (*Tess of the D'Urbervilles* by Thomas Hardy)

timbrel NOUN timbrel is a tambourine ❑ *What pipes and timbrels?* (*Ode on a Grecian Urn* by John Keats)

tin NOUN tin is slang for money/cash ❑ *Then the plain question is, an't it a pity that this state of things should continue, and how much better would it be for the old gentleman to hand over a reasonable amount of tin, and make it all right and comfortable* (*The Old Curiosity Shop* by Charles Dickens)

tincture NOUN a tincture is a medicine made with alcohol and a small amount of a drug ❑ *with ink composed of a cephalic tincture* (*Gulliver's Travels* by Jonathan Swift)

tithe NOUN a tithe is a tax paid to the church ❑ *and held farms which, speaking from a spiritual point of view, paid highly-desirable tithes* (*Silas Marner* by George Eliot)

towardly ADJ a towardly child is dutiful or obedient ❑ *and a towardly child* (*Gulliver's Travels* by Jonathan Swift)

toys NOUN trifles are things which are considered to have little importance, value, or significance ❑ *purchase my life from them bysome glass bracelets, glass rings, and other toys* (*Gulliver's Travels* by Jonathan Swift)

tract NOUN a tract is a religious pamphlet or leaflet ❑ *and Joe Harper got a hymn-book and a tract* (*The Adventures of Huckleberry Finn* by Mark Twain)

train-oil NOUN train-oil is oil from whale blubber ❑ *The train-oil and gunpowder were shoved out of sight in a minute* (*Wuthering Heights* by Emily Brontë)

tribulation NOUN tribulation means the suffering or difficulty you experience in a particular situation ❑ *Amy was making this distinction through much tribulation* (*Little Women* by Louisa May Alcott)

trivet NOUN a trivet is a three-legged stand for resting a pot or kettle ❑ *a pocket-knife in his right; and a pewter pot on the trivet* (*Oliver Twist* by Charles Dickens)

trot line NOUN a trot line is a fishing line to which a row of smaller fishing lines are attached ❑ *when he got along I was hard at it taking up a trot line* (*The Adventures of Huckleberry Finn* by Mark Twain)

troth NOUN oath or pledge ❑ *I wonder, by my troth* (*The Good-Morrow* by John Donne)

truckle NOUN a truckle bedstead is a bed that is on wheels and can be slid under another bed to save space ❑ *It rose under my hand, and the door yielded. Looking in, I saw a lighted candle on a table, a bench, and a mattress on a truckle bedstead.* (*Great Expectations* by Charles Dickens)

trump NOUN a trump is a good, reliable person who can be trusted ❑ *This lad Hawkins is a trump, I perceive*

(*Treasure Island* by Robert Louis Stevenson)

tucker NOUN a tucker is a frilly lace collar which is worn around the neck ❑ *Whereat Scrooge's niece's sister—the plump one with the lace tucker: not the one with the roses—blushed.* (*A Christmas Carol* by Charles Dickens)

tureen NOUN a large bowl with a lid from which soup or vegetables are served ❑ *Waiting in a hot tureen!* (*Alice's Adventures in Wonderland* by Lewis Carroll)

turnkey NOUN a prison officer; jailer ❑ *As we came out of the prison through the lodge, I found that the great importance of my guardian was appreciated by the turnkeys, no less than by those whom they held in charge.* (*Great Expectations* by Charles Dickens)

turnpike NOUN the upkeep of many roads of the time was paid for by tolls (fees) collected at posts along the road. There was a gate to prevent people travelling further along the road until the toll had been paid. ❑ *Traddles, whom I have taken up by appointment at the turnpike, presents a dazzling combination of cream colour and light blue; and both he and Mr. Dick have a general effect about them of being all gloves.* (*David Copperfield* by Charles Dickens)

twas PHRASE it was ❑ *twas but a dream of thee* (*The Good-Morrow* by John Donne)

tyrannized VERB tyrannized means bullied or forced to do things against their will ❑ *for people would soon cease coming there to be tyrannized over and put down* (*Treasure Island* by Robert Louis Stevenson)

'un NOUN 'un is a slang term for one—usually used to refer to a person ❑ *She's been thinking the old 'un* (*David Copperfield* by Charles Dickens)

undistinguished ADJ undiscriminating or incapable of making a distinction between good and bad things ❑

their undistinguished appetite to devour everything (*Gulliver's Travels* by Jonathan Swift)

use NOUN habit ❏ *Though use make you apt to kill me* (*The Flea* by John Donne)

vacant ADJ vacant usually means empty, but here Wordsworth uses it to mean carefree ❏ *To vacant musing, unreproved neglect* (*The Prelude* by William Wordsworth)

valetudinarian NOUN one too concerned with his or her own health. ❏ *for having been a valetudinarian all his life* (*Emma* by Jane Austen)

vamp VERB vamp means to walk or tramp to somewhere ❏ *Well, vamp on to Marlott, will 'ee* (*Tess of the D'Urbervilles* by Thomas Hardy)

vapours NOUN the vapours is an old term which means unpleasant and strange thoughts, which make the person feel nervous and unhappy ❏ *and my head was full of vapours* (*Robinson Crusoe* by Daniel Defoe)

vegetables NOUN here vegetables means plants ❏ *the other vegetables are in the same proportion* (*Gulliver's Travels* by Jonathan Swift)

venturesome ADJ if you are venturesome you are willing to take risks ❏ *he must be either hopelessly stupid or a venturesome fool* (*Wuthering Heights* by Emily Brontë)

verily ADV verily means really or truly ❏ *though I believe verily* (*Robinson Crusoe* by Daniel Defoe)

vicinage NOUN vicinage is an area or the residents of an area ❏ *and to his thought the whole vicinage was haunted by her.* (*Silas Marner* by George Eliot)

victuals NOUN victuals means food ❏ *grumble a little over the victuals* (*The Adventures of Huckleberry Finn* by Mark Twain)

vintage NOUN vintage in this context means wine ❏ *Oh, for a draught of*

vintage! (*Ode to a Nightingale* by John Keats)

virtual ADJ here virtual means powerful or strong ❏ *had virtual faith* (*The Prelude* by William Wordsworth)

vittles NOUN vittles is a slang word which means food ❏ *There never was such a woman for givin' away vittles and drink* (*Little Women* by Louisa May Alcott)

voided straight PHRASE voided straight is an old expression which means emptied immediately ❏ *see the rooms be voided straight* (*Doctor Faustus 4.1* by Christopher Marlowe)

wainscot NOUN wainscot is wood panel lining in a room so wainscoted means a room lined with wooden panels ❏ *in the dark wainscoted parlor* (*Silas Marner* by George Eliot)

walking the plank PHRASE walking the plank was a punishment in which a prisoner would be made to walk along a plank on the side of the ship and fall into the sea, where they would be abandoned ❏ *about hanging, and walking the plank* (*Treasure Island* by Robert Louis Stevenson)

want VERB want means to be lacking or short of ❏ *The next thing wanted was to get the picture framed* (*Emma* by Jane Austen)

wanting ADJ wanting means lacking or missing ❏ *wanting two fingers of the left hand* (*Treasure Island* by Robert Louis Stevenson)

wanting, I was not PHRASE I was not wanting means I did not fail ❏ *I was not wanting to lay a foundation of religious knowledge in his mind* (*Robinson Crusoe* by Daniel Defoe)

ward NOUN a ward is, usually, a child who has been put under the protection of the court or a guardian for his or her protection ❏ *I call the Wards in Jarndyce. They*

are caged up with all the others.
(Bleak House by Charles Dickens)

waylay VERB to waylay someone is to lie in wait for them or to intercept them ❑ *I must go up the road and waylay him (The Adventures of Huckleberry Finn by Mark Twain)*

weazen NOUN weazen is a slang word for throat. It actually means shrivelled ❑ *You with a uncle too! Why, I knowed you at Gargery's when you was so small a wolf that I could have took your weazen betwixt this finger and thumb and chucked you away dead (Great Expectations by Charles Dickens)*

wery ◼ ADV very ❑ *Be wery careful o' vidders all your life (Pickwick Papers by Charles Dickens)* ◼ *See* wibrated

wherry NOUN wherry is a small swift rowing boat for one person ❑ *It was flood tide when Daniel Quilp sat himself down in the wherry to cross to the opposite shore. (The Old Curiosity Shop by Charles Dickens)*

whether PREP whether means which of the two in this example ❑ *we came in full view of a great island or continent (for we knew not whether) (Gulliver's Travels by Jonathan Swift)*

whetstone NOUN a whetstone is a stone used to sharpen knives and other tools ❑ *I dropped pap's whetstone there too (The Adventures of Huckleberry Finn by Mark Twain)*

wibrated VERB in Dickens's use of the English language 'w' often replaces 'v' when he is reporting speech. So here 'wibrated' means 'vibrated'. In *Pickwick Papers* a judge asks Sam Weller (who constantly confuses the two letters) "Do you spell it with a 'v' or a 'w'?' to which Weller replies 'That depends upon the taste and fancy of the speller, my Lord' ❑ *There are strings . . . in the human heart that had better not be wibrated (Barnaby Rudge by Charles Dickens)*

wicket NOUN a wicket is a little door in a larger entrance ❑ *Having rested*

here, for a minute or so, to collect a good burst of sobs and an imposing show of tears and terror, he knocked loudly at the wicket (Oliver Twist by Charles Dickens)

without CONJ without means unless ❑ *You don't know about me, without you have read a book by the name of* The Adventures of Tom Sawyer *(The Adventures of Huckleberry Finn by Mark Twain)*

wittles ◼ NOUN wittles is a slang word which means food ❑ *I live on broken wittles–and I sleep on the coals (David Copperfield by Charles Dickens)* ◼ *See* wibrated

woo VERB courts or forms a proper relationship with ❑ *before it woo (The Flea by John Donne)*

words, to have PHRASE if you have words with someone you have a disagreement or an argument ❑ *I do not want to have words with a young thing like you. (Black Beauty by Anna Sewell)*

workhouse NOUN workhouses were places where the homeless were given food and a place to live in return for doing very hard work ❑ *And the Union workhouses? demanded Scrooge. Are they still in operation? (A Christmas Carol by Charles Dickens)*

yawl NOUN a yawl is a small boat kept on a bigger boat for short trips. Yawl is also the name for a small fishing boat ❑ *She sent out her yawl, and we went aboard (The Adventures of Huckleberry Finn by Mark Twain)*

yeomanry NOUN the yeomanry was a collective term for the middle classes involved in agriculture ❑ *The yeomanry are precisely the order of people with whom I feel I can have nothing to do (Emma by Jane Austen)*

yonder ADV yonder means over there ❑ *all in the same second we seem to hear low voices in yonder! (The Adventures of Huckleberry Finn by Mark Twain)*